Since 2010, **Ryan Lambie** has served as the deputy editor of denofgeek.com, a Dennis Publishing-owned entertainment website that has a global reach of around 5 million unique users per month. Specialising in feature-writing, primarily about genre movies, he has interviewed all kinds of actors, directors and producers in the course of his work, including Ridley Scott, Donald Trumbull, Alejandro Iñárritu, Rutger Hauer and Denzel Washington. As a freelance writer, his other work has included pieces on movies and video-games for such publications as the *Guardian*, the *Mirror*, *Bizarre*, *Mental Floss* and the *Escapist*. In 2014, Ryan received the Richard Attenborough Award for best blogger at the FDA Regional Critics Film Awards.

The Geek's Guide
to SF Cinema

Ryan Lambie

ROBINSON

ROBINSON

First published in Great Britain in 2018 by Robinson

1 3 5 7 9 10 8 6 4 2

A CIP catalogue record for this book
is available from the British Library.

ISBN: 978-1-47213-985-6

Typeset in Whitman by Hewer Text UK Ltd, Edinburgh
Printed and bound in Great Britain by Clays Ltd, St Ives plc

Papers used by Robinson are from well-managed forests and other responsible sources.

Robinson
An imprint of
Little, Brown Book Group
Carmelite House
50 Victoria Embankment
London EC4Y 0DZ

An Hachette UK Company
www.hachette.co.uk

www.littlebrown.co.uk

For Sarah, Kathy, David and Simon

Contents

Introduction

In 1977, a truck driver bought a cinema ticket and sat down to watch a brand-new film called *Star Wars*. As the grand, vivacious space opera unfolded on the screen, the young man was filled with wonderment, but also frustration. Why was he driving trucks for a living when he could be making movies? He loved science fiction, so how come this George Lucas guy got to make a space opera and he didn't? Within seven years, James Cameron had given up truck driving for good and directed his first feature film, *The Terminator*. Twenty-five years later, he finally got to direct a space opera of his own: *Avatar*.

One of the beautiful things about science fiction is that one great piece of filmmaking inspires another. The dreamlike stories of pioneering director Georges Méliès inspired the filmmakers who followed him to make great movies of their own. There's a clear line from Fritz Lang's *Metropolis* to Ridley Scott's *Blade Runner*; from Méliès's *Trip to the Moon* to *2001: A Space Odyssey*, from *Frankenstein* to *Ex Machina*.

This very book exists thanks to the inspiring work of other filmmakers. When I was a young boy growing up in a very grey part of the UK, my earliest memories were of science-fiction films. I shuddered at *The Creature from the Black Lagoon*; I hid my eyes behind my hands at *Dr Who and the Daleks*. I cheered at *Star Wars*. I cried at *Silent Running*. I shrank in fear from *Invaders from Mars*, a film where a young boy's father is turned into a pitiless, violent drone by aliens at the bottom of his garden. The latter film left me awestruck: I was used to seeing sci-fi films unfold in exotic settings beyond the stars. Here was an invasion story in a domestic setting, where a little kid is the only one who knows about the presence of evil aliens – and nobody will listen to him.

It's science fiction's inspiring sense of limitless possibility that makes it such a vibrant and important genre. At its most basic level, sci-fi is about humankind's relationship with technology, how it moulds us and changes us, and how – for better or worse – it might affect us in the future. Ray guns, spaceships, robots, aliens with tentacles and multiple eyes – these are the garnish around the edges of sci-fi, but not the meal itself; at their core, sci-fi movies are about ourselves, about the very best and very worst of our natures.

This is something I first realised when I saw *Invaders from Mars*: whether its writer and director meant it to or not, that movie expressed what it's like to be a child in a world of grown-ups who are taller and stronger than you are, whose moods and concerns are inscrutable. The boy's father may have been a simulacrum created by aliens, but his shift in behaviour could have just as easily been caused by depression, or rage, or too much alcohol. Such is the brilliance of sci-fi: it can explore subjects that might be too disturbing or unpalatable to reach a wide audience in a contemporary drama.

That's the aim of this book: to not only highlight thirty key movies from sci-fi's long history, but also to demonstrate how each has in some way inspired the other, and, moreover, pushed cinema forward as a whole. Some of the movies in this book are classics; others less so. Some have elements that are timeless; plenty of them have areas that look glaringly dated. Note, too, that the most popular and financially successful sci-fi movies aren't always the most influential or revolutionary; Steven Spielberg's *Close Encounters of the Third Kind* and *E.T. The Extra-Terrestrial*, for example, are rightly regarded as classics yet their influence arguably pales when compared to the genre-defining *Star Wars*. What all these films have in common is their strength of vision and the extraordinary ripple effect they have had on the movies which came after them. This is why, as well as such movies as *Metropolis* and *Alien*, this book will also explore films such as *Things to Come* and *The Incredible Shrinking Man* – features that haven't necessarily defined the genre as we know it, but nevertheless contain moments of genuine wonder.

What you'll find in the following chapters, then, is not just a list of films, but a guided tour of a genre that has continuously evolved and redefined itself over the past one hundred years.

1. The silent-era pioneer

A TRIP TO THE MOON (1902)

The story of sci-fi cinema begins in a Frenchman's back garden. It was in Montreuil, nestled among the trees of this quiet Paris suburb, that filmmaker Georges Méliès built the first movie studio in Europe. From the outside, the building didn't so much resemble a studio as a greenhouse; completed in 1897, its glass roof and walls allowed natural light to bathe the hand-painted sets created by Méliès and his small crew. It was here, on what was once a vegetable patch, decades before Neil Armstrong first climbed down from his lunar lander in July 1969, that cinema first put a human being on the Moon.

Exactly how humanity could launch itself into space was something writers had pondered for centuries. In his second-century work, *A True History*, Greek writer Lucian thought we could journey to the Moon on a boat carried aloft by a jet of water. In the seventeenth century, Francis Godwin wrote that we might be able to visit Earth's nearest neighbour if we had enough geese to carry us there. Jules Verne's seminal novel *From the Earth to the Moon* (1865) saw American astronauts launched towards the Moon from a giant cannon; H. G. Wells's adventurers in *The First Men in the Moon* (1901) made their trip in a metal sphere painted with a gravity-defying substance named Cavorite.

When it came to the emerging medium of film, however, sending an explorer into space would take something entirely new: the very first visual effects.* At the end of the nineteenth century, the language of cinema was only

---

* See: Helen Powell, *Stop the Clocks! Time and Narrative in Cinema* (London: I. B. Tauris, 2012), https://books.google.co.uk/books?id=PA83d5HLDhIC&pg=PA47&redir_esc=y#v=onepage&q&f=false.

just being written; for the most part, the earliest movies were concerned with capturing scenes from everyday life: workers leaving a factory, a train pulling into a station. On either side of the Atlantic, pioneering filmmakers were working in parallel lines; in the United States, inventor Thomas Edison's studio was making brief movies of boxers and scenes of everyday life, which could be viewed on a device called a kinetoscope. In Paris, brothers Auguste and Louis Lumière were thrilling audiences with their cinematograph, another early version of the modern film projector.

Theatre owner and stage magician Georges Méliès was among the first to experience one of the Lumière brothers' movies. Intent on making and presenting films at his own venue, the Théâtre Robert-Houdin, Méliès tried and failed to purchase one of the Lumière brothers' projectors, but eventually obtained a similar projection device, called an Animatograph, from the British inventor Robert W. Paul. Méliès demonstrated a flash of his own technical ingenuity when he stripped the Animatograph down and, by studying its components, worked out how to turn it into a film camera.

Within a year of seeing the Lumière brothers' demonstration, Méliès was making his own movies, which initially followed the popular convention of pointing the camera at an everyday subject. Méliès' first film, for example, simply showed a trio of gentlemen relaxing in the afternoon sun, one reading a newspaper while the other two play cards. Méliès quickly moved beyond this, however, as he began to employ his skills as a magician in his films: at first, he simply captured himself performing conjuring tricks, but gradually came to realise that the camera could be used to create a new kind of visual sleight of hand.

In his 1896 film *The Haunted Castle*, Méliès uses a carefully timed cut to create the illusion of a bat turning into the demon Mephistopheles – an editing technique that, according to filmmaking legend, Méliès discovered by accident. The story goes that, a few months before he made *The Haunted Castle*, Méliès was filming passing traffic in a busy part of Paris when his camera unexpectedly jammed. When Méliès watched the footage back, he noted that a passing horse-drawn bus appeared to turn into a hearse – an illusion created by the camera abruptly stopping and then starting again a few seconds later. Whether this oft-repeated story is true or not – and Helen

Powell's book, *Stop the Clocks!*, casts a certain level of doubt on it[*] – Méliès would use editing to repeated and pioneering effect throughout his filmmaking career. He also used multiple exposures and other in-camera tricks to experimental effect, such as an 1898 film in which Méliès appears to pull his own head off and switch it with a selection of other heads sitting on a table. Méliès made around 240 films between 1896 and 1900, which drew ever greater audiences with their visual trickery. As his filmmaking evolved, Méliès realised that the techniques he had developed could be used not merely to create isolated illusions, but to tell stories where incredible, unpredictable things could happen. In *Cinderella* (1899), Méliès uses editing and whimsical set designs to retell the folk tale of a lowly woman magically transformed into a princess. With the viewpoint dissolving from location to location as we follow the heroine's progress, *Cinderella* was Méliès's most ambitious undertaking up to that point, and his first major success in both the United States and Europe.

It was Méliès's 1902 film, *A Trip to the Moon*, however, that really broke new ground. Not only was it one of the longest films of its era – lasting around nine minutes at a time when most films lasted mere seconds – but it was also one of the most expensive and ambitious. By this stage, Méliès had established the Star Film Company, and built the airy, glass-roofed studio on his Montreuil vegetable patch.

A Trip to the Moon borrows liberally from Jules Verne's *From the Earth to the Moon* – specifically, Verne's idea of blasting explorers into space via a huge cannon. Yet Méliès also appears to take inspiration from H. G. Wells's *The First Men in the Moon*, first published just one year before his film. Whereas Verne's fanciful adventure saw its pioneers slingshot around the Moon and return home again, Wells's story had its explorers land on the lunar surface and meet its inhabitants – an insect-like species Wells dubs Selenites. Méliès appears to take this latter part of the novel for his own adventure, since *A Trip to the Moon* shows its eccentric-looking explorers (among them Méliès himself, heavily

---

[*] Powell, *Stop the Clocks!*, https://books.google.co.uk/books?id=PA83d5HLDhIC&pg=PA47&redir_esc=y#v=onepage&q&f=false.

disguised) meeting some athletic Moon people and even killing a few with the swipe of an umbrella. As in Wells's novel, the explorers later meet the king of the Selenites (whom they also kill).

Compact though it is by modern standards, A Trip to the Moon is a landmark achievement in special effects. Not only is it the first true science-fiction movie, but it's also the first film to depict the initial contact between humans and an alien species. Little wonder, then, that it caused such a fuss when it first played in Méliès's theatre in the autumn of 1902. A true transatlantic film phenomenon, it managed to draw crowds in the United States as well as Europe. A Trip to the Moon's popularity was such that it was widely bootlegged, with counterfeit copies of the movie proving to be so rife that Méliès opened a branch of his company in the United States to help stem the flow.

Just six years after A Trip to the Moon came out, however, Méliès's popularity began to wane – and, incredibly, his pivotal achievement in cinema very nearly vanished forever. When the First World War broke out in 1914, Méliès's theatre was shut down, his film studio turned into a makeshift hospital and hundreds of his movies melted down for their minerals. When the war ended, Méliès spent several years in obscurity, and with money tight, he was forced to work as a shopkeeper at a Paris train station. (It was this part of Méliès's life that director Martin Scorsese told in his uncharacteristically mellow 2011 drama, Hugo.)

Of the dozens of Méliès's films lost to history, A Trip to the Moon might have vanished too, were it not for a renewed interest in his work at the end of the 1920s. With that critical reassessment came a drive to find and catalogue the Méliès films that still survived, and A Trip to the Moon was one of several prints discovered and preserved for future generations. Remarkably, films previously thought lost to history are still being found today, decades after Méliès's death in 1938. A hand-coloured print of A Trip to the Moon emerged in 1993; in October 2016, a film called Match de Prestidigitation (or Conjuring Contest) was handed to archivists in the Czech Republic.

In the twenty-first century, A Trip to the Moon is rightly regarded as providing a pivotal moment in cinema. The film's fame is such that, from 1999 onwards, an effort began to digitise and restore the hand-tinted print discovered six years earlier. Each of *A Trip to the Moon*'s 13,000 frames was scanned and carefully cleaned by film specialists – a process which took a staggering ten years to complete. The restored print was first screened at the Cannes Film Festival in 2011 and, for the first time in over a century, audiences could see this sci-fi milestone as it looked when it was originally shot. Cinema and visual effects may have moved far beyond the relatively simple techniques Méliès employed in his film, but it was here, in this playful, dreamlike film shot in a Paris suburb, that sci-fi cinema began.

Silent sci-fi

To understand just how rapidly the new language of cinema evolved in the early twentieth century, you only have to look at the sci-fi and fantasy films that emerged from 1900 to 1920. For all their technical ingenuity, Georges Méliès's earliest movies followed the traditions of the theatre, with actors performing in front of painted backdrops – the filmmaking concepts of long shots, close-ups and tracking shots hadn't yet been invented.

Gradually, however, we see Méliès experimenting with some of the filmmaking techniques that would soon become vital to the language of cinema. In *The Impossible Voyage* (1904), what we might now think of as a sequel to *A Trip to the Moon*, a group of scientists build a rocket and blast off for the heart of the sun. In several sequences, Méliès uses simple miniature effects to create long shots, providing his story with a greater sense of scale. In one scene, Méliès illustrates a journey through the Swiss Alps with an effects shot of a train crossing a bridge and trundling through snow-capped mountains. A few shots later, a group of travellers clatter off through the Alps in a charabanc, and Méliès depicts this with a long tracking shot, the camera following the vehicle's progress up and down steep alpine mountainsides. Compare *The Impossible Voyage* to *A Trip to the Moon* from just two years earlier, and it's easy to see how Méliès's style developed; that earlier fantasy featured just one instance of what appears to be a camera movement – the famous sequence where the ship strikes the Man in the Moon directly in the eye. Méliès heightens the humour by having the camera close in on the Moon, illustrating the craft's approach. In reality, the camera is static, and Méliès simply moves his subject – a heavily made-up actor's face and a painted backdrop – towards the lens.

Méliès comes up with a similar but far more elaborate gag in *The Impossible Voyage*. A train full of adventurers speeds up the side of a mountain, using it as a ramp to launch them into space; Méliès creates the illusion of another long tracking shot, as the train passes mountains, then clouds, before racing on into the depths of space. In the next shot, we see the sun pass through clouds and then slowly approach the camera; as the sun yawns, the train flies straight down its throat.

By 1912, we can see how Méliès continued to evolve his filmmaking techniques, even as his adventures remained as whimsical as ever. *The Conquest of the North Pole*'s major set-piece is a flying sequence, which lasts for approximately ten minutes, as a plane flies past a procession of strange phenomena on its way to the Arctic. Méliès's most lengthy and ambitious film, *The Conquest of the North Pole* was also, sadly, one of his last; it was far less successful than his earlier fantasies and, like so many of his films, its true value was only fully appreciated many years later. By 1915, American director D. W. Griffith had made *The Birth of a Nation* – a movie that, for all its horrendous racism, was breathtaking in its scale, ambition and filmmaking invention. Méliès's whimsical adventures, by this point, had begun to look rather old-fashioned.

The language of cinema was also advancing rapidly in Europe by the time the First World War broke out in 1914. Adapted from Bernhard Kellermann's bestselling novel *Der Tunnel*, published in 1913, the film of the same name was a technical marvel. Directed by German filmmaker William Wauer, it details the construction of a huge transatlantic railway tunnel between France and the United States and the dangers that go into building it. Unlike Méliès's films, *Der Tunnel* is starkly realistic in tone and execution; Wauer uses close-ups and low camera angles to create a sense of heat and claustrophobia as workers carve their way through earth and rock.

Within little more than a decade, cinema had transformed almost beyond recognition. Early, five-minute vignettes of everyday life or conjuring tricks had given way to stories of exploration and adventure, and then three-hour-long historical epics. Cinema moved from the simple camera set-ups and staging of Méliès's breakthrough films and towards location filming and hugely detailed sets. In such films as *Der Golem* and *The Cabinet of Dr Caligari* (both 1920), German Expressionist filmmakers experimented with stylised set design, lighting and camera angles to create drama and suspense – techniques that would pass over to the United States later in the century.

If Méliès's films were only tangentially sci-fi, in the sense that they were created to entertain rather than provoke thought about the realities of human experience, they nevertheless set the groundwork for what was to come later in the century. Thanks to Méliès and pioneering filmmakers like him, cinema had found its own language and voice. The stage was set for the next pivotal sci-fi film: *Metropolis*.

Selected SF films mentioned in this chapter:

The Haunted Castle (1896)

Cinderella (1899)

The Impossible Voyage (1904)

The Conquest of the North Pole (1912)

Der Tunnel (1914)

Der Golem (1920)

The Cabinet of Dr Caligari (1920)

2. Revolutionary cinema

METROPOLIS (1927)

'What if one day those in the depths rise up against you?'

Fritz Lang nods politely but, inwardly, he's panicking. The director is sitting opposite Joseph Goebbels, the Nazi Party's Minister of Propaganda, who's talking enthusiastically about Lang's movies. But Lang isn't really listening to Goebbels – he's looking through the window over Goebbel's shoulder, at the clock in the street outside. Lang originally showed up at Goebbels's office to argue the case for his latest film, *The Testament of Dr Mabuse*, which has just been withdrawn for its anti-fascist sentiments (the director had, admittedly, placed Nazi Party slogans in the mouth of its title criminal). Instead, Lang is surprised – and more than a little alarmed – to hear that Adolf Hitler is a fan of his work. Worse still, Goebbels reveals that the Führer wants a propaganda film – and that Hitler thinks Lang should be the one to direct it. Lang sits quietly, wondering whether he can get to the bank, withdraw his savings and flee Berlin; but as Goebbels talks and talks, closing time draws ever closer. Quietly, Lang begins to perspire.*

Five years earlier, Lang had made one of the films so avidly watched by Hitler: *Metropolis*. Even today, its bold, stark images hold a magnetic power: art-deco buildings soaring into the sky. An elegant robot sitting on a throne, gazing back at us with unblinking eyes. An unending row of workers dressed in black, heads bowed, shuffling to the city's great engine rooms. For these

---

* See:https://cinephiliabeyond.org/mise-en-scene-fritz-lang-invaluable-short-lived-magazines-article-master-darkness.

extraordinary images alone, *Metropolis* deserves its status as one of the most important films of twentieth-century cinema. In technical terms, it was nothing less than groundbreaking – its visual effects paving the way for sci-fi movies still to come. At the time, however, this grand future vision was far from celebrated.

Born in Austria in 1890, Fritz Lang had already lived an eventful life by the time of his thirtieth birthday. When he was twenty, Lang went travelling in Europe and Asia for three years before heading to Paris to study painting in 1913. After the First World War broke out, he served for two years before his injuries – suffered while fighting in Russia and eastern Europe – led to his honourable discharge.

Lang started writing screenplays while he was still in the army, and directed his first feature, the silent picture *Halbblut* (or *Half-Breed*), in 1919. From that point on, Lang continued writing and directing films at a prodigious rate, and in 1920 he met Thea von Harbou, a successful actress and novelist who would play an instrumental role in the director's career. The pair collaborated on some of the most popular German films of the decade: *Dr Mabuse, The Great Gambler* (1922), which led to a whole series of movies, and *Die Nibelungen* (1924), an epic fantasy released in two parts. All the same, Lang and von Harbou's relationship had a darker side. Both were already married when they embarked on a passionate affair; years later, it emerged that Lang's then-wife, Lisa Rosenthal, had discovered the pair's secret relationship and had tragically shot herself. (Patrick McGilligan, who wrote the exhaustively detailed biography *Fritz Lang: The Nature of the Beast*, raised the disturbing possibility that Lang may have pulled the trigger himself.)

From Lang and von Harbou's partnership came one of the most important science-fiction films of all: *Metropolis*. In interviews, Lang liked to say that the film was inspired by a visit to New York in 1924; he gazed at the Manhattan skyline, with its buildings clawing at the sky, and the idea for a story set in a futuristic city began to formulate in his mind. In reality, von Harbou was already well into writing the story by October 1924, since the novel was serialised in *Illustriertes Blatt* magazine the following year, and first published in book form in 1926.

The novel and the resulting movie share the same basic plot. Set in the distant year 2026, *Metropolis* imagines a sprawling city of sharp social divisions: the rulers and the wealthy live in their glittering towers like gods on Mount Olympus; the vast sea of ordinary workers live underground, powering the great engines that keep the metropolis in motion. Following a chance encounter, a member of the wealthy elite, Freder, falls in love with Maria, a member of the working class. Journeying into the world of machines below, Freder witnesses firsthand the suffering of the workers, and learns that Maria is a kind of freedom fighter who predicts that a messianic figure will one day emerge – a leader capable of forging a union between the upper and lower classes. Meanwhile, Freder's father, Fredersen, plans to disrupt the workers' gathering, and has his scientist underling Rotwang build a robot capable of impersonating Maria and upending her revolutionary antics. What Fredersen doesn't realise is that Rotwang harbours a longstanding grudge against his master, and plans to use the robot to bring the metropolis to its knees.

A sci-fi fantasy of romance, black magic and futuristic technology, *Metropolis* was an unusually ambitious movie for its time. Not only would it require the kind of set building and army of extras that pioneering director D. W. Griffith employed a decade earlier, but it would also require the creation of new photographic and miniature effects – techniques that were still in their relative infancy. Little wonder, then, that *Metropolis*'s budget would begin to swell after filming began in the spring of 1925; originally set at 1.5 million Reichsmarks, the investment quickly rose to 5.1 million – making it one of the most expensive movies of its day, and reckoned to equate to around $200 million in 2010.*

Nevertheless, Lang used all that money to striking and often ingenious effect. During *Metropolis*'s production, effects artist Eugen Schüfftan would prove to be pivotal to the film's design: he oversaw the creation of the scale models that created the illusion of a bustling city; beneath the art-deco towers, dozens of tiny planes and vehicles were carefully manipulated, one frame at a time. These stop-motion sequences took months to prepare, build and execute; heartbreakingly, one sequence had to be shot all over again when the

* See: https://www.theguardian.com/film/2010/oct/21/metropolis-lang-science-fiction.

footage was accidentally destroyed by the film lab. Schüfftan also came up with a technique that used mirrors to place actors in the same shot as a scale miniature, creating the illusion of huge sets at a fraction of the cost of building full-size ones. Although later supplanted by more modern compositing techniques, the Schüfftan process was truly pioneering.

Another of *Metropolis*'s most memorable images – the curvaceous robot, or 'Maschinenemensch', created by Rotwang – was designed by Walter Schulze-Mittendorff. He came up with a very different design from the one described in von Harbou's book; she had imagined the robot as svelte and semi-translucent. Schulze-Mittendorff instead came up with something far more imposing; made from an early form of plastic, it was precisely modelled from a plaster cast of actress Brigitte Helm's body. Originally, Schulze-Mittendorff had planned to craft the robot suit out of metal, before he realised it would be too heavy and cumbersome to wear. Casting around for another suitable material, he chanced on a newly invented substance he dubbed 'plastic wood' – a kind of filler that hardened when exposed to the air.* Even with this canny use of modern materials, the robot suit remained painful to move around in, and Helm was left sore and exhausted after wearing the outfit in take after take. (One behind-the-scenes photograph from the shoot shows a wan-looking Helm being attended to by a crewmember holding a hairdryer.)

That Lang was a fiercely committed perfectionist hardly helped. Indeed, the director's seeming intent on making a film larger and more spectacular in scale than his previous one, *Die Nibelungen*, was a major reason why *Metropolis* ran so wildly over schedule and over budget. Filming took the best part of a year, and employed tens of thousands of extras – including 750 children – for a dramatic sequence in which the city is subjected to a devastating flood. The youngsters, brought in from the poorer areas of Berlin, were repeatedly drenched by water cannon over a gruelling fourteen-night shoot.† Lang, in his

---

* See: https://web.archive.org/web/20151004213042/http://www.walter-schulze-mittendorff. com/EN/robot02.html.

† See: https://web.archive.org/web/20140316012144/http://www.tcm.com/this-month/article/ 25817%7C0/Metropolis.html.

merciless pursuit of the perfect shot, sat high up on his director's chair, pointing and shouting.

After repeated delays, *Metropolis* finally had its premiere in Berlin on 10
January 1927, and it was a grand occasion befitting a film of its scale. The
UFA-Palast am Zoo, then Germany's largest cinema, must have looked a spectacular sight to the moviegoers filing into the 600-seat theatre. The building
was painted silver; above the door hung a huge bronze gong, a reference to a
major set-piece from the movie. In huge letters, the words '*Metropolis*: Ein
Film Von Fritz Lang' spanned the width of the cinema's facade. By most
accounts, the reaction from the public was rapturous, with *Metropolis*'s futuristic visuals frequently punctuated by applause.

The film's distributors were, however, less enamoured with Lang's epic
concoction: because of its towering expense, *Metropolis* was bankrolled and
distributed by three companies – Germany's UFA (Universum-Film
Aktiengesellschaft), and over in Hollywood, Metro-Goldwyn-Mayer and
Paramount Pictures. One of the stipulations in the *Metropolis* contract was
that UFA reserved the right to alter the movie in order to 'ensure profitability'.
With *Metropolis* costing UFA an unprecedented *sum* of money, and its duration coming to a lengthy 153 minutes, the decision was made to cut the movie
down. Shortly after the premiere, the movie was withdrawn and heavily
rewritten by American playwright Channing Pollock, resulting in a much-
simplified story told over a more compact 115 minutes. This was the version
screened in the USA and UK to decidedly mixed reviews – including one by
eminent writer H. G. Wells, who dismissed *Metropolis* as an 'unimaginative,
incoherent, sentimentalising and make-believe film'.*

The movie was cut yet again in 1927 when businessman Alfred Hugenberg
took over UFA; the version of *Metropolis* put on general release in German
cinemas that October lasted just ninety-one minutes. This meant that the
audiences who saw *Metropolis* on its premiere were the only people ever to see
the film entirely uncut. Over the next few decades, *Metropolis* would gradually
be restored to something close to its former glory, but even at the time of

---

* See: http://www.openculture.com/2016/10/h-g-wells-pans-fritz-langs-metropolis.html.

writing, the original 153-minute cut shown in January 1927 remains lost – perhaps forever.

Towards the end of his life, Lang himself seemed to disavow the picture, describing it as a 'fairy tale' that he 'detested' in an interview with Peter Bogdanovich.[*] It's certainly true that *Metropolis*'s ending seems naive in the extreme, given everything that comes before it: Freder becomes what Maria predicted all along – a mediating voice between the rich and powerful, represented by his father, and the underclass, represented by machine operator Grot (Heinrich George). Exactly how this future society's gross inequalities will be resolved is left hanging, rather unconvincingly, in the air. But while it's true that Lang and von Harbou's movie is as much fantasy as sci-fi, and that its story elements aren't necessarily all that original – Rotwang is evidently inspired by Doctor Frankenstein, and the story of a futuristic workers' uprising appears to be taken from Karel Capek's play, *R. U. R.* – *Metropolis* remains a powerhouse of imagination. More than any other movie of its era, the film would inspire the look and feel of sci-fi cinema for decades to come; as critics began to rediscover and reappraise Lang's film, it grew in reputation from a fragmented product of a bygone era to a timeless classic, its central image of the wealthy living high above the poor coopted by such directors as Ridley Scott and Neill Blomkamp.

Lang's view of *Metropolis* may have changed, but that probably had something to do with the events that occurred in the build-up to the Second World War. The relationship between Lang and von Harbou, who by this point were married, began to sour by the time they collaborated on *The Testament of Dr Mabuse* in 1933. Lang often liked to repeat the story of his meeting with Goebbels, and his subsequent flight from Germany to Paris, and then to America. But like his *Metropolis* creation myth, where the sight of the Manhattan skyline planted the seed for his movie, the effusive Goebbels, the ticking clock and the perspiration may have been just another tall tale. Whatever the truth was, Lang soon began a new career in Hollywood, while von Harbou continued writing and

---

[*] Peter Bogdanovich, *Who the Devil Made It?: Conversations with Legendary Film Directors* (London: Arrow, 1998).

occasionally directing movies in Nazi Germany. Hitler, meanwhile, turned to the filmmaker Leni Riefenstahl to make the propaganda movie he had long dreamed of: *Triumph of the Will* (1935).

Metropolis therefore emerged at a unique point in history; between two immensely destructive world wars, at the end of the Expressionist era of film-making, and at a time when the creative partnership between Lang and von Harbou was still at its height. If Lang later shunned *Metropolis*, the film nevertheless remains one of the most important movies in German cinema, and a landmark in sci-fi movie-making.

BEYOND *METROPOLIS*

After the completion of *Metropolis* in 1927, Fritz Lang and Thea von Harbou, it seemed, still had sci-fi imagery stirring in their heads. Perhaps they were still thinking about an ending they had once planned for *Metropolis* – one very different from the shaking of hands between the workers and the elites. Rather than reunite the city, leading couple Maria and Freder would have escaped in a space rocket. The ending was soon dropped, yet the idea of a movie about space travel remained so insistent that, within two years, Lang had made *Woman in the Moon* (1929).

Although less widely celebrated than *Metropolis*, *Woman in the Moon* is nevertheless a key part of early SF cinema – largely thanks to its special effects and scientific rigour. Unlike the fanciful romances of Wells and Verne, published just a couple of decades earlier, Lang's film used cutting-edge scientific breakthroughs to depict a realistic space mission; between the two world wars, Germany led the way in astrophysics, and Lang cannily employed rocket scientist Hermann Oberth as an advisor on his movie.

While *Woman in the Moon* didn't get all its details right – there's breathable air on one side of the Moon – its depiction of a rocket launch is eerily accurate and, as you would expect from Lang, beautifully staged. Anticipating the real space rockets that launched decades later, Lang's craft is multistage, with its main booster breaking off in orbit and leaving the front-most section to continue on its path to the Moon.

Metropolis and *Woman in the Moon*, with their lavish budgets and huge sets, were products of a country that had dramatically reshaped itself in the decades following the First World War. These years of renewed growth resulted in similarly ambitious genre films appearing across Europe. In Russia, 1924 saw the release of the pioneering silent film *Aelita*, based on the novel of the same name by Alexei Tolstoy. What's surprising about *Aelita*, directed by Yakov Protazanov, is how honestly it depicts the austerity of the Soviet Union of the early 1920s, when the revolution had only occurred a few years earlier. The wine tastes like vinegar; food is scarce; rations of sugar are furtively stashed away. *Aelita* contrasts what its Soviet audience would have recognised as humdrum everyday life with a decadent society on Mars; the ruling class live a gilded existence in their huge, angular palaces, while a penniless working class are kept on ice deep underground. Eventually, the Martian society and its statuesque queen, *Aelita*, are revealed to be the reverie of the film's protagonist, Los (Nikolai Tsereteli). At the film's conclusion, Los rejects his selfish ambition to build a rocket, and instead vows to dedicate his energies to serving the greater good. It's a moral that probably won't do much for modern audiences, but in terms of its elegant, futuristic visuals – which had a clear influence on Lang's *Metropolis* – *Aelita* remains a vitally important film in early twentieth-century cinema.

Likewise *Cosmic Voyage* (1936), a Soviet film that depicts a flight to the Moon in extraordinary detail. The story itself is pure fantasy; a luxuriously bearded professor boards his rocket with an intense young boy and a female assistant, and their adventures on the Moon see them rescue a cat left stranded following an earlier test flight. In terms of design, however, *Cosmic Voyage* is a technical marvel. Director Vasili Zhuravlov films his detailed miniatures from a low angle, creating a grand sense of scale as the camera tracks across the rocket in its hangar. Sequences on the Moon use stop-motion animation to depict the cosmonauts' tripping and bouncing along the lunar surface. This commitment to realism was thanks in part to rocket scientist Konstantin Tsiolkovsky, who served as the film's science consultant, just as Hermann Oberth had on Lang's *Woman in the Moon*. Withdrawn from cinemas by Soviet censors shortly after its release, *Cosmic Voyage* thankfully survives today.

Released the same year as *Cosmic Voyage*, *Things to Come* was a similarly ambitious depiction of scientific progress. Written by the great sci-fi author H. G. Wells and directed by William Cameron Menzies, *Things to Come* could be described as Britain's answer to *Metropolis* – a movie Wells was rather scathing about several years earlier. Beginning in 1940, Menzies's film charts the rise and fall of a British city – called Everytown – over the course of almost a hundred years. Destroyed by a great war, the city reflects a wider apocalypse where humanity backslides into chaos; after decades of war and death, a new, more peaceful civilisation emerges, packed into pristine cities constructed deep underground. A mission to send a rocket to the Moon is briefly disrupted by protestors who have grown nervous about all the unfettered scientific progress. The flight nevertheless proceeds as planned, and the city's governor sombrely warns us that humanity must remain on its path of progress, or instead risk sinking back into intolerance and war. Originally running to a length of 117 minutes, *Things to Come* was edited to 108 minutes by the time of its release; other cuts brought its duration down to as low as 72 minutes. That original cut, regrettably, no longer survives.

Things to Come wasn't a financial success in its day, and even in its edited form, it's a slow and ponderous film. But in visual terms, its image of a clean subterranean utopia is unforgettably striking; an early shot of fighter planes flying over the cliffs of Dover, created years before the Battle of Britain, is chillingly prophetic.

Selected SF films mentioned in this chapter:
Aelita (1924)
Woman in the Moon (1929)
Cosmic Voyage (1936)
Things to Come (1936)

3. Creator and creation

FRANKENSTEIN (1931)

'Now I know what it feels like to be a god!'

Decades before *Blade Runner* or *RoboCop*, there was *Frankenstein*: a pioneering story of creator and nightmarish creation. Mary Shelley's seminal gothic novel was a milestone in literature, yet it's Universal's 1931 movie that gives us much of the imagery we now associate with the *Frankenstein* tale: the scientist in his lab coat, joined by his hunchbacked assistant. The creature stretched out on an operating table, lit up by great arcs of electricity. That lofty forehead, the bolts through the neck, those half-closed eyes, at once disturbing and sympathetic. Directed by James Whale, *Frankenstein* introduces all kinds of ideas that weren't in Mary Shelley's source novel. Never mind the common mistake that Frankenstein is the name of the monster's creator, not the monster itself; in Shelley's novel, first published in 1818, Victor Frankenstein (not Henry, as he's named in the movie) doesn't have a hunchbacked assistant. The creation of the monster is left ambiguous; the bolts through the neck and the lofty forehead are nowhere to be found. Whale's movie, however, remains one of the most compelling and urgent adaptations of the original text – a cautionary sci-fi tale that soon flips over into pure horror.

The science-fiction label did not even exist when Shelley first put pen to paper at the age of just eighteen. But while *Frankenstein: or, The Modern Prometheus*, to give the novel its full title, takes in elements from gothic horror, it's undoubtedly a sci-fi story. Unlike tales from folklore, such as the Golem, *Frankenstein* takes the idea of a man creating life from the realms of magic and into the arena of scientific speculation. Victor Frankenstein is, after all, a scientist – an expert in biology, chemistry and physics. When Shelley started writing her novel, she drew on the work of such real-life scientists as Humphry Davy and Erasmus Darwin. (In the preface to the first edition of *Frankenstein*, Shelley's husband, Percy Bysshe Shelley, writes, 'The event on which this fiction is founded, has been supposed, by Dr Darwin, and some of the physiological writers of Germany, as not of impossible occurrence . . .')

Adapted from a stage play by Peggy Webling, Whale's *Frankenstein* is more contained than Mary Shelley's work. Where the novel moved from Europe to Scotland to Ireland to the North Pole, the movie takes place in and around a single (unnamed) European village. As in the book, Frankenstein (Colin Clive) is a scientist obsessed with the idea of creating life. Working in an abandoned watch tower with his assistant Fritz, Frankenstein stitches together a tall, makeshift human form from purloined body parts and, one tempestuous evening, brings his creature (Boris Karloff) to life in a burst of lightning. Unlike the articulate monster in the book, Frankenstein's creation is a mute, pitiful thing; tall, capable of miraculous feats of strength, yet hardly malicious or cunning (one of the monster's first actions in the book is to frame Frankenstein for murder). Nevertheless, Frankenstein becomes fearful of his creation, much as his counterpart in the book was; thinking the monster capable of murder, Frankenstein claps the poor creature in irons. The monster does eventually kill, but only after Frankenstein's old mentor Dr Waldman (Edward Van Sloan) makes an attempt to dissect it. Again, as in the book, the monster becomes a shunned, tragic figure – in this instance, cornered by an angry mob of villagers and burned alive in a windmill. An ending was originally devised in which Frankenstein met a fiery death at the same time; this was removed after test screenings found it to be too downbeat, and the scientist is instead allowed to live in happiness with his wife Elizabeth – a far cry from the icy gloom of Shelley's final chapter.

Frankenstein's iconic makeup effects were conceived by Jack Pierce, who had previously worked on *The Man Who Laughs* (1928) and Universal Studios' adaptation of *Dracula* (1931), and his monster makeup is ingenious in its simplicity. The flat-topped head and heavy eyelids give Karloff's already distinctive features an unnatural quality, while at the same time giving the actor the freedom to express himself; those strange, hollow cheeks were achieved with an even simpler approach – Karloff simply removed his dentures.

The monster's birth scene is equally striking, thanks in no small part to Colin Clive's fevered performance as Frankenstein and some stunning production design. The effects of lightning and electricity – which recall the creation of the robot in Fritz Lang's *Metropolis* – were the creation of Kenneth Strickfaden, who was himself a kind of Frankenstein figure. Like Herr Frankenstein, Strickfaden showed a talent for physics and chemistry at school and, as a teenager, became fascinated by electricity and gadgets. Strickfaden's inventiveness led to a job at a travelling sideshow, for which he designed some eye-catching attractions: one took in spinning circular saws, dancers and flashes of light emanating from a Tesla coil.*

Strickfaden later took his knowledge of science and mechanics into the film industry, and his work on Frankenstein's laboratory is arguably his most famous contribution to cinema. If audiences didn't believe they were witnessing a scientific breakthrough, the rest of the story's impact would be lost; thanks to Strickfaden's electrical effects – all flickering gadgets and blinding arcs of light – it became the archetypal mad scientist's lab, cluttered to the rafters with test tubes and sparking electrical devices. (Decades later, Mel Brooks's affectionate parody, *Young Frankenstein*, reused these exact same setpieces – incredibly, Strickfaden had kept all the old apparatus hoarded in his garage.)

As for *Frankenstein*'s shadowy and beautifully stark imagery, we have British director James Whale to thank. Like many European filmmakers of his era, Whale was influenced by the Expressionist filmmakers of Germany, and there's much of the dreamlike quality of *The Cabinet of Doctor Caligari* and *Der Golem* (both 1920) in his *Frankenstein*. Whale began his career as a director of

* See: Harry Goldman, *Dr Frankenstein's Electrician* (Jefferson, CA: McFarland, 2005), https://books.google.co.uk/books?id=1FKDBAAAQBAJ&pg=PA24&lpg=PA24&dq=kenneth+strickfaden+carnival&source=bl&ots=7YMgsYpSo-&sig=1CYOJrCVASGdXJMk2k5mtXefAKQ&hl=en&sa=X&ved=0ahUKEwj-4aiR8uTRAhVFIsAKHUnbDeYQ6AEIIzAB#v-onepage&q-kenneth%20strickfaden%20carnival&f-false.

stage plays, and the success of *Journey's End*, about veterans of the First World War, was met with critical and popular acclaim on both sides of the Atlantic. As cinema was making the transition from the silent era to the sound age, Hollywood studios were casting around for directors who had experience of working with dialogue. Whale was duly signed up to direct an adaptation of *Journey's End* for the cinema, and he brought actor Colin Clive, who had played the lead on stage, to reprise the part for the silver screen. Clive, of course, would go on to play the title role in *Frankenstein*.

By modern standards, *Frankenstein's* production was remarkably brief. Filming got under way in the summer of 1930 and lasted barely six weeks; by the early part of the following year, it was out in cinemas. A massive hit for Universal, *Frankenstein* – along with *Dracula*, also released in 1931 – prompted the studio to invest further in crowd-pleasing genre films. Whale, under a five-picture contract, made several in the years following *Frankenstein*; *Bride of Frankenstein* (1935), in which the monster is revealed to have survived his fiery brush with fate, is one of the director's very finest movies. It's inspired by a part of Shelley's novel where the monster demands that Frankenstein builds him a mate; at first, the scientist acquiesces, only to destroy his latest creation when he realises that the pair might spawn yet more monsters. In the movie, written by William Hurlbut and John L. Balderston, it's the monster who rejects his bride, and the pair wind up dying together in Frankenstein's crumbling lab. Once again, Frankenstein dodges the lonely fate suffered by his literary counterpart.

Both the *Frankenstein* book and movie have since become shorthand for scientific hubris, whether it's through genetic engineering or machine intelligence. Yet *Frankenstein* is more than a cautionary story about the dangers of playing God. It also raises moral questions about scientific responsibility – in both versions of the story, Frankenstein is, among other things, an unloving father. In Shelley's novel, the monster is eloquent enough to express his sense of isolation, both from his creator and the rest of humanity. Like Caliban in Shakespeare's *The Tempest*, self-knowledge is a curse for the monster: 'The red plague rid you,' Caliban tells Prospero, the wizard who gives him the power of speech, 'for learning me your language!'

The monster of James Whale's movie lacks that gift of articulation, but we can sense his loneliness through Karloff's quietly brilliant physical performance; certainly, he's a more innocent, sympathetic figure than the creature in the book.

Decades later, *Frankenstein* still poses difficult questions: if science could create a sentient being, whether out of purloined body parts or lines of code on a computer, what rights would it have? What would its existence mean for us as humans? It's those questions that make *Frankenstein* so timelessly resonant, and so commonly used as inspiration for other stories of scientific discovery.

From page to screen

After *Frankenstein*, Hollywood developed an appetite for larger-than-life stories of mad scientists and their twisted creations – and inspiration for these stories was frequently found in the pages of nineteenth-century literature. Released a matter of months after *Frankenstein*, Paramount's adaptation of Robert Louis Stevenson's *Strange Case of Dr Jekyll and Mr Hyde* was a similarly big hit. Fredric March plays the dapper scientist whose experimental drug unleashes the vicious id within – his hairier alter-ego, Edward Hyde. For the time, the transformation sequences were sensational; March's dual performance was similarly lauded, and landed him an Oscar.

Paramount's next sci-fi shocker was, if anything, even more potent. The novel the studio chose was H. G. Wells's controversial *The Island of Doctor Moreau* – perhaps the most disturbing work of its kind since *Frankenstein*. On a remote island in the South Pacific, Moreau subjects wild animals to lengthy, painful experiments, which twist them into humanoid, talking creatures – they're no longer beasts, but then, they're not quite human, either.

Directed by Erle C. Kenton and beautifully shot by cinematographer Karl Struss, *Island of Lost Souls* (1932) plays fast and loose with Wells's text, but nevertheless captures its nightmarish tone. The island is a place of screams and unspeakable suffering; the protagonist, Parker (Richard Arlen), is chilled to the core by the bloodcurdling cries of Moreau's victims. The doctor himself, played by a coolly charismatic Charles Laughton, is utterly indifferent to the cruelty he metes out in his experiments. Like the literary Dr Frankenstein, Moreau is ultimately done in by his own creations; in his desire to turn animals into people, he misplaces his own humanity.

Island of Lost Souls was sold on the alluring presence of Lota, a feline woman created specifically for the movie; played by Kathleen Burke, she was billed as a scantily clad seductress wont to destroy men 'body and soul'. What movie-goers got instead was one of the most effective and disquieting genre films of its era; so effective, in fact, that it was banned for decades in the UK. By the time an uncut version of the movie emerged on disc in 2011, two further adaptations of *Doctor Moreau* had come out of Hollywood. Neither could match *Island of Lost Souls* for sheer coiled menace.

One year after *Island of Lost Souls*, James Whale tackled another of Wells's great novels in *The Invisible Man* (1933), starring Claude Rains as Dr Griffin, another scientist whose experiments leave him on the darker reaches of the moral divide. Rains, who spends much of the film either offscreen or clad in bandages, nevertheless projects a magnificent performance through the eye-popping invisibility effects.

In 1935, Whale returned – reluctantly, at first – to the story of the sensationally popular monster he had brought to the screen just four years earlier. *Bride of Frankenstein* reunited Boris Karloff's creation with Colin Clive's excitable maker; in a dark echo of Dr Frankenstein's relationship with his fiancée Elizabeth (here played by Valerie Hobson), the monster is given a mate of his own – the nameless bride, played by Elsa Lanchester in unforgettable makeup by a returning Jack Pierce. *Bride of Frankenstein* cemented the monster's status as a pop-culture icon, and Karloff would reprise the role in a string of decreasingly expensive sequels, released up until the 1950s.

Gradually, the fertile period of early 1930s genre cinema, which so frequently took inspiration from literature and gave us such indelible films as *Frankenstein*, *Island of Lost Souls* and *The Hands of Orlac* (also known as *Mad Love*) gave way to a slew of sequels that emphasised spectacle over story. Meanwhile, an increasingly overbearing American ratings board ensured that films as disturbing – and potentially blasphemous – as *Island of Lost Souls* were *verboten* by the end of the decade. As the Second World War loomed, European filmmakers could ill-afford to make the kinds of ambitious genre movies that had lit up the 1920s and 1930s; American theatres, meanwhile, were largely filled with low-budget, escapist fare with lurid titles: *Man-Made Monster* (1941), *The Purple Monster Strikes* (1945). It wasn't until the 1950s that a new golden age of sci-fi cinema would finally dawn.

Selected SF films mentioned in this chapter:

Dr Jekyll and Mr Hyde (1931)

Island of Lost Souls (1932)

The Invisible Man (1933)

Bride of Frankenstein (1935)

The Hands of Orlac/Mad Love (1935)

Man-Made Monster (1941)

The Purple Monster Strikes (1945)

4. Cinema's first sci-fi hero

FLASH GORDON (1936)

'Take him to a laboratory. Give him everything
he requires . . . except his freedom!'

Audiences were hungry for escapist entertainment in the era of the Great Depression, but science fiction remained an expensive and often risky genre for film studios on both sides of the Atlantic. Britain's *Things to Come* (1936), as ambitious and often stunning to look at as it was, failed to make much money. Similarly, *The Tunnel* (1935) – a third adaptation of Bernhard Kellermann's novel – proved to be a box-office misfire. In the United States, 20th Century Fox suffered an even bigger blow with *Just Imagine* (1930), a sci-fi musical set in the distant year of 1980.* Its production values were high, and its depictions of svelte hovering aircraft and art-deco Manhattan towers were dazzling enough to garner an Academy Award. Once again, however, cinemagoers failed to show up; the waning popularity of musicals may have been a factor, but as a result of its low turnout, *Just Imagine* would be the last big-budget sci-fi film to emerge from an American studio for more than twenty years. But while the film itself was a failure, *Just Imagine's* sets – and even some of its footage – lived on in an unexpected arena.

---

* See: Tobias Hochscherf and James Leggott, *British Science Fiction Film and Television: Critical Essays* (Jefferson, CA: McFarland, 2005),
https://books.google.co.uk/books?id=JVqg-LWs5JYC&pg=PA18&lpg=PA18&dq=science+f
iction+box+office+poison&source=bl&ots=oxsHlGnzGO&sig=YcgIlzoxNg9AoXgJIp5eP
n2EK_k&hl=en&sa=X&ved=0ahUKEwjApL32_qrSAhXkL8AKHUc5AMcQ6AEIQDAG#v
=onepage&q=science%20fiction%20box%20office%20poison&f=false.

In the mid-1930s, Universal acquired the rights to *Flash Gordon* – an enormously popular comic strip created by artist Alex Raymond. Flash Gordon was the epitome of the all-American hero: square-jawed, well-educated and as adept at playing polo as he was punching aliens with his bare fists. In an era when pulp stories about alien planets and brave heroes were at the height of their popularity, *Flash Gordon* soared on the wings of Raymond's exotic, striking artwork. In theatres, film serials offered a similar diet of action, mystery and suspense: divided into chapters generally lasting between twenty to thirty minutes each, they offered, like the pulp magazines filling newsstands through the Depression era, a cheap form of mass entertainment.

For Universal, *Flash Gordon* presented something of a challenge: how could the planets and ships depicted in Raymond's artwork be brought to the screen without running up a huge budget? The investment set aside to make the film was higher than most serials, but still lean by the standards of most studio feature films. During the making of *Just Imagine*, 20th Century Fox spent a reported $168,000 on constructing a miniature Manhattan skyline – more money than a studio like Republic Pictures typically spent on a fifteen-chapter serial like *Dick Tracy* in 1937. In order to make *Flash Gordon*'s $350,000 budget stretch further, Universal therefore made cunning use of music and set-pieces from other serials and movies – including *Just Imagine*.* A metallic, bulbous rocket, which would soon become famous as the ship built by Dr Zarkov (Frank Shannon) in *Flash Gordon*, was originally constructed for Fox's ill-fated sci-fi musical; both the scale miniature and its full-scale interior set were among the props and other pieces purchased by Universal. The laboratory set and its equipment – created by Kenneth Strickfaden, who also worked on *Just Imagine* – were recycled from *Frankenstein* and *Bride of Frankenstein*. Several effects shots and other bits of footage were taken from Universal's 1936 film, *The Invisible Ray*, and even the music was taken from other films in Universal's back catalogue.

Flash Gordon may have been something of a Frankenstein's monster, but under the control of veteran serial producer Henry MacRae and director

* See: http://www.imagesjournal.com/issue04/infocus/flashgordon.htm.

Frederick Stephani, the serial nevertheless felt like a comic-book adventure drawn to life. One element vital to the serial's success was its casting; in the title role, MacRae and Stephani hired Larry 'Buster' Crabbe, a former Olympic swimmer and trainee lawyer. Crabbe had previously played the title role in another serial, *Tarzan the Fearless*, and his athletic prowess meant that he was a perfect match for the chiselled hero depicted in Raymond's comics.

First appearing in theatres in April 1936, *Flash Gordon* brought with it an exoticism that was absent from the cheaper westerns and thrillers of rival serials. The story begins as an alien planet, Mongo, closes in on Earth. While a meteor strike causes chaos across the United States, polo-champ Flash, his love interest Dale Arden (Jean Rogers) and scientist mentor figure Dr Zarkov blast off for Mongo. There, Flash and his friends encounter the planet's evil dictator, Ming the Merciless (Charles Middleton), his duplicitous daughter Princess Aura (Priscilla Lawson) and a small army of strange and aggressive monsters. Each episode offered an unpredictable grab-bag of pulp SF and surreal fantasy; ray guns and gravity-defying vehicles were everywhere on Mongo, yet soldiers also fought with swords and spears. Sets in one episode might look metallic and futuristic; in another, they might look like something from antiquity. This was, of course, because of all those recycled props from other movies, yet the eclectic mix of the Egyptian, the Roman and the futuristic all formed a part of *Flash Gordon*'s escapist appeal. Besides, despite the cheap special effects – giant lizards are evidently small reptiles with horns glued to their heads – the episodes were made and acted with such pace and brio that audiences were simply swept along by it all. The undercurrent of simmering eroticism also helped; Universal commissioned *Flash Gordon* as an attempt to hook a more adult audience for a genre increasingly watched by children, which explains the love rivalry between the demure Dale Arden and Princess Aura, the tight costumes and Crabbe's frequent toplessness.

To modern eyes, *Flash Gordon*'s less pleasant undercurrents are difficult to ignore. Ming, played with imposing enthusiasm by Middleton, is an oriental caricature in the Fu Manchu mould; the female characters are generally there to swoon or be rescued by the hero just in the nick of time. Yet *Flash*

Gordon's cultural importance shouldn't be underestimated, either; in the comic-book realm, Flash was created as a rival to Buck Rogers, a similar pulp SF hero created by Philip Francis Nowlan in 1929. Buck Rogers got a film of his own before Flash did, but it was merely a ten-minute short screened at the Chicago World's Fair in 1933. It was therefore Flash Gordon who became cinema's first true sci-fi action star. The first serial's thirteen-episode run was so popular – it was Universal's second most profitable release of 1936 – that Crabbe returned to play the hero again in the fifteen-episode *Flash Gordon's Trip to Mars* (1938) and the twelve-episode *Flash Gordon Conquers the Universe* (1940).

Flash Gordon's popularity lingered long after the age of the matinee serial passed, and far outlived its creator, Alex Raymond, who sadly died in a car crash in 1956. By then, the original serial had reappeared in multiple guises, sometimes edited down to feature-film length and issued under such titles as *Rocket Ship* or *Spaceship to the Unknown*. A television series, which ran for thirty-nine episodes, first aired in 1954 and starred Steve Holland. Like Crabbe before him, Holland looked like he had stepped straight out of a comic book – partly because he had been the model for a number of pulp-magazine illustrations – yet the series around him, shot in post-Second World War Germany and France, looked decidedly threadbare.

Regular reruns of the original Buster Crabbe serials, the syndicated 1954 series and the continued popularity of the comic strips meant several generations of Americans kids grew up with *Flash Gordon* as a part of their cultural backdrop. The writer Ray Bradbury and Italian filmmaker Federico Fellini were both open about their admiration for *Flash Gordon* in their youth; meanwhile, in 1950s Modesto, California, a shopkeeper's son named George Lucas enthusiastically devoured Flash's adventures on the page and screen. As we'll later see, *Flash Gordon* became one of the key ingredients in Lucas's phenomenal *Star Wars* saga, which, like *Flash Gordon* before it, is a pop-cultural blend of fantasy, fairy tale, war movie and space opera. Just as *Flash Gordon* was fashioned from a piece of a forgotten musical here or a bit of *Bride of Frankenstein* there, so *Star Wars* borrowed freely from fairy tales, literature, pulp fiction and 1930s matinees.

Ironically, it might have been *Flash Gordon*, and not *Star Wars*, that became the special effects blockbuster of the 1970s. Italian producer Dino De Laurentiis had been trying to get a new adaptation of *Flash Gordon* onto the screen through much of the decade; Lucas himself famously wanted to direct a *Flash Gordon* movie, but finding the rights too expensive, came up with a space-opera premise of his own. In the interim, an animated TV series emerged and, most curiously of all, so did an erotic parody called *Flesh Gordon* (1974). The latter brought the kinky undercurrent of the original serial right into the foreground, and contained such character names as Emperor Wang and Dr Jerkoff. Meanwhile, behind the scenes, young artists Rick Baker and Dennis Muren worked on *Flesh Gordon*'s special effects; within three years, they would be working with George Lucas on *Star Wars*.*

De Laurentiis's *Flash Gordon* movie finally emerged in 1980 – three years after *Star Wars* broke records, and on a somewhat larger budget than Lucas's space fantasy. Directed by Mike Hodges, *Flash Gordon* was an exercise in vibrant high camp, with former *Playgirl* centrefold Sam J. Jones playing a conspicuously muscular Flash. Max von Sydow, previously better known for his work with Ingmar Bergman, played the glowering Ming, while Brian Blessed chewed scenery as the winged Prince Vultan. Not a smash like *Star Wars*, *Flash Gordon*'s tongue-in-cheek tone, screenwriter Lorenzo Semple Jr's wilfully ripe dialogue ('Flash, I love you, but we only have 14 hours to save the Earth!') and Queen's thumping rock soundtrack still earned it a devoted cult audience.

In the twenty-first century, *Flash Gordon* has become somewhat eclipsed by more modern comic-book creations like DC's *Superman* and Marvel's *Avengers*; nevertheless, the space-opera hero has continued to ride the changing tides of pop culture, appearing in a 1996 animated TV series and a live-action show in 2007. As recently as 2015, British director Matthew Vaughn announced his intention to make a new big-screen version of *Flash Gordon*, based on a

---

* See: http://variety.com/2014/film/news/comic-con-flesh-gordon-star-to-join-autograph-seekers-in-pressing-the-flesh-1201266935.

screenplay by Mark Protosevich.* More than seventy years on from his debut, Flash Gordon remains the archetypal space adventurer.

SERIAL SCI-FI

Flash Gordon may have got to the United States' theatres first, but his success meant that Buck Rogers wasn't far behind. Universal, eager to get more space opera before its moviegoing public, brought Rogers to the screen in 1939 – and, rather than fix something that wasn't broken, the studio cast Buster Crabbe in the title role. Like Flash, Buck Rogers was an all-American hero, but this time a veteran of the First World War rather than a champion polo player. Rogers is a hero displaced in time rather than space; a freak accident leaves him in a state of suspended animation for 500 years and, after waking up in the twenty-fifth century, he discovers that the entire planet is in the thrall of a criminal organisation and its despotic leader, quaintly named Killer Kane (Anthony Warde).

Buck Rogers's tale of freedom fighting and bravery stretched across twelve chapters of about twenty minutes each and, once again, the serial's producers used stock footage and recycled props to save costs. Crabbe only appeared in one *Buck Rogers* serial, but the character remained almost as enduring as Flash Gordon; a new TV series appeared in the early 1950s, while the 1979 TV movie and series, which starred Gil Gerard as Rogers and Erin Gray as Wilma Deering, arrived in the wake of *Star Wars*-mania.

For most, *Flash Gordon* and *Buck Rogers* remain the most famous examples of science fiction from the serial era, and while their production values weren't exactly top-notch even in the 1930s, they were nevertheless a world away from the cheap westerns, mystery thrillers and aviation adventures more commonly seen at matinees of the period. Nevertheless, other SF serials popped up both before and after *Flash Gordon*. *The Invisible Ray* (1920), not to be confused with the 1936 film of the same name, was a sci-fi thriller about a

* See: http://uproxx.com/hitfix/mark-protosevich-hired-to-rewrite-matthew-vaughns-flash -gordon-for-fox.

weapon that could prove deadly in the wrong hands – a popular theme in these old serials, since *The Power of God* (1925) was also about a scientist whose invention could prove dangerous if seized by criminals. Like so many films from the early decades of cinema, *The Invisible Ray* is sadly lost.

One of the first serials from the sound era also concerned a threatening invention: *The Voice from the Sky* (1929) begins with an ominous broadcast from a scientist who threatens to destroy the world's vehicles and weapons.

It was after *Flash Gordon*, however, that makers of serials began to explore science fiction more commonly. One of the most entertaining was *The Phantom Creeps* (1939), starring Bela Lugosi. Once again, mad scientists try to conquer the world with their evil intentions, which included an invisibility belt, giant mechanical spiders and an eight-foot-tall robot with a face that resembles a Japanese kabuki mask.

By the time *The Monster and the Ape* came out in 1945, the popularity of serials had begun to wane. While such studios as Republic and Columbia continued to make serials well into the 1950s – *Radar Men from the Moon* was one SF example – the rising number of televisions in American households meant that serialised dramas increasingly began to appear on the small screen. The simplistic plots and low production values of most serials also made them look increasingly old-fashioned as feature films introduced things like widescreen, Technicolor and surround sound to entice audiences back into theatres. By 1956, what was once a staple of American cinema had reduced to a trickle; the fifteen-part western *Blazing the Overland Trail* was the last major serial of its kind.

Of the dozens of chapter-plays produced in the first half of the twentieth century, only a tiny fraction of them could be considered science fiction – and, even then, they were intended to thrill rather than delve deep into the human condition. All the same, *Flash Gordon* and *Buck Rogers*, plus later serials based on comic-book characters, like Superman and Batman, were the popcorn cinema of their day. With their stories led by action and special effects, they were the forerunner of today's superhero movies – and, indeed, their episodic nature anticipated the 'Cinematic Universe' concept established by Marvel Studios, in which a wide story arc is told over a series of movies.

It's also worth noting, on the other hand, just how few and far between science-fiction movies were in American cinema between the 1930s and 1940s. While previous decades had seen the release of such touchstones as *Metropolis*, *Things to Come* and *Aelita*, the genre was studiously avoided by American studios from 1930 to the end of the Second World War. It wasn't until the boom years of the 1950s, and the advent of the atomic bomb, that a golden age of science-fiction cinema would begin in the United States. The age of the pulp matinee hero was over by 1951, but he would soon be replaced by a new form of big-screen sci-fi that was bigger, deeper and spectacularly diverse.

Selected SF films mentioned in this chapter:
The Invisible Ray (1920)
The Power of God (1925)
The Voice from the Sky (1929)
The Tunnel (1930)
Just Imagine (1930)
The Invisible Ray (1936)
The Phantom Creeps (1939)
The Monster and the Ape (1945)
Radar Men from the Moon (1952)
Flesh Gordon (1974)

5. UFO-era classics

THE DAY THE EARTH STOOD STILL (1951)

'We have come to visit you in peace and with goodwill.'

In March 1948, the first issue of *Fate* magazine appeared on American news-stands. Its cover, with yellow type set against a thick vertical red band, carried a striking image: a light aircraft dwarfed by three bronze flying discs. The illustration could have come from one of the pulp SF stories that were so popular in the 1930s and 1940s, but it was intended as the depiction of a real event: one described by amateur pilot Kenneth Arnold.

In June the previous year, Arnold caused a sensation when he claimed to have spotted a chain of unidentified objects in the sky over Mount Rainier in Washington state. Arnold described the objects as metallic, fast and crescent-shaped, and compared their movement to a saucer skipping across a stretch of water. The story spread through the nation's newspapers and, within weeks, reports grew of similar sightings. By 8 July, the *Roswell Daily Record* had run a front-page story claiming that the US Air Force had recovered a crashed flying saucer from a desolate stretch of land in New Mexico. The military later denied the claim, revealing that the 'saucer' was in fact the remains of a crashed weather balloon – nevertheless, the story of a crashed disc and alien occupants persisted.

The tall tales of alien visitors told in the pulps were, it seemed, bleeding into the skies above America. The planet as a whole appeared to be on the cusp of both scientific opportunity and imminent destruction: in 1945, the atom bombs dropped on Hiroshima and Nagasaki had brought the Second World War to a close, but the conflict was soon replaced by increasing tensions between the USA and the Soviet Union. There were breakthroughs in supersonic aircraft and the United States' nascent space programme – a V-2 rocket carrying plants and fruit flies was launched in February 1947 – but a background noise of paranoia and uncertainty was quietly growing.

It was against this backdrop that, in 1949, movie producer Julian Blaustein began thinking about making a science-fiction movie. At the time, the genre was largely ignored by Hollywood's major studios, as it had been since the 1930s. Blaustein, on the other hand, noted both the growing popularity of SF and the fractious mood of the time: the Soviet Union had recently tested its first atom bomb, triggering a nuclear arms race that would dominate the rest of the twentieth century. Blaustein saw science fiction as the perfect means of delivering a message of peace in a climate that seemed dangerously close to fostering another war.

The result was *The Day the Earth Stood Still*. Directed by Robert Wise, who had previously worked as an editor for Orson Welles on *Citizen Kane* and *The Magnificent Ambersons*, it was the first sci-fi film from a major Hollywood studio since the ill-fated *Just Imagine* twenty years earlier (see Chapter 4). Unlike other genre films released in 1951, *The Thing from Another World* and *The Man from Planet X*, *The Day the Earth Stood Still* imagined the occupant of its flying saucer as benign rather than aggressive: in Wise's film, it's we earthlings who pose the biggest threat.

British actor Michael Rennie stars as Klaatu, an alien who, one fine day, serenely steps from a flying saucer parked in the middle of a Washington, DC baseball field. Klaatu comes bearing some kind of gift, which the trigger-happy soldiers surrounding the ship assume to be a weapon. A shot is fired, Klaatu is injured, and Gort (Lock Martin) – a towering robot who serves as Klaatu's bodyguard – responds defensively, obliterating the soldiers' guns with a laser from his single eye.

Later escaping from the military's clutches and assuming the civilian identity of Mr Carpenter, Klaatu learns more about Earth's occupants, striking up a friendship with a young woman, Helen (Patricia Neal) and her son, Bobby (Billy Gray), before revealing the reason behind his visit: he's the representative of a united group of planets who have become fearful of Earth's growing nuclear arsenal. There's the possibility, Klaatu says, that Earth's internal aggressions could one day turn out towards space, endangering other planets – and that, Klaatu says, makes Earth a threat. Klaatu therefore issues a warning: a worldwide blackout of all mechanical activity, bringing the planet to a halt. The message is clear: the Earth must mend its warlike ways or perish.

Wise, who went on to make *The Sound of Music*, *The Andromeda Strain* and *Star Trek: The Motion Picture*, directed *The Day the Earth Stood Still* with a sober clarity and realism. The movie's generous use of real locations rather than studio backlots grounds the movie in contemporary America; the effect is further compounded by the use of real radio and TV news people, who babble urgently about the alien visitor in their midst.

The Day the Earth Stood Still was adapted from the short story 'Farewell to the Master', written by Harry Bates in 1940 and first published in *Astounding Science Fiction*. In expanding it for the screen, scriptwriter Edmund H. North changed a considerable amount; in Bates's story, the world doesn't grind to a halt, Klaatu has no message of peace to deliver, and the film's sprinkling of Christ metaphors (death, resurrection, Klaatu's 'Carpenter' pseudonym) were all North's. What North did retain, however, was the moment that enticed Blaustein to option the story in the first place: the overzealous soldier who shoots Klaatu. For Blaustein, that image seemed perfect for a world that itself seemed to have an itchy trigger finger.

Indeed, what's surprising about *The Day the Earth Stood Still* is that it succeeded in emerging at all, given the hawkish climate of the time. As we'll see in Chapter 7, Hollywood filmmakers were being scrutinised for any trace of communist sympathies at the end of the 1940s; not only did *The Day the Earth Stood Still* dare to add a character plainly modelled on the scientist Albert Einstein (played by Sam Jaffe), a figure known for his socialist leanings, but it also contained scenes in which the character arranges a peace conference with scientists from both sides of the Cold War.* As the *New York Times* writer J. Hoberman pointed out in 2008, this peace conference had clear echoes of a real-world summit held at New York's Waldorf Astoria hotel in

---

* See: http://monthlyreview.org/2009/05/01/why-socialism.

1948.* Organised by the American Communist Party, the event was picketed by anti-Stalinists who considered it an attempt to promote communist ideals on American soil. Like Klaatu, Blaustein wanted to make the case for stronger ties between nations – hardly a popular opinion among Americans at the time.

Thanks to Blaustein, *The Day the Earth Stood Still* managed to mix big-screen spectacle with a seriousness of intent. Gort, the sleek robot with the killer eye, was a fearsome yet likeable creation, and both he and the phrase used to deactivate him – 'Klaatu barada nikto' – have long since entered the sci-fi pantheon. Indeed, the movie's difficult to fault in any department; Bernard Herrmann's score, which mixes the distinctive sound of the theremin with a traditional orchestra, is both lavish and otherworldly. The acting and characterisation is unusually considered for a genre film of its era; where most sci-fi films were filled with cyphers, Klaatu emerges as a tender, captivating figure; the slight, sad-eyed Rennie is perfect casting, and it's hard to imagine Spencer Tracy – a star initially considered for the role – bringing quite the same air of quiet sensitivity. Jaffe is similarly effective as the scientist who befriends Klaatu; fresh from an Oscar-nominated performance in *The Blackboard* (1950), he lends Professor Barnhardt a childlike humanity that is a world away from the hubristic 'mad scientist' archetype that so often appeared in movies of the era. Tragically, *The Day the Earth Stood Still* would be Jaffe's last major film role for nearly seven years; in 1950, Jaffe's name appeared in *Red Channels*, a pamphlet listing 151 alleged communist sympathisers within the US entertainment industry. That Jaffe wasn't a communist hardly mattered; the actor was made a pariah, and didn't appear in another American movie until 1958.

A regular fixture on cable television after it left theatres, *The Day the Earth Stood Still* soon became one of the most revered genre films of the 1950s flying-saucer cycle; there was even talk, at 20th Century Fox, of producing a sequel. According to Robert Wise, author Ray Bradbury had written a treatment for a follow-up, but the resulting project failed to bear fruit. Like so many SF movies

* See: http://www.nytimes.com/2008/11/02/movies/moviesspecial/02hobe.html?_r=0.

of the 1950s, *The Day the Earth Stood Still* was eventually remade: released in 2008, the new version of the film was given an environmentalist slant, and a reimagined, much taller Gort was joined by a cloud of deadly nano insects. Directed by Scott Derrickson, the remake doubled down on flashy special effects, which meant that much of the dramatic understatement of the 1951 film was lost; Keanu Reeves, the new Klaatu, was a pale substitute for the dignified Rennie.

Decades later, Robert Wise would reflect that, in a glittering career studded with such classics as *West Side Story* and *The Sound of Music*, it was *The Day the Earth Stood Still* that people asked him about most often. Even now, it isn't difficult to see why; in the midst of the Cold War, *The Day the Earth Stood Still* pleaded for calm and tolerance in an age that appeared to have little of either.

Movies of the saucer age

The flying-saucer flap of the 1940s and 1950s was bound up with Cold War anxieties from the very beginning. For evidence, take a look at the very first movie to deal with the subject of mysterious discs in the sky: 1950's *The Flying Saucer*. A low-budget B-movie made by actor Mikel Conrad, it wasn't about aliens at all; instead, the title craft is the secret invention of an American scientist, which quickly becomes the target of Soviet agents who want to use its technology for their own communist ends. The film glided by largely unnoticed, but was illustrative of the uncertainty and paranoia of the age: were these lights and discs in the sky extraterrestrial or were they experimental spy-craft created by the Russians?

The flying saucer became one of the dominant sci-fi motifs of the 1950s. In *The Thing from Another World*, the first sci-fi horror adaptation of John W. Campbell's story *Who Goes There?*, an alien being is found frozen in the icy Antarctic landscape. A brief scene memorably indicates that the creature crawled from a large, circular vehicle also entombed beneath the ice. The decade's films were full of alien visitors with mischief in mind, whether they arrived quietly in their craft and plotted world domination, as in *Invaders from Mars*, or arrived noisily, as seen in Byron Haskin's colourful H. G. Wells adaptation, *The War of the Worlds* (1953). Produced by George Pal, *The War of the Worlds* was noteworthy not only for its production values, but also its inventive visual effects; the Martian vehicles, with their curved wings and cobra-like death rays, stood out in an era of shiny flying saucers. It's worth noting that, while the invaders' craft appear to float, they're really supported by three invisible legs, just like the tripods in Wells's novel – the film's effects designer Al Nozaki opted to make the legs invisible because they were too difficult to animate. The Martian war machines were so effective that, not only did they wind up winning *The War of the Worlds* an Oscar for visual effects, but director Byron Haskin also wound up recycling the designs for his later sci-fi film, *Robinson Crusoe on Mars* (1964).

One of the most lavishly produced American sci-fi movies of the 1950s also featured a handsome-looking flying saucer. *This Island Earth* (1955), adapted from the novel by Raymond F. Jones, offered a refreshingly different perspective on interplanetary war. With its home planet ravaged by a rival alien race, a group of lofty-foreheaded beings from the planet Metaluna have plans to migrate to Earth. Square-jawed scientist Dr Meacham (Rex Reason) is initially unaware of this, until he and Dr Ruth Adams (Faith Domergue) are whisked up in a flying saucer belonging to Exeter, played by Jeff Morrow. Shot in glorious Technicolor, where most other 1950s sci-fi films made do with black-and-white, *This Island Earth* was marked out by its impressive scenes of devastation on Metaluna, and its towering monster (or 'Mutant'), added at the behest of its studio, Universal International. The film's true star, though, is Exeter, who's the rare example of an alien with a conscience; his fate, at the end of the film, is an unexpectedly moving one.

The cruel invaders were back in force, meanwhile, in 1956's *Earth vs the Flying Saucers*. In it, an armada of aliens descends on our planet's capital cities; the story is thin to say the least, but the movie remains notable for Ray Harryhausen's miniature effects. His images of saucers destroying famous landmarks – Washington, DC doesn't come off well – had a clear impact on the 1990s invasion movies *Independence Day* and *Mars Attacks!*

By the end of the 1950s, the growing number of movies featuring bug-eyed aliens in circular craft had already threatened to fall into self-parody. Such films as *Invasion of the Saucer Men* (1957), *Teenagers from Outer Space* and director Ed Wood's gloriously inept *Plan 9 from Outer Space* (both 1959) could be politely described as cheap and cheerful. *Teenagers from Outer Space* was distinguished by a remarkable scene in which a barking dog is reduced to a skeleton by an alien ray gun.

While the flying saucer survived on television in the 1960s – examples could be seen in *The Invaders* and *Lost in Space* – its increasing association with the low-budget end of filmmaking saw it fall out of favour with filmmakers. The concerns of sci-fi movies also shifted as the McCarthyist Red Scare waned towards the end of the 1950s; stories of invasion gave way to movies about the space race, experiments gone awry and giant monsters.

Cinema's fascination with UFOs never quite went away, however, and in 1977 the sub-genre got a late – and perhaps definitive – entry. Steven Spielberg's *Close Encounters of the Third Kind* deals in awestruck terms with some of the theories set out by ufologists: that the lights in the sky spotted by thousands of Americans are indeed alien spacecraft, and that the government is covering up the regular contact between humans and unearthly visitors. Belief in UFOs, *Close Encounters* appears to suggest, requires faith, and everyman Roy Neary (Richard Dreyfuss) eventually has his faith spectacularly rewarded in the film's final act. The quaint silver discs of old are imagined by effects designer Douglas Trumbull as huge, glittering objects that descend from the sky like inverted cathedrals; Neary is swept up in one of the craft and whisked away to parts unknown to the strains of John Williams's triumphant score. For those who had looked up at the night sky with hope and wonder rather than fear, *Close Encounters of the Third Kind* provided the ultimate wish-fulfilment.

Selected SF films mentioned in this chapter:

The Flying Saucer (1950)
The Thing from Another World (1951)
The Man from Planet X (1951)
The War of the Worlds (1953)

This Island Earth (1955)

Earth vs the Flying Saucers (1956)

Invasion of The Saucer Men (1957)

Teenagers from Outer Space (1959)

Plan 9 from Outer Space (1959)

Robinson Crusoe on Mars (1964)

Close Encounters of the Third Kind (1977)

6. Atomic monsters

GODZILLA (1954)

'When it can't find fish in the sea, it finds men on the land . . .'

On 1 March 1954, a small fishing boat sailed by the Marshall Islands in the South Pacific. Its twenty-two-strong crew had lived cheek-by-jowl on the tiny wooden vessel for three months, and with food supplies running low, this would be the final day's fishing before they started the two-week journey back to port.

At 6.45 that morning, the dark autumn sky to the west lit up like a crimson sunset, illuminating the horizon and stirring the boat's crew from their bunks. It was an apocalyptic sight, but not an unexpected one: the USA had been testing nuclear weapons on the nearby Bikini Atoll since 1946, and the *Daigo Fukuryu Maru*'s captain, Hisakichi Tsutsui, had guided his boat to a part of the ocean that was close but nevertheless outside the danger zone established by the US Navy.

The device detonated on 1 March was, however, far more powerful than the ones set off in earlier tests – more powerful, even, than US scientists had predicted. The 15-megaton blast flung nuclear fallout far beyond the exclusion zone, and the crew of the Japanese tuna boat could only watch as the pale dust fell softly from the sky. On the long journey back to port, crewmembers began to suffer from radiation sickness; several months later, the boat's radio operator died from complications hastened by his exposure to the fallout.

For a country still reeling from the bombs that fell on Hiroshima and Nagasaki in August 1945, the incident was like salt in a raw wound, and placed renewed strain on the diplomatic relationship between the United States and

Japan. Anti-nuclear sentiment rapidly grew after the incident, both in Japan and elsewhere – and its shockwaves would soon rumble through cinemas across the world.

Mere weeks after the explosion in the South Pacific, producer Tomoyuki Tanaka began thinking about making a monster movie. He wanted to emulate the success of an American film, *The Beast from 20,000 Fathoms* (1953), in which a nuclear test wakes an angry dinosaur from its millennia-long slumber. Featuring stop-motion special effects work by Ray Harryhausen, the movie was *King Kong* for the post-war era: a story about a devastating power unleashed by science. In Tanaka's mind, the giant reptile in *20,000 Fathoms* fused with the fate of the fishing vessel, the *Daigo Fukuryu Maru*; within days, he had come up with a towering monster of his own, perhaps subconsciously inspired by the name of the tuna boat itself. In English, *Daigo Fukuryu Maru* roughly translates to 'Lucky Dragon 5'.

The result was *Gojira* – renamed *Godzilla* in the West – a movie that emerged from Japan like a cry of anguish in November 1954. *The Beast from 20,000 Fathoms* may have come first, but it was *Godzilla*, the marauding, radioactive lizard from the depths, that most effectively captured the mood of its age. Directed by Ishiro Honda, *Godzilla* was successful enough to spark an entire genre in its native country: the *kaiju eiga*, or 'strange beast movie', with *Godzilla* sequels, spin-offs and outright copies appearing annually (and sometimes even more regularly) from the mid-1950s onwards. With such sensational titles as *The War of the Gargantuas*, *Destroy All Monsters* and *Gappa: The Triphibian Monster*, Japanese *kaiju* films attracted a cult following in the West, and were generally known for their melodrama and distinctive special effects: an actor in a monster suit stomping on model cities and military vehicles.

Revisit the original *Godzilla*, meanwhile, and you'll find a movie entirely devoid of the camp excess that defined its successors. The film's seriousness of intent is marked out in its opening scenes, in which a fishing vessel not unlike the *Lucky Dragon* is destroyed by a flash of light emerging from the ocean. On nearby Odo Island, village elders begin to talk darkly of an ancient menace revived from its sleep: predictions that soon come to pass, as a colossal beast rises from the sea one night, lays waste to the island and then turns its eyes toward Tokyo.

Even with a then-unprecedented budget (estimated to have been around $1 million), *Godzilla*'s filmmakers couldn't afford to recreate the expensive and time-consuming stop-motion techniques that Ray Harryhausen had brought to *The Beast from 20,000 Fathoms*. But the production's secret weapon was cinematographer and special effects genius Eiji Tsuburaya. During the Second World War, he had worked on a string of propaganda movies that were widely praised for the quality of their visuals. In 1944's *Kato hayabusa sento-tai* (*Colonel Kato's Flying Squadron*), for example, Tsuburaya mixed live-action footage with scale miniatures to create the film's dogfights and bombing runs – sequences that were unusually realistic for their time. Tsuburaya, who had been itching to make his own monster movie since he saw the classic *King Kong*, brought all his creative skill to bear on *Godzilla*, and together with designers Teizo Toshimitsu and Akira Watanabe, built a movie monster just as iconic as the giant ape animated by Willis O'Brien two decades earlier. Although the Godzilla suit, worn by actors Haruo Nakajima and Katsumi Tezuka, was modelled after the form of dinosaurs, its most telling attribute is its skin: Tsuburaya's beast isn't covered in lizard-like scales, but in a strange mottled texture like the bark of a tree. Legend has it that Godzilla's skin was designed to resemble the scar tissue of atom-bomb survivors.

It's details like these that made *Godzilla* more than a monster movie: Honda's film was a despairing symbol of a country left shattered by the atom bomb. Unlike later films in the series, the title creature is barely seen: it's often shrouded in shadow, lit from behind by an explosion or obscured by smoke. Instead, Honda focuses his camera on the terror of its victims: Tokyo residents fleeing for their lives or staring up in awe and disbelief. It's worth noting that, from the end of the Second World War until the start of the 1950s, America's occupying forces expressly forbade Japanese filmmakers from mentioning nuclear bombs in their movies. While that ban had been lifted by the time *Godzilla* emerged, there's still the sense that a repressed terror had found its release in Honda's film.

The movie's human characters also seem haunted by memories of the bomb. Reclusive scientist Dr Serizawa (Akihiko Hirata), a survivor of the war left with a radiation scar on his face, creates a device called an Oxygen Destroyer; like Robert Oppenheimer, he's horrified by his invention's destructive power, and initially refuses to use it against Godzilla. Similarly, the palaeontologist Dr Yamane (Takashi Shimura) states that the creature should be allowed to live so it can be studied.

Just as Honda depicts the destruction of Tokyo as a tragedy rather than an entertaining firework display, so Godzilla's defeat is shown as a Pyrrhic victory. Dr Serizawa sets off his Oxygen Destroyer, a device that strips all living things to the bone, killing both himself and Godzilla. It's a cruel death for a creature summoned by a destructive act; for all its terrifying power, Godzilla is still a noble beast, and its death is portrayed as an undignified end.

With its recurring images of the dead and injured lying in hospitals, and a mesmerising sequence where 2,000 schoolchildren sing a prayer of peace, *Godzilla* is the most resonant and emotionally charged monster movie of the post-war era. Its raw power was such that, when the film arrived in the United States under the title *Godzilla: King of the Monsters*, it was heavily re-edited to remove some of its spikier, more disturbing edges. Around forty minutes of drama were cut out, with actor Raymond Burr edited in as a journalist following Godzilla's trail of destruction. All mention of nuclear weapons or radiation burns were also excised, along with Dr Yamane's salutary line at the end of the film, in which he predicts that further nuclear tests will give rise to more monsters.

After the 1954 original, subsequent *Godzilla* movies gradually shifted the creature's persona from merciless destroyer of worlds to benign mascot, a towering warrior that defends the Earth from the giant aliens that threaten its cities. Yet even this gradual transformation provides a sense of catharsis; the walking embodiment of destruction becomes an ally. Through cinema, the savage beast is tamed.

MONSTERS OF THE NUCLEAR AGE

Some emerged from the murky depths, while others scuttled in from the desert. Some arrived from other planets, while still others awoke from our own prehistory. Through the 1950s and 1960s, our world was bombarded again and again by huge and terrifying monsters, some insectoid, others reptilian, just about all of them intent on destroying everything in their path.

King Kong may have been almost twenty years old by the 1950s, yet its central image of an uncontrollable beast wreaking havoc in the middle of a city proved to be timeless – so much so that it was reissued in US cinemas no fewer than five times between the 1930s and the 1950s. When the United States and the Soviet Union began their atomic weapons tests, giant monsters became an apt metaphor: a seemingly unstoppable destructive power unleashed by science. Pandora's box was opened, and from 1953's *The Beast from 20,000 Fathoms* onwards, the giant monster sub-genre evolved rapidly in both the United States and Japan.

Them!, released in 1954, was one of the most effective American monster films of the 1950s, thanks to some terrifically atmospheric filmmaking from director Gordon Douglas. Atom-bomb tests in the New Mexico desert give rise to an army of giant, ferocious ants; they quickly head for the network of storm drains beneath Los Angeles, where their queen rears her offspring. The giant monster effects have less character and class than Ray Harryhausen's stop-motion creature in *The Beast from 20,000 Fathoms*, but *Them!* benefits from keeping its killer ants off the screen for long stretches. Instead, their presence is made known by an eerie, high-pitched insect noise or a huge shadow passing across the screen. The film's opening third, in which a girl is discovered wandering traumatised through a stormy desert, is a terrific exercise in tension building; the third act – a shootout between US soldiers and monstrous ants beneath the streets of LA – could be seen as the dry run for a noticeably similar scene in 1986's *Aliens* (see Chapter 20).

Whether it was a giant octopus with six legs attacking San Francisco in *It Came from Beneath the Sea* (Ray Harryhausen's budget couldn't stretch to eight legs), colossal spiders in *Tarantula* or irradiated locusts in *The Beginning of the End*, the monsters in American movies were subtly different from the ones that marched angrily through Japanese cinema. As we've already seen, the death of Godzilla in his 1954 debut wasn't greeted with a cheer, but a sense of tragedy – the beast is simply another victim of human folly. *Godzilla* wasn't the first film to show empathy for its title monster – *King Kong* arguably did the same – but the Japanese *kaiju* pictures of the 1950s overwhelmingly depicted their creatures as noble and sometimes even heroic. From *Godzilla Raids Again* (1955) onwards, Godzilla is depicted as a warrior as much as a destructive force; large parts of the film see him do battle with a second monster awoken by the Bomb – a spiky, crocodile-like beast named Anguirus. *Godzilla* began a rich tradition of Japanese *kaiju* movies that remains popular in the twenty-first century: *Rodan* (1956), *Mothra* (1961) and *Gamera* (1965) introduced monsters of their own, with each of them either spawning their own franchises or appearing in other movies as combatants. Flying monstrosity Rodan, for example, was one of an army of creatures that clashed in 1968's *Destroy All Monsters*. Far from the faceless, identical ants of *Them!*, the monsters in Japanese monster movies are more akin to Roman gladiators – big, powerful, but also individual and majestic. That majestic quality may come from Japan's location in such a volcanic region; in the Far East, nature is both beautiful and terrifying. Or perhaps Godzilla and his fellow monsters are an embodiment of scientific progress as both destroyer and saviour. Japan knew all too well that a new, cutting-edge weapon like a nuclear bomb could bring about terrible suffering and loss of life; but in the wake of the Second World War, Japan's remarkable explosion of growth, which saw the country transformed from a largely agricultural society to an industrial powerhouse, meant that scientific progress was also its salvation.

The *kaiju* genre continued in Japan long after interest in giant monsters ebbed in Western cinema. The melancholy and class of the first *Godzilla* may have been lost in the later *kaiju* movies, but they are steeped in a warmth and charm that make them unlike the monster movies from any other country. In the United States, the sub-genre descended into B-movie goofiness even more rapidly, with its best, classiest examples – *The Beast from 20,000 Fathoms*, *Them!*, *20 Million Miles to Earth* – closely followed by entertainingly low-rent films like *The Giant Claw*, *Earth vs the Spider* and *The Monster that Challenged the World*.

One of the great monster movies of the atomic age wasn't, strictly speaking, a giant monster movie at all. *The Incredible Shrinking Man* (1957), directed by Jack Arnold and adapted by Richard Matheson from his own novel, was a giant monster film in reverse. Its protagonist, Carey (Grant Williams) encounters a radioactive cloud while at sea, which gradually makes him shrink in size. Carey decreases in stature at the rate of an inch a day; we watch as his relationships subtly change, as his wife begins to treat him like a child – rarely has a kiss on the cheek looked so emotionally loaded. Eventually, Carey shrinks to such an extent that he becomes hunted by his own domestic cat, and later does battle with a colossal house spider. Thrilling and thought-provoking, *The Incredible Shrinking Man* also contains one of the most satisfyingly downbeat endings of a 1950s sci-fi movie. What begins as a typical atomic-age B-picture ends as an unusually poignant musing on the nature of existence itself.

Selected SF films mentioned in this chapter:

King Kong (1933)

The Beast from 20,000 Fathoms (1953)

Them! (1954)

It Came from Beneath the Sea (1955)

Tarantula (1955)

Rodan (1956)

The Incredible Shrinking Man (1957)

The Beginning of the End (1957)

20 Million Miles to Earth (1957)

The Giant Claw (1957)

The Monster that Challenged the World (1957)

Earth vs the Spider (1958)

Mothra (1961)

Gamera (1965)

The War of the Gargantuas (1966)

Gappa: The Triphibian Monster (1967)

Destroy All Monsters (1968)

7. The quiet invaders

INVASION OF THE BODY SNATCHERS (1956)

'I don't want to live in a world without love or grief or beauty. I'd rather die.'

In 1947, the same year that Kenneth Arnold's UFO sighting ushered in the flying-saucer age, a ripple of suspicion and fear rolled across America. As tensions between the United States and the Soviet Union rose in the wake of the Second World War, so too did anxieties within the USA about the spread of communism. That November, the House Un-American Activities Committee, a government body set up to sniff out communist leanings among US citizens, began its investigations into the activities of Hollywood writers and filmmakers.* A pamphlet published in 1950 summed up the mood of the time: 'Right now films are being made to craftily glorify Marxism, UNESCO and one-worldism,' it read; 'and via your TV set [. . .] they are poisoning the minds of your children under your very eyes'.†

Not even the Hollywood dream factory, it seemed, was safe from communism's insidious threat. Little surprise, then, that the Second Red Scare became a prominent backdrop for so many American sci-fi movies in the

---

* Paul Buhle and Dave Wagner, *Hide in Plain Sight: The Hollywood Blacklistees in Film and Television, 1950–2002* (New York: Palgrave Macmillan, 2005), https://books.google.co.uk/books?id=g2WluH1AARoC&pg=PA73&lpg=PA73&dq=daniel+mainwaring+blacklisted&source=bl&ots=_AmJXp2BVh&sig=nTKX_I_NjHvtwsbmzpYATAqu5Ec&hl=en&sa=X&ved=0ahUKEwing5CWzN_PAhVlCcAKHS1iCbIQ6AEIMzAE#v=onepage&q=daniel%20mainwaring%20blacklisted&f=false.
† See: https://en.wikipedia.org/wiki/McCarthyism#/media/File:Anticommunist_Literature_1950s.png.

1950s. Some, like *Red Planet Mars*, released by United Artists in 1952, were so flatly anti-communist that they functioned more as hysterical propaganda pieces than actual movies. *Invasion of the Body Snatchers*, on the other hand, tapped into the mood of the era so powerfully that its paranoid air still feels relevant over sixty years later.

First came Jack Finney's novel, *The Body Snatchers*, published in 1955. Alien seed pods, capable of copying and replacing humans with physically identical yet soulless clones, emerge in a small American town. The silent invasion threatens to engulf the planet, before sheer human fortitude sees the alien menace beat a hasty retreat.

Taking Arnold's premise, director Don Siegel and screenwriter Daniel Mainwaring forged one of the most nightmarish movies of the 1950s. The story takes place in Santa Mira, a sleepy Californian town small enough that Dr Miles Bennell (Kevin McCarthy) knows most of his patients by name. Gradually, Bennell's patients start to complain that their friends or loved ones aren't who they appear to be: they may look the same, but the spark of life has gone. The growing phenomenon is initially dismissed as hysteria, until Bennell realises, seemingly too late, that Santa Mira's residents are being replaced by emotionless pod people. The invasion could soon sweep across the whole of California – and possibly the world.

Don Siegel began his career in the Montage Department at Warner Bros – the opening to *Casablanca* (1942) was his – before he moved into directing features of his own. A couple of great noir thrillers followed in the 1950s, including *Night unto Night*, starring Ronald Reagan, and *The Big Steal*, starring Robert Mitchum and Jane Greer. *Invasion of the Body Snatchers* was Siegel's first science-fiction film, and he shoots it like a noir thriller: filmed in moody black-and-white, *Body Snatchers* is all heavy shadows, low camera angles and brooding tension. Siegel also eschews special effects for the most part, and instead uses suggestive imagery to imply the alien threat: silhouetted figures, close-ups of stars McCarthy and Dana Wynter staring in horror. It's well over half an hour before we see something resembling an effects shot, and the build up to it is so perfectly escalated that it kicks the movie into another, horrifying gear. Bennell and his unaffected friends (played by King Donovan and Carolyn Jones) find a collection of pods lurking in an outbuilding, and watch aghast as they ooze and pulsate. A few scenes later, the pods' vague forms have coalesced into identical copies of Bennell and the other survivors. From this moment on, *Body Snatchers* barely pauses for breath; as the army of pod people grows, the net around Bennell closes in, building to the most startling scene in the entire film: the doctor trying in vain to warn drivers on a highway of the invasion.

'They're here already!' Bennell screams into the lens. 'You're next, you're next . . .'

That sequence was originally intended to be *Body Snatchers'* last, and would have certainly left moviegoers with an unforgettable final image. If anything, the ending was too effective; the film's studio, Allied Artists Pictures, balked at releasing such a downbeat movie. Against the wishes of Siegel and producer Walter Wanger, a wrap-around sequence was therefore added, in which the main bulk of the movie is told in flashback from a hospital ward; the scene following Bennell's primal scream on the highway reveals that the invasion was halted in the nick of time thanks to the FBI.

Since *Body Snatchers'* release, there have been differing readings of its underlying theme: is it an anti-communist movie or is it, like Arthur Miller's 1953 play *The Crucible*, a scathing critique of the blacklist and the actions of senator Joseph McCarthy? Siegel denied that there was any political subtext to *Body Snatchers*, but a clue to the film's leanings could be inferred from the history of its screenwriter. Daniel Mainwaring was, like Siegel, steeped in noir thrillers, having written the classic *Out of the Past* (1947), Siegel's *The Big Steal* (1949) and *The Phenix City Story* (1955). One of the most significant films in Mainwaring's career, however, was 1950's *The Lawless*, a thriller about a Californian newspaper writer who becomes embroiled in the racist and cruel treatment of migrant workers. *The Lawless* was directed by Joseph Losey, a director whose leftist politics made him a person of interest for the House Un-American Committee. One year after *The Lawless*, Losey was blacklisted and, suddenly unable to find work, spent the rest of his career making movies in Europe.

Losey once commented in an interview that Mainwaring had also been blacklisted, though it seems likely that he was mistaken; what is known is that

Mainwaring lent his name to the work of other authors who couldn't work because of the blacklist, including TV writer Adrian Scott.

Taken together, it doesn't seem too much of a stretch that, in adapting Jack Finney's novel, Mainwaring had in mind an America succumbing to a disturbing kind of groupthink: a populist movement that turns friend against neighbour. This certainly echoes what was happening in the 1940s and 1950s, as Hollywood's close-knit community was torn apart by paranoia and political fervour. Actors were encouraged to inform on their colleagues in the hope of salvaging their livelihoods; some, like screenwriter Dalton Trumbo, found themselves exiled from the business for years. Little wonder, then, that so many sci-fi films of the 1950s dealt with the subject of a formless, silent menace – beings capable of infiltrating our towns, our houses, perhaps even our beds.

When McCarthyism withered at the end of the 1950s, *Invasion of the Body Snatchers'* concept proved to be such an irresistible one that it was remade three times: once in 1978 by Philip Kaufman, in 1993 (as simply *Body Snatchers*) by Abel Ferrara, and again in 2007 (as *The Invasion*) by Oliver Hirschbiegel. Of these, Philip Kaufman's version is the most satisfying, and approaches the 1956 original in its escalating sense of dread. As reworked by screenwriter W. D. Richter, the 1978 *Body Snatchers* sees the alien seeds descend on San Francisco, where the flower-power era has given way to a new epoch of pop psychology and self-help books. The hero in Kaufman's film isn't an upstanding family doctor, but a somewhat petty health inspector played by Donald Sutherland. Again, a small group of Americans find themselves hemmed in by emotionless pod people – these ones equipped with a disturbing tendency to point and scream when they spot a human interloper.

Offbeat both in its writing and casting – Sutherland is joined by Leonard Nimoy, Brooke Adams, Veronica Cartwright and a young Jeff Goldblum – the 1978 *Body Snatchers* is a witty, disturbing remake for the Watergate era. Running counter to Siegel's version, where the alien threat turns friends and neighbours into drones, the invasion in Kaufman's film takes place under the cloak of urban anonymity: everyone's so busy and self-absorbed that the pod people have managed to take over half of San Francisco before anyone begins to notice.

Like the original, which featured a brief appearance from a young Sam Peckinpah, Kaufman's *Body Snatchers* has a nice line in cameos: look out for an uncredited Robert Duvall as a creepy priest in a children's playground, Don Siegel as a taxi driver and, best of all, Kevin McCarthy in a cheeky reprisal of the 1956 film's most powerful scene.

Less essential than Kaufman's *Body Snatchers*, the 1993 remake nevertheless has a few clever twists on the established formula. This time, the invasion takes place at an army base in the United States' Deep South: a setting ripe for commentary on the dehumanising effect of the military. The story diverges from the previous two movies by telling it from a teen's perspective – Marti, played by Gabrielle Anwar. If the second remake's less satisfying and surefooted than the first two movies, it's at least shot through with the same sense of dread: Meg Tilly, who plays Marti's mother, turns in a magnificently eerie performance.

The less said about 2007's *The Invasion*, meanwhile, the better. More generously budgeted than the earlier films, *The Invasion* reworks the threat as a space virus, which is brought to Earth by a crashed space shuttle. The virus then spreads from person to person until Dr Carol Bennell (Nicole Kidman) finds a means of wiping it out.

The Invasion followed the tradition of the previous movies in filmmaking terms, in that none of the directors that made them were pigeonholed as sci-fi directors; prior to his *Body Snatchers*, Philip Kaufman was best known for such acclaimed dramas as *Goldstein* (1964) and *The White Dawn* (1974). Abel Ferrara was previously known as the wayward director of such uncompromising films as *The Driller Killer* and *Ms 45*; one year before *Body Snatchers*, he made the controversial cop drama *Bad Lieutenant*. Those appointments resulted in distinctive, individual movies, and it briefly looked as though the 2007 movie might go the same way; director Olivier Herschbiegel's prior movie was 2004's *Downfall*, an Oscar-nominated drama about the collapse of the Third Reich. The mix of Herschbiegel and science fiction didn't, it's fair to say, bear creative fruit – not least because *The Invasion*'s studio, Warner Bros, ditched approximately 30 per cent of the film and had a new ending reshot by director James McTeigue. The result is a curious Nicole Kidman vehicle that reads more like a disease thriller than sci-fi allegory. Its plot flirts with the notion that our planet may be more peaceful under the control of the pod people, but this is quickly abandoned in favour of a far cosier ending than any other *Body Snatchers* movie to date.

The twenty-first century may still be waiting for its own classic *Body Snatchers* film but, then again, the ideas and themes presented in Siegel's movie – and the 1978 remake for that matter – make them timeless. Intolerance, mob mentality, hatred of the other: these are the fears that *Body Snatchers* explores, and they are as urgent as ever today. As Dr Bennell wisely put it back in 1956, 'In my practice, I've seen how people have allowed their humanity to drain away – only it happened slowly instead of all at once. All of us, a little bit, we harden our hearts, grow callous. Only when we have to fight to stay human do we realise how precious it is to us, how dear.'

In plain sight

The fear of invasion ran deep in the science-fiction films of the post-war era, and while such movies as *Earth vs the Flying Saucers* and *The War of the Worlds* delivered big-screen spectacle, others imagined a far more insidious kind of alien menace. *Invasion of the Body Snatchers* was arguably the finest of this small sub-genre, but others were minor classics in their own way. One of the most visually arresting was *Invaders from Mars*, released in 1953. It was directed by the production designer William Cameron Menzies, who had woven his magic on such films as Alfred Hitchcock's *Spellbound* (he shot its celebrated dream sequence, conceived by artist Salvador Dalí) and previously directed H. G. Wells's *Things to Come* (1936). Menzies brought a deliciously surreal quality to his invasion movie, which looks at times like a children's picture book splashed across the screen: appropriate, given that it's told entirely from the perspective of a small boy, David MacLean (Jimmy Hunt).

During a savage thunderstorm one night, David wakes up to see a flying saucer descend into the field behind his house. The next day, David's father goes to investigate, and returns from the end of the garden a changed man: distant, dead-eyed and aggressive. One by one, the authority figures around

David fall victim to the flying saucer's spell and David realises they're being controlled by a jewel-like device implanted at the base of their necks.

For the first half an hour, *Invaders from Mars* builds up a nightmarish atmosphere, until the army sweeps in on a wave of stock footage and saves the day from a group of alien 'mute-ants' with plainly visible zips on their costumes (the tallest of these was played by Lock Martin, the actor inside the Gort suit in *The Day the Earth Stood Still*). But before that, *Invaders* bewitchingly evokes the mood of the communist-panic era. By telling the story from a child's level, the film also takes on an almost Kafka-esque tone: the figures who protect and care for David succumb to the aliens' influence, and the result is, for a time, truly unnerving.

Released the same year as *Invaders from Mars*, *It Came from Outer Space* imagined an alien takeover of a very different kind. What appears to be a meteorite crashes on the outskirts of a small Arizona town, and a local author, John (Richard Carlson) goes to investigate. The realisation soon hits that the crashed object is an alien spaceship, and John tries to warn the townsfolk that there's a mysterious craft buried out in the desert. Like little David in *Invaders*, John's news is roundly ignored – and then, one after another, various locals begin to vanish and reappear as emotionless figures. There is, however, a twist that sets *It Came from Outer Space* apart from other invasion movies of its time: the aliens are later revealed to be benign, and simply borrow the inhabitants of the town to help them repair their damaged ship.

It Came from Outer Space was directed by Jack Arnold, one of the most talented and prolific genre directors of the era. Its story, meanwhile, sprang from the pen of Ray Bradbury, one of America's finest writers working in sci-fi and fantasy. His collection of short stories, *The Martian Chronicles*, vividly imagined all the cruel ways mankind might treat the inhabitants of Mars during a future colonisation. Similarly, in *It Came from Outer Space*, it isn't the aliens who are the true threat, but our species' fear of the Other.

The common theme in all these movies is the loss of self, whether through the complete replacement by an alien imposter (as in *Invasion of the Body Snatchers* and *It Came from Outer Space*) or via some other means of mind control. Anxieties about the loss of free thought were another artefact of the early Cold War era, with the term 'brainwashing' first entering the English language in the early 1950s. Like the UFO phenomenon, brainwashing soon became fodder for movies, whether in thrillers – *The Manchurian Candidate*, *The Ipcress File* – or in sci-fi. *The Brain Eaters*, a low-budget 1958 movie by Roger Corman, saw several characters' minds controlled by parasites burrowing into their necks; the concept was considered so close to Robert A. Heinlein's novel *The Puppet Masters* that Corman was eventually forced to settle out of court.

In the 1950s, even household pets weren't safe from alien possession. In *The Brain from the Planet Arous* (1957), an alien being called Vol takes control of a scientist's faithful dog. Fortunately, Vol's on the side of the human race: he's only possessed the mutt to warn us about Gor, a criminal alien who has possessed the canine's owner, Steve. The invader is later revealed to be an outsized floating brain: literally a mind capable of controlling minds.

Of all the killer-brain films of the 1950s, the most entertaining and controversial was surely *Fiend without a Face* (1958). Shot in the UK on a shoestring budget, it sees a swarm of invisible parasites attack an American airbase. Attracted by atomic power, the invisible creatures set upon and kill several of the base's servicemen, removing and inhabiting their brains and spinal cords. As animated by German duo Karl Ludwig Ruppel and Baron Florenz von Fuchs-Nordhoff, the monsters in *Fiend without a Face* are mesmerisingly icky, and a final showdown, where the film's heroes gun down the slithering creatures in great showers of blood and goo, was considered outrageous enough that it was brought up in the British Parliament. The twist in *Fiend* is that the parasites aren't alien at all but, rather like the id monster in *Forbidden Planet* (see Chapter 8), a projection of a scientist's mind, summoned up by his investigations into telekinesis.

Telekinetic powers were deployed to chilling effect in *Village of the Damned* (1960), based on John Wyndham's novel, *The Midwich Cuckoos*. In a sleepy, quintessentially British village, the inhabitants unaccountably fall asleep one day; a few months later, the female residents are all revealed to be pregnant. Later still, the women all give birth to identical, rapidly growing babies with glowing eyes and blond hair ('Beware the stare!' warned the film's tagline).

Like the pod people of *Invasion of the Body Snatchers*, the village's progeny prove to be emotionless and calculating; it falls to neatly dressed Professor Gordon Zellaby (George Sanders) to figure out how to repel the alien menace. Directed by Germany's Wolf Rilla, *Village of the Damned* is an invasion movie about the post-war generation gap; there's an amusing disconnect between the somewhat stiff grown-ups and their children, with their weird hair and hidden agendas. Just as British kids in the late 1950s and early 1960s were baffling their parents by listening to noisy rock-and-roll, so the blond aliens in *Village of the Damned* are staging their own kind of rebellion: they may wear the neat little suits given to them by their parents, but secretly they are plotting to take over the world. Older members in the audience may have felt reassured, then, by the conclusion, where the professor thwarts the youthful invaders and restores the natural order. The film was followed by a sequel, *Children of the Damned* (1963), which cast the adults as villains rather than the kids. In 1995, director John Carpenter helmed a disappointingly flat remake, also called *Village of the Damned*, in which the wigs and glowing eyes look glaringly unconvincing. The 1960 original, on the other hand, remains a sharply effective example of the quiet invader sub-genre. 'Beware the stare', indeed.

Selected SF films mentioned in this chapter:
Invaders from Mars (1953)
It Came from Outer Space (1953)
The Brain Eaters (1958)
The Brain from the Planet Arous (1957)
Fiend without a Face (1958)
Village of the Damned (1960)
Children of the Damned (1963)

8. Voyages among the stars

FORBIDDEN PLANET (1956)

'Guilty! Guilty! My evil self is at that door, and I have no power to stop it!'

Against a glimmering backdrop of stars, we hear an unearthly sound: dissonant, echoing, yet strangely melodic, it's like a symphony from an alien world. So begins *Forbidden Planet*, the most expensive American SF movie of the 1950s. There was much that was groundbreaking about *Forbidden Planet*, but nothing quite as daring as that extraordinary score: created by Bebe and Louis Barron, a married couple who pushed the boundaries of experimental music, it was cinema's first entirely electronic soundtrack.

Forbidden Planet was virgin territory for MGM, a studio better known at the time for its lavish musicals. In an era when sci-fi films were generally low-budget B-pictures, the studio set aside around $2 million for *Forbidden Planet* – not too far behind the sums the studio was spending on such musicals as *The Band Wagon* and *Seven Brides for Seven Brothers*. The result was one of the most sumptuous-looking genre films of the decade – and, despite some of its less convincing elements, one of the most intelligent.

As conceived by screenwriters Irving Block and Allen Adler (and later rewritten by Cyril Hume), *Forbidden Planet* takes the skeleton of Shakespeare's *The Tempest* and places it in the twenty-third century. The sorcerer Prospero becomes a scientist named Dr Morbius; his virginal daughter, Miranda, becomes Altaira; the island on which they are trapped becomes the distant planet, Altair IV.

Leslie Nielsen plays John J. Adams, the commander of the faster-than-light spaceship, *C-57D*. He and his crew are despatched to discover the fate of a seemingly doomed expedition sent to Altair IV a couple of decades earlier. Adams's saucer-like ship sets down on the planet's dusty surface and is greeted by Robby, a hulking yet benign robot created by Morbius (Walter Pidgeon). The scientist explains that he and Altaira (Anne Francis) are the only survivors of that earlier, ill-fated expedition; he claims that an alien force on the planet killed the others and destroyed their fleeing ship. A romance develops between Adams and Altaira: at the same time, the crew of C-57D are attacked by a huge, invisible monster – the same threat that wiped out the earlier expedition has, it seems, sprung back to life.

Taking its cue from numerous pulp-magazine covers, Forbidden Planet's original poster is a clever piece of misdirection. Depicting Robby the Robot clutching an unconscious female (who barely resembles Anne Francis), the artwork might imply that the automata is the movie's main villain. In the movie itself, Robby could be the equivalent of Caliban, the island native in The Tempest who serves as Prospero's unwilling servant.

Ultimately, the film's villain isn't the robot or an alien; it's a beast from Morbius's subconscious mind, generated by a piece of technology left behind by the planet's long-dead aliens. In using that technology to boost his intellect, Morbius unleashes 'monsters from the Id' – a manifestation of his repressed thoughts that killed the other members of his expedition years earlier, and is now killing Adams's crew. Continuing the film's Freudian theme, it seems that Morbius's repressed feelings for his daughter, and his rage at the crew's lust for her, has hastened the beast's awakening.

The Id monster is a fearsomely cinematic creation, brought to life in dazzlingly original style. Director Fred M. Wilcox suggests its unseen presence with huge footprints and buckling steel staircases; the Barrons' throbbing soundtrack gives it weight and an otherworldly presence. In Forbidden Planet's most thrilling set-piece, the monster finally appears, illuminated by the laser blasts of Adams's crew. It was an ingenious piece of special effects work in 1956, and remains striking today. Disney animator Joshua Meador, who had previously worked on Snow White and Fantasia, lent his talents to the production, drawing the individual frames of the Id monster, which were then composited into the live-action footage.

Designed by Robert Kinoshita, Robby the Robot was no less a technical feat. At a cost of an estimated $100,000, Robby was one of the most expensive movie props ever built – and certainly the most detailed and realistic-looking automata seen on the screen up to that point. With his distinctive domed head revealing a network of internal mechanisms, Robby was both functional-looking and oddly charismatic; little wonder that, after *Forbidden Planet*'s release, Robby became a minor celebrity, given his own spin-off movie, *The Invisible Boy* (1957), and occasionally made appearances in such TV shows as *The Addams Family* and *Columbo*.

Robby's design proved to be enormously influential, too, both on the Japanese toy industry and the dozens of Robby-inspired miniature robots produced in that country, and on TV and filmmakers. Producer Irwin Allen hired Kinoshita to design the robot for his TV series *Lost in Space* – a character who bore more than a passing resemblance to Robby. *Forbidden Planet*'s most memorable character would, as we'll later see, also have an effect on George Lucas when he came to make *Star Wars*.

Forbidden Planet wasn't a huge hit for MGM, but the movie would have a considerable impact on two of the biggest franchises of the late twentieth century. When asked about the similarities between *Forbidden Planet* and the hit 1960s TV series *Star Trek*, Gene Roddenberry initially denied that there was a creative link between the two. Nevertheless, internal letters written by Roddenberry in 1964 reveal that he had recommended a screening of *Forbidden Planet* for his crew while *Star Trek* was still in its design stages, and there are certainly clear similarities between some of the sets and props in *Star Trek* and MGM's sci-fi movie. The macho John J. Adams is a ship's captain very much in the mould of Captain Kirk, while the plot itself, with its exploration of human failings and allusions to Shakespeare, wouldn't look out of place in a *Star Trek* episode. (Later episodes of *Star Trek* often borrowed from Shakespeare, whether for their stories or in their titles: 'Dagger of the Mind', 'All Our Yesterdays' and so on.)

Then there was *Forbidden Planet*'s extraordinary soundscape, which soon set imaginations soaring. One of the impressionable young minds in the cinema when the film first emerged was a boy named Ben Burtt. Later, after studying physics at the University of Pennsylvania, Burtt went into film-making, and the impact of *Forbidden Planet* still resonated more than twenty years later when he created the unforgettable sound effects for *Star Wars*.

Beneath *Forbidden Planet*'s lavish production values, meanwhile, lay a sentiment that would return again and again in 1950s sci-fi films: the destructive power of technology when it's misused. One image aptly sums this up: straight after the roaring Id monster has despatched several of Adams's crew, the scene cuts to a shot of Morbius, asleep at his desk, surrounded by alien machines. It appears to be a reference to a famous engraving by the Spanish artist Goya: a slumbering artist surrounded by demonic creatures. The picture's caption reads, 'The sleep of reason begets monsters.'

In an age of seemingly boundless scientific progress – nuclear power, the space programme – and also the looming possibility of atomic annihilation, *Forbidden Planet* offered a fitting allegory.

AD ASTRA

From the earliest sci-fi novels to the first silent films, filmmakers and story-tellers dreamed of leaving our planet long before the space race finally began in earnest. And as the Second World War gave way to a new period of prosperity in the United States, storytellers again turned their gaze to the sky.

It's perhaps fitting that, just as many of the scientists in the US space programme were brought in from Europe, one of the most important sci-fi producers in American cinema was himself a migrant. George Pal, born György Pál Marczinksak in 1908, was a Hungarian animator who, like so many artists of his generation, fled to the United States to escape the rise of Nazism. Thereafter, Pal began his career making television commercials, before shooting to prominence with a string of genre films through the 1950s and early 1960s, including the 1951 adaptation of H. G. Wells's *The War of the Worlds*.

Pal's earliest big Hollywood hit was *Destination Moon* (1950), loosely based on the novel *Rocket Ship Galileo* by Robert A. Heinlein. Like Fritz Lang's *Woman in the Moon* two decades earlier, *Destination Moon* was distinguished by its unusual commitment to realism; as directed by Irving Pichel, it attempted to depict what humanity's first exploration of the Moon might look like, and what hazards we might encounter along the way. To modern eyes, the ponderous dialogue and wooden characters may seem quaint, but its special effects were considered something of a breakthrough at the time, and went on to win an Academy Award. With a budget of $500,000, *Destination Moon* was considerably more expensive than *Rocketship X-M*, a rival film from Lippert Pictures, which managed to sneak into cinemas just one month before Pal's film. That *Rocketship X-M* was rushed through to completion is evident in its effects sequences, and while the film's plot is ostensibly the same – it concerns the first mission to the Moon – the plot soon veers off (literally) in a more fanciful direction. The title ship's explorers – led by Lloyd Bridges, who plays the pilot – find themselves on Mars, where they discover the remains of a lost civilisation, apparently killed by a weapon akin to our atom bomb. These sequences on Mars, co-written by blacklisted screenwriter Dalton Trumbo, remain eerily effective, as does the movie's unusually downbeat conclusion, which still packs a punch all these years later. There can be no space travel, it seems, without sacrifice. George Pal's next exploration film, the similarly expensive *Conquest of Space* (1955), carried a similar sentiment; from a new space station orbiting Earth, the first mission to Mars blasts off, but it's threatened from the outset by acts of God and human madness. The explorers eventually reach their destination, but again, not without some losses in the process. Far less successful than *Destination Moon*, *Conquest of Space* was a disappointment to Pal; when he finally returned to the SF genre five years later, it was with a far less scientifically rigorous movie: a colourful adaptation of H. G. Wells's *The Time Machine* (1960), which he also directed.

Some of the most beautiful space-exploration films of the era emerged not from the United States, but from the Eastern bloc. In the Soviet Union, a generation of movie directors were creating their own dreams of rocket ships and adventures among the stars. Often made with far higher budgets than their American counterparts, these movies offered a utopian vision of selflessness and bravery in the face of the unknown. Indeed, while Stanley Kubrick's *2001: A Space Odyssey* (see Chapter 10) was considered the first truly cerebral science-fiction film from the States, the Soviets began their cinematic space programme much earlier. Directed by Pavel Klushantsev, 1958's *Doroga k Zvezdam* (*Road to the Stars*) is an extraordinarily ambitious film – part science lesson, part SF exploration story, it was reportedly made over the course of three years, and the special effects remain truly extraordinary. We watch as multistage rockets leave Earth; cosmonauts float in the weightlessness of space; later, we see what life might be like on a rotating space station with artificial gravity, science labs and a video-link system back to Earth. A full decade before Kubrick's *A Space Odyssey*, *Road to the Stars* provided a convincing, graceful look at the future of space exploration.

Perhaps the most accomplished Soviet sci-fi film of the late 1950s was director Valery Fokin's *Nebo Zovyot* (*The Heavens Call*). In it, the USSR is in the process of sending its first manned mission to Mars (like *Conquest of Space*, from a space platform), when Russian scientists discover that the Americans are also planning to rush ahead and get their own rocket to the Red Planet before them. When the USA's mission goes wrong, the Soviet cosmonauts bravely switch course and make a rescue attempt – only to wind up stuck in a similarly parlous situation themselves. Fokin's film takes the time to distinguish between the competitive spirit of the capitalist Americans and the collectivist Soviets; between the moments of pro-communist propaganda, however, *Nebo Zovyot* contains some quite stunning sets and effects sequences.

Unfortunately, much of the film's majestic tone was mislaid in its journey to the United States. Purchased by producer Roger Corman, the film was given the more eye-catching title *Battle Beyond the Sun*, had its USSR–USA space-race dialogue erased, and some dubious monster footage added in its place. Shot on a Hollywood sound stage, these suggestive creature effects were devised by a twenty-four-year-old Francis Ford Coppola – the future director of *The Godfather* and *Apocalypse Now*.

Other films from the Eastern bloc were reworked for American audiences in a similar way, including 1962's *Planeta Bur* (which arrived in the USA under the assumed identity *Voyage to the Prehistoric Planet*) and the superb Czech film *Ikarie XB-1* (1963), based on a novel by Stanisław Lem – it emerged in the United States as *Voyage to the End of the Universe*. For decades, the original cuts of these films were difficult to find, yet have thankfully been revived in the twenty-first century; in 2011, the British Film Institute ran a season of Soviet genre films to coincide with the fiftieth anniversary of Russian cosmonaut Yuri Gagarin's first spacewalk. Belatedly, the Eastern bloc's essential contribution to SF cinema is being appreciated.

Selected SF films mentioned in this chapter:

Destination Moon (1950)

Rocketship X-M (1950)

Conquest of Space (1955)

Road to the Stars (1958)

Nebo Zovyot (The Heavens Call) (1959)

The Time Machine (1960)

Planeta Bur (1962)

Ikarie XB-1 (1963)

9. In the shadow of the bomb

Dr Strangelove; or, How I Learned to Stop Worrying and Love the Bomb (1964)

'Gentlemen, you can't fight in here! This is the War Room!'

Dr Strangelove is many things: Cold War thriller, political satire, bawdy comedy. But it is also an incisive and vital work of science fiction: a deceptively detailed look at the processes that might lead our species to stumble towards its own destruction. The notion that humanity might destroy itself wasn't a far-fetched one in the early 1960s; just two years before *Dr Strangelove*'s release, the Cuban Missile Crisis had almost triggered a nuclear conflict between the USA and the USSR. (In 2002, it was additionally revealed that a Russian submarine had come within a hair's breadth of launching its payload of missiles at the United States during that crisis; the world was far closer to complete annihilation than anyone realised at the time.)

Director Stanley Kubrick's style of filmmaking is so sober and, in some sequences, akin to a documentary that *Dr Strangelove* may not even resemble sci-fi at first glance. Yet so much of its visuals and story are speculative: the film's major setting, the War Room, set deep beneath the Pentagon, is entirely fictional. Kubrick and his team had no idea what the controls of a US bomber looked like, so they had to be fabricated. At the time, the concept of a 'Doomsday Device', which could automatically trigger a retaliatory strike in the event of a conflict, was pure science fiction. *Dr Strangelove* is therefore an imaginative film based on a kind of war that was only just becoming possible as the Second World War gave way to the Cold War: a conflict that wouldn't just mean the deaths of hundreds of thousands of soldiers, but also millions of innocent civilians. Kubrick looked at this looming threat and saw its frightening reality, but also its absurdity.

Indeed, Kubrick's initial idea was to make a straight drama about nuclear war, but he quickly changed his mind when he started researching the subject. In particular, he became fascinated by the concept of mutually assured destruction: the bizarre equilibrium where two opponents are armed with such deadly force that both sides are frozen in a permanent state of fear. If both parties possess armaments that could result in their own destruction as well as their enemy, then the result is what was described in the mid-1950s as 'the balance of terror'. The more Kubrick thought about this paradoxical situation, the more blackly comic it seemed; to this end, he took the 1958 novel *Red Alert* by Peter George and began reworking it according to his own stark, absurdist vision. The result is *Dr Strangelove*; co-written by Kubrick and Terry Southern, it ranks among the most important and best-made films about the Cold War.

Dr Strangelove imagines a nuclear crisis that is brought about not through a breakdown in diplomacy or a technical malfunction, but through paranoia, cowardice and outright stupidity. The trigger for the whole scenario is the dangerously unstable Brigadier General Jack D. Ripper (Sterling Hayden), a glowering lunatic who is convinced that fluoridation of the American water supply is a communist attempt to pollute the nation's 'pure fluids'. From Ripper's initial order on down, *Dr Strangelove* provides a catalogue of mistakes that lead to the inevitable. Aboard a B-52 bomber bound for Russia, the crew coolly execute their orders. In the Pentagon's War Room, ineffectual president Merkin Muffley (Peter Sellers) makes feeble attempts to placate the Russian premier by telephone, before engaging in a string of increasingly panicked and futile discussions with his advisors over how to prevent the destruction of the planet. Back at the US Army base where Ripper's holed up, RAF officer Lionel Mandrake (Sellers, this time hidden behind a thick moustache) makes his own flailing attempts to avert the crisis, only to realise just how sociopathic Ripper actually is.

When a Russian ambassador gently explains to President Muffley that a US attack will automatically trigger the Soviets' secret Doomsday Device, the full horror of the situation becomes clear. Fortunately, wheelchair-bound German scientist Dr Strangelove (Sellers yet again, this time wearing glasses and a shock of white hair) is on hand to provide a silver lining: Earth's elite – which includes everyone in the War Room, of course – can survive underground, and will have to spend the next 100 years or so procreating to repopulate the planet. Hence the film's subtitle: *How I Learned to Stop Worrying and Love the Bomb*.

When Kubrick embarked on *Dr Strangelove* in the early 1960s, he was already a filmmaker of both renown and no small amount of controversy. The former photographer had crashed onto the world stage with the historical epic *Spartacus*, before tackling Vladimir Nabokov's taboo novel *Lolita* – his first collaboration with Sellers. *Spartacus* gained Kubrick the plaudits, but it was his smaller films, like *Lolita*, *The Killing* and *Paths of Glory*, that best showcased his style as a filmmaker: the coolness and precision of his cinematography rubbing up against the dark irony and sly comedy of the situations he captures.

It's this friction that creates the brightest sparks in *Dr Strangelove*. Kubrick's oppressive lighting and extraordinary set design suggest a drama of absolute seriousness; for the most part, his actors, who include George C. Scott, Slim Pickens and James Earl Jones as well as Sellers, play their roles straight; it's the inherent absurdity of the dialogue and situations that results in the movie's blackest, most pointed humour.

Dr Strangelove's set design was the brainchild of Ken Adam, the production designer who would later become famous for his work on the Bond movies. In 1962, Adam had just created the angular, futuristic sets for *Dr No*, the first of Ian Fleming's novels to appear on the silver screen. Kubrick had seen that movie, and hired Adam to apply his design flair to the War Room; Kubrick's brief was to create a set that was triangular, since he argued that such a shape would be strong enough to withstand a nuclear blast if constructed out of enough concrete and steel. The result is one of the most distinctive and oft-borrowed set designs in movie history. With its irregular walls and imposing screens beaming out the paths of American bombers above a circular conference table, it's one of *Dr Strangelove*'s most arresting images: President Muffley and his advisors, lit from above by a ring of light, playing poker with the fate of humanity.

There's a matter-of-fact elegance to Kubrick's style that masks just how difficult *Dr Strangelove* was to make behind the scenes. Adam later admitted that he found Kubrick hard to work with, and recalled a hair-raising moment where, having built one iteration of the War Room with a large catwalk populated by dozens of extras, the director turned around and said it didn't work. Adam was forced to swallow his panic and rework the design.* Kubrick and cinematographer Gilbert Taylor clashed over the use of overhead lighting on that huge round table, which Taylor argued made the scenes impossible to shoot. The colossal screens – or 'big board' as George C. Scott's General Turgidson describes them – were prone to overheating, and had to be cooled down with air-conditioners. The black floor was so prone to scratches that cast and crew were forced to wear velvet-soled shoes – which explains why Scott accidentally falls head-over-heels in one scene. (Like much of Scott's scenes, this was meant to be an outtake; when Scott learned that Kubrick had tricked him into providing a broader performance, Scott vowed never to work with the director again.)

Beneath *Dr Strangelove*'s cool interiors and bickering characters, Kubrick's movie also follows in the lineage of Fritz Lang's *Metropolis*. The asymmetrical set design is a homage to the expressionist angles seen in *Metropolis* and *The Cabinet of Dr Caligari*, while Dr Strangelove himself is a mad scientist in the mould of *Metropolis*'s Rotwang. Like Rotwang, Strangelove possesses a shock of white hair and a black glove on one hand – the latter belonged to Kubrick, which Sellers borrowed to make an allusion to *Metropolis*'s scientist.

Kubrick's exacting approach extended to the movie's final scene as originally scripted. *Dr Strangelove* was once supposed to end with a huge food fight, with the leaders of the free world pelting each other with custard pies as mushroom clouds bloom in the world above. Kubrick and his crew spent a week filming this final battle sequence, in which the cast spent take after take

* See: http://www.bbc.co.uk/news/entertainment-arts-23698181.

throwing around 3,000 pies. Kubrick later cut the scene, much to Adam's chagrin; these days, most agree that Kubrick's second choice of ending, which cuts from Dr Strangelove's Nazi salute to chilling footage of nuclear explosions, is the better conclusion.

It's Dr Strangelove's imagination and black comedy that make it such an enduring and oft-referenced classic. Like Joseph Heller's novel Catch-22, another product of the early 1960s, Dr Strangelove dares to suggest that those in power may not be the civic-minded, noble leaders they claim to be, but rather self-possessed, vain, arrogant and dangerously unstable. Technology may move forward, but the base desires of grasping, simple-minded men seldom keep pace; from its suggestive use of stock footage in its opening title sequence, Dr Strangelove displays a thinly veiled obsession with sex: planes refuelling in mid-air, phallic nose cones on an aircraft, a Playboy model spread out on General Turgidson's bed, even Merkin Muffley's suggestive name, all slyly point to a collection of generals and politicians obsessed with their own libido – or lack of it.

When Dr Strangelove came out in 1964, both critics and members of the military denounced it as both 'dangerous' and 'evil'; several experts disregarded the film's events as 'impossible'. Yet history would eventually bear Kubrick and his collaborators out; despite the US military's protestations, it emerged that, in the 1950s and 1960s, it really was possible for an American general to launch a nuclear strike without the president's approval. In the 1970s, Russian scientists were also working on something called Dead Hand – a device remarkably like the doomsday weapon described in Dr Strangelove.[*] Also known as Perimeter, the device, completed in 1985, was designed to automatically launch a strike against the United States if it detected a nuclear attack on Russian territory. Incredibly, knowledge of this device didn't come to light until the end of the Cold War; again, like Dr Strangelove, the Russians had built an ultimate deterrent – but hadn't bothered to tell the world of its existence.

* See: http://www.newyorker.com/news/news-desk/almost-everything-in-dr-strangelove-was-true.

In many respects, *Dr Strangelove* is a perfect piece of science fiction: a meditation on the dark turns technology might take in the imminent future, and a salutary warning about the people who might misuse it.

VISIONS OF WAR

Standing before the United Nations on 25 September 1961, John F. Kennedy made one of the most famous speeches in his tenure as American president. 'Every man, woman and child lives under the nuclear sword of Damocles,' Kennedy said, 'hanging by the slenderest of threads, capable of being cut at any moment by accident, or miscalculation, or madness. The weapons of war must be abolished before they abolish us.'

It was a speech that crystallised the scale of the nuclear threat – a subject tackled by a host of filmmakers, both before and after Stanley Kubrick's *Dr Strangelove*. Directed by Oscar-nominated director Sidney Lumet, *Fail Safe* (1964) – based on a novel by Eugene Burdick and Harvey Wheeler – might have been the bigger hit had Stanley Kubrick not insisted (with the help of his legal team) that *Dr Strangelove* had its release first. *Fail Safe* was certainly the starrier picture, featuring as it did Henry Fonda and Walter Matthau, and the movie treated its subject in less playfully grotesque terms than Kubrick's dark satire. A mixture of human and computer error results in an American nuclear bomber being despatched to Moscow; the US President (Henry Fonda) stands aghast as the Soviets threaten to launch an all-out counterattack. To reassure the Russians that the imminent destruction of Moscow was triggered acciden-tally, the President opts to make a horrifying sacrifice: he orders a nuclear strike on New York City. Throughout, *Fail Safe*'s politicians and military lead-ers talk in grave terms about the nature of nuclear war; critics at the time gave *Fail Safe* glowing notices, but it's striking just how much more dated the movie looks when compared to *Dr Strangelove* – although well shot and chilling in places, the absence of Kubrick and Terry Southern's biting dialogue makes for a gruelling, sombre movie.

Then again, few movies about the possibility of nuclear Armageddon held out much hope. *On the Beach*, released two years before *Dr Strangelove* and based on the novel by Nevil Shute, is a startlingly bleak account of life after a nuclear war. As the movie opens, the countries of the northern hemisphere have already destroyed themselves; in Australia, survivors wait as a deadly cloud of nuclear fallout drifts ever southwards. Like the book, *On the Beach*, directed by Stanley Kramer, contains all kinds of unforgettably ghoulish moments: a deserted San Francisco, apparently undamaged yet eerily deserted. A grand prix race in which its competitors no longer care whether they live or die. That the winner is none other than Fred Astaire (he plays a scientist named Julian Osborn) does little to lift the doom-laden tone; indeed, the presence of such stars as Gregory Peck, Ava Gardner and Anthony Perkins in such an apocalyptic film only serves to make it feel all the more unnerving.

Although made for a fraction of *On the Beach*'s budget, *Panic in the Year Zero!* (1962) is a similarly effective look at the societal fallout from a nuclear war. It was directed by Ray Milland, the star of such films as *The Lost Weekend* (1945) and Alfred Hitchcock's *Dial M for Murder* (1954), who also takes the leading role as Harry, the patriarch of a middle-class family that unwittingly embarks on the holiday from hell. As Harry, his wife and two kids drive out of Los Angeles, they narrowly avoid the devastation of a nuclear bomb; instead, they live to see the aftermath, where robbers roam the countryside and clouds of deadly radiation gather in the skies above.

In the 1980s, renewed East–West tensions reawakened old nightmares about the threat of the bomb; it's telling that TV broadcasters on both sides of the Atlantic were making films about nuclear war in the early part of the decade. In the USA, *Testament* (1983) was shot as a TV movie yet wound up receiving a theatrical release. Like *Panic in the Year Zero!*, it's about another average American family caught in the afterglow of the bomb; directed by Lynne Littman, the drama is made all the more powerful for its largely interior, low-key storytelling and some great acting from its cast, which includes Jane Alexander (who was nominated for an Oscar) and appearances from a young Kevin Costner and Rebecca De Mornay.

The Day After (1983), directed by genre filmmaker Nicholas Meyer (*Time After Time*, *Star Trek II: The Wrath of Khan*) tells a similarly uncompromising story on a more sweeping scale; taking in an airbase, a hospital and a town in Missouri, it again underlines the powerlessness of individuals in the face of war.

In the UK, director Mick Jackson's feature-length docudrama *Threads* (1984) provided a grim account of societal collapse; the population dwindles from sickness and disease and the country drifts back to a tough, pre-industrial state. In the years after its first airing, *Threads* became infamous as a film that scarred the memories of a generation of schoolkids.

Hailing from the other side of the Iron Curtain, *Dead Man's Letters* (1986) is equally downbeat. Co-written by Boris Strugatsky (who wrote *Roadside Picnic*, adapted by Andrei Tarkovsky as the classic arthouse sci-fi film, *Stalker*), it's set in the aftermath of a nuclear conflict. The central character, a scientist played by Rolan Bykov, does his best to help out his fellow survivors, while occasionally writing letters to his absent son. Beautifully shot by director Konstantin Lopushansky – once an assistant to Tarkovsky – *Dead Man's Letters* is perhaps the most oppressive film ever made about nuclear conflict. Every frame feels infused with sickness and disease, yet Lopushansky also finds beauty among the desolation and hope amid despair.

One of the most effective American tales of nuclear apocalypse arrived just as the Cold War began to wind down towards the end of the 1980s. Written and directed by Steve De Jarnatt, *Miracle Mile* (1988) is a quirky blending of genres; it's at once a thriller, a romance and a blackly comic apocalypse saga. A rather self-possessed jazz musician, Harry (Anthony Edwards) falls in love with a waitress and would-be-novelist, Julie (Mare Winningham). They plan to meet for their first date at an LA diner at midnight, but a series of mishaps means they wind up missing each other. In the weird hours between midnight and dawn, word spreads around Los Angeles that a nuclear strike is imminent; against a ticking clock, Harry resolves to track Julie down and head to safety before the missiles land. So begins a tender, unexpectedly disarming movie, which mixes Cold War fear with the kind of philosophical humour of Kurt Vonnegut. Sometimes circuitously, often with a powerful blow to the gut, *Miracle Mile* exposes the delicacy of human existence.

According to a newspaper report in 1989, an early screening of *Miracle Mile* in a Toronto cinema ended first with a dazed silence, and then a spontaneous burst of applause.* Even today, the film retains its startling impact.

Selected SF films mentioned in this chapter:

On the Beach (1962)

Panic in the Year Zero! (1962)

Fail Safe (1964)

Testament (1983)

The Day After (1983)

Threads (1984)

Dead Man's Letters (1986)

Miracle Mile (1988)

* See: https://news.google.com/newspapers?nid=1917&dat=19881014&id=9HwhAAAAI BAJ&sjid=vogFAAAAIBAJ&pg=4239,4039836&hl=en.

10. Into the unknown

2001: A Space Odyssey (1968)

'No 9000 computer has ever made a mistake or distorted information. We are all, by any practical definition of the words, foolproof and incapable of error . . .'

A broom flies up into the air, cartwheeling end over end. The person who threw it is none other than Stanley Kubrick, who is round the back of a sound stage, taking a break from his latest movie, *2001: A Space Odyssey*. Kubrick picks up the broom and throws it again, gazing as it spins into the air and falls back to the tarmac. This, according to author Arthur C. Clarke, was the genesis of one of the most famous edits in cinema history: a cut that whisks us from our prehistory to the early years of the twenty-first century.

Having already flirted with sci-fi in his biting political satire *Dr Strangelove*, Stanley Kubrick embarked on his magnum opus in 1964. Contrasting with the handheld cameras, minimalist interiors and stark black-and-white of his previous movie, *2001: A Space Odyssey* was envisioned as a widescreen epic with groundbreaking special effects. Kubrick spent four years and around $12 million developing and filming *A Space Odyssey*, and while the movie was initially met with a tepid reception from critics, it was soon embraced by younger moviegoers, and was, in time, the movie that cemented Kubrick's status as a cinema auteur. But while it's Kubrick's name that looms large on the posters, it's the collaborators he astutely chose that ultimately helped make *A Space Odyssey* a genre classic.

First, there was Arthur C. Clarke, the British sci-fi author who by 1964 was already known for such novels as *Childhood's End* (1953) and *A Fall of Moondust* (1961). Although frequently published in pulp magazines, Clarke was one of a number of writers who emphasised technical realism over gaudy action and bug-eyed alien invaders. His approach struck a chord with Kubrick, who approached the author with the aim of making, to cite a particularly famous quote, 'The proverbial good science fiction movie' – a piece of cinema that gave a sense of awe and grandeur to the universe and the mysteries it might hold. Looking through a number of Clarke's short stories, Kubrick eventually chose 'The Sentinel' as a potential candidate for his movie; written in 1948, it concerned the discovery of a mysterious, alien object on the Moon. On further investigation, lunar explorers conclude that the object – large, tetrahedral, like polished stone – was left behind by aliens thousands of years before as a kind of beacon. This sentinel, the narrator posits, is an early warning system, designed to warn other worlds that a new, possibly dangerous civilisation has risen up. 'Perhaps they wish to help our infant civilisation,' Clarke writes, 'but they must be very, very old, and the old are often insanely jealous of the young.'

That alien artefact provided the seed for 2001: A Space Odyssey's story, on which Kubrick and Clarke collaborated for over a year. Together, they worked up a loose narrative in three parts, all linked by the single image of the artefact – reworked in the movie as a rectangular black slab. The monolith first appears in Earth's prehistory, its eerie noises apparently educating and guiding humanity on its evolution from chattering ape to deep-space explorer. With a single breathtaking cut from a bone tumbling through a blue sky to a military satellite orbiting Earth, we jump ahead to the year 2001, where another monolith is discovered on the Moon, buried deep beneath the dusty lunar surface. Again emitting its eerie signal, the monolith triggers the film's second act: a voyage to Jupiter, where astronauts Dr David Bowman (Keir Dullea) and Dr Frank Poole (Gary Lockwood) are on the first leg of a mission whose details are initially obscure. After the ship's computer, HAL 9000 (voiced with eerie calm by Douglas Rain) goes dangerously haywire, Bowman discovers they have been dispatched to investigate another monolith, this one orbiting the Jovian planet.

On approaching the object, Bowman is sucked into a stargate, which appears to take him beyond time and space and into a dimension where temporal laws no longer apply. After observing himself at various stages of his life, Bowman seemingly experiences a cosmic rebirth, and floats back to Earth as a colossal foetus: a symbol of humanity's transcendence from ignorant beast to enlightened being.

Visitation by ancient aliens wasn't an entirely new concept by the 1960s – screenwriter Nigel Kneale's *Quatermass and the Pit*, which used a similar idea, was first broadcast on British television in 1959 – but Kubrick's visually bombastic treatment of it was nothing short of groundbreaking. Those visuals were thanks in no small part to a filmmaker named Douglas Trumbull, who was still in his early twenties when he joined the production as a background artist. His contributions would ultimately become pivotal to some of the film's most striking effects sequences.

In 1964, Trumbull was working at a small company in Hollywood called Graphic Films, which had just created a movie about space travel called *To the Moon and Beyond*. Kubrick had seen the film at that year's New York World's Fair, and was so impressed by its visuals and filmmaking techniques – it used a fisheye lens and 70 mm film to project a 360-degree image onto a concave screen – that he enlisted the company to consult on *A Space Odyssey*'s design. Trumbull was one of thirty-five designers hired to work on Kubrick's movie as production began in 1965. Originally thinking he would only be in the UK for a few months, Trumbull wound up spending two-and-a-half years working on the film, gradually climbing the ranks to become one of the film's four main effects supervisors.

Trumbull, it turned out, had just the right mix of art and engineering in his blood. His father Donald worked on the visual effects for 1939's *The Wizard of Oz*. A fan of science fiction since childhood, Trumbull suddenly found an outlet for his abilities on *2001: A Space Odyssey*, as he moved between departments during its lengthy production: building scale miniatures, working on sets, and coming up with inventive new photographic techniques for the film's third act. Trumbull's crowning achievement was his pioneering split-scan effect, which used a complex photographic technique to create the illusion of flying through a mesmerising tunnel of light. This image, like so many others in the film, would be copied and referenced by dozens of other filmmakers in the years ahead.

It was Kubrick's attention to detail and desire to push technical boundaries that made *A Space Odyssey* the seminal genre film it would soon become. As an example of how Kubrick's uncompromising style resulted in a stunning image, there is a moment in the second act where we see what everyday life is like aboard the *Discovery One*. The ship uses centrifugal force to simulate gravity, meaning that the crew essentially live and work on the hub of a huge spinning wheel. On one of Shepperton Studios' sound stages, Kubrick had a 38-foot-high section of the *Discovery*'s interior built at full size, capable of rotating as actor Keir Dullea ran inside it, like a hamster on a wheel. This expensive feat of planning and engineering resulted in some breathtaking illusions, particularly a sequence where the camera appears to follow Dave Bowman as he jogs around the entire 360-degree set. Other effects were simpler to pull off, but hardly less bewitching: a pen stuck to a piece of glass and rotated in front of the camera provided the illusion of an object floating in space.

For all of Kubrick's technical ingenuity and obsession with accuracy, however, *2001: A Space Odyssey* is above all science fantasy. It imagines, often with wonder and sometimes with fear, what the space age might look like in the near future, and what we might find on our travels. Like *The Day the Earth Stood Still* before it – a movie that, incidentally, Kubrick didn't particularly like – *A Space Odyssey* suggests that our encounters with extraterrestrials could be enlightening rather than disastrous. According to the film, the alien monolith helped us through our hairy formative years, and when the time came for us to fly the nest, beckoned us from the Moon to the edge of our solar system and out towards the stars. It's worth noting that, as Kubrick shaped his film, he gradually whittled away the scientific explanation and dialogue and focused instead on his visuals and music. Earlier versions of the script contained a voiceover; one cut of the movie included brief interviews with scientists. Gradually, these were all dropped, along with a more detailed explanation for HAL 9000's malfunction. Shorn of its exposition, *A Space Odyssey* instead opens as a silent movie, its story told entirely with visuals and sound: the shriek of apes, the disquieting howl of the monolith. It was a bold move, particularly for a movie with a budget approaching Kubrick's name-making biblical epic, *Spartacus*. Kubrick made *A Space Odyssey* into a movie to be experienced and interpreted rather than understood; a kind of cinematic opera cut to the music of Johann and Richard Strauss. The movie reaches a crescendo in its last half-hour, as Bowman is subjected to an experience beyond words: a riot of colour and weird imagery, accompanied by the unearthly tonal shifts of Gyorgy Ligeti's *Lux Aeterna*.

When *2001: A Space Odyssey* finally emerged in the spring of 1968, it was both praised for its scale and imagination and taken to task for its glacial pace. Kubrick's wife, Christiane, once recalled that some older executives at MGM walked out of an early screening; 'The film was actually launched by young people,' she later said.* One young person who understood the potential of Kubrick's movie was Mike Kaplan, an MGM publicist. While several mainstream critics – most prominently Pauline Kael – had given the film a mauling, Kaplan championed the film, and understood its potential as a counter-culture film.

By the time *2001: A Space Odyssey* was re-released one year later with the tagline, 'The Ultimate Trip',† Kubrick's movie had begun to gain traction among audiences, and its fame as a singular cinematic experience had grown. Indeed, the film was commonly cited as a formative experience for a generation of filmmakers growing up in the late 1960s and 1970s, including George Lucas and James Cameron, who would soon go on to make vital sci-fi movies of their own. It was *2001: A Space Odyssey*, with its majestic scenes of spacecraft and planets in motion, that showed just how startling visual effects could be in the right hands. Kubrick and Clarke's story of evolution, space travel and scientific discovery brought a seriousness of intent and intelligence that was comparatively rare in American cinema.

A Space Odyssey also launched Douglas Trumbull's career, whose contribution outside the film shouldn't be underestimated. After working with Kubrick, Trumbull directed the spectacular eco-fable *Silent Running* (1972), which starred Bruce Dern as a space explorer tending his garden in deep

---

* See: http://www.denofgeek.com/movies/kubrick/30844/a-closer-look-at-taschens-deluxe-book-the-making-of-2001-a-space-odyssey.
† See: https://www.theguardian.com/film/2007/nov/02/marketingandpr.

space. In 1977, Trumbull again broke new ground with his special effects for *Close Encounters of the Third Kind*, Steven Spielberg's UFO fantasy about a blue-collar worker (Richard Dreyfuss) and his quasi-religious meeting with benign aliens. Trumbull's extraterrestrial craft, as baroque as a cathedral and as beautifully lit as a city skyline, provided the film with some moments of genuine wonder.

A *Space Odyssey* was, therefore, more than just a seminal sci-fi movie: it also served as a lens for other filmmakers. Like the shiny black monolith, *2001: A Space Odyssey* appeared at the tail end of the 1960s and invited its audience to look and think in a different way. Afterwards, cinema would never be quite the same again.

THE LONELINESS OF SPACE

In his *Space Odyssey*, Kubrick depicted the exploration of the solar system as a grand, stately ballet. Even as Dave Bowman journeyed off into a potentially terrifying unknown, enlightenment and rebirth were awaiting at the end. But in certain moments, Kubrick also imagined the chillier side of space travel: the isolation, the detachment from the comforts of home and society, the boredom, the terror when apparently foolproof mechanisms break down. From an early scene where Dr Floyd (William Sylvester) is shown slumped, fast asleep in his chair on a trip to the Moon, to the eerie silence of Bowman and Poole's journey in *Discovery One*, the film imparts the sense of isolation in a great vacuum, of the infeasible distance between planets. Other filmmakers have taken these notions even further, and used space travel as a stress test for our human frailties.

In Andrei Tarkovsky's peerless *Solaris* (1972), adapted from the novel by Polish author Stanisław Lem, the scientific investigation of an alien planet brings its researchers face to face with their own subconscious. A psychologist, Kris Kelvin (Donatas Banionis) is sent to the space station orbiting the planet Solaris to find out why a trio of otherwise rational scientists have started to transmit bizarre, indecipherable messages. Kelvin gradually learns that the station's inhabitants are being haunted by figures from their past

– Solaris isn't merely a planet, but a vast, conscious organism capable of reading human memories and, from them, creating physical copies of those long gone. For Kelvin, this means the sudden reappearance of his late wife, Hari (Natalya Bondarchuk), who had committed suicide years earlier. Their reunion is one of bitter pain; both for Kelvin, whose grief is suddenly brought roiling back to the surface, and also for Hari, who at first has no idea that she's the creation of an alien entity. In the context of a sci-fi movie, *Solaris* deals with weighty themes about the nature of existence and memory; it's a quiet, cerebral movie, but also a beautifully human one.

As we saw in Chapter 8, the SF movies of Europe and the Soviet Union were unafraid to explore complex and lofty themes, and such movies as Czechoslovakia's *Ikarie XB-1* (also known as *Voyage to the End of the Universe*, 1963) and *Planet of Storms* (1962) depicted the monotony of space travel as well as the dangers. Inevitably, their special effects can't compare to Kubrick's expensive and rigorously researched scenes of spacecraft and planets, but their imagery and atmosphere are, in their own way, similarly awe-inspiring.

It wasn't until after *2001: A Space Odyssey* that American cinema began to explore the psychological tolls of interstellar travel in quite the same depth. *Dark Star* (1974), the low-budget debut from director John Carpenter (see *The Thing*, Chapter 17) may be a black comedy, but it also convincingly depicts space exploration as cramped, frustrating and punishingly dull. Likewise Douglas Trumbull's *Silent Running* (1972), in which Bruce Dern's space-faring eco-warrior finds himself cooped up with a bunch of guys he can't stand; when events drive him to kill his co-workers and head off into unknown space with humanity's last remaining plant specimens, he instead finds companionship through three adorably stumpy robots, which he reprograms and dubs Huey, Duey and Louie. Operated by three amputees, *Silent Running*'s robots are clear forerunners of R2-D2 and the other droids in the *Star Wars* universe; it's a testament to the power of their design that, when something awful happens to one of them, it's a heart-wrenching moment. Indeed, few other American films have so powerfully depicted a sense of loneliness as effectively as *Silent Running*.

Moon (2008), the debut from British director Duncan Jones, is a low-budget sci-fi film in the vein of those 1970s classics. It stars Sam Rockwell as a blue-collar worker who oversees a lunar mining base; he's already served three years on his shift, and now, bearded and lonely, he's seeing out the final few days before he can return to Earth. But then a chance discovery leads him to rethink his relationship with the Moon base and his role there. Like *Solaris* and *Silent Running* before it, *Moon* functions both as believable sci-fi – it seems increasingly likely that we'll be mining the lunar surface for minerals before too long – and as an emotionally charged human drama. Through Sam Bell, sublimely played by Rockwell, we're confronted with some difficult philosophical questions: what is it that makes us unique as human beings? Are we really much more than the sum of our memories and experiences?

Like other sci-fi films about life outside our planet, *Moon* isn't so much about journeying into the stars as journeying into our psyches. As one scientist in *Solaris* so eloquently puts it, space exploration isn't so much about finding strange new life forms on other planets as it is about trying to understand ourselves.

'We don't want to conquer space at all,' says Dr Snaut. 'We want to expand Earth endlessly. We don't want other worlds; we want a mirror.'

Selected SF films mentioned in this chapter:
Solaris (1972)
Silent Running (1972)
Dark Star (1974)
Moon (2008)

11. An evolving franchise

PLANET OF THE APES (1968)

'Man is a nuisance. The sooner he is exterminated, the better.'

In the searing heat of an Arizona summer, a small army of oddly dressed actors shield themselves from the sun. One holds an umbrella. Another wears shades. Still another wears a broad-brimmed hat, and passes the time by reading a newspaper. Faces clad in latex and paint, heads and hands obscured by thick black hair, the actors are ill-equipped to deal with the 150 °F temperatures in the desert. They have already spent about four hours in a makeup chair, but there's more to come: a full day's shooting, a lunch break where they will have to use a mirror to help shovel food through their latex masks and into their mouths, and then, after all that, a further hour to have all the prosthetics, hair and paint carefully stripped off again.

It's the shoot of *Planet of the Apes*, and the entire movie hinges on whether audiences will accept all that painstakingly applied makeup. By this point, producer Arthur P. Jacobs had already fought long and hard to get his sci-fi adventure in front of the camera; he had shopped the project around Hollywood earlier in the decade, and pitched it to 20th Century Fox no fewer than four times before finally getting it accepted.

Like most studios, Fox took a dim view of science fiction, and its dealings with the genre had largely been restricted to such fare as Irwin Allen's *Voyage to the Bottom of the Sea* (1961, which formed the basis for a later TV series) and the distribution of such low-budget movies as *The Day Mars Invaded Earth* (1963), the little-seen *Curse of the Fly* (1965), and *Spaceflight IC-1* (1965), a British space-exploration movie directed by Bernard Knowles. Nevertheless,

Jacobs remained convinced that *Planet of the Apes* could be a hit, just as he was when he first read its source novel in 1963.*

Written by Pierre Boulle, French author of *The Bridge Over the River Kwai*, *La Planète des Singes* (or *Monkey Planet*) tells the story of three astronauts who travel to a distant world where apes are the dominant species; while humans are mute and savage, apes have advanced to the point where they wear clothes, drive vehicles and live in cities. Through this ape society, Boulle crafts a deft satire about our species' darker impulses. Jacobs, who by 1963 was in the midst of producing an expensive adaptation of *Doctor Dolittle* for Fox, read *La Planète des Singes* shortly after its publication that same year, and quickly purchased the rights to turn it into a movie. Looking back, it's remarkable just how much faith Jacobs had in his apes project; Boulle considered it to be one of his lesser works, while studios balked at the potentially huge cost of realising its vision of a primate society. Still, Jacobs pressed on: he hired a team of concept artists to create a kind of brochure that showed how his movie could look – a quite unusual approach to selling a movie at the time. He then turned to Rod Serling, the gifted sci-fi writer behind TV's *The Twilight Zone*, to adapt *La Planète des Singes* into a screenplay. Even a writer as talented as Serling appeared to struggle with the task of turning Boulle's allegory into a workable movie, however; after one year and a reported thirty drafts, Serling's version of the story was rejected.

Meanwhile, studio bosses all over Hollywood were telling Jacobs that nobody would accept a film about talking apes. 'I went to every film company I could think of, hoping to get them interested,' Jacobs told the magazine *Big Screen Scene Showguide* in 1968. 'But they all said it couldn't be made.'

Things began to move forward when Jacobs took a different approach: he began hawking the concept around various Hollywood stars, including Marlon Brando and Paul Newman – all of whom passed – but he found an unexpectedly receptive figure in Charlton Heston, a star with the kind of clout that

* *Big Screen Scene Showguide* magazine (1968),
http://pota.goatley.com/cgi-bin/pdfview.pl?uri=misc/screenguide/screenguide-uk-1968-04.pdf.

could make a studio executive sit up and take notice. Around the same time, the $5-million sci-fi adventure *Fantastic Voyage* was a sizeable hit for Fox – about a team of scientists shrunk down and injected into a desperately ill scientist, it proved that audiences would pay to see an imaginative genre film.

As *Planet of the Apes* finally got the go-ahead, Jacobs hired screenwriter Michael Wilson to overhaul Rod Serling's script. A Hollywood veteran, Wilson had worked on such acclaimed movies as *It's a Wonderful Life* (1946) before he became one of several writers whose careers were all but ruined by the anti-communist blacklist. Unperturbed, Wilson moved to Europe and continued writing under a pseudonym; one of his most successful works of the 1950s was his adaptation of Boulle's *The Bridge on the River Kwai*, co-written with Carl Foreman. It was Wilson's idea to take the apes from their more high-tech society, as described in both Boulle's novel and Serling's drafts, and instead place them in a pre-industrial setting. The apes retain their intelligence and their class structure, but the absence of vehicles and sophisticated architecture meant the film could be made on a much lower budget.

By the time *Planet of the Apes* appeared in cinemas in 1968, it was evident that change was in the air, both in Hollywood and the world at large. Just three months before, Jacobs's *Doctor Dolittle* adaptation (directed by *Fantastic Voyage*'s Richard Fleischer), which had cost a staggering $17 million due to star Rex Harrison's salary and numerous production setbacks, had proved to be a costly misfire. That same year, *Bonnie and Clyde*, a seethingly violent drama about depression-era bank robbers, had gone on to make $70 million on a fraction of *Doctor Dolittle*'s budget. The New Hollywood era was dawning, and audiences were, it seemed, ready for movies that reflected the complexity and turmoil of the real world.

The 1960s had already seen the assassination of President John F. Kennedy, the rise of the civil rights movement, and protests over the United States' costly involvement in the Vietnam War. Science would soon put man on the Moon, yet back on Earth, the threat of nuclear Armageddon was still ever-present.

In the context of escapist entertainment, *Planet of the Apes*, directed by Franklin J. Schaffner, dealt with the fears of its era through the prism of a thrilling genre movie. If Charlton Heston's astronaut Taylor feels taken aback at finding himself in a world where everything he understands has been thrown out of line, then that only reflected the sense of upheaval sweeping America in the late 1960s.

Hurtling through time and space, Taylor and his fellow explorers Landon (Robert Gunner) and Dodge (Jeff Burton) crash on the titular planet, their ship immediately sinking irretrievably in the middle of a lake. Having learned that humans on the planet are little more than wild animals, the astronauts are captured by a phalanx of apes on horseback, and Taylor eventually finds himself alone, surrounded by a society of intelligent orangutans and chimpanzees who regard him with hatred and suspicion. Dr Zaius (Maurice Evans), a member of the ruling orangutan class, regards humans as a dangerous threat that needs to be exterminated. Thanks to a sympathetic pair of scientists, Zira (Kim Hunter) and Cornelius (Roddy McDowall), Taylor manages to escape the apes' clutches, and journeying into an area known as the Forbidden Zone, learns a bitter truth: the planet of the apes is Earth, some 2,000 years into the future.

Planet of the Apes's ending is among the most powerful, well-known and oft-lampooned in all cinema. There is, however, some disagreement as to its origins; according to the book *Planet of the Apes: The Evolution of a Legend*, the conclusion first surfaced during a conversation between Jacobs and director Blake Edwards, who at one early stage considered making the movie himself.[*] Yet the ending undoubtedly exists in early drafts of Serling's screenplays, and was retained when Michael Wilson made his rewrites. Whether the famous image of the Statue of Liberty jutting out of a desolate beach was Serling's idea or not, there were precedents for it on the covers of pulp sci-fi books and magazines published many years earlier.[†] More than one edition of John Bowen's book, *After the Rain*, published in 1958, show strikingly similar

[*] Joe Fordham and Jeff Bond, *Planet of the Apes: The Evolution of a Legend* (London: Titan, 2014).

[†] See: https://sciencefictionruminations.wordpress.com/2012/10/01/adventures-in-science -fiction-cover-art-the-statue-of-liberty.

images, while the February 1941 edition *of Astounding Science Fiction* depicts the statue standing, apparently eroded by time, in a far-future landscape. As the final shot of a major Hollywood movie, however, *Apes*'s ending was bravely downbeat; coming as it did just a few years after the Cuban Missile Crisis almost triggered a nuclear war, the notion that humanity might eventually destroy itself was chillingly believable.

Planet of the Apes's prosthetic effects, meanwhile, devised by John Chambers, broke new ground. To create them, Chambers devised new and ingenious techniques that resulted in thinner latex, allowing the actors' expressions to be seen through the makeup – an advance that rightly earned Chambers an Academy Award for his work.

Planet of the Apes was hugely successful, and sparked something comparatively new in Hollywood: a multimedia franchise, which would soon take in comics, toys, live-action and animated television spin-offs, and a string of movie sequels. *Apes* therefore paved the way for *Star Wars* less than a decade later; a movie which would itself rely hugely on special effects to tell its story of a familiar yet topsy-turvy world, and which would also go on to spawn a colossally popular franchise.

Remarkably, the entire franchise owes its existence to a single moment. Long before director Franklin J. Schaffner and his cast and crew headed off to shoot on location in Arizona, Pierre Boulle visited a zoo in France. Peering into an enclosure, he observed an ape's uncannily human expressions, and wondered what it might be like if their positions were reversed: Boulle in the enclosure and the ape outside, staring back at him. That was the seed that led to *La Planète des Singes*, a story that explores the dark side of human nature from a playfully skewed perspective. In the same fashion, the *Planet of the Apes* movies offer up a mirror to our own society – and what an ugly reflection it can be.

ASCENT OF THE APES

The idea of multiple sequels and franchises was a relatively unexplored one when *Planet of the Apes* emerged in 1968. Yet *Apes* proved so immediately popular that, within two months of its release, 20th Century Fox told producer Arthur P. Jacobs that it wanted a follow-up. So began a pattern that has repeated itself in Hollywood ever since: Jacobs had to find a means of continuing a story that had already come to a natural conclusion in the first film. And so it was that a string of writers – including Pierre Boulle, the mind behind the original novel, *The Twilight Zone*'s Rod Serling and finally British screenwriter Paul Dehn were drafted in to work out how the *Apes* saga could be continued.

The result, 1970's *Beneath the Planet of the Apes*, was inevitably compromised by its status as a studio-mandated follow-up – like so many sequels after it, *Beneath* has some work to do in order to justify its existence. Charlton Heston's reluctance to reprise his role as Taylor didn't help, either; with Heston eventually agreeing to appear in the film for a few brief scenes, the story's forced to introduce a new protagonist: space traveller Brent, played by Heston-a-like James Franciscus, who is sent to find out what happened to Taylor and his fellow astronauts.

Less satisfying though it is, the sequel nevertheless succeeds in being even more bleak than its predecessor. *Beneath the Planet of the Apes* carries the theme of mankind's self-destructive nature to its absolute conclusion, with Brent discovering a subterranean tribe of human survivors who worship a recovered nuclear bomb. As we'll see in Chapter 12, *Beneath*'s explosive final sequence inadvertently fired the starting pistol on a decade of downbeat sci-fi movies – not least *Soylent Green*, also starring Heston. But once again, *Beneath* appeared to present Fox's nascent series with a narrative dead end. How do you continue the story once you've blown up the entire planet?

Nevertheless, the franchise continued, with three further sequels – *Escape from the Planet of the Apes*, *Conquest of the Planet of the Apes* and *Battle for the Planet of the Apes* appearing annually between 1971 and 1973. Although the budget on each gradually fell and the once spectacular makeup effects degraded with each movie, the films followed the previous entries' line in bleak social commentary. *Escape from the Planet of the Apes* reversed the first film's premise, with three apes travelling back in time to 1970s Los Angeles in Taylor's old spaceship. There, the ape visitors – Zira (Kim Hunter), Cornelius

(Roddy McDowall) and Dr Milo (Sal Mineo) – briefly become celebrities among the humans, before the planet's uglier, fearful tendencies take over. Fearing for the future of the human race, the US government – represented by the President (William Windom) – decides the apes' lives must be extinguished.

From *Escape from the Planet of the Apes* onwards, the franchise became a kind of movable feast, as recurring writer Paul Dehn used the saga to explore such themes as racism, the Cold War and Vietnam-era political tension. After 1974, the saga migrated to television, both as a live-action TV series, which ran for a fourteen-episode season on CBS, and then as an animated show, *Return to the Planet of the Apes*, which was similarly short-lived. (The latter was noteworthy, however, for depicting some of the ideas from the original book that were deemed too expensive to recreate in the movies.)

Efforts were made to bring *Planet of the Apes* back to cinemas throughout the 1980s and 1990s, yet a revolving door of directors, producers and writers failed to get the revival into production. Director Tim Burton finally succeeded where others failed in 2001, and the result was a lavish reworking of Schaffner's 1968 film rather than a bold reinterpretation of Boulle's book. Mark Wahlberg plays the astronaut hero who winds up on the ape planet; once again, he discovers that humans have become subservient to a hairier dominant species, which, like the original movie, has yet to emerge from a pre-industrial age. The makeup effects work by Rick Baker is spectacular, and Tim Roth makes for an imposing villain as the military-caste chimp, General Thade. Overall, however, Burton's film bears the scars of its lengthy pre-production, with the superb production design let down by some muddled storytelling. Commendably, the film at least attempts to come up with a different ending to the 1968 movie, but even its less harsh critics would probably agree it entirely lacked the earlier film's impact.

The franchise got a far less tentative reimagining in 2011, thanks to screenwriters Rick Jaffa and Amanda Silver and British director Rupert Wyatt. Serving as a prequel of sorts to the 1968 film, *Rise of the Planet of the Apes* provides an alternate explanation for how the apes wound up running the entire planet. A genetic scientist named Will Rodman (James Franco) is the nominal protagonist, before it emerges that the story's true hero is Caesar (a motion-captured Andy Serkis), a chimpanzee granted super-intelligence by Rodman's experiments. Rallying his fellow primates in captivity, Caesar leads a charge across San Francisco and off into the mountains; human forces fight back, unaware that they are already too late – Rodman's research has also unleashed a deadly virus, and our species is on borrowed time.

An unusually bleak film for a summer studio piece, *Rise of the Planet of the Apes* breathed new life into an ailing series. *Dawn of the Planet of the Apes* (2014) and *War for the Planet of the Apes* (2017), directed by Matt Reeves, pushed the franchise into even darker arenas. In the decades after the fall of humanity, an uneasy equilibrium between species is broken by zealotry on both sides; through it all, Caesar struggles to balance his loyalty to his own kind while retaining a shred of empathy for humans. Superbly acted by Serkis and fellow ape performers Terry Notary, Toby Kebbell and Karin Konoval, *Dawn* and *War* took the bold step of shooting their effects sequences in harsh, real-world conditions. The resulting sequences are eerily photoreal, and do much to sell the idea of humans coming face to face with their own tribal instincts.

Fifty years on, *Planet of the Apes* retains the crown as one of the most technically daring and intelligent franchises in sci-fi cinema.

Selected SF films mentioned in this chapter:
Beneath the Planet of the Apes (1970)
Escape from the Planet of the Apes (1971)
Conquest of the Planet of the Apes (1972)
Battle for the Planet of the Apes (1973)
Planet of the Apes (2001)
Rise of the Planet of the Apes (2011)
Dawn of the Planet of the Apes (2014)
War for the Planet of the Apes (2017)

12. Bleak futures

A CLOCKWORK ORANGE (1971)

*'Goodness is something to be chosen. When a man
cannot choose he ceases to be a man.'*

It's little coincidence that two great dystopian novels of the twentieth century were written while their authors were desperately ill. George Orwell suffered from tuberculosis while writing *Nineteen Eighty-Four*; the book was published in 1949, just six months before his death. Anthony Burgess wrote *A Clockwork Orange* (1962) shortly after he was misdiagnosed with an inoperable brain tumour. Mistakenly believing that he had a matter of months to live, Burgess crafted a considerable part of *A Clockwork Orange* in a fevered year of writing, in which he penned a handful of other novels in short order – his aim being to leave his wife with a steady stream of royalties after his death.

The result was an aggressive rush of words: written, according to Burgess, in just ten days. *A Clockwork Orange* is a futuristic fable told from the perspective of its teen anti-hero, Alex, and written in his distinctive voice, dubbed Nadsat – a mangled argot that sounds like cockney rhyming slang mixed with Russian. Burgess was partly inspired to write the book by a horrific attack on his wife, Lynne; in 1944, she was viciously beaten by a gang of men, and the assault, Burgess said, tragically resulted in a miscarriage. That attack fuelled a stomach-churning sequence in *A Clockwork Orange*, where Alex and his gang break into an author's home and sexually assault his wife; in a bold leap of imagination, Burgess writes the incident from the attackers' perspective.

Alex's violent rampages are brought to an abrupt end when he's arrested and subjected to an experimental form of rehabilitation called the Ludovico

Technique. Alex is strapped to a chair and forced to view violent imagery while he's given drugs and assaulted with loud music by Beethoven – who happens to be Alex's favourite composer. The treatment successfully 'cures' Alex of his desire to rape, assault or kill, but also obliterates his agency; when he's attacked by former members of his own gang later in the story, the mere thought of trying to defend himself leaves him incapacitated. For those in power who want to end the teenage violence on their streets, the Ludovico Technique's side effect is perfectly justified. Burgess, on the other hand, makes his own view perfectly clear: it's better to have the will to do evil than no will at all.

When *A Clockwork Orange* was published in 1962, its literary reception was mixed. Some complained about the impenetrable vocabulary. Others condemned the nastiness of its violence. The book was better received in the United States, though oddly, readers there wound up with a very different version of the story than in its native Britain: at the behest of its publisher, *A Clockwork Orange*'s final chapter, in which Alex rejects a life of violence of his own volition, was cut out. Burgess later wrote, in a 1988 preface, that his book 'Was Kennedyan and accepted the notion of moral progress. What was really wanted was a Nixonian book with no shred of optimism in it.'

It was this 'Nixonian' edition of the book that Stanley Kubrick adapted for the screen in 1971, and while Burgess may have disapproved of the movie's icy violence and pessimism, it undoubtedly chimed with the post-Nixon, post-Vietnam War climate of recession and decline. Largely shot in and around outer London locations near Kubrick's home, the director's rendering of the novel reflects the failed utopia of the post-war housing boom. As its backdrop, *A Clockwork Orange* uses Thamesmead South housing estate: a modernist sprawl of cold concrete arrayed across the marshes of the Thames that was already beginning to look wan and unwelcoming at the start of the 1970s.

Kubrick's vision of a concrete dystopia anticipated the wave of electronic music that would capture Britain's zeitgeist in the wake of punk at the end of the 1970s. Indeed, the harshness of the visuals are entirely bound up with the film's pioneering score, created by Wendy Carlos on a Moog synthesiser. Like *Forbidden Planet* all those years earlier, Carlos's music – derived from classical pieces by Beethoven, Rossini and Elgar – created a disturbing aural landscape quite unlike anything heard in a movie before. Like the architecture, and like Alex (played by Malcolm McDowell), it's the sound of a culture stripped of its humanity. Less than a decade after *A Clockwork Orange*, the falling prices of synthesisers saw British musicians and bands like the Human League, Gary Numan and Depeche Mode write their own electronic songs with a dystopian edge. Human League band member Martyn Ware later said that the cover of their first album, *Reproduction*, was supposed to look like 'some kind of dystopian vision of the future'.*

After the lengthy shoot on 2001: *A Space Odyssey* (see Chapter 10), which dragged on for four years, Kubrick attacked *A Clockwork Orange* with a rigour approaching the pace of Burgess's writing. The movie's shoot was completed in about eight months, which, by the director's standards, was unusually concise. This in turn feeds into the film's frenzied tone: loud, grandiose performances, confrontational camerawork and harsh edits. On a comparatively low budget, Kubrick (who also adapted the screenplay) creates the impression of a near-future Britain that feels at once familiar and unsettlingly alien. The gang violence, crumbling buildings and homeless sleeping under bridges suggest a society falling apart at the seams; the pervasiveness of sexual imagery – like the huge phallus owned by one of Alex's female victims – hint at a culture nakedly obsessed with sex.

Kubrick's film retains the moral sentiment from the book – that violence is a part of human nature, that technology might take away our freewill, and might in turn open the door to totalitarianism – but his depiction of that violence is profoundly unsettling. As in Burgess's writing, we see the attacks from the perspective of Alex and his gang of droogs, but without the novel's slang to provide a protective gauze from the violence, it takes on an even more voyeuristic hue. The use of the theme song from *Singing in the Rain* – belted out by Alex in one sequence – could be interpreted as Kubrick's own version of the Ludovico Technique: it turns a once innocent piece of music into something far more horrifying through simple association.

* See: https://www.creativereview.co.uk/the-human-league-and-a-vision-of-the-future.

A Clockwork Orange emerged in the midst of a growing wave of explicitly violent films in the United States, which sprang up as censorship laws were relaxed. The American New Wave of directors, which included Dennis Hopper (*Easy Rider*), Francis Ford Coppola (*The Godfather*), Martin Scorsese (*Taxi Driver*) and Arthur Penn (*Bonnie and Clyde*), brought a harsher, uncompromising kind of movie with them – movies that were unafraid to tell their stories from the perspective of outsiders, gangsters, bikers or killers. *A Clockwork Orange*, whether Kubrick consciously intended it to or not, may have been his response to that wave sweeping Hollywood; Alex DeLarge is certainly an antagonist every bit as spiky and challenging as *Taxi Driver*'s Travis Bickle. The violence proved to be as controversial as that in Sam Peckinpah's *Straw Dogs*, also released in 1971, or Michael Winner's *Death Wish* (1974) – another film about rape, violence and urban malaise.

A Clockwork Orange, however, became the flashpoint for a far more pronounced media backlash than even those films. There were inaccurate newspaper reports that the movie had provoked a copycat crime against a nun in the USA, while in the UK, *A Clockwork Orange*'s name was brought up in two cases of teenage boys accused of assault and manslaughter. With debate surrounding the film's events even reaching the British Houses of Parliament, Kubrick's family reportedly began to receive threats from protestors against the movie. In response, Kubrick contacted Warner Brothers and, using his formidable standing at the studio, had the film withdrawn from British cinemas. For twenty-seven years, *A Clockwork Orange* was unavailable to watch, either in cinemas or on home video, in the UK. Inevitably, a mystique built around the film, which only grew until the film was finally released again after Kubrick's death in 1999.

Time may have done much to erode *A Clockwork Orange*'s shock value, but much of its disturbing potency remains – not least in its unsettling juxtaposition of violence, rape and apparent black comedy. At the same time, its imagery has furtively pervaded our culture: that opening shot of Alex, glaring defiantly back at us with one eye caked in eyeliner, is as eloquent in its own way as Burgess's pitch-perfect writing.

Unlike Orwell, Burgess lived to see the impact his book would have. Later in life, he expressed his ambivalence at its depiction of violence, and a certain amount of frustration that his own work had been eclipsed to an extent by Kubrick's adaptation.* In any event, *A Clockwork Orange* is an intelligent and prescient film; a reflection of the 1970s cultural climate, and a thought-provoking warning of state control versus individual freedom.

GLOOM AND PARANOIA IN 1970S SCI-FI

First published in 1976, Bill Kaysing's book *We Never Went to the Moon* helped perpetuate a conspiracy theory that still has some currency in certain corners of the web: that one of the greatest scientific achievements of the twentieth century was a hoax. The book is perhaps a symbol of the souring public mood in the 1970s, where the peace-and-love optimism of the previous decade began to buckle under the weight of the Vietnam War and the Watergate scandal. With an oil crisis, recession and high unemployment in both the USA and UK, the 1970s was, to paraphrase Hunter S Thompson, an era of increasing fear and loathing.

Little wonder, then, that the mood of the era seeped into movies. While *A Clockwork Orange* imagined a future of cultural decline and state-sponsored mind control in the UK, George Lucas's *THX 1138*, also released in 1971, depicts a subterranean dystopia where technology has made everything colourless and sterile. In a nod to Aldous Huxley's *Brave New World*, emotions and procreation are strictly controlled via medication; surveillance and police presence is ubiquitous; religion and consumerism have congealed into an unholy mass. It's a nightmarishly cold future vision, Lucas's stark imagery married to some oppressive sound design by Walter Murch, who co-wrote the screenplay. In the end, the story's hero, THX 1138 (Robert Duvall) escapes from the city and heads off into an uncertain future. Like *A Clockwork Orange*, Lucas suggests that a life of uncertainty and individuality is preferable to mindless conformity.

The growing environmental movement of the 1970s also fed into the decade's movies. Director Douglas Trumbull's *Silent Running* (1972) is set in a

* See: http://www.thewrap.com/sexplosion.

future where Earth's plant life has gone the way of the dodo; all that remain are a few samples of flora, floating among the stars in giant greenhouses. In *Soylent Green* (1973), based on the 1966 novel *Make Room, Make Room*, twenty-first-century Earth is wracked by ecological disaster and overpopulation. While investigating the murder of a wealthy New York businessman, detective Frank Thorn (Charlton Heston) uncovers a conspiracy involving Soylent Green: an artificial foodstuff supposedly derived from plankton. While the elite of 2022 dine on fresh beef and vegetables, the rest of the world's population, Thorn discovers, have subsisted on something far less palatable.

The wealthy and powerful are hardly more compassionate in *Rollerball* (1975), a bruising dystopia directed by Norman Jewison. In a near future controlled by rival corporations, the masses are kept anaesthetised by a violent televised sport, Rollerball – a brutal mix of roller derby and American football. Veteran player Jonathan E (James Caan) is the sport's rising star, which poses something of a problem for those in power; Rollerball is supposed to demonstrate the helplessness of the individual against the state, and Jonathan's maverick style of play is a breathing, roller-skating contradiction of that idea. When Jonathan defies repeated attempts to force him out of the game, the corporations respond by making the sport ever more gladiatorial. What begins as a diversion ends as a bloodcurdling war of man versus state.

Conspiracies and apocalypses were running themes in many of the 1970s genre films. The deliciously weird *Zardoz* (1974), directed by John Boorman, sees a post-apocalyptic Earth divided between 'Eternals', who live in luxury, and a lower class of violent, ill-educated 'Brutals' over whom they rule. In the little-seen *Damnation Alley* (1977), a nuclear disaster leaves the planet overridden by giant cockroaches and scorpions.

The air of cynicism permeating the 1970s was neatly crystallised in one movie: *Capricorn One* (1977). A mix of sci-fi and conspiracy thriller, it concerns a government attempt to fake the first manned mission to Mars; to prevent the truth coming out, assassins are despatched to silence the astronauts involved. Writer-director Peter Hyams first came up with the idea for *Capricorn One* while working at CBS television in the 1960s. As he watched an Apollo mission unfold, he wondered: what if this was all just a hoax?

'I remember sitting there thinking, that's a one-camera story,' Hyams recalls. 'And if you could screw with the camera, you could screw with the story. When my parents grew up, they were the generation that felt that, if you read it in the papers, it was true. I was the generation that thought if you saw it on television, it was true. Then we found out that what the papers said was sometimes untrue, and later, we found out that television could do the same thing."*

For much of the 1970s, sci-fi movies looked at the narratives spun by politicians, the media and the wealthy with distrust. Even *Star Wars* and *Close Encounters of the Third Kind*, which ushered in a lighter, more escapist kind of sci-fi fable at the tail end of the decade, carried some of that distrust along with them. In *Close Encounters*, the government cover up the arrival of alien craft by faking a gas leak in Wyoming; in *Star Wars*, the Empire covers up the murder of Jawas on the planet Tatooine by making their deaths look like the work of Tusken raiders. Lucas would one day suggest that his space opera was a Vietnam protest movie in disguise; it is, after all, about a technically superior power fighting a group of less well-equipped rebels. It's an example of how, even in the midst of the most light-hearted genre movies, the concerns and ideals held by their creators can't help but find their way to the surface.

Selected SF films mentioned in this chapter:
THX 1138 (1971)
Silent Running (1972)
Soylent Green (1973)
Zardoz (1974)
Rollerball (1975)
Damnation Alley (1977)
Star Wars (1977)
Close Encounters of the Third Kind (1977)
Capricorn One (1977)

* See: http://www.denofgeek.com/movies/peter-hyams/27854/director-peter-hyams-outland-2010-gravity-kubrick.

13. Galactic adventures

STAR WARS (1977)

'A long time ago in a galaxy far, far away . . .'

Tensions were rising at Elstree Studios in the spring of 1976. At the studio in Hertfordshire, England, thirty-two-year-old director George Lucas was trying to film the exteriors for his third feature, a space opera called *Star Wars*. By this point, he had already endured two weeks of shooting in Tunisia: a tortuous period that took in props that wouldn't work, searing heat and torrential rainfall.

Long before that, he had spent months shopping his sci-fi concept around Hollywood studios, and found himself rejected by almost all of them; even Alan Ladd Jr, the boss of 20th Century Fox who gave it the green light, admitted that he didn't really understand exactly what Lucas was trying to make. All Ladd knew was that Lucas was a promising filmmaker, having shown off his skills as a visual stylist in the chilly dystopia *THX 1138* (1971), starring Robert Duvall, and having captured the 1950s nostalgia zeitgeist with his freewheeling – and highly successful – drama, *American Graffiti* (1973).

Now, Lucas had a demoralised cast and a sceptical crew with which to contend. Lucas's head may have been bursting with ideas, but he felt awkward on set and found communicating with his actors difficult. Just about everyone, from the higher-ups at Fox to the cast down to the set builders, thought they were working on some sort of eccentric disaster. The script was full of weird lines like, 'I should have known better than to trust the logic of a half-sized thermocapsulary dehousing assister.' The story was a mix of eastern mysticism, European fairy tale and staples from old serials and westerns. Even the costumes were strange; there goes Peter Mayhew, a seven-foot-tall Londoner clad from head to foot in a suit made of brown yak hair. Here comes the six-foot-six-tall bodybuilder David Prowse, dressed in a black cape and an awkward pointy mask that muffles his distinctive West Country accent.

Harrison Ford, co-starring as the smuggler and loveable rogue Han Solo, was grumbling about the dialogue and relieving his boredom between takes by taking a saw to chunks of the set. With the production running behind schedule, Lucas tried to convince the crew to stay behind to keep shooting. The union boss said the crew wouldn't want to do that, so Lucas put it to a vote, thinking they would back him. The crew voted to go home.

Meanwhile, Lucas had his film's special effects to worry about. Back in the old studio days, there were in-house workshops dedicated to creating special effects; by the mid-1970s, they had all closed. Lucas therefore took the unusual step of setting up his own: Industrial Light & Magic (ILM), which was a grand-sounding name for a bunch of twenty-somethings in a warehouse in Van Nuys, California. Initially headed up by John Dykstra – Douglas Trumbull's assistant on *Silent Running* – it was their task to create the hundreds of visual effects shots that would bring Lucas's space fighters and moon-sized battle stations to life. It's worth comparing the number of effects shots in *Star Wars* to *2001: A Space Odyssey*, which had set such a high watermark for miniature effects less than a decade earlier. Kubrick's movie had around 200 shots; *Star Wars* required 360. Worse still, Lucas didn't have the fearsome clout of Kubrick, nor the luxury of time the auteur's reputation afforded; all told, ILM had a year to get all those shots in the can.

The team at ILM did, however, have new technology on their side: by using computer-controlled cameras, they could take separate shots of miniatures and composite them together with a precision that wasn't available to Kubrick or his effects genius Douglas Trumbull in the 1960s. In simple terms, this meant that the effects team could have multiple miniature ships all moving around in the same frame, seemingly passing over each other or even appearing to fly directly over the camera. Actually implementing this technology wouldn't be without its teething problems, however; Dykstra and his team spent the first six months producing four effects shots, which Lucas considered unusable. This left ILM six months to go back and get all the sequences finished; the team completed their final shot – the first scene in the movie – just days before the *Star Wars* premiere.

Without those effects sequences, the film looked skeletal; it needed the ships and the starry backdrops to add flesh to its bones. This might partly explain why, as *Star Wars* reached the editing stage, the spectre of failure still hung over it. One day, Lucas famously screened a rough cut for some of his filmmaking friends, including Francis Ford Coppola, Steven Spielberg and Brian De Palma. In place of the incomplete effects shots, Lucas had spliced in black-and-white dogfight sequences from old war movies.[*] Lucas's peers were far from convinced.

Cutting Lucas's space opera together also proved to be a headache, as he repeatedly clashed with veteran editor John Jympson over the movie's tone and pace. Jympson was eventually replaced by editors Richard Chew, Paul Hirsch and Lucas's then wife, Marcia, who had just won an Oscar for her cutting on Martin Scorsese's *Alice Doesn't Live Here Anymore*. Working in tandem, the editing team began stripping *Star Wars* back down and building it back up again, tightening its pace and removing extraneous scenes.

Star Wars made its release date, opening at Grauman's Chinese Theatre in Los Angeles on 25 May 1977. Lucas may have dragged the film over the finish line, but he still wasn't convinced that it was going to do much more than open, get a few stinging reviews and fade from view. With their work done, George and Marcia went off on holiday to Hawaii, hoping to put the long days and sleepless nights behind them. All of this meant that Lucas was oblivious to the reaction *Star Wars* was getting back in the States: audiences cheered as John Williams's triumphant march blared out in theatres. They gasped at the first shot of an Imperial Star Destroyer cruising over the top of the camera like a gigantic arrowhead. Word was spreading; queues were building outside theatres. The summer of *Star Wars* mania had begun.

All told, *Star Wars* made $775 million on its initial release in 1977, replacing *Jaws* as the biggest film of all time. But *Star Wars* was more than a hit, and

* See: http://www.starwars.com/news/from-world-war-to-star-wars-dogfights.

more even than a merchandising phenomenon (due to his deal with Fox, Lucas would soon become a multi-millionaire thanks to toy sales alone). *Star Wars* crossed over into wider culture as few other science-fiction properties had done before, with a disco version of its theme appearing in clubs and comedians making jokes about the movie on TV.

Star Wars also marked a shift in tone for Hollywood movies. Before *Star Wars*, a wave of filmmakers had directed movies that were tough, uncompromising and keyed into the mood of the late 1960s and 1970s: Arthur Hill horrified an older generation with the violent gangster romance, *Bonnie and Clyde*; Dennis Hopper got the motor running with *Easy Rider*; William Friedkin thrilled and terrified with *The French Connection* and *The Exorcist*. All of these films were not only critically acclaimed, but also a hit with audiences. In an era of Watergate, the Vietnam War, recession and fuel crises, these were unvarnished films for troubled times.

Star Wars, on the other hand, offered the kind of light-hearted escapism that hadn't been seen since the matinee serials that blossomed in the wake of the Great Depression. Far from the anti-heroes of *Taxi Driver* or *Easy Rider*, the characters in *Star Wars* were divided cleanly into the good and the bad; the brave Rebels on one side, the evil Darth Vader on the other. Audiences, it seemed, were waiting to be whisked away from their troubles and off to a simpler, more innocent time and place.

Star Wars wasn't the only sci-fi fairy tale around in 1977, either. Steven Spielberg's *Close Encounters of the Third Kind* was an expression of the director's fascination with UFOs. What might have been a fairly serious thriller about saucers and government conspiracy (screenwriter Paul Schrader wrote a draft at one point) wound up as a mixture of family drama and religious experience. Richard Dreyfuss starred as a blue-collar worker whose contact with strange lights in the sky leads him on a quest to Wyoming, where he meets angelic beings and, eventually, ascends to the heavens in glittering chariots designed by Douglas Trumbull. George Lucas, fatalistic to the last, bet Spielberg that *Close Encounters* would be a bigger hit than *Star Wars*. Needless to say, it wasn't, and Lucas is still paying Spielberg a percentage of *Star Wars*'s gross to this day.

That *Star Wars* continues to be a pop-culture phenomenon hardly needs saying. Its first two sequels, *The Empire Strikes Back* (1980) and *The Return of the Jedi* (1983) were both huge hits, if not quite of the same magnitude as the original. Even a trilogy of inferior prequels – *The Phantom Menace, Attack of the Clones* and *Revenge of the Sith* – couldn't quite extinguish the public affection for the universe and characters Lucas created. Following Lucas's retirement in 2012, the *Star Wars* franchise – and its creator's company Lucasfilm – were passed over to Disney in a $4 billion deal. Under Disney's stewardship, the franchise has continued to thrive, with such directors as J. J. Abrams, Gareth Edwards and Rian Johnson bringing their own slants to Lucas's saga.

Beyond the confines of the franchise itself, the *Star Wars* movies helped usher in a special effects revolution. ILM quickly became the most respected and famous effects company in the United States, and from its collective brain came such things as Photoshop, an industry standard piece of photo-editing software, and Pixar, the animation studio which began as an offshoot of ILM. Beyond the first film's technical achievements, there was the detail and thought that went into its design. It was George Lucas who came up with the idea that the *Star Wars* universe should look tired and lived-in; an idea that still informs the look of science-fiction films to this day, as Professor Will Brooker, the author of *Using the Force*, points out.

'I think [*Star Wars*] was incredibly innovative, bold and inventive in terms of its effects,' Professor Brooker tells me. 'Beyond its technical achievements in terms of (for instance) filming miniatures, creating convincing matte paintings and rotoscoping, the care, detail and imagination that went into its design of ships, costumes and props seems outstanding to me. Perhaps above all, the "used universe" aesthetic was radical and influential – the idea that technology should look battered and dirty.'

Lucas himself was changed forever by the power of his creation. He often talked about returning to experimental movies after he finished *Return of the Jedi* in 1983 but, to date, the director who brought us the disturbing images of *THX 1138* and the sparky, loose comedy-drama of *American Graffiti* has never re-emerged. Some of Lucas's later creative decisions also made him a controversial figure among *Star Wars*'s fans, particularly from the late 1990s onwards:

these include the added CGI sequences and reworked scenes in the 1997 reissue of *Star Wars* (most infamously, the reworking of a shootout between Han Solo and bug-eyed bounty hunter, Greedo); the introduction of the comedy sidekick Jar Jar Binks in *The Phantom Menace*: rushed CGI movie *The Clone Wars*, originally developed as a TV pilot before being retooled as a theatrical release at Lucas's insistence. Nevertheless, Lucas redefined American cinema more drastically than perhaps any other filmmaker of the late twentieth century; the effects of *Star Wars* are still being felt today, both within the movie industry and without. By dreaming up his space fantasy world, Lucas changed the real world, too.

RETURN OF THE SPACE OPERA

Largely forgotten by Hollywood for decades, the space opera soon came back into vogue thanks to *Star Wars*. From 1977 onwards, movies that would never have been given multimillion-dollar budgets were suddenly given the green light; James Bond, who was originally supposed to embark on the adventure *For Your Eyes Only* in 1979, instead blasted off into space with *Moonraker*.

Star Trek, with a cult following that had grown continuously since its cancellation in the 1960s, was originally going to be brought back to the small screen with a new television series. In March 1978, Paramount boss Michael Eisner announced that the original cast of *Star Trek* were indeed set to make a triumphant return – not to the small screen, but to cinemas. In fact, work on a *Star Trek* movie had begun three years earlier as an aborted project named *Planet of the Titans*; this in turn gave way to a TV series called *Star Trek: Phase II*, before Paramount abruptly decided to switch back to making a movie again.

Star Trek: The Motion Picture, directed by Robert Wise and released in 1979, was in many ways the antithesis of *Star Wars*. Moving at a stately pace, it offered a journey into the unknown more akin to *2001: A Space Odyssey* than the lightsabre-flashing *Star Wars*. The movie proved expensive for Paramount, too, with a $46 million budget; a sum run up in no small part because of a costly problem with its special effects. When Paramount parted company with the original studio commissioned to create *Star Trek*'s numerous effects shots,

Douglas Trumbull, whose work had lit up the screen in *2001: A Space Odyssey*, stepped in to fill the breach. His work would, thankfully, prove to be stunning.

Beautifully shot and mounted though it was, *Star Trek: The Motion Picture* wasn't quite the *Star Wars*-beater Paramount might have hoped; with a take of $139 million, it was a success rather than a zeitgeist-capturing phenomenon. All the same, the *Enterprise* had finally re-emerged from dry dock: *Star Trek* was back. Some critics may have joked about *The Motion Picture*'s pace, or maybe the advancing years of its cast in the sequels, but Paramount managed something no other studio could in the wake of *Star Wars*: it successfully launched a space-opera franchise of its own. Many others tried and failed.

Disney, one of the studios who had turned down *Star Wars* in the mid-1970s, earmarked a then-huge $20 million to make up for lost ground with *The Black Hole* (1979) – a space adventure where goofy-looking robots voiced by Slim Pickens and Roddy McDowall sat awkwardly alongside violent deaths and references to hell. More creepy than exhilarating, Disney's unexpectedly dark adventure was fated to become a cult item rather than a financial success.

Dune, adapted from Frank Herbert's bestselling novel and directed by David Lynch, was supposed to be the movie that launched a string of sequels. Reports around the time of its release in 1984 suggested that as many as five movies were planned – all the better to realise Herbert's story of spice mining and warring clans on distant planets. Rumours of production difficulties plagued *Dune* for months, however, and critics rounded on the finished film when it finally appeared. Universal, which had spent a reported $40 million in the hope of getting its own merchandise-selling space saga, instead got a baroque, eccentric and faintly disturbing epic with horror overtones – hardly the kind of thing that shifts sticker books or bedspreads. Ironically, Lynch had turned down the chance to direct *Star Wars* sequel *Return of the Jedi* to make *Dune*.

Dune, like so many would-be blockbusters of the 1980s, would eventually become a cherished cult film. Likewise *The Last Star Fighter*, a sci-fi film which might have sounded like a sure-fire hit on paper: a space adventure akin to *Star Wars* that also tapped into the exploding popularity of videogames. Released in

1984, *The Last Star Fighter* is particularly noteworthy for its extensive use of CGI in place of miniature effects; movies like *Tron* and *Star Trek II: The Wrath of Khan* may have used computer imagery first, but only in a handful of scenes (much of *Tron* was created using traditional animation techniques).

If major studios were disappointed by the tepid responses to their space movies, small independents were quite happy to appeal to grindhouse cinemas or the VHS market. Veteran B-movie filmmaker Roger Corman once complained that, in the wake of *Jaws* and *Star Wars* in the 1970s, Hollywood was starting to take all his ideas and remake them with huge budgets. This didn't, however, stop Corman or independent filmmakers like him from wresting the same ideas back again and swiftly making cheap adventure movies with wobbly sets and effects. Some of the most noteworthy space operas from the post-*Star Wars* era were *Starcrash* (1978), directed by Italy's Luigi Cozzi, distributed by Corman and starring David Hasselhoff and Christopher Plummer; *Battle Beyond the Stars* (1980), a quasi-remake of Akira Kurosawa's *Seven Samurai* with spaceships; and *Space Raiders* (1983), which recycled footage from *Battle Beyond the Stars*. Whether they meant to or not, many of these movies wound up looking far more like the old matinee serials from the 1930s than *Star Wars* did; yes, those are spray-painted McDonalds burger boxes you can see on the walls in *Battle Beyond the Stars*.

As the 1990s tipped over into the new millennium, making space adventure films remained a risky proposition. *Wing Commander* (1999), based on the hit videogame series and starring Mark Hamill, was a critical and financial disappointment; in a final humiliation, reports circulated that moviegoers were buying tickets, watching the trailer for *The Phantom Menace* at the beginning, and promptly walking back out again. *Battlefield Earth* (2000), based on a novel by L. Ron Hubbard and starring an almost unrecognisable John Travolta, was an unintentionally amusing disaster.

It was the digital effects explosion sparked by *Jurassic Park* (1993), and George Lucas's *Star Wars* prequel trilogy, released from 1999 onwards, that prompted a renewed interest in the space opera. The most successful was James Cameron's *Avatar* (see Chapter 29), which defied expectations and became the highest-grossing movie of all time when unadjusted for inflation.

Given all that came before it, maybe it was inevitable that Disney's *John Carter* (2011), based on Edgar Rice Burroughs's series of pulp novels, failed to make the same impression. Rice's books had been plundered of so many ideas by subsequent storytellers – including the creators of *Superman*, *Flash Gordon*, *Star Wars* and *Avatar* – that *John Carter* looked almost quaint to modern eyes.

Marvel Studios went out on something of a limb when they made a space adventure of their own in 2014. Yet *Guardians of the Galaxy*, directed by James Gunn, proved to be another major hit to match Marvel's other comic book blockbusters; full of quirky characters and knowing humour, Gunn's film – and his 2017 sequel, *Guardians of the Galaxy Vol. 2* – hark back to the exoticism and fun of matinee serials and 1980s *Star Wars* knock-offs.

Disney, just over four decades after it turned down the chance to make *Star Wars*, now owns both Lucasfilm and Marvel – and by extension, two of the biggest space-opera franchises on the planet. With *Star Wars* movies planned for release on an annual basis following the franchise's relaunch with *The Force Awakens* in 2015, the space opera is likely to thrive for years to come.

Selected SF films mentioned in this chapter:

Starcrash (1978)

Moonraker (1979)

Star Trek: The Motion Picture (1979)

The Black Hole (1979)

Battle Beyond the Stars (1980)

Space Raiders (1983)

Dune (1984)

The Last Star Fighter (1984)

Wing Commander (1999)

Battlefield Earth (2000)

John Carter (2011)

Guardians of the Galaxy (2014)

Star Wars: The Force Awakens (2015)

Guardians of the Galaxy Vol. 2 (2017)

14. Star beasts

ALIEN (1979)

'I admire its purity . . .'

In the late 1970s, a young writer named Dan O'Bannon found himself lying on a friend's couch, jobless, anxious and depressed. For almost a year, he had been working on a movie that could have been the making of his career: an ambitious, sprawling adaptation of James Herbert's epic sci-fi novel, *Dune*. Director Alejandro Jodorowsky, the Chilean filmmaker behind such eccentric cult hits as *The Holy Mountain* and *El Topo*, had assembled an extraordinary team of artists and designers from all over Europe – and O'Bannon was given the job of overseeing them all.

Fresh from co-writing, editing and acting in the 1974 SF comedy *Dark Star*, directed by John Carpenter on a shoestring budget, O'Bannon was given the task of coordinating artists as diverse as the UK's Chris Foss, Jean 'Moebius' Giraud from France and H. R. Giger from Switzerland. Jodorowsky's *Dune* screenplay ran to around 300 pages; the movie's budget was set at just under $10 million, while the eclectic cast was set to include Mick Jagger, Orson Welles and surrealist artist Salvador Dalí.

For six months, O'Bannon's Paris-based art department worked on an extraordinary array of production designs and concept drawings for Jodorowsky's space opera. The entire script was storyboarded in detail, and hinted at a genre film with the kind of scale rarely seen since the days of Fritz Lang. The expense and sheer unbridled scale of *Dune* was what killed the project in the end; funding for the movie fell apart, and O'Bannon had little choice but to head back to the United States.

The death of *Dune* would, however, bear the kind of creative fruit that

O'Bannon could never have predicted. O'Bannon's friend, who generously lent him the use of his couch, was Ronald Shusett, a fellow writer with ambitions of breaking into Hollywood. Together, the pair began work on a project initially named 'Starbeast'; a horror film set on a spacecraft where the crew are hunted down by a vicious alien. When O'Bannon struggled to think of a creative way to get the monster on to the ship, Shusett came up with a grimly creative solution: the alien is a parasite, which impregnates a crewmember. Back on the ship, the creature hatches from its host and begins terrorising everyone else on board.

This was the kind of visceral, button-pushing concept that separated O'Bannon and Shusett's story from other monster-in-space movies, from *This Island Earth* to *It! The Terror Beyond Space*. When the pair began hawking the script around Hollywood, it was certainly the horrific birth sequence that attracted producers Gordon Carroll and David Giler when the screenplay landed on their desk in the mid-1970s. Now called *Alien*, the script had many of the trappings of a low-budget B-movie – indeed, it came close to being bought up by Roger Corman at one point – yet the thin sliver of body horror made it seem more closely attuned to a decade that produced such graphic movies as *Last House on the Left*, *The Exorcist* and *The Texas Chain Saw Massacre*.

There was already a precedent for a parasitic organism that hatches from its victim's stomach by the late 1970s, in fact. *Shivers*, the first feature from the Canadian filmmaker David Cronenberg, featured a leech-like creature that passed from human to human, incubated in their stomachs and eventually burst through their skin – but not before it had turned them into sex-obsessed zombie maniacs. (Cronenberg once suggested that O'Bannon had seen *Shivers* and that *Alien* was inspired by it; neither O'Bannon nor Shusett admitted as much themselves.)

Of *Alien*'s creative origins, O'Bannon once said that his story 'wasn't stolen from anybody; it was stolen from *everybody*'.* It's certainly true that there are

---

* See: Chris Taylor, *How Star Wars Conquered the Universe: The Past, Present and Future of a Multi-Billion Dollar Franchise* (London: Head of Zeus, 2015), https://books.google.co.uk/books?id=z7GbBAAAQBAJ&pg=PT234&lpg=PT234&dq=I+didn%27t+steal+alien+from+anybody+shusett&source=bl&ots=9Ijq9KZsoL&sig=ps6zRltdPJTSAzXWYUoggGPkwME&hl=en&sa=X&ved=0ahUKEwjO39jouLPUAhXIK1AKHfwHB0cQ6AEIJDAA#v=onepage&q=I%20didn't%20steal%20alien%20from%20anybody%20shusett&f=false.

elements in common with a section of A. E. van Vogt's book, *Voyage of the Space Beagle* – the author was eventually given a credit at the end of the movie as part of a settlement with 20th Century Fox. The difference between *Alien* and most other monster movies of its period, however, was that it emerged from a major Hollywood studio. The success of *Star Wars* had made sci-fi a viable genre, while the box-office success of *Jaws*, *The Omen* and *The Exorcist* indicated that audiences would pay to see a horror movie with an A-picture budget. And so it was that, in 1977, Fox studio head Alan Ladd Jr gave *Alien* the green light, setting aside a budget of $4.2 million. By this point, the screenplay had been rewritten by David Giler and Walter Hill – much to O'Bannon's chagrin. Hill had already written such gritty films as *The Getaway* and *The Driver* (which he also directed), and was quite candid about his lack of interest in science fiction. O'Bannon bristled when Hill changed all the character names from things like Melkonis and Robie to Parker and Dallas, but Hill's earthier, more grounded angle would prove vital to *Alien*. It was Hill's idea that the ship be a kind of interplanetary oil refinery, and that its crew were 'truckers in space' – a mismatched bunch who bickered about bonuses and low pay. Hill then had the idea of the ship being the property of a heartless company who regarded its employees as a secondary concern; in an era of fuel shortages, post-Watergate fallout and union strikes, it was the perfect backdrop for a turbulent decade.

When Walter Hill passed on the opportunity to direct *Alien* himself, production company Brandywine eventually settled on Ridley Scott, a forty-year-old former maker of commercials (his promo for Hovis was screened on British television for years) whose debut feature, *The Duellists* (1977), had recently appeared at film festivals. Starring Harvey Keitel, *The Duellists* may have been a low-budget period piece, but there was something about the precision of Scott's direction that appealed to *Alien*'s producers. As it turned out, Scott's flair for art and design was just what *Alien* needed to elevate it far above the level of B-grade schlock – indeed, the clarity of Scott's ideas for *Alien*, set down in a set of storyboards, convinced Fox to almost double *Alien*'s budget. Under Scott's aegis, O'Bannon – by then hired as visual effects supervisor – managed to assemble a group of world-class artists and designers, many of whom he had already met on the ill-fated *Dune*. Chief among them was the eccentric H. R. Giger, the Swiss artist who, using acrylic paints and an airbrush, specialised in visualising his nightmares as freakish, biomechanical landscapes. It was O'Bannon who first handed Scott a copy of *Necronomicon*, a 1977 book containing much of Giger's major work up to that point. In a pivotal moment in SF movie history, Scott flicked through page after page of surreal, largely monochrome images, and settled on a painting titled *Necronom IV*. It showed a bizarre creature in profile, its humanoid body covered in bony outcroppings, its shiny, insectoid head elongated and suggestively phallic. Like much of Giger's work, the creature was at once grotesque and beautiful; mechanical yet also fleshy.

Scott and his team had laboured for months over what the title creature in *Alien* might look like; early drawings by Ron Cobb had the beast looking like a cross between a featherless turkey and a crab. But here, in the pages of Giger's book, was something that genuinely looked like a monster from a fever dream. Scott had found his *Alien*.

In 1979, *Alien* appeared in US cinemas on 25 May – the same date as *Star Wars* two years earlier and Fox boss Alan Ladd Jr's lucky day. Critical notices were initially lukewarm, but audiences responded more vocally; according to one account, several moviegoers at *Alien*'s Dallas premiere were seen fleeing up the aisles in terror. Part of *Alien*'s brilliance is the immersion created by Ridley Scott's measured, prowling direction, matched by Jerry Goldsmith's eerily understated score and Michael Seymour's gritty production design. Unlike the sparse, angular spaceship sets of the 1950s and 1960s, *Alien*'s craft, the *Nostromo*, is a claustrophobic, oppressively cold hive of long corridors and mess rooms with low ceilings. By the time the *Nostromo* reaches LV-426, a forbidding moon covered in claw-like rocks and swirling fog, the sense of foreboding already hangs thickly in the air.

Scott's casting and the terse quality of the screenplay also run counter to most sci-fi movies that came before *Alien* – the sense of low-key, lived-in realism is closer to *2001: A Space Odyssey* (a film that Scott prized) than *It! The Terror from Beyond Space*. Lacking outright A-list stars, actors such as Sigourney Weaver, Yaphet Kotto, Ian Holm and Veronica Cartwright add to the film's stark ordinariness. Much of the dialogue is muttered, or overlaps, or simply vanishes beneath the hiss and whine of the cavernous ship. Together, Scott and his cast manage to create the impression that this group of tired, scruffy astronauts have been trapped together for years, the tensions between them slowly beginning to tell in their irked exchanges.

It's nearly an hour into *Alien* before the crew of the *Nostromo* finally discover the source of the beacon that woke them from their slumber: a ship that doesn't look so much built as grown. Like all the extraterrestrial elements in *Alien*, this ship – dubbed the Juggernaut – was designed and built by Giger, who worked feverishly with piles of bones, polystyrene, clay and spray paint at Shepperton Studios. With his slicked-back hair and black leather jacket, which he refused to take off even in the clammy summer heat, Giger was often compared to Peter Lorre by his fellow crewmembers. Yet Giger, in all his eccentricity, proved to be the movie's secret weapon; his ship, with its ribbed interior and strange, long-dead pilot, looked unlike anything seen in a movie before.

Then there's the alien itself, which Kane (John Hurt) discovers in the bowels of the ship: a spider-like parasite, which springs from a leathery egg and attaches itself to his face. Against their better judgement, Kane's colleagues drag him back to the *Nostromo*, where it's revealed that the parasite has deposited something in Kane's viscera. The ship's science officer, Ash (Ian Holm) seems to know what it is; clearly, the movie is building up to something dreadful. Audiences in 1979 were unprepared for what would come next.

Kane barely gets more than a few mouthfuls of his final meal before the birth pains begin. In one of the most infamous scenes in sci-fi cinema, an alien foetus erupts from Kane's chest, tearing and gnashing through his blood-spattered shirt. It's a startlingly violent sequence, both visually and in its implications: between them, the artists, writers and technicians behind *Alien* manage to dredge up a hideous artefact from the human subconscious. It's a manifestation of all our mortal fears of disease, sexual violence, birth and death. It is, as Ash glibly puts it, 'Kane's son.'

Worst of all, the alien's horrible life cycle feels so utterly convincing: it's a parasite that can lie dormant, perhaps for centuries, before it springs out and impregnates its prey. Once hatched, the alien grows to a huge size, and then . . . well, Scott's film leaves the creature's activities largely obscure, at least in *Alien*'s theatrical cut. A deleted scene shows Ripley (Weaver) discovering a kind of nest where the Starbeast has cocooned several members of the crew, who appear to be turning into eggs capable of spawning more face-hugging spores – all the better to perpetuate its species. The alien's motivations are elaborated on rather differently in James Cameron's 1986 sequel (see Chapter 20), but for audiences back in the late 1970s, the creature remained chillingly ambiguous. Flashes of gore are, birth scene aside, fleeting; we're left to decide for ourselves whether the alien is blood-sucking, or flesh-eating, or uses its victims for even more disturbing ends.

Alien's major coup, however, was its casting of Sigourney Weaver as the *Nostromo*'s only survivor. It was reportedly Alan Ladd Jr who suggested that Ripley should be a female character after reading an early draft of the script; Ladd was, he later admitted, influenced by the popularity of a number of female-led movies in the 1970s, such as *Julia*, starring Vanessa Redgrave and Jane Fonda, and *The Turning Point*, starring Shirley MacLaine and Anne Bancroft – both films he had greenlit at Fox. But while Ladd's suggestion may have been led at least in part by his commercial instinct, the result was something vanishingly rare in science-fiction cinema before 1979: a heroine as sharp and capable as any of the male characters surrounding her. Audiences watching *Alien* in the 1970s might have assumed that Dallas (Tom Skerritt), the *Nostromo*'s alpha male, might be the one who would vanquish the ship's ferocious eighth passenger; instead, he meets a grim fate while crawling around in an oily ventilation system. It's Ripley – shrewd, smart, even somewhat aloof – who ultimately outwits this seemingly indestructible creature.

Almost by accident, the makers of *Alien* created a perfect mirror image in Ripley and the alien. Like Dr Morbius in *Forbidden Planet*, Giger conjures up a horrifying beast from his subconscious: a slithering embodiment of distinctly masculine fears about sex, defilement and childbirth. Perhaps it's only fitting, then, that a woman expels this violent monster from the male psyche.

THE BEST AND WORST OF SPACE HORROR

Before *Alien*, space-horror movies were generally inexpensive affairs, charac-terised by wobbly sets and less than convincing monsters. One notable excep-tion was *Planet of the Vampires*, directed by Italy's Mario Bava and released in 1965. While it bears many of the hallmarks of a B-movie – wooden acting from a less than charismatic cast, uneven special effects – it also contains moments of genuine unease. Like *Alien*, *Planet of the Vampires* sees a group of explorers land on a windswept planet; there, an unseen force causes them to turn violently on one another. Lit with Bava's typically sumptuous colour and featuring some striking costume and set designs, *Planet of the Vampires* has much in common with *Alien*, and some shots even look markedly similar.

After *Alien*, space horror struck back with a vengeance. Varying wildly in quality and budget, none of them could match Scott's classic in terms of detail or suspense, so many opted for gross-out gore instead. The UK's *Inseminoid* (1981) was a bad-taste *Alien* knock-off, right down to its title monster, which impregnates its victims and turns them into raving zombies. Stephanie Beacham stars, and spends much of the film stumbling about in the tunnels of what is evidently an abandoned mine.

Hollywood's mogul of the zero-budget flick, Roger Corman, responded with a few *Alien* clones of his own. The best of these was arguably *Galaxy of Terror* (1981), which sees a group of neurotic explorers touch down on a planet where their worst fears are realised. It's an enjoyably rough-edged, schlocky film, and notable for several reasons: first, it provides an early genre outing for future Freddy Krueger star Robert Englund; second, it has a scene where the head of Erin Moran from *Happy Days* explodes. Finally, take a look at the end credits: the effects designer and second unit director on *Galaxy of Terror* was one James Cameron.

Other *Alien* clones from the 1980s included *Titan Find* (also known as *Creature*, 1985), featuring a typically deranged performance from Klaus Kinski, and *Forbidden World* (also known as *Mutant*, 1982), which features one of the most startling bad-taste endings of them all. Director Tobe Hooper, whose *Texas Chain Saw Massacre* had provided much inspiration to Ridley Scott in the 1970s, tried his hand at a quasi-space-horror movie of his own in 1985.

Lifeforce, based on Colin Wilson's novel *The Space Vampires*, sees a team of astronauts retrieve a trio of humanoid aliens from a ship hiding in Halley's Comet. The astronauts are mysteriously killed on the trip back to Earth, while the aliens – chief among them a profoundly nude Mathilda May – turn out to be energy-sucking predators who bring chaos to London.

Like most post-*Alien* horror movies, *Lifeforce* failed to make much of an impression at the box office and, to modern eyes, it seems borderline shocking that so much money – a then-considerable $25 million – would be lavished on such a bizarre film. All the same, *Lifeforce* has survived as a cult oddity, much like the other movies mentioned so far. Even the space-horror films released more recently, such as 1997's *Event Horizon*, a kind of gothic, space-faring version of *The Shining*, have struggled to make the same kind of impression as *Alien*, even if they do occasionally produce some mesmerising images of their own.

In 2012, Ridley Scott made *Prometheus*, the first in a planned trilogy of *Alien* prequels. Once again, the crew of a spaceship make an ill-fated voyage to a faraway planet, where all kinds of monsters from the id await. Its imagery was often spectacular, but even Scott couldn't replicate *Alien*'s coiled menace with *Prometheus*. Its plot, which echoes *Planet of the Vampires* and even *Galaxy of Terror*, has a tendency to demystify the *Alien* universe even as it expands it. Its monsters, for all their pale skin, tentacles and sharp teeth, are but a shadow of Giger's terrifying alien. In fact, Ash's description of *Alien*'s monster also applies to the movie itself: 'It's the perfect organism. Its structural perfection is matched only by its hostility.'

Selected SF films mentioned in this chapter:

Planet of the Vampires (1965)

Inseminoid (1981)

Galaxy of Terror (1981)

Forbidden World (1982)

Titan Find (1985)

Lifeforce (1985)

Event Horizon (1997)

Prometheus (2012)

15. It came from the desert

MAD MAX (1979)

'Any longer out on that road and I'm one of them, you know? A terminal crazy. Only I got a bronze badge to say I'm one of the good guys.'

From an early age, George Miller had something of a love-hate relationship with cars. He grew up in Chinchilla, a small town outside Queensland, Australia, where young men raced up and down the dusty roads at terrifying speed. By the time Miller left Queensland to study medicine, he had already lost several friends in motor accidents; during his residency at St Vincent's, a hospital in Sydney, he noted the number of people wheeled into the emergency department having been involved in high-speed crashes.

'The USA has its gun culture,' Miller once told the Australian film publication *Cinema Papers*, 'we have our car culture.'*

While Miller practised medicine, his other passion lay in filmmaking. His short film *Violence in Cinema: Part I*, made with his creative partner Byron Kennedy in 1971, earned several awards – not to mention a ripple of controversy for its explicit bloodshed. Miller was by no means the first Australian filmmaker to explore his country's attitude to violence; director Ted Kotcheff's fearsome 1971 cult horror-drama *Wake in Fright* explored the hard-drinking, bare-knuckle culture of a small Antipodean town to mesmerising effect. Peter Weir's debut, *The Cars that Ate Paris* (1974) was about a hermetic town whose inhabitants run unwary visitors off the road, plunder their wrecked vehicles

---

* See: https://issuu.com/libuow/docs/cinemapaper1979mayno021.

and cart the drivers off to use in weird medical experiments. (Weir's film, it seems, inspired Roger Corman to make a film about vehicular carnage himself: 1975's *Death Race 2000*.)

It was Miller's 1979 film *Mad Max*, however, that really captured cinema-goers' imaginations, and from its humble beginnings as a low-budget exploitation picture, wound up becoming a multimillion-dollar franchise – and, in the process, made a Hollywood star of its leading man, Mel Gibson.

Mad Max's plot is as stripped down as a racing car. In a near-future Australia, a dwindling supply of fuel has left society in complete disarray. Assorted gangs of robbers and maniacs roam the long stretches of tarmac like highwaymen, or bandits in the Old West; a law enforcement group called the Main Force Patrol does its best to keep a lid on all the anarchy. Officer Max Rockatansky (Gibson) is one of MFP's finest – that is, until he sees his partner, Goose (Steve Bisley), and then his own family murdered by a vicious gang led by the maniacal Toecutter (Hugh Keays-Byrne). A red mist descends, and Max heads off on a revenge-fuelled rampage.

From this wilfully simple premise, Miller delivers a kinetic exercise in low-budget filmmaking. With a handful of cars and meagre resources, Miller creates the impression of a world on the verge of collapse; *Mad Max* is a violent film not just in terms of its content, but in its sound, filming and editing. There's a blunt ruthlessness to the way one sequence flows into the next; like the great white shark in Steven Spielberg's *Jaws*, *Mad Max* never stops moving. As Miller himself once put it, *Mad Max* has 'the impact of being in a car accident'.

Incredibly, *Mad Max* was made for almost nothing at all – Miller places his budget at around $300,000, which is roughly what Roger Corman was spending on making his movies in the late 1970s. That small sum of money was dragged together largely from private investors, and also by Miller and producer Byron Kennedy; for three months, the pair worked as a first-response medical emergency team, Kennedy driving the car and Miller jumping out to provide assistance. 'We got a lot of anecdotes and stories for the film by visiting road accident victims who'd come through traumatic experiences,'

Kennedy later recalled. 'In that short period, we were able to earn a fair bit of money, too . . .'*

Nevertheless, $300,000 was a tiny sum, particularly given the number of stunts the plot required. Time and money were so tight, in fact, that numerous scenes were shot without permits, with Miller and his crew closing off roads, stealing a few shots and moving on; by tuning in to police frequencies, they successfully avoided getting caught by the law. Still, the low budget contributed to the film's gritty style, right down to some of the incidental details in the stunts: in one sequence in the finished movie, you can clearly see a stuntman being struck on the head by his own motorcycle. In another scene, a car travelling in excess of 100 mph slides perilously out of control – a mishap Miller left in the final cut. The film's rough-and-ready approach extended to the sets: art director Jon Dowding 'borrowed' signs from a local milk bar to use in a handful of scenes, used them to dress his set, and returned them after filming the next morning.

In 1979, George Miller and his crew returned from the scrubland outside Melbourne with a buzzing, fractious genre film that tapped into the 1970s zeitgeist. Conflict in the Middle East and declining oil production in the United States led to a pair of fuel crises in 1973 and 1979; supplies dwindled, the cost of oil soared, stock markets faltered.

'I'd lived in a very lovely and sedate city in Melbourne,' Miller later explained to the *Daily Beast*, 'and during OPEC and the extreme oil crisis, where the only people who could get any gas were emergency workers, firemen, hospital staff, and police, it took ten days in this really peaceful city for the first shot to be fired. So I thought, "What if this happened over ten years?" '†

Against this global backdrop, and from his own experiences as an Australian, Miller forged a highly personal mixture of sci-fi dystopia, western, horror, revenge thriller and biker movie. Although he lacked the resources available to the directors of such films as *Planet of the Apes*, *Soylent Green* or the

---

* See: https://issuu.com/libuow/docs/cinemapaper1979mayno021.
† See: http://www.thedailybeast.com/articles/2015/05/16/mad-max-fury-road-how-9-11-mel-gibson-and-heath-ledger-s-death-couldn-t-derail-a-classic.html.

little-seen *Damnation Alley*, Miller succeeded in creating an absorbing sense of the apocalyptic. *Mad Max* is at once a movie that takes a gloomy look at what a resource-drained future might produce, and perhaps also a damning satire of a particular kind of masculinity; the film paints a darkly amusing portrait of the male as pack animal, wont to follow a charismatic leader – in this case, Toecutter – and fetishise cars, weapons and cold acts of violence. And as we'll soon see, *Mad Max*'s down-at-heel, grungy style would quickly spawn a series of imitators from all corners of the globe.

With an estimated box-office take of $100 million, *Mad Max* still ranks among the most profitable independent movies of all time. As a result, humanity descended further into chaos two years later with *Mad Max 2: The Road Warrior*, in which Max Rockatansky again does battle with maniacal gangs on Australia's desolate highways. Less profitable than *Mad Max*, *Road Warrior* is, if anything, even more spectacular than its predecessor. The somewhat less satisfying *Mad Max Beyond Thunderdome* followed in 1985; co-starring Tina Turner as the magnificently named Aunty Entity, it shifts focus from vehicular action to gladiatorial combat in a hemispherical arena. The most expensive *Mad Max* movie in the series at that point, it was also the most muted in box-office terms – though Miller's unwavering eye for action and world-building mean it has a devoted cult following.

From the late 1990s onwards, Miller struggled in vain to make a fourth *Mad Max* movie, with everything from financing to the weather repeatedly thwarting his plans. Shooting on what would become *Mad Max: Fury Road* finally began in earnest in 2012, with Miller and his crew spending the best part of four months in the Namibian desert, repeatedly crashing cars in the searing heat. By this point, Miller was approaching his seventies; his cinematographer, John Seale, had to be coaxed out of retirement to join him on the production. Such a shoot would have been gruelling for filmmakers half their age, yet still they persisted; by the time filming ended in mid-2013, Miller and his crew had generated a startling 480 hours of footage. From this bizarre cloud of sand, dust, fire and metal came another febrile rave of a movie, impeccably edited by Miller's partner Margaret Sixel: an operatic chase movie, which updates the madness of the 1979 original for a modern multiplex audience. British actor Tom Hardy replaces Mel Gibson as a new, monosyllabic Max Rockatansky, but the film's plot really belongs to Charlize Theron as Furiosa, a haunted, wounded truck driver who steals a group of captive 'wives' from a warlord, Immortan Joe (Hugh Keays-Byrne, back from the first *Mad Max* in a new guise), kick-starting an apocalyptic pursuit, which barely lets up for two solid hours.

Fury Road's critique of masculinity is, if anything, even more scathing than it was over three decades earlier. Through his twisted apocalyptic world, Miller comments on man's tendency to turn everything into a commodity – water is branded 'Agua Cola' by Immortan Joe – and the grim inevitability of violence. In 1979, Miller came out of nowhere with a breakthrough hit that became one of the most influential films of its era; that he could make another film with such energy and verve over thirty-five years later is a testament to his filmmaking skill.

Post-apocalyptic action

In its depiction of a society hurtling towards collapse, *Mad Max* didn't need special effects shots of cities in ruins or expensive sets. Rather, its use of real, backwater locations gives the film a sense of abandoned grubbiness; with the addition of some ramshackle, modified vehicles and a handful of brave (and quite possibly crazy) stunt performers, *Mad Max* proves that you can make a futuristic action thriller on a shoestring budget.

George Miller's movie inspired other filmmakers to head off into the middle of nowhere with a bunch of actors, some props and a camera, and come back with their own apocalyptic thriller. The result was a surprisingly vibrant sub-genre, which covered the Antipodes, Europe, the Philippines and America. While few – if any – of the directors behind these movies had the intelligence and craft displayed by Miller, they often made up for their lack of storytelling skill with sheer reckless abandon.

Europe's great powerhouse for *Mad Max* rip-offs was Italy, a country which chased its proud 1960s and 1970s line of classic westerns, thrillers and horror films with a procession of cheap clones of Hollywood movies. One of the earliest was *1990: The Bronx Warriors* (1982), a movie that borrows the dusty post-apocalypse of *Mad Max 2* and throws in a bit of Walter Hill's 1979 gangland thriller *The Warriors* for good measure. Shot on a visibly low budget, *The Bronx Warriors* nevertheless goes all-out to entertain: its compact ninety minutes takes in high-octane chases between motorcycle gangs and hoodlums in vintage cars, shootouts, swordfights, explosions and liberal sprinklings of gore. Director Enzo G. Castellari, who had previously directed, among other things, the 1977 cult film *The Inglorious Bastards*, made two further post-apocalyptic films in quick succession: *The New Barbarians* (1983) and *Escape from The Bronx* (1983), each with their own rough-and-ready charm: one of the big stunts in *The New Barbarians* involves a car driving through some empty beer barrels.

The most rough-and-ready clone to hail from Italy was, perhaps, *Exterminators of the Year 3000* (1983), a ninety-minute orgy of long-haired men crashing cars in the wilds of Italy and Spain. Like so many of these movies, the plot is almost non-existent; what distinguishes *Exterminators* is its procession of genuinely dangerous-looking stunts. In the film's final battle, a high-octane clash between two armies of rusty vehicles breaks out, resulting in a comical yet vaguely terrifying carnival of twisted metal and flying bodies. At one point, a stuntman explodes for no identifiable reason.

Across the pond in the United States, meanwhile, filmmakers were trying their hands at *Mad Max* homages of their own. *Steel Dawn* (1987) was so intent on channelling *Max*'s spirit that its makers hired that film's Australian composer Brian May (not to be confused with the Queen guitarist) to write the soundtrack. Set in another sandy post-war wasteland, *Steel Dawn* is a somewhat classier affair than its brethren from Italy. First, there's the cast, which features Patrick Swayze as the hero, Nomad, Anthony Zerbe as the boss of an evil gang terrorising a small town of settlers, and character actors Brion James (*Blade Runner*) and Arnold Vosloo. With a slightly more generous budget than most *Mad Max* clones (about $3.5 million), *Steel Dawn* boasts some impressive production values and competent framing (curiously, the movie also happened to be shot in Namibia, the same desert location Miller used for *Mad Max: Fury Road* nearly thirty years later). *Steel Dawn* was but one in a small wave of post-apocalyptic action films, though, with such cult gems as *Cherry 2000* (directed by *Miracle Mile*'s Steve De Jarnatt), *Hell Comes to Frogtown* and *The Salute of the Jugger* (starring Rutger Hauer) all following on its heels. If the producers behind them were hoping to capitalise on the muted success of *Mad Max Beyond Thunderdome*, however, they would soon be disappointed – although these films would find a loyal cult following on videotape, none captured the broader public's imagination like Miller's nightmarish series.

All the same, *Mad Max* continued to be a fertile source of inspiration for filmmakers all over the world. The Japanese manga and anime series *Hokuto no Ken*, known in the West as *Fist of the North Star*, was a post-apocalyptic western saga in the *Mad Max* tradition. Extraordinarily gory and violent – it's about a warrior class that is able to kill its opponents by hitting certain pressure points on the body – *Fist of the North Star* got an animated feature film in 1986, a low-rent live-action movie adaptation in 1995 and a small army of spin-off videogames that still continues today.

Perhaps the biggest *Mad Max*-inspired film of them all, though, was *Waterworld*. Made for what was in 1995 an extraordinary amount of money ($172 million), its action is set in a future world drowned by melting ice caps; with nowhere to drive a truck or motorbike, lawless gangs have instead migrated to the high seas, where they stage violent attacks on artificial islands populated by ragged survivors. Kevin Costner plays the Mariner, a terse hero with some of the swimming abilities of comic-book hero, Aquaman, while Dennis Hopper plays his cackling nemesis, Deacon. Marred by a troubled shoot and cost overruns, *Waterworld* made its money back, but struggled to shake off the stigma of a fraught production covered in gleeful detail by the press.

To date, no other post-apocalyptic action film has quite matched *Mad Max* and its sequels in terms of wit and iconic imagery. The series' imitators hungrily latched onto its idea of heroes and villains fighting for scraps at the end of the world, but tended to overlook the deeper meaning of George Miller's movies: their bitingly funny critique of macho idiocy – an obsession with guns, cars and violence; a desire to grab land and dominate the less able;

a tendency to mindlessly follow a leader, like a pack animal. That satirical streak was back in full force in *Mad Max: Fury Road* – and once again, other filmmakers have attempted to follow in its slipstream. In late 2016, a Chinese production company announced *Mad Shelia: Virgin Road*,* which is as blatant a rip-off of *Fury Road* as those old Italian movies were of *Mad Max 2*. It only proves, once again, that imitation is the sincerest form of flattery.

Selected SF films mentioned in this chapter:

1990: The Bronx Warriors (1982)

The New Barbarians (1983)

Escape from the Bronx (1983)

Exterminators of the Year 3000 (1983)

Fist of the North Star (1986)

Steel Dawn (1987)

Cherry 2000 (1987)

Hell Comes to Frogtown (1988)

The Salute of the Jugger (1989)

Waterworld (1995)

* See: http://edition.cnn.com/2016/11/25/asia/china-mad-max-mad-shelia.

16. More human than human

BLADE RUNNER (1982)

'If only you could see what I've seen with your eyes . . .'

There must have been a point during the making of *Blade Runner* where Ridley Scott wondered what he'd gotten himself into. The director was clashing with producers and studio heads, who wanted to know where all their money was going. He wasn't getting on with the movie's star, Harrison Ford. A writer's strike erupted in the middle of production. The shoot took place almost entirely at night, with rain machines drenching the cast in gallons of water. Perhaps worst of all, Scott was facing a mutiny from his crew, who had taken exception to certain statements the filmmaker had made to the UK press about working in United States. After the success of *Alien*, Scott himself became the stranger in a strange land: a British director working in Los Angeles on his first proper American movie. *Alien* may have been financed by 20th Century Fox, but it was shot at Shepperton Studios in the UK; *Blade Runner*, on the other hand, was shot entirely in California, either on Warner Bros's backlot or on location around LA.

Maybe all this explains why, in a thriller about a detective-assassin tasked with hunting down a gang of artificial humans – or Replicants – Scott's film identifies so strongly with the prey rather than the hunter. Harrison Ford is *Blade Runner*'s nominal hero, Rick Deckard, but the movie spends just as long with Roy Batty (Rutger Hauer) and his trio of non-human outlaws. Based on the novel *Do Androids Dream of Electric Sheep?* by influential sci-fi author Philip K. Dick, *Blade Runner* is set in a twenty-first century ravaged by pollution and war. Much of humanity has migrated to colonies on other planets, leaving the streets of Los Angeles populated by all the criminals and weirdos who have failed to fly the toxic nest. By 2019, the Tyrell Corporation has perfected the craft of making artificial humans who are all but indistinguishable from the rest of us. Created as soldiers, labourers or prostitutes, these Replicants are effectively slaves for off-world colonists; forbidden to set foot on Earth, they're considered problematic enough that there's even a special branch of the police, nicknamed Blade Runners, dedicated to hunting them down.

The taciturn Deckard is one such Blade Runner, dragged out of retirement by his sleazy chief (M. Emmet Walsh) and teamed with an enigmatic younger partner, Gaff (Edward James Olmos) to hunt a dangerous quartet of Replicants. The problem for Deckard is that the Tyrell Corporation has become a little too good at its job; its Replicants are now so lifelike that the only scientific way to detect them is by using a device called a Voight-Kampff machine – a kind of polygraph that measures tiny emotional reactions in its subject. The process remains a slow one, however, and fraught with danger. A colleague of Deckard is shot repeatedly by Leon (Brion James), a Replicant uncovered during one of these interrogations. Leon is a Nexus 6, and one of the four surviving 'skin jobs' at large on the benighted streets of Los Angeles.

Blade Runner's detail and sense of breadth are such that entire movies could have been spun out of just one of its story elements. It isn't difficult to imagine an alternate version of the story that is simply about Blade Runners using the Voight-Kampff machine to smoke out their prey; a kind of Agatha Christie whodunnit crossed with the Spanish Inquisition. How the Replicants are made is fascinating in itself; the movie implies that they are constructed in a similar way to clocks in the eighteenth century, where craftsmen work away on individual organs and body parts in private workshops; presumably, the parts are all shipped off to a Tyrell lab somewhere for assembly. We only meet two of these craftsmen in *Blade Runner* itself; Chew (James Hong), who specialises in making eyes, and J. F. Sebastian (William Sanderson), a genetic designer. The movie leaves us to imagine all those other artisan organ-makers and what they get up to in their labs.

Much of this detail can be found in Philip K. Dick's source novel and, indeed, there's plenty that the film either sketches in or omits entirely. That animal life on Earth is largely extinct, and that humans have taken to making artificial creatures instead, is only a brief background detail in *Blade Runner*; in the book, it's far more pivotal. Owning a genuine pet is seen as a status symbol in *Do Androids Dream of Electric Sheep?*; in a quirky flourish typical of the author, Deckard's motivation for hunting down the Replicants is to raise funds for a flesh-and-blood animal. Other elements from the book, such as a machine that allows its users to 'dial in' emotions, and a futuristic religion called Mercerism, are left out altogether.

In adapting Dick's book, screenwriters Hampton Fancher and David Peoples work in elements of hard-boiled detective fiction, with Deckard portrayed as a hard-drinking gumshoe akin to Raymond Chandler's Philip Marlowe. Deckard's search for the Replicants takes in abandoned apartments and unseemly clubs; the reclusive Eldon Tyrell (Joe Turkel), the corporation boss who makes the artificial humans, is akin to the old millionaire in Chandler's *The Big Sleep*. (Coincidentally, *Blade Runner* was filmed on the very same Warner backlot as that book's 1946 adaptation.) Even the movie's title was taken from elsewhere; in 1974, author Alan E. Nourse wrote a sci-fi novel called *The Bladerunner*, which was turned into a film treatment called *Blade Runner (A Movie)* by *Naked Lunch* writer William S. Burroughs. Hampton Fancher, hunting around for a satisfying name, eventually settled on Burroughs's snappy, evocative title.

The result is a movie that varies quite a bit from its source in terms of plot and details. But as writer and academic Professor Will Brooker points out, *Blade Runner* successfully captures the tone and loose structure of Dick's novel. '*Blade Runner* [. . .] retains the fascinating incoherence and jumbled ideas of Philip K. Dick,' Professor Brooker tells me, 'and perhaps also, because of the differences between the versions, it embodies a Dickian sense of paranoia and hallucination. Between one and the other versions of *Blade Runner*, we can't be sure what we saw, heard or experienced, and might think we are developing false memories.'

Throughout Dick's work, there's the repeated suggestion that it isn't what we're made of that makes us uniquely human, but the way we treat each other. In the author's stories, artificially intelligent cab drivers can prove to be as wise as any flesh-and-blood counsellor; an alien can turn out to be a better, more sensitive husband than the person he's replaced. In both *Do Androids Dream of Electric Sheep?* and *Blade Runner*, we're told that the only reliable way to distinguish between a human and a Replicant is by using a machine that measures a Replicant's empathy, yet it's demonstrated throughout the film that humans are just as capable of lacking empathy as Replicants. How else do we account for Deckard's ability to coldly shoot a fleeing, unarmed woman in the back? In a climactic pursuit between Deckard and Rutger Hauer's dying Roy Batty, we see a Replicant perform an act that can only be described as empathetic: Deckard stumbles and almost falls to his death; Batty, even having seen Deckard murder his compatriots one by one, reaches down and saves him. *Blade Runner*'s third act therefore sees Deckard complete his journey from cold-blooded killer to a new understanding: that Replicants are really no different from us.

Like *Metropolis* nearly seventy years before it, *Blade Runner* was far from an immediate success. Test screenings were disastrous and, after a bruising and difficult shoot, Scott was forced to heavily modify the film, adding a narration (intended to clarify the plot) and an entirely new, less ambiguous ending. In the theatrical cut, as released in 1982, Deckard drives off into the countryside with his Replicant lover, Rachael (Sean Young) – a sunny conclusion entirely at odds with the rest of the movie. These late changes did little to help *Blade Runner* at the box office; in a year packed with genre fare, the movie was largely dismissed by critics and audiences alike. For Professor Brooker, the widespread assumption that *Blade Runner* would be another upbeat adventure film like *Star Wars* may have been a factor in the film's icy reception.

'My personal theory is that audiences were expecting another Harrison Ford vehicle like the *Star Wars* movies and didn't get it,' Brooker says. '*Raiders of the Lost Ark* had also confirmed Ford's star persona and the kind of films he appeared in – action-adventure, drawing on and reworking 1930s serial movies, with a knowing smirk and a lot of charm – and *Blade Runner* is not that, at all.

'If you were told that after the retro derring-do of *Star Wars* and *Raiders*, Ford was next going to appear in a version of the 1940s noir, but set in the future, you would be expecting that kind of sly grin, affectionate pastiche, with a lot of gunplay, stunts and romance.'

'Blade Runner was a disaster,' Ridley Scott told me in 2015. 'It didn't play. People didn't get it. That was when I learned to move on and not read press. You can't read the press – it'll destroy you."*

Blade Runner found an appreciative audience on VHS and, gradually, its images of a downbeat, neon future began to filter into popular culture; Scott started to notice his movie's subtle influence on MTV.

'It grew out of rock-and-roll bands, definitely,' Scott said. 'It grew out of MTV. Isn't it musicians and those kinds of guys who get things more quickly than other people? I always remember seeing videos for various groups and going "Oh!" Because I used to watch MTV [. . .] I suddenly thought, "Oh, that looks like *Blade Runner*," but it wasn't. It started to happen – I realised it was a huge influence on other filmmakers.'

All the same, it seemed as though the damage to *Blade Runner* had already been done. For years, the modified theatrical cut of Scott's film was all that existed, and it wasn't until the 1990s that an earlier print – a cut of the film that more closely matched the director's original intentions – was finally located.

'It was without a voiceover, and with no silly ending driving into the mountains,' Scott said. 'It was the cut where I really thought I'd got it; it ends with Harrison gazing at the piece of origami, then joining Rachael. Close the door – it's film noir.'

When the director's cut of *Blade Runner* emerged in 1991, it cemented the film's rising status as a classic of its kind. With its original, more ambiguous ending, which heavily implies that Deckard himself is an android, *Blade Runner* has been dissected and pored over by fans and academics alike. The stunning set designs and visual effects, created by Douglas Trumbull, have proved to be as influential as Fritz Lang's *Metropolis*. And while *Blade Runner* drew on Lang's film, *Blade Runner*'s atmosphere, soaring electronic music – by

* See: http://www.denofgeek.com/movies/the-martian/37130/ridley-scott-interview-the-martian
-prometheus-sequels.

Greek composer Vangelis – and sheer detail have had a profound impact on the future visions in other movies, books and videogames.

'Culturally, it's certainly a frequent and important reference,' says Professor Brooker, whose book *The Blade Runner Experience* examines the film's legacy in depth. 'I think the Voight-Kampff test has become a familiar-enough cultural touchstone that people refer to it fairly regularly, in terms of technology such as Captcha (which asks explicitly "Are you a robot?"). I would say it's very quotable and that its key speeches are often repeated.'

The most important speech of them all comes from Roy Batty, played with disarming eccentricity by Dutch actor Rutger Hauer. Partly written by Hauer himself, it comes in the concluding scene that cuts to the heart of *Blade Runner*'s timeless allure. As Batty lies dying, his desperately brief four-year lifespan nearly at an end, he reflects on all the things he's seen and done – and how the memories that have defined him will soon vanish forever.

'In his makeup, in his program, there was a sense of poetry,' Hauer said of his character in 2016. 'A sense of soul. There's, like, twenty ingredients that make no sense. He has a conscience. So that's where the idea came from.'*

Originally, Batty's dying monologue would have been much longer – approximately twenty lines, according to Hauer. But as the final day of filming loomed and Scott fell under increasing pressure to get *Blade Runner* finished, the actor spent a sleepless night reworking what would become the most important speech in the movie.

'At the last day of shooting, I still had this page in front of me with so many lines that I didn't like,' Hauer told me. 'So that night I didn't sleep, I got up and I wrote. The only line I came up with was, "All those moments will be lost in time like tears in rain." That's all. That came from my heart and my soul and my frustration.'

It's a line that also encapsulates the air of existential longing that runs through the entire film: beneath the stark beauty of *Blade Runner*'s future vision, there runs a vital thread of humanity.

* See: http://www.denofgeek.com/movies/alien/40184/rutger-hauer-interview-alien-out-of -the-shadows.

HUMANITY AND MACHINES

At a Canadian SF convention in 1972, Philip K. Dick delivered a talk on a subject close to his heart: the relationship between humans and robots.* Echoing one of the recurring themes in his novels, Dick asked: what would the difference be between an ordinary, flesh-and-blood person and an artificial one?

To illustrate the question, Dick described a scenario that could have emerged from one of his stories. A human encounters an android that has recently emerged, shiny and new, from a factory; for some reason, the human – let's call him Fred – shoots the android and, to Fred's surprise, the android starts to bleed like a real, living being. As the android crumples to the floor, in clear agony, it pulls out a gun and returns fire; Fred looks down and sees that, through the ugly wound in his chest, an electric pump throbs where his heart should be . . .

This matchbox-size story emphasises what is likely to become an increasingly urgent philosophical question in the twenty-first century: the boundary between human and machine. From *Frankenstein* to *Blade Runner* and beyond, the same subject has long been interrogated from multiple angles: what is it that makes us human? Through the history of science fiction, we have seen artificial humans created in a multitude of ways, from the cobbled-together remains of corpses to robots built on a production line. But invariably, the stories aren't concerned with how these artificial humans are created so much as how they behave and how we treat them. Their behaviours reflect our failings as humans; similarly, the cruel, indifferent way we treat our creations often says something deeply disquieting about us as a species.

Such 1970s genre highlights as *The Stepford Wives* (first adapted in 1975 from the novel by Ira Levin) and *Westworld* (1973) suggest that we would use artificial beings for pleasure. In the former, a suburb of men, apparently fed up with their wives having a will of their own, replace them with demure,

* See: http://1999pkdweb.philipkdickfans.com/The%20Android%20and%20the%20Human. htm.

pleasure-giving robots. In *Westworld*, robots are used as target practice or as sex objects for decadent humans on vacation. *Blade Runner*, of course, holds a similarly grim view: its replicants are little more than slaves, fated to be hunted like animals should they visit Earth.

More recently, there's the superb *Ex Machina* (2014), written and directed by novelist and screenwriter Alex Garland (*28 Days Later*, *Sunshine*). Computer whiz Caleb Smith (Domhnall Gleeson) is asked to engage in a series of interviews with an android named Ava (Alicia Vikander) knowing full well that she's not human. Ava's creator, the reclusive web billionaire Nathan Bateman (Oscar Isaac), gives Caleb the task of concluding whether or not the android has genuine consciousness, or whether it's a sophisticated programming trick. Gradually, it's Ava who begins to interview Caleb as the human falls under the machine's spell; the movie poses pertinent, difficult questions not just about artificial intelligence, but also the way men objectify women. Indeed, current technology suggests that such writers as Philip K. Dick, Isaac Asimov and Michael Crichton weren't too far from the mark in their stories about robots and how we might use them. Companies in Japan are already producing humanoid robots that can serve as secretaries or sex partners. In modern videogames, we take delight in blasting soldiers or aliens that possess increasingly sophisticated artificial intelligence.

From a moral and philosophical perspective, the creation of an artificial intelligence raises other hypothetical questions. What would it be like to possess consciousness, but not the other attributes associated with being a human? Without the ability to procreate, even the ability to grow old and die, what would existence even mean? Sci-fi stories commonly illustrate this as a kind of emptiness or longing; just as Roy Batty sought to find an extension on his all-too-brief lifespan in *Blade Runner*, so the artificial life forms in other movies have gone on philosophical quests of their own. Steven Spielberg's *A.I.* (2001) sees its young android hero, David, embark on a quest to discover how to become a real human boy. Likewise, the innocent leads in *D.A.R.Y.L.* (1985), *Short Circuit* (1986) and *Chappie* (2015) who are each created by the military but wind up escaping to pursue their own destiny. *Chappie*, in particular, asks a pertinent philosophical question about the value of artificial life. Through the film's central character – a childlike, sentient robot – director Neill Blomkamp argues that any form of consciousness, whether it's human, animal or artificial, has the same value.

'If something else is sentient or conscious,' Blomkamp said in 2017, 'is it any more or less important than a human consciousness or sentience? To me, the answer is an obvious no. Everything that is aware is as valuable as any other thing.'*

In these films and others in the same vein, including Brad Bird's animated feature *The Iron Giant* (1999), based on Ted Hughes's poem 'The Iron Man', the human characters are the true menace.

All of this brings us back to Philip K. Dick's talk about the human and the android. Time and again in his work, Dick suggested that the two might be interchangeable; whether a being is born or artificially created, it's empathy that truly defines a human. Through selfishness, cruelty, or by mindlessly following orders, people are wont to become as cold and emotionless as machines; as Dick once observed, Nazism encouraged people to think mechanically rather than with compassion. In an era of online cybercrime and internet trolling, where anonymity gives some people the licence to destroy the lives of others, perhaps the need for empathy is the most important philosophical question of our age. Whether we interact through social media or, looking further into the future, replace our failing body parts with mechanical ones – a prosthetic arm here, a cybernetic eye there – ultimately, it's our empathy and compassion that we must retain at all costs.

Selected SF films mentioned in this chapter:
Westworld (1973)
The Stepford Wives (1975)
D.A.R.Y.L. (1985)
Short Circuit (1986)
The Iron Giant (1999)

---

* See: http://www.denofgeek.com/uk/movies/chappie/49924/looking-back-at-chappie-with-director-neill-blomkamp.

A.I. (2001)
Ex Machina (2014)
Chappie (2015)

17. A classic revived

THE THING (1982)

'Why don't we just wait here for a little while . . . see what happens?'

When offered the choice between nihilistic terror or childlike awe, movie-goers roundly plumped for the latter in the summer of 1982. Steven Spielberg's *E.T. The Extra-Terrestrial*, released that June, was a box-office phenomenon; John Carpenter's *The Thing*, released the same month and battered by hostile reviews, soon faded from view.

Neither critics nor audiences, it seems, were prepared for the oppressive atmosphere and graphic violence offered up by *The Thing*. It didn't help that Carpenter's film was a remake of *The Thing from Another World*, a much-loved sci-fi horror produced by Howard Hawks – one of the most respected film-makers of the classic Hollywood era. Hawks's film, directed by Christian Nyby, was about a group of servicemen who discover a frozen alien in the ice near their outpost in Alaska. When the thawed-out alien (played by a hulking James Arness) turns out to be hostile, the servicemen work together to cut the menace down to size. *The Thing from Another World* had its shocks and jump-scares, but its overall tone was one of courage under fire rather than despair, all capped off by the closing refrain, 'Keep watching the skies.'

Carpenter's film, on the other hand, was a more faithful adaptation of *The Thing*'s original source, *Who Goes There?*, a novella written by John W. Campbell and published in 1938. Where the 1951 movie imagined the title alien as an aggressive, humanoid vegetable ('An intellectual carrot – the mind boggles,' one character exclaims), the creature thawed out in Campbell's story is a formless, shape-shifting creature capable of perfectly imitating any life form it touches. With the help of the twenty-two-year-old special effects artist Rob Bottin, Carpenter resolved to bring the creature onto the screen for the first time.

The Thing was Carpenter's sixth feature as director, but his first for a major Hollywood studio. As a result, he had access to the kind of budget and resources that had eluded him when making such cult films as *Dark Star* or *Assault on Precinct 13*. Carpenter had long admired both the original *Thing* and the short story on which it was based; Hawks's film even made a cameo in Carpenter's 1978 slasher hit, *Halloween*. When Universal offered Carpenter the chance to remake *The Thing*, however, the director initially balked at the idea. It was when Bottin – fresh from his extraordinary werewolf effects on *The Howling* – came up with the concept of a creature whose true form is never seen that Carpenter finally relented. What if the monster had encountered and mimicked all kinds of other creatures from across the galaxy, and was capable of transforming into any one of them at any time?

As written by Bill Lancaster and Carpenter, *The Thing* plays up the mystery and paranoia of Campbell's original story. Frustrated and bored after months of being cooped up in their Antarctic research outpost, a group of American scientists gradually realises that at least one of their number could be a shape-shifting monster. Otherwise indistinguishable from the hosts it imitates, the alien assumes all kinds of grotesque forms when cornered; in one standout scene, a severed human head sprouts eyes and arachnid legs before scuttling to safety. In another, a husky's body erupts in a tangle of writhing tentacles.

The 1970s and early 1980s saw new breakthroughs in special makeup effects, with such movies as William Friedkin's *The Exorcist*, John Landis's *American Werewolf in London* and David Cronenberg's *Videodrome* all featuring stunning examples of an evolving artform. Dick Smith made Linda Blair's head spin in *The Exorcist*, and created one of the most iconic exploding heads in cinema for Cronenberg in *Scanners*. Rick Baker created a startlingly graphic werewolf transformation in Landis's comedy horror, before assaulting the screen with fleshy guns and pulsating televisions in Cronenberg's wayward *Videodrome*.

Practical makeup effects arguably reached their peak in *The Thing* – a film remarkable for both its technical ingenuity and its outrageous, unfettered imagination. Bottin worked so hard on sculpting and designing his monster's various forms, even sleeping under a bench in his workshop, that he almost wound up in hospital from sheer exhaustion; his workload was such that another genius of makeup effects, Stan Winston, came in to help him create one or two shots – a sequence involving a squealing, mutated husky was his.

Cinematographer Dean Cundey's prowling, eloquent lighting and framing also play a role. *Halloween* had begun with a celebrated POV shot where we share the viewpoint of the killer Michael Myers; Cundey and Carpenter create a similarly effective moment in *The Thing*, where the creature, in its guise as a husky, treads softly through the Antarctic outpost, the smooth glide of the camera suggesting that the title monster could strike anywhere and at any time. When Bottin's creature bursts into view, Cundey uses tiny lights and harsh shadows to pick out individual, queasy details: a throbbing vein here, a bony leg there. Thanks to Bottin and Cundey's combined talents, it's easy to believe that the creature exists in that camp with the huskies, the scientists, the drunken helicopter pilots and the chef on roller skates.

The Thing also reaches further back to the chilly horror literature of H. P. Lovecraft. Lovecraft's novella *At the Mountains of Madness*, first published in 1931, shares a number of similarities with *The Thing*: it concerns a scientific expedition that uncovers something ancient and alien buried beneath the ice; later, the narrator is pursued through the snowy wastes by a tentacular, hideous being. Campbell occasionally cited Lovecraft's story as an inspiration for *Who Goes There?*; whether Carpenter meant to or not, he also captures the grim, chilly tone of that narrative and other Lovecraftian tales. In *Who Goes There?*, the scientists successfully prevent the alien from leaving the camp and reaching the civilised world, the story ending on a note of quasi-religious optimism ('By the grace of God [. . .] we keep our world'). In Carpenter's movie, MacReady (Kurt Russell) succeeds in preventing the monster from escaping, but decides that the only way to ensure that its virus-like threat can't spread is by burning the entire station to the ground. Even then, the movie ends on a note of uncertainty: MacReady and Childs (Keith David) sitting among the embers of the camp, unsure whether one can trust the other.

It was such a gloomy ending that even Carpenter wasn't entirely sure whether it would work; he filmed a second final scene as a back-up, in which MacReady wakes up in a hospital bed, a test confirming that he's still human. Ultimately, Carpenter chose the ending that better reflected the movie's apocalyptic tone – something that evidently proved too much for both audiences and critics. *The Thing* was condemned by *New York Times* reviewer Vincent Canby as 'Instant trash'; even genre magazines, like *Starlog* and *Cinefantastique*, wrote scathing notices. One issue of the latter carried the cover story, 'Is this the most hated movie of all time?'

The Thing was ultimately bested not by MacReady's flamethrower or the bitter chill of the Antarctic, but the cuddly alien in *E.T.* Carpenter, left reeling from the unexpectedly toxic response to his film, largely withdrew from studio filmmaking. His next project, the Stephen King adaptation *Firestarter*, was taken away from him in the wake of *The Thing*'s financial failure.

It was thanks to VHS and cable that *The Thing* gradually began to be discovered and re-evaluated. By the end of the 1980s, the aspects that were once condemned by critics were beginning to be seen as virtues: for all the blood and quivering internal organs, the visual effects are some of the best of the decade. The performances from the ensemble cast may be low-key, but their terse conversations and bickering lend the film a pleasing unpredictability. To this day, fans of the film argue over who was infected by the monster and when. Was Childs really *The Thing* at the end of the movie? Was MacReady? Or maybe both of them?

The Thing's fleshy effects had a clear and lasting effect on filmmakers and videogame designers. Chris Carter's hit TV series *The X-Files* paid homage to Carpenter's movie in the episode 'Ice'. The Japanese feature-length anime *Wicked City* (1987), directed by Yoshiaki Kawajiri, featured some transformation sequences taken directly from *The Thing*, including a severed head with wriggling spider's legs. In 2002, *The Thing* got a video-game adaptation of the same name, its events taking place straight after those of the movie.

Universal paid Carpenter the ultimate compliment in 2011 when it released *The Thing* – a prequel directed by Matthijs van Heijningen Jr. Just as the 1982 film cleverly tucked allusions to the 1950s movie into its story – as seen in the grainy footage of the monster's crashed saucer, a shot taken directly from the Hawks–Nyby classic – so *The Thing* 2011 contains repeated references to the imagery and tone of Carpenter's film. It stars Mary Elizabeth Winstead as an American scientist stationed in Antarctica, and tells the story of what happened to the devastated Norwegian camp discovered by MacReady in 1982. It's far from a bad movie, but *The Thing* 2011 suffered from problems of its own; the movie's creature effects were originally created with the kind of traditional techniques Rob Bottin had used almost thirty years earlier, but Universal came to the conclusion that modern audiences wouldn't accept something so retro-looking. So it was that the practical visual effects made by Amalgamated Dynamics – the team behind the monsters in such films as *Tremors* and *Alien 3* – were overlaid with CGI. With cinematography and lighting that apes John Carpenter and Dean Cundey's deliberate, slow-burn style, and scenes of mutation and gore that look glaringly digital, *The Thing* 2011 is as much soulless imitation as affectionate homage. Indeed, the film merely serves to highlight how superbly formed Carpenter's sci-fi horror was. Critics may have railed against the 1982 film's graphic violence and terse characters but, viewed today, Carpenter's movie takes on an almost blackly comic edge. There's a grotesque beauty, too, in Rob Bottin's monster, as it contorts, shudders, oozes and creeps; the advent of CGI means filmmakers can create all kinds of strange visuals with ease, but making something that looks as physical and individual as *The Thing*'s creature is evidently difficult to achieve with computer graphics.

In TV, movies, games and comics, storytellers have often tried to come up with their own protean monsters like the one in *The Thing*. Indeed, there's a certain irony to the level of reverence artists, filmmakers and fans have for *The Thing*, given how roundly shunned it was in 1982. But while *The Thing* has many imitators, Carpenter's film has yet to be surpassed.

RISE OF THE SCI-FI REMAKE

The sci-fi genre, once regarded as box-office poison by Hollywood, was suddenly hot property in the late 1970s, ignited as it was by *Star Wars*, *Close Encounters of the Third Kind* and *Alien*. Those movies proved that concepts once thought of as the preserve of B-movies and cheap matinee serials could be A-picture hits if they were given shiny enough production values.

So it was that, just a few years after Philip Kaufman's exemplary reworking of *Invasion of the Body Snatchers* in 1978, Hollywood caught the remake bug. *The Thing* may have been a failure from Universal's perspective, but it didn't deter other studios from dipping into the archives to find their own properties to remake.

David Cronenberg's *The Fly* (1986) was arguably among the finest and most considered remakes of the 1980s. Like the 1958 original, directed by Kurt Neumann, the 1986 version is a sci-fi horror about a scientist who invents a revolutionary matter transporter. When the scientist tests the machine on himself, his DNA is fused with that of a common housefly. Neumann's film (based on the George Langelaan story of the same title) had David Hedison's scientist step out of a transporter with a giant fly's head and one claw-like hand. Cronenberg's scientist, Seth Brundle (Jeff Goldblum), meanwhile, undergoes a slower and more painful transformation. At first, the infusion of fly DNA leaves Brundle invigorated and marvelling at his newfound strength; gradually, however, the insect within begins to take over, and his journalist girlfriend (Geena Davis) can only watch as her lover's body begins to mutate into something new and horrifying.

On the surface, *The Fly* is a schlock-horror about scientific hubris, and its success at the box office made it the most successful – and mainstream – movie of Cronenberg's career to date. But *The Fly* is also a tragic relationship drama and, like Franz Kafka's novella *The Metamorphosis* before it, a powerful metaphor for sickness and disease. Audiences could thrill at the goo, the detached limbs and gore, but beneath the splatter, *The Fly* is also an existential parable about ageing and death – all sold brilliantly by Goldblum and Davis's natural, sparky performances.

No other remake of the era could match *The Fly* for pathos or intelligence, but one or two others provided plenty of gruesome entertainment. Chuck Russell's *The Blob* (1988), a remake of the 1958 film featuring a pre-stardom Steve McQueen, was a riot of blood and post-*Thing* practical makeup effects. Once again, a deadly gob of ooze terrorises a small American town, and Kevin Dillon plays a young tearaway who dares to cross its path. The twist is that this particular blob doesn't merely swallow its prey, but also has the ability to dissolve bodies like acid, sprout tentacles or hide inside its victims and kill them from within. The movie offers little in the way of subtlety, but it is a likeably grotesque thrill train ride: among the imaginative deaths, the true standout is a sequence involving Candy Clark's hapless waitress; in a shot captured from above, we see Clark cowering in a telephone box as the blob engulfs her in a pulsating geyser of ooze. *The Blob*'s cinematographer was Mark Irwin, who had previously made David Cronenberg's movies look so unforgettably visceral, while its co-writer was Frank Darabont, who would go on to direct such Stephen King-derived movies as *The Shawshank Redemption* and *The Mist*. Curiously, *The Blob*'s eagerness to please didn't particularly endear it to moviegoers; unlike *The Fly*, it barely made back half of its $19 million investment.

Tobe Hooper's 1986 remake of William Cameron Menzies's *Invaders from Mars* didn't fare well, either, despite its pedigree. The combined talents of Stan Winston and John Dykstra should have meant that *Invaders* looked as unforgettably stylish as the 1953 original; instead, it ended up looking even more wobbly and uneven. That *Invaders from Mars* was produced by Cannon Films, a firm more famous for the quantity of its output than its quality, hardly helped.

In the twenty-first century, we have now reached the point where movies from the 1980s and 1990s are being given the remake treatment. Paul Verhoeven's *Total Recall* (1990) was tepidly remade in 2012 by director Len Wiseman, and it's an example of how hollow a movie can be when it's made for the wrong reasons. The story is almost identical – an ordinary man (played here by Colin Farrell) discovers that his life isn't all it appears – but without Verhoeven's blackly comic, outrageously violent excesses, the film quickly devolves into a generic action-thriller.

As films like Carpenter's *The Thing* and *The Fly* prove, remakes needn't necessarily be a crutch for film studios who have run out of original ideas. The best remakes take existing stories and tell them from a new perspective, or update them to address more modern concerns. Where remakes can go wrong, however, is when films are flattened out by studio executives who are more interested in branding than telling stories. The remake of *RoboCop*, directed by Brazil's José Padilha and released in 2014, has much to recommend it: again about a law enforcer who is transformed into an armoured cyborg, it adds commentary on drone warfare, American foreign policy and the nature of freewill into the story established by Paul Verhoeven in 1987. Reviving old movies may sound like a safe option in an increasingly risk-averse Hollywood, but as lesser movies like the 2011 version of *The Thing* and many others prove, remakes are often doomed to live in the shadow of their predecessors.

Selected SF films mentioned in this chapter:

The Fly (1986)

Invaders from Mars (1986)

The Blob (1988)

RoboCop (2014)

18. Assassins and time travel

THE TERMINATOR (1984)

'Come with me if you want to live . . .'

The crash of a door and the startled yelp of a receptionist marked the beginning of a particularly strange Hollywood meeting. It was 1982, and John Daly, the film producer and boss of independent studio Hemdale, had just received an unexpected visitor: as Daly sat at his desk, a black-clad figure marched into his office and sat in the chair opposite. Looking the intruder up and down, Daly noted some fake-looking injuries on the intruder's forehead, a tatty leather jacket . . . and was that foil from a cigarette packet covering his teeth?

For fifteen minutes, the two sat and stared at each other uneasily, before a second, younger man ran into the office and started talking hurriedly about his idea for a science-fiction film. It was about a killer cyborg from the future – a figure resembling the one sitting in the chair and glowering at John Daly. The guy doing all the talking, Daly would later learn, was a young filmmaker named James Cameron; his associate, with the bit of cigarette packet glinting in his mouth, was Lance Henriksen – an actor Cameron, at least at the time, thought would be perfect to play the title role in his project, *The Terminator*.

This bizarre episode emerged in Rebecca Keegan's book on James Cameron, *The Futurist* – and it's here, in front of a surprisingly receptive independent movie producer, that the director's career turned a corner. Cameron's first film was, after all, little short of a disaster. *Piranha II: The Spawning* (1981) was a low-budget, low-rent sequel to Joe Dante's toothsome horror comedy, produced by Italy's Ovidio Assonitis. Cameron was fired just two weeks into the production; Assonitis insisted that the footage Cameron had shot up to that point didn't cut together. Cameron countered that Assonitis really wanted to direct the film himself.

At any rate, 1981 saw Cameron stuck in Rome, penniless, his hopes of a film career seemingly in tatters. It was around this time that, stressed and stricken by fever, Cameron had a fateful dream: a gleaming metal skeleton, wielding a knife, crawling from a curtain of fire. This nightmare image would prove to be pivotal in the development of *The Terminator*, the movie that in turn defined the shape of Cameron's career.

Before the *Piranha II* debacle, Cameron had made the short film *Xenogenesis* (1978), an ambitious nugget of science fiction about humans battling a giant robot. Funded by a consortium of dentists and shot in just a few days, the film provided an early glimpse of Cameron's technical ingenuity, with its matte paintings and miniature effects, and contained several elements that would appear in his later films: the theme of humanity against machine, killer robots with tank-like tracks, and powerful mecha (giant robots) that can be moved around by a pilot's arms and legs. *Xenogenesis* caught the eye of low-budget movie-maker Roger Corman, who hired Cameron as a model-maker and special effects designer on such cut-price films as *Battle Beyond the Stars* (1980) and *Galaxy of Terror* (1981). Around the same time, Cameron also landed a job as a matte painter for John Carpenter's cult sci-fi thriller, *Escape from New York* (1982).

Cameron, his mind set on becoming a director, knew he had to come up with a script for a low-budget film in order to break into the industry. Not long before, John Carpenter had defined the slasher-horror genre with *Halloween* (1978), a slick thrill-ride that launched a long line of imitators. The script Cameron wrote in the wake of his Roman nightmare was an ingenious sci-fi twist on the slasher genre. In the near future, the human race has been decimated by an artificially intelligent computer called Skynet and its army of machines. Determined to crush the human resistance, Skynet sends a cyborg back in time to kill Sarah Connor – the mother of freedom-fighter John Connor, who will one day change the tide of the war. In response, the resistance storms Skynet and sends a soldier back to protect Sarah. Thus begins a relentless and bloody pursuit through 1984 Los Angeles, with a waitress hunted by an emotionless and seemingly unstoppable assassin.

On a budget of just \$6.4 million, Cameron managed to craft one of the most influential sci-fi movies of the mid-1980s. A background in visual effects allowed Cameron to imagine a vision of the future with relatively meagre resources: armoured, sentient tanks crush piles of skulls under their wheels, while colossal drones patrol the skies.

Then there's the Terminator himself, so imposing and unforgettable that, like *Jaws* and *Alien*, he gets top billing. Living flesh over a gleaming metal chassis, the Terminator is a grim reaper for the computer age; a steely killer who views the world through a filter of pixels and scrolling lists of data. As played by former Mr Universe-winning bodybuilder Arnold Schwarzenegger, the Terminator's implacable strut recalls Yul Brynner's robot cowboy in Michael Crichton's *Westworld*, released in 1973. (Writer Harlan Ellison also noted a distinct similarity between Cameron's movie and his *Outer Limits* episodes 'Soldier' and 'The Glass Hand'; Ellison was later credited and the matter settled out of court.*)

The Terminator was also the product of an age when computers were moving into people's homes, and when the Cold War was again beginning to rear its head. In 1983, John Badham's sci-fi thriller *WarGames* saw a tech-savvy schoolkid hack into the United States' defence computers and inadvertently drag the planet to the brink of nuclear Armageddon. In *The Terminator*, Cameron suggests that our machines, for all their cold logic, might also inherit some of our faults: not least our capacity to kill.

Ironically, Michael Crichton, who had become a celebrated writer and director thanks to his novels and movies about science gone awry, also had a sci-fi film out in the autumn of 1984. *Runaway*, made with a considerably larger budget than *The Terminator*, depicted a near-future where robots are almost ubiquitous. Boxy, cumbersome things resembling 1980s music systems, they tend our crops, prepare our meals and even babysit our children. A renegade terrorist (Gene Simmons, of the rock band Kiss) turns these normally docile robots into lethal killing machines, and so an electronics expert and cop – played by Tom Selleck – resolves to track him down. For all its nifty gadgets,

---

* See: http://harlanellison.com/heboard/archive/bull0108.htm.

including deadly robot spiders and guns with heat-seeking bullets, *Runaway* looks rather pedestrian when placed alongside *The Terminator*. Cameron's movie, with its street-level view of Los Angeles, brings with it a tough, gritty edge where sci-fi collides with the grubbily everyday. The look of the film is summed up best by the phrase Tech Noir – the name of the nightclub where Sarah Connor (Linda Hamilton) is first attacked by her cyborg assassin. *The Terminator* owes its success not just to Cameron's confident direction, but also to effects artist Stan Winston's cyborg design, from the makeup, which gives the illusion of the robot skull and bones glinting beneath damaged skin, to the stop-motion endoskeleton that comes limping out of a ball of fire at the movie's conclusion: a powerful rendering of Cameron's original nightmare image.

Although drawing from a large mix of influences, *The Terminator* would itself inspire a score of imitations. Movies such as *Eve of Destruction* (1991) and Italy's *Alien Terminator* (1988) were blatant rip-offs; the low-budget British film *Hardware* (1990), directed by Richard Stanley, echoes both its first-person shots and robot design.

The Terminator's reach extends far beyond movies, however. While not the first genre film to imagine an uprising by sentient machines, it has permeated the public consciousness like few other movies of its kind; articles about the possible rise of AI will often reference Skynet and its army of drones and hunter killers. Indeed, Professor Noel Sharkey, a computer scientist at the University of Sheffield, has repeatedly written about the dangers of mindless killer robots. An entity like Skynet may not exist in the twenty-first century, but the use of drones in warfare and even policing – a robot was used to kill a suspect in Dallas in 2016 – means that some of the ideas in *The Terminator* are far from outdated.

The Terminator was also the film that launched both Cameron and Schwarzenegger's careers. Schwarzenegger had already made his mark in Hollywood thanks to his sword-twirling title performance in *Conan the Barbarian*, but the breakout success *of The Terminator* cemented his status as a star – and gave him his immortal catchphrase: 'I'll be back.'

As for Cameron, he had been writing the treatment for another sci-fi film at the same time he was developing *The Terminator*. Once again, he was keen to direct, but getting the gig hinged on how well *The Terminator* performed; shortly after the movie landed in US cinemas on 26 October 1984, Cameron got a call from 20th Century Fox: the studio had given him the green light. His next film would be *Aliens*.

JOURNEYS THROUGH TIME

As the machine's great disc hums, buildings spring up and collapse, the sun dawns and sets, entire civilisations rise and fall. Such is H. G. Wells's vivid description of travelling through history in his seminal novel, *The Time Machine*, first published in 1895. Written near the start of his career, this was the novel that finally brought Wells the success he craved – and, more broadly, introduced the science-fiction concept of a machine that could physically carry a traveller to different points in history. Such stories as Dickens's *A Christmas Carol* (1843) and Mark Twain's *A Connecticut Yankee in King Arthur's Court* (1889) featured time travel, but like Wells's *The Invisible Man*, *The Time Machine* gave a fantasy concept an air of scientific plausibility.

The Time Machine has itself been adapted for the screen more than once, most famously in 1960, with Rod Taylor as the traveller, and less successfully in 2002 by director Simon Wells – H.G. Wells's great-grandson. Yet the dramatic possibilities of time travel have been mined in a startling variety of ways by generations of storytellers on the large and small screen, from TV's evergreen *Doctor Who* to the *Terminator* franchise. The sheer number of films that have used time travel as their foundation is so vast that it would be impossible to do them justice here; the *Back to the Future* trilogy brought with them equal parts adventure and nostalgia. The micro-budget indie thriller *Primer* (2004), by filmmaker Shane Carruth, explored the implications of time travel in such mathematical detail that it almost defies description – it's perhaps sufficient to say that, if such a device were to exist, its effect on the course of history could be dangerously difficult to control.

While time travel has often been the fodder for big-budget action thrillers, including *Timecop* (1994) and *Déjà Vu* (2006), some of the most compelling uses of the concept have, like *Primer*, come from independent filmmakers.

Chris Marker's 1962 French film *La Jetée* uses little more than narration and black-and-white still photographs to powerfully evoke a post-apocalyptic world. From a bunker beneath the remains of Paris, scientists send a volunteer back in time to help avert the catastrophe; in just thirty minutes, Marker weaves a bewitching and deeply satisfying mystery. *La Jetée* was famously the inspiration for Terry Gilliam's *12 Monkeys* (1995), a sci-fi thriller with broadly the same premise; directed with Gilliam's unfailing eye for the bizarre and disturbing, it's arguably the most intelligent sci-fi thriller to emerge from Hollywood in the 1990s.

Shot for just $2.6 million, Spanish writer-director Nacho Vigalondo's *Timecrimes* (2007) serves as a nightmarish cousin to Carruth's *Primer*. An act of voyeurism leads a lazy, plain-looking man, Hector (Karra Elejalde), into the path of a terrifying maniac swathed in bandages and brandishing a pair of scissors. Fleeing in terror, Hector discovers a nearby building and hides inside what turns out to be a time machine. Thus begins an increasingly knotty causal loop, where Hector's efforts to undo one mistake lead to several more unforeseeable ones. The pace is dizzying, the atmosphere drips with dread; we may get to the end and start to poke holes in Vigalondo's tangle of a plot, but his journey through time remains an unforgettable one.

If time travel's the perfect fodder for thrillers, that's because the concept allows us to ask all kinds of questions about ourselves; if we could go into the past, what would we change? If we were to meet our younger self, what would we say to them? Would we even get on? Such is the basis for *Looper* (2012), a refreshingly gritty spin on established sci-fi concepts. In a twenty-first-century Kansas, where the young have few work opportunities, twenty-somethings like Joe (Joseph Gordon-Levitt) take on the role of Loopers – essentially hitmen for the Mafia. If some schmuck has crossed the mob, they're trussed up, hooded, taken back in time and coldly shot by one of these Loopers. But then something disturbing happens to Joe: on a regular hit, the schmuck he's supposed to shoot turns out to be none other than his older self, played by Bruce Willis. Thus begins a rip-roaring thriller steeped in post-financial crisis uncertainty; aside from all the action, the film's most effective scene takes place in a diner. The two Joes, one in his twenties, the other in his fifties, sit opposite one another and pick at each other's failings: the former at the latter's age and cynicism, the latter at the former's laziness and naivety. *Looper* uses science fiction as shorthand for a generation's bitterness and disillusionment.

Likewise *Predestination* (2014), a little-seen but superbly effective thriller about a group of characters affected by a time loop. Based on a story by Robert A. Heinlein, it stars Ethan Hawke as an agent sent back in time to 1970s New York to track down a terrorist; there, he encounters a man in a bar whose tragic story intertwines with his own in unexpected ways. Featuring a peerless performance by Australian actress Sarah Snook, and taut direction by the Spierig Brothers, *Predestination* is a thriller with a poignant, human edge: a mind-bending story of tragedy and regret. Such films as *Predestination* and *Primer* toy with our everyday relationship with time; how we may wish we could turn back the clock and undo past mistakes, and how our experiences, for better or worse, shape us as individuals.

Selected SF films mentioned in this chapter:
The Time Machine (1960)
La Jetée (1962)
Back to the Future (1985)
Timecop (1994)
12 Monkeys (1995)
Primer (2004)
Déjà Vu (2006)
Timecrimes (2007)
Looper (2012)
Predestination (2014)

19. Brave new worlds

BRAZIL (1985)

'This is your receipt for your husband. And this is my receipt for your receipt.'

Just as the detonation of the first nuclear bomb triggered the atomic age, so the advent of the integrated circuit in the 1950s hastened the information age. As computers became smaller, faster and more affordable in the late 1970s and early 1980s, this new technology was, predictably enough, greeted with both enthusiasm and suspicion. On one hand, there were the predictions that computers would revolutionise everything from education to business; on the other, there were suggestions that computers could be misused by hackers – the 1983 film *WarGames*, for example, floated the notion that a smart enough kid, armed with a computer and a phone line, could hack into American's military defence systems.

Long before the internet became ubiquitous, writers and filmmakers were already thinking about the possibilities of an interconnected planet; in his imaginative novels, such as the seminal *Neuromancer* (1984), William Gibson wrote about the technologies, counter-cultures and criminal activities that might spring up in the computer age. Even before Gibson, George Orwell had written presciently in *Nineteen Eighty-Four* (1949) about how new technologies might be used as a means of control: through protagonist Winston Smith, we discover a future society in which a citizen's every move is recorded and scrutinised, and where individual thought is regarded as a crime.

Filmmakers had adapted Orwell's novel in the past, including director Michael Radford, whose earthy adaptation, starring John Hurt as Winston Smith and Richard Burton as O'Brien, emerged – appropriately enough – in 1984. And yet, by filtering Orwell's dystopia through his own eccentric imagination, director Terry Gilliam gave us what might be the ultimate cautionary SF movie about totalitarianism: *Brazil*.

In Gilliam's hands, *Brazil*'s future world becomes as absurd as Orwell's was terrifying; here, everything is governed by a chaotic web of machines and information. There are lengthy databases about everyone and everything, and much of the populace, it seems, is packed into grey offices sifting through paperwork or wrestling with elephantine computers in a vain attempt to process it all. Society is drowning in data and bureaucracy – a Babylon of confusing and often bogus information.

The result is a film with the thematic heft of Orwell's work and the surreal irony of Gilliam, the former member of the Monty Python troupe who crafted its unforgettably eccentric animated sketches. In order to get *Brazil* released, however, Gilliam had to first navigate a Hollywood studio that was almost as labyrinthine and inscrutable as the one depicted in his movie. Indeed, it's a minor miracle that *Brazil* exists at all.

Brazil began not with a reading of *Nineteen Eighty-Four* – Gilliam has long said he didn't read Orwell's novel until after he had made the movie – but with a visit to Port Talbot in Wales. A steel town with a beach left blackened by coal dust, Port Talbot etched an enticing image in Gilliam's mind: a man sitting on the soot-covered shore, fiddling with the dial of a radio and hearing the 1930s song, 'Aquarela do Brasil'. That song, Gilliam later said, was unlike anything the lonely man on the beach had ever heard before – a piece of music that transported him to another, better world.

'That was America in the Forties,' Gilliam told Salman Rushdie at the 2002 Telluride Festival. 'We were always going south to Rio, and I grew up in that dream time. And it seems like the dream world was somewhere in South America, where everything would be perfect.'*

From that tiny seed came a much bigger, grotesque dystopia about an unremarkable, thirty-something man – Sam Lowry, played by Jonathan Pryce – who is relatively happy with his status as a cog in a machine. Born into a privileged family – the vanity of his bourgeois elderly mother (Katherine

---

* See: http://www.believermag.com/issues/200303/?read=interview_gilliam.

Helmond) is a recurring joke – Sam leads a life of humdrum complacency. It's only in his dreams that his imagination takes flight, as he repeatedly dreams of an alternate life as an Icarus-like hero who rescues a beautiful woman (Kim Greist) from a string of bizarre near-death experiences. At Sam's day job, a computing error results in state forces battering their way into the house of an innocent cobbler instead of a suspected terrorist. At the behest of his boss, Mr Kurtzmann (Ian Holm), Sam is despatched to tidy up the error – that is, to wipe the torture and execution of an innocent man from the government record. As a result, Sam's drawn ever further into an oppressive machine that he has always kept at arm's length; along the way, he encounters an oddball enemy of the state, Archibald Tuttle (Robert De Niro), and the woman of his dreams, who turns out to be a tough resistance fighter. Meanwhile, Sam's competitive yet seemingly benign schoolfriend Jack Lint (Michael Palin) is revealed to be the regime's sadistic torturer-in-chief.

Although rooted in the past, with its city of failing machines, ducts and gadgets resembling an America of the 1930s and 1940s as much as a dystopian future, *Brazil* is also disturbingly prescient. Not only does the film explore themes of mass surveillance and state control, but it also shows how a totalitarian regime could cement its power by fostering a sense of apathy. In one hilariously pointed sequence, Sam, his mother and her upper-crust friends are ordering dinner in a high-tech restaurant when terrorists detonate a bomb mere feet away; sitting amid the dust and corpses, the diners barely flinch. One of *Brazil*'s most urgent sentiments, then, is its warning about complacency; how public indifference, as much as a Big Brother figure with a lust for power, could bring about totalitarianism. It's significant that the overall leader in *Brazil*'s future state barely even figures in the story; it's the blandly evil middlemen, like Palin's Jack Lint, who keep the engine of power running.

Brazil was a brave film to even attempt to get through the Hollywood system, yet thanks to Israeli producer Arnon Milchan, Gilliam very nearly got away with it. In February 1985, 20th Century Fox released the film to great acclaim in Europe and the rest of the world; it was because of Gilliam's souring relationship with co-financier Universal, who had signed a deal to distribute the movie in the United States, that things grew more complicated.

A private screening for Universal executives in the middle of 1984 resulted in the conclusion that *Brazil* was rather too dark and lacking in commercial prospects for comfort. Studio boss Sid Sheinberg therefore came up with a suggestion: cut out all the depressing events after Sam makes love to his dream woman, Jill (Greist), and end the story on a happy note. When Gilliam resisted, Universal replied that the director had broken a clause in his contract that demanded that he deliver a cut of the movie running to 127 minutes or less; Gilliam's cut ran to 142 minutes.

With both director and studio digging in their heels, a public feud spilled out into Hollywood's trade papers. Gilliam and Sheinberg refused to engage with one another directly, but openly aired their grievances to *Los Angeles Times* writer Jack Mathews. Mathews, knowing he was on to the entertainment story of the year, happily played arbitrator, and published the pair's increasingly bitter back-and-forth spats in his column. Unbeknown to Gilliam, Universal already had a team of editors working on its own cut of *Brazil*. Meanwhile, Gilliam spent several thousand dollars on a full-page advert in *Variety*: a single, almost blank page with the words, 'Dear Sid Sheinberg, When are you going to release my film, "Brazil"? Terry Gilliam'.

What Universal didn't know was that, while it was working on an alternate cut, Gilliam was getting his original edit of the film in front of as many critics as he could, either by flying them to Europe to watch it on its official release, or by holding secret screenings in the United States. At one US college, Gilliam held a Q&A for a group of students and said he was permitted to show only a clip from his latest film – it just so happened that the clip comprised the 142-minute cut of *Brazil* in its entirety.

Ultimately, Gilliam got his own way: at the Los Angeles Film Critics Association awards in 1985, the still-unreleased *Brazil* won Best Picture – beating Universal's big Oscar contender for that year, *Out of Africa*. In the face of growing praise for *Brazil* in its original form, Universal therefore had little choice but to rush the movie for release uncut. Sheinberg's shorter edit with the happy ending – popularly dubbed the 'Love Conquers All cut' – was eventually screened on cable television. Today, that version is largely remembered as the by-product of a very odd Hollywood battle. Poor Sam Lowry may have been crushed between the gears of a brutal regime, but *Brazil*, thankfully, survived the Hollywood machine unscathed.

THE POWER OF THE DYSTOPIA

'In Newspeak,' George Orwell wrote in his novel *Nineteen Eighty-Four*, 'there is no word for science.'

At first, it might sound like an oddly paradoxical statement, since the future world in which *Nineteen Eighty-Four* is set is full of technology: televisions and microphones monitor its citizens' every move; books are written automatically by some form of strange computer. Orwell understood that while technology can be used to spread information – as the printing press had in the Enlightenment – it can also be used as a tool of oppression. With technology and information in the hands of the powerful few, the ordinary people of Airstrip One live in a state of enforced ignorance, where rules are obeyed without a thought, vocabularies are gradually whittled down, and 'two plus two equals five' is a popular phrase in the media.

As director José Padilha once said shortly after the release of his *RoboCop* remake, 'Technology can give you freedom – you could be free to get in a spaceship and go somewhere else – but on the other hand, technology can take freedom away. The key that opens the door to heaven also opens the door to hell.'*

Fritz Lang's *Metropolis* (1927) was one of the first movies to show how a technologically advanced society could be sharply divided between the wealthy and the poor, and it's a motif we have seen in dystopian sci-fi movies ever since. Jean-Luc Godard's *Alphaville* (1965), a low-budget collision of sci-fi and noir thriller, ingeniously depicts a future city without using special effects; Godard imagines a city run by a sentient computer, Alpha 60, which runs its infrastructure and strictly forbids individual thought. One of its most forward-thinking, memorable scenes involves a dictionary connected to the computer

* See: http://www.denofgeek.com/movies/jose-padilha/29178/jose-padilha-interview-robo-cop-elite-squad-philosophy.

mainframe; with a single update, banned words can vanish from its pages. (In a weird, real-world echo of this, a 2012 news story related the plight of Linn Jordet Nygaard, a Norwegian woman whose Kindle was suddenly locked, without explanation, by the device's vendor, Amazon. For weeks, her virtual library of books remained out of bounds while Nygaard navigated through layers of corporate bureaucracy.*)

Fahrenheit 451, François Truffaut's 1966 adaptation of Ray Bradbury's novel, also dealt with the control of information. In its totalitarian future vision, a special team of firemen are tasked not with putting out fires, but lighting them – collecting all forms of literature from people's houses and burning them in the streets. It's a characteristically poetic image from Bradbury, and a less brutal depiction of a future state than Orwell's; its sentiment, that fascist states will always try to limit our access to knowledge, remains a potent one.

As we saw in Chapter 12, the 1970s brought with it a wave of nightmarish future visions, from the concrete Britain of *A Clockwork Orange* via the overcrowded America of *Soylent Green* to the city in *Logan's Run*, where getting old is literally punishable by death. Interestingly, an adaptation of the twentieth century's other great dystopian novel, Aldous Huxley's *Brave New World*, never surfaced, save for a low-budget TV movie which aired on NBC in 1980. It took until 1997 before writer-director Andrew Niccol, through *Gattaca*, explored Huxley's idea of a future society 'purified' by eugenics – much in the way that *Brazil* filtered *Nineteen Eighty-Four* through Terry Gilliam's eccentric filmmaking style.

In *Gattaca's* near-future, society is divided cleanly between valids – those that are genetically pure and therefore qualify for high-ranking jobs – and in-valids – those with inherited disorders, such as heart conditions, who are forced to take on low-level jobs such as cleaning. Vincent Freeman (Ethan Hawke) is an in-valid who has dreamed of becoming an astronaut since child-hood, but finds himself locked out of the profession due to his poor genetic provenance. Determined to fulfil his ambition, Vincent joins forces with another outsider – genetically perfect valid, Jerome (Jude Law), whose

---

* See: http://www.nbcnews.com/technology/technolog/you-dont-own-your-kindle-books-amazon-reminds-customer-1c6626211.

sporting career was destroyed following a car accident. Jerome, now an embittered recluse, agrees to supply Vincent with the daily DNA samples he needs to pass off as a valid – thus allowing Vincent to pursue the career he's always wanted. But as meticulous as Vincent is in his deception, a police investigation at his workplace leaves him under increasing scrutiny; throughout the story, he teeters between achieving his dreams and being caught by a terrifyingly incisive system. Beautifully written, shot and acted, *Gattaca* was a tragic box-office misfire. It remains an intelligent and lastingly relevant film, however, and is still discussed and cited by scientists for broaching modern questions about genetic testing and what it might mean for our individual freedom.*

Today, internet surveillance, drones and mechanised warfare are common topics in dystopian films and literature. Suzanne Collins's hit series of novels, *The Hunger Games*, adapted as a similarly successful film franchise, is a dystopia for young adults growing up in an age of social media and reality TV. To survive a brutal televised game show and overthrow a despotic regime, heroine Katniss Everdeen (Jennifer Lawrence) soon realises that a carefully managed public image is a vital part of securing victory.

In both fiction and the real world, oppressive regimes frequently attempt to limit our access to knowledge or alter the language we might use to define and describe our oppression. The Nazis burned books and banned 'degenerate' art in the 1930s; Soviet leader Josef Stalin attempted to change history by executing political opponents and airbrushing their faces out of photographs. Whether they are books or movies, the great dystopias serve a vital function: they give us the vocabulary to recognise and describe the Big Brother in our midst.

Selected SF films mentioned in this chapter:
Alphaville (1965)
Fahrenheit 451 (1966)
Gattaca (1997)
The Hunger Games (2012)

* See: http://www.depauw.edu/sfs/essays/gattaca.htm.

20. This time it's war

ALIENS (1986)

'What do you mean they cut the power? They're animals . . .'

A monster, a spaceship, an unsuspecting crew waiting to be torn apart. What more was there to do with Ridley Scott's *Alien*? For five years, the question was left hanging in the air, seemingly waiting for a smart-enough filmmaker to come along and answer it. When *The Terminator* became a surprise hit in 1984, 20th Century Fox and production company Brandywine gave Cameron and producer partner Gale Anne Hurd the keys to the *Alien* franchise: less than four years after he first pitched *The Terminator* to Hemdale, Cameron was at the helm of a major Hollywood movie.

The budget for *Aliens* was more generous than *The Terminator* but still lean, given Cameron's ambitious ideas. Cameron's concept took place fifty-seven years after the events of *Alien*, and returns Ripley to the planet LV-426, where an army of xenomorphs have engulfed a mining colony set up by her old employers, Weyland-Yutani. *Aliens* therefore required a wider variety of sets, a larger cast, more special effects and many times more creatures to design and construct than the 1979 original. But once again, Cameron's background in low-budget filmmaking meant that he and his crew managed to come up with numerous ways of stretching Fox's $18 million investment. When the budget wouldn't stretch to building twelve cryotubes with functioning lids, a mirror was carefully positioned to make a row of six chambers look twice as long. The pace and editing of the movie may have created the impression of a planet overrun by toothsome monsters but, in reality, only eight 'soldier' aliens were built for the movie.

A key factor in *Aliens*'s success is the way it expands on the original film. Where most sequels might be content to regurgitate everything that came before it, *Aliens* cleverly switches pace from creeping horror to gun-blazing action. *Alien* was a masterpiece of atmosphere and mood; its slowly building sense of dread as important as the implied violence oozing from its title monster. Realising that he couldn't pull off the same trick twice, Cameron turned *Aliens* into a film of motherhood and survival. Having survived one encounter with the Starbeast, Lieutenant Ripley drifts through space for decades until she's finally woken up on a space station in Earth's orbit. Her reputation and career seemingly in tatters – Weyland-Yutani, her employers, are unimpressed by her claim that she blew up their expensive ship because it had an alien running around it – Ripley is plagued by nightmares and a gnawing sense of loss. (In a longer cut of the movie released on video in 1992, we learn that Ripley had a daughter, Amanda, who had died of old age while Ripley was drifting through space.)

Ripley's shaken from her torpor by the news that Weyland-Yutani has lost contact with the mining colony located on LV-426. As a detachment of Colonial Marines is assembled to head off and search for survivors, slick company executive Carter Burke (Paul Reiser) invites Ripley along as a consultant; Ripley, keen to see the planet's alien threat wiped out, reluctantly agrees to join the mission. So begins a relentlessly exciting action thriller in which Ripley's survival instinct is repeatedly proven to be a greater asset than the Marines' bristling firepower. As the group finds itself stranded on the planet with acid-spitting parasites closing on all sides, Ripley gradually shifts from haunted survivor to fearless warrior. In this regard, *Aliens* functions as the second half of Ripley's story, leading her away from the inescapable terror of *Alien* and towards something akin to a happy ending. As the rest of the cast is gradually whittled down, as much through their own human failings as the xenomorphs' hunting abilities, Ripley emerges as the indomitable hero. She forges a maternal bond with a survivor on the planet – twelve-year-old Newt (Carrie Henn), and there's a spark of affection between Ripley and quietly spoken marine, Hicks (Michael Biehn). Ripley's final confrontation with the Alien Queen – a triumph of puppetry and design – becomes a symbol of her completion; by slaying this twisted reflection of a human mother, Ripley finally lays her trauma to rest.

When Dan O'Bannon and Ronald Shusett conceived *Alien* in the 1970s, they drew on decades of pulp fiction and genre films, and Cameron follows suit. His depiction of armoured, space-faring warriors is redolent of Robert A. Heinlein's novel *Starship Troopers*, adapted in mischievous style as a movie by Paul Verhoeven in 1997. A line uttered by one Colonial Marine in *Aliens* – 'Is this a stand-up fight, sir, or just another bug hunt?' – could even be a conscious nod to Heinlein's novel, since its plot involved the mass extermination of giant insects on a distant planet. In his depiction of the aliens as an insectoid hive – something entirely absent from *Alien* – Cameron also appears to draw from the 1954 sci-fi horror, *Them!*, which saw an army of giant, mutant ants menace California. That film's third act, where the US Army fight its way into the ants' shadowy nest with machine guns and flamethrowers, is remarkably akin to *Aliens*'s dramatic midpoint, where the ill-prepared squad are assaulted from all sides by xenomorphs in their biomechanical lair.

By the same token, Cameron also drew considerably on the language and iconography of the Vietnam War.[*] His Colonial Marines all talk in the manner of American soldiers of the 1960s and 1970s – something he's readily admitted in interviews – and the outfits, weapons and ships all carry echoes of military hardware from the same era: the Dropship, which takes Ripley and the marines to the planet surface, for example, bears a passing resemblance to a Huey helicopter. It's probable that some of the military ideas Cameron put into *Aliens* arose as a result of his research for *Rambo: First Blood Part II*, which he wrote for action star Sylvester Stallone at the same time he wrote his *Alien* sequel. Like Vietnam veteran John Rambo in the latter film, Ripley is a traumatised survivor; something that was downplayed in the rewritten shooting script for *First Blood Part II*, but remained intact in *Aliens*.

The rich imagery Cameron conjures up for *Aliens* has affected popular culture in ways that he couldn't have predicted. Released less than one year later, the videogame *Contra*, by Japanese company Konami, draws freely on

[*] See: http://www.lofficier.com/cameron.htm.

the biomechanical monsters and futuristic artillery of *Aliens*; its muscular pair of heroes, named Bill Rizer and Lance Bean, are a mangled amalgam of four actors in Cameron's movie: Bill Paxton, Paul Reiser, Lance Henriksen and Michael Biehn.

That arcade hit was but one of a large number of videogames that have borrowed from *Aliens* over the past thirty years. *R-Type*, *Doom*, *Halo*, *Metroid* and *Gears of War* are just a few titles that have been inspired by *Aliens*'s weapons, characters, creatures and dialogue – or, in some instances, all four. Indeed, the concept of the bull-necked, tough-talking, Pulse Rifle-toting space marine has become such a genre cliché that it has since drifted into self-parody. Ironically, the game designers and filmmakers who have mined *Aliens* for their own work largely missed the point of the original movie: its Colonial Marines all wind up dying because of their bravado and over-reliance on military technology. Once the Marines' numbers begin to fall, we see their morale and egos collapse, and Ripley – the whip-smart survivor – again comes to the fore as the story's true warrior. *Alien* established Ripley, but it was *Aliens*, in the midst of a decade dominated by macho action heroes like Arnold Schwarzenegger and Sylvester Stallone, that turned her into a pop-culture icon.

To this day, Ripley remains one of the great female leads in a genre movie, and it's possible to see hints of her spirit and inner resolve in such varied characters as Katniss Everdeen in *The Hunger Games*, truck-driving road warrior Furiosa in *Mad Max: Fury Road* and Rey in *Star Wars: The Force Awakens*. Like Sarah Connor before her, Ripley is depicted as a fighter rather than a victim – a heroine who, through keeping hold of her humanity rather than giving into pure killer instinct, succeeds in meeting her nemesis head on and defeating it.

Alien and *Aliens* are therefore an unusual example of a pair of movies that complement one another. They essentially form two halves of one seamless story when watched back-to-back, which might explain why, when 20th Century Fox ordered a sequel to *Aliens* in the late 1980s, a succession of writers and directors struggled to figure out where to take the franchise next. What would eventually become *Alien 3*, released in 1992, was developed over approximately five tempestuous years, with talents as wide-ranging as William Gibson, *Die Hard 2* director Renny Harlin and New Zealand's Vincent Ward trying their luck and subsequently leaving. First-time director David Fincher eventually signed on to the sequel late in production, by which point Fox were desperate to get *Alien 3* in the can for a predetermined release date. With Ripley having found completion at the end of *Aliens* – surrogate daughter, lover, sweet dreams and all – the only way *Alien 3*'s writers could make her face her deadliest enemy again was by taking everything away. After the triumph of *Aliens*, its 1990s sequel sends Ripley to a nihilistic purgatory: abandon hope all ye who enter here.

Even in death, Ripley couldn't find rest. *Alien: Resurrection* (1997), directed by *Delicatessen* auteur Jean-Pierre Jeunet, saw Ripley revived through the miracle of genetic cloning, her DNA fused with that of a xenomorph and trapped in yet another ship full of monsters. That the *Alien* franchise has endured, despite the disappointments of the film spin-offs *Alien vs Predator* (2004) and *Aliens vs Predator: Requiem* (2007) – which crossed over with another 20th Century Fox sci-fi franchise, *Predator* – is a testament to the power of the monster originally brought to life by H. R. Giger in the late 1970s. Ridley Scott's series of prequels to *Alien*, which began with *Prometheus* in 2012 and continued with *Alien: Covenant* in 2017, aims to explore the dark corners of the franchise's universe, and has thus far uncovered giant, hairless humanoid entities called Engineers – which have, in a touch inspired by Erich von Däniken and H. P. Lovecraft, spawned life on Earth – deadly black goo and slithering, vicious, great-great-grandparents of the Starbeast itself.

H. R. Giger sadly died in 2014, not long after he had made a few final, small contributions to *Prometheus*. Nearly forty years on, his creature retains a horrifying allure, even as decades of exposure have threatened to make it as familiar and oft-parodied as Dracula or Frankenstein's monster.

It's arguable, however, that the alien would be nothing without Ripley, the creature's resourceful and compassionate mirror image. If the xenomorph represents everything that is grotesque and horrifying about being a living, breathing creature – our capacity for violence, our vulnerabilities to disease and old age – then Ripley represents our more noble qualities. *Aliens* is famous for its tough-talking marines and military imagery, but it's Ripley who reflects the best of us.

THEY COME FROM WITHIN: SCI-FI AND BODY HORROR

It all began with a single image: a spider emerging from the mouth of a sleeping victim. From this tiny seed, Canadian director David Cronenberg's first feature film emerged: 1975's *Shivers*. A taboo-busting spin on George A. Romero's *Night of the Living Dead* (1968), it was a horror film with a sci-fi twist that would soon become synonymous with Cronenberg's name. In a luxury apartment block, a scientist's experiments result in a parasite that passes from victim to victim, spreading a disease that turns the afflicted into raving, sex-obsessed maniacs. In a curious echo of British author J. G. Ballard's *High-Rise*, published the same year, *Shivers* sees the politely structured society of retirees, families and young professionals fall apart as the beasts within are unleashed.

Shot on a tiny budget, *Shivers* couldn't afford to show the spiders from Cronenberg's original vision, but the writhing maggots that replaced them are hardly less disturbing: wont to emerge and enter from just about every orifice, Cronenberg's parasites are a masterfully repulsive creation. One scene, in which a parasite emerges from a bath plug and inches its way towards horror icon Barbara Steele's nether regions, was so unforgettably effective that it not only appeared on *Shivers*'s poster, but also inspired an almost identical sequence in the 2006 sci-fi horror comedy *Slither*, directed by James Gunn. Indeed, Cronenberg's debut was quietly influential even in the 1970s; as we saw earlier in Chapter 14, a scene in which dozens of parasites emerge from the belly of actor Allan Kolman predates the chest-bursting creature in 1979's *Alien* by about four years.

The incisive horror of *Shivers* – released in Canada as *They Came from Within* and also known as *The Parasite Murders* – set the tone for much of Cronenberg's early career. In its native country, it was considered sordid and violent enough to be brought up in Parliament (that it was partly funded by taxpayers' money was a particularly sore point, though *Shivers* was notable for being one of the few Canadian films to make a return on its investment). The similarly gut-wrenching sci-fi horror *Rabid* followed in 1977, and it is in many ways a companion piece to *Shivers*. An experimental skin-graft operation, carried out on a young woman badly injured in a motorcycle accident, causes a blood-sucking, parasitic organism to emerge from beneath her armpit. As the woman goes from place to place, sating her need for blood, her attacks spread a disease that hastens a wider societal breakdown in downtown Montreal.

In these early films, Cronenberg's filmmaking style emerged fully formed, establishing a unique sub-genre widely termed 'body horror'. The writer-director's films function like slides under a microscope, each one studying such topics as birth, death, ageing, disease and identity in ways that are often shocking, assaultive but seldom less than electrifying. *Videodrome* (1982) sees a sleazy cable TV executive, Max Renn (James Woods) attempt to discover the origins of an illicit TV show, which appears to depict the torture and death of real people. Renn's investigations lead him into the path of a reclusive media prophet who only appears on television and, worse, a kind of terrorist organisation that aims to cleanse North America of anyone sick enough to watch a show like *Videodrome*. With special effects by Rick Baker, *Videodrome* is a grotesque, extraordinary film, both reflective of its era – where the spread of violent and sexually explicit videotapes was creating a media panic, particularly in the UK – and strikingly relevant for the twenty-first century.

After *The Fly* (1986), which turned the 1950s B-movie into an existential and explosively bloody relationship drama, Cronenberg began to move away from sci-fi and horror, though 1999's *eXistenZ* emerged as a potent kind of *Videodrome* for the PlayStation era. As Cronenberg moved into other territories, whether it was the profoundly tragic *Dead Ringers* (1988) or the blackly comic Hollywood satire, *Maps to the Stars* (2014), his body-horror ideas continue to inspire other filmmakers.

Japanese director Shinya Tsukamoto's *Tetsuo* (1989) is a black-and-white, stomach-churningly surreal horror in the Cronenberg vein, as an ordinary salaryman (Tomorowo Taguchi) gradually transforms into a huge, biomechanical creature that threatens to destroy Tokyo. The sequels *Tetsuo II: The Body*

Hammer (1992) and *Tetsuo: The Bullet Man* (2009) continued the same unsettling themes of man and machine, each one nightmarishly depicting the consumption of humanity by technology.

One of the most striking body-horror movies hails from the UK. Directed by Jonathan Glazer and loosely adapted from the novel by Michel Faber, 2013's *Under the Skin* is a one-of-a-kind arthouse sci-fi movie. Scarlett Johansson stars as an enigmatic alien entity who moves like a wraith through modern Glasgow. In the guise of an ordinary woman, she drives around autumn streets, picking up unsuspecting men and luring them back to her house – their fate, behind closed doors, is disturbing and unearthly in a way that defies description. Gradually, however, the alien's movements among humans causes something to rub off; as we watch, she becomes more curious, warmer, seemingly growing in empathy for the people she meets. By the end of the movie, we come to realise that the alien is far less predatory than some of the people around her.

Selected SF films mentioned in this chapter:
Night of the Living Dead (1968)
Shivers (1975)
Rabid (1977)
Videodrome (1982)
Dead Ringers (1988)
Tetsuo (1989)
Tetsuo II: The Body Hammer (1992)
Slither (2006)
Tetsuo: The Bullet Man (2009)
Under the Skin (2013)

21. Brutal satire

RoboCop (1987)

'They'll fix you. They fix everything.'

A single photograph sums up both *RoboCop*'s tone and the personality of its director, Paul Verhoeven. It shows the Dutch filmmaker standing in front of a towering robot, which looks like a bipedal tank, bristling with machine guns. The most fearsome thing in the picture, however, is Verhoeven himself: teeth bared, arms waving, fingers crooked like the talons of a hawk. Brilliantly, *RoboCop*'s set photographer has captured a moment where the director is attempting to provoke a terrified response from his cast, standing just outside the frame. In the finished movie, the robot, ED-209, goes berserk in its creators' corporate headquarters and trains its twin cannons on a terrified executive.

On the film set, the full-sized ED (Enforcement Droid) is just a motionless prop; the droid's movements will be created later by the stop-motion animator Phil Tippett. So, to get the quaking reaction he needs, Verhoeven starts screaming and waving his arms about, mimicking the rolling movements of the robot, stomping about like a heavyweight boxer. It's an example of Verhoeven's fierce, confrontational attitude to filmmaking: at once intelligent and larger-than-life, humanistic yet startlingly violent.

Released the same year as *RoboCop*, Oliver Stone's stockbroking drama *Wall Street* attempted to crystallise the go-go 1980s in the figure of its corporate-raider villain Gordon Gecko, who even had a motto to go with his aggressive style of operation: 'Greed, for want of a better word, is good.' Yet *RoboCop* is arguably *Wall Street*'s equal in summing up a decade of Reaganomics and wild excess: in *RoboCop*, there's literally blood in the boardroom.

Wrapped up in *RoboCop*'s ultra-violent revenge story there are themes of death and resurrection, the decay of the US steel and automotive industries, gentrification, Cold War-era politics, numbing commercialism and, yes, corporate greed. Set in a near-future Detroit, *RoboCop* sees idealistic law enforcer Alex Murphy (a steely-eyed Peter Weller) brutally shot to death by a gang of thugs led by the sadistic Clarence Boddicker (Kurtwood Smith). Murphy's tortured body is carted off by a company called Omni Consumer Products (OCP), which is attempting to create a private army of police robots – the first step in its stated aim to tear down old Detroit and replace it with gleaming towers for the rich. OCP's first prototype, ED-209, is an exercise in comic overkill: dreamed up by OCP executive Dick Jones (Ronny Cox), it's the cybernetic equivalent of a gas-guzzling American saloon car. Murphy, meanwhile, is resurrected as a cyborg sheriff in shining armour: a cold, sleek automaton with no memory of the husband and father he once was. But as Murphy makes his first neighbourhood patrols as RoboCop, images of his murder gradually resurface. Together with his old partner Anne Lewis (Nancy Allen), Murphy resolves to bring his killers to book; dead or alive, they're coming with him.

RoboCop was Verhoeven's second US film, the director having been the subject of both praise and controversy for such movies as *Spetters* (starring Rutger Hauer), *The Fourth Man* and *Soldier of Orange* in his native Holland. A filmmaker with an eye for the extreme and outrageous, Verhoeven brings a febrile quality to *RoboCop*'s set-pieces, which are so graphic and gory that they read as a satire of other 1980s action movies: an era where muscles bulged and heroes shot first and left the questions for the sissies on Capitol Hill. That scene where ED-209 malfunctions and shoots an OCP employee sets the tone early, as the robot's chattering machine-gun fire reduces the executive's body to what amounts to a pile of crimson goo and a shredded grey suit. Set against the impotent cry of, 'Will someone call a goddamn paramedic?', Verhoeven establishes a blackly comic tone.

Even the casting goes against the grain of a straight sci-fi movie. Ronny Cox, the gaunt corporate villain Dick Jones, was better known as one of the duelling banjo players in *Deliverance* than as a bad guy. Verhoeven also appears to take great delight in taking actor Paul McCrane (Montgomery from the TV series *Fame*), covering him in toxic waste, and having him smashed to a pulp by Boddicker's out-of-control car. (In a brilliant touch, Boddicker turns on his windscreen wipers to clear the view.)

The grotesquery and satire recall the British comic-book character Judge Dredd and, indeed, the influence of the dystopian judge, jury and executioner extended to the character design. Behind-the-scenes photos show that Rob Bottin's early concepts for RoboCop's armour were extremely close to the Judge Dredd outfit as drawn by comic-book artist Carlos Ezquerra: the broad shoulders, the helmet that covers the character's eyes. The RoboCop design seen in the movie is less obviously modelled on Dredd, yet the obscured face and stern voice ('Come with me or there will be trouble') still bear echoes of the comic.

As written by screenwriter Ed Neumeier, *RoboCop* followed *Alien* and *Aliens* in its depiction of a future world controlled by uncaring corporations. But Neumeier takes the notion of corporate indifference one step further: after his death, Alex Murphy's shattered body and mind become the property of OCP; in a clever twist on Isaac Asimov's Three Laws of Robotics, Murphy's free will is constrained by five directives, which dehumanise him to the point where only the wisps of his original personality remain. If we humans have a soul at all, *RoboCop* seems to suggest, then maybe it too can be captured, modified and turned into a commodity.

RoboCop's mixture of ideas is easy to miss at first glance and, indeed, Verhoeven may never have made the film at all if he had gone with his initial response to Neumeier's screenplay. Scoffing at its daft title and B-movie plot, Verhoeven promptly threw the script in the bin; it was his wife Martine Tours who, after retrieving the stack of papers and reading them herself, prompted Verhoeven to read the script again. It was on his second readthrough that Verhoeven began to see the layers beneath the gunplay: the ingenious use of adverts, news broadcasts and clips from TV shows, which suggest a society in which information itself is filtered and repackaged; disturbing stories about an escalating nuclear crisis in South Africa are glibly relayed by news anchors, and contrast ghoulishly with adverts for Cold War-themed board games

('Nukem! Get them before they get you!') and replacement mechanical hearts sold by a doctor in an ill-fitting wig. The result is a quite unique mix of action and satire, as *RoboCop* does for a post-industrial, 1980s America what *Dr Strangelove* did for the politics of mutually assured destruction in the 1960s.

Neumeier's endlessly quotable script is undoubtedly a cornerstone, but it's difficult to imagine another director rendering *RoboCop* quite so well as Verhoeven. A lesser director would have played up the violence and likely skated over the commentary; worse still, a more earnest director might have tried to serve up its story of death, revival and revenge straight. Instead, Verhoeven deepens the ideas present in the screenplay and introduces plenty of his own; he accentuates the quasi-religious imagery that was already latent in *RoboCop*'s tale of science-assisted resurrection, turning its metal-clad hero into a mixture of straight-shooting sheriff from the Old West and a modern Christ – the sly implication being that an American saviour would likely carry a gun.

'The point of *RoboCop*, of course, is it is a Christ story,' Verhoeven once told MTV. 'It is about a guy that gets crucified after 50 minutes, then is resurrected in the next 50 minutes and then is like the super-cop of the world, but is also a Jesus figure as he walks over water at the end.'[*]

RoboCop is also a 1980s riff on Mary Shelley's *Frankenstein*. Like *Frankenstein*'s monster, RoboCop is constructed from the remains of the dead and, in another parallel, lacks his own name: instead, he's given a brand name by OCP – the company even takes the time to have its corporate logo emblazoned on the side of his helmet. RoboCop is, therefore, a Frankenstein's monster created by committee: a product engineered with directives – serve the public trust, protect the innocent, uphold the law – but no real will of its own. Gradually, however, the humanity inside the machine begins to resurface, and in the film's final scene, *RoboCop*'s overarching theme is laid bare: it's about Alex Murphy wresting his identity back from the people who took it from him. The villains who roam Detroit's streets may have destroyed

---

[*] See: http://moviesblog.mtv.com/2010/04/14/paul-verhoeven-robocop-christ-story-remake -update.

Murphy's body, but it was OCP that took and manipulated his mind. In that final scene, the hero is asked what his name is.

'Murphy,' he replies with a wry smile: the soul within the machine has been freed, and Murphy has found completion.

With a story as perfectly tied up as that, it's unsurprising that *RoboCop*'s various sequels, spin-offs and 2014 remake felt so superfluous. *RoboCop 2*, directed by *The Empire Strikes Back*'s Irvin Kershner and released in 1990, had a few ideas of its own – even commenting on its own status as a sequel – but lacked its predecessor's depth. *RoboCop 3* followed three years later, and was little more than a glorified toy commercial (in a sure sign that the series had drifted into self-parody, one sequence sees *RoboCop* fly around via jetpack). By the time a Canadian TV series emerged in 1994, *RoboCop* had itself become a consumer product: tamed, packaged, merchandised, a shadow of its former self.

Brazilian director José Padilha attempted to bring some of the old Verhoeven bite back in his 2014 remake, simply titled *RoboCop*, which reworked the story for an era of drone warfare, Foxconn and smartphones. Unfortunately for Padilha, *RoboCop* was the property of a major Hollywood studio, MGM, and not a plucky mini-major like Orion, the company behind the 1987 original. Padilha's film sees technology as a possible conduit for totalitarianism: as drones and robots engage in an endless war in the Middle East, and OCP plans to expand its army of automatons to the USA. RoboCop is essentially developed as a publicity stunt: a human face (or, at least, a handsome chin) to parade in front of the media. Unfortunately for Padilha, MGM appeared to want the new *RoboCop* to appeal to kids who flocked to see Marvel's *Iron Man* movies, and the film emerged as a bloodless and somewhat sterile PG-13 action flick – another consumer product. Exasperated, Padilha later said that making *RoboCop* was one of the most stressful experiences of his life.

Verhoeven's original *RoboCop*, on the other hand, is among the best SF films ever made. Absurd in its tone and still startlingly brutal today, *RoboCop* remains one of the great stories about the fault lines between humanity, capitalism and technology.

Verhoeven's sci-fi

If Paul Verhoeven's wife was instrumental in getting the Dutch director to make *RoboCop*, we have Arnold Schwarzenegger to thank for Verhoeven's next foray into the SF genre. Schwarzenegger, who in the late 1980s was a bona-fide superstar thanks to the success of his post-*Terminator* action movies, watched *RoboCop* and was hugely impressed by it. For some years, Schwarzenegger had a pet project he had been trying to get off the ground, only to see it fail on several occasions. It was called *Total Recall*, an action thriller loosely based on the short story 'We Can Remember It for You Wholesale' by Philip K. Dick. A project that had been through many drafts and numerous lead actors since producer Ronald Shusett acquired it in the late 1970s, *Total Recall* had come close to fruition under movie mogul Dino De Laurentiis's studio, DEG. Weeks before production was due to begin in Rome, however, De Laurentiis went bust, leaving *Total Recall* in limbo. Schwarzenegger moved quickly, encouraging Hollywood mini-major Carolco – the studio behind the *Rambo* movies – to purchase the rights to *Total Recall* from the failing DEG, while Schwarzenegger coaxed Verhoeven into agreeing to step in as director.

The result is another mix of black comedy and thunderous violence, where the spirit of Philip K. Dick's concept still sings through the gunfire. Schwarzenegger plays Douglas Quaid, a construction worker distracted by recurring dreams of a more exotic, exciting life on Mars. Intent on bringing that dream a little closer to reality – and too broke to afford a real trip to the colonies on the Red Planet – Quaid visits Rekall, a company dedicated to planting memories into the heads of its customers. During the implantation procedure, Rekall's technicians discover that Quaid's mind has already been tampered with: he's apparently a former spy who has had his memory wiped.

Thereafter, Quaid finds himself in the midst of a conspiracy that involves the fate of Mars, ancient alien technology and a small army of assassins presided over by Cohaagen (Ronny Cox, returning from *RoboCop*) and his angry henchman, Richter (Michael Ironside). Even Quaid's once demure wife, Lori (Sharon Stone) is out to kill him. But is everything Quaid is experiencing real, or is it part of the flawlessly convincing 'ego trip' implanted by Rekall?

Total Recall has less thematic depth than *RoboCop*, but Verhoeven still exercises his impish sense of humour within the context of a beefy Schwarzenegger star vehicle. As originally written, *Total Recall* – like Dick's short story – portrayed Quaid as a regular guy with a desk job. With Arnold looking more like someone who had just stepped down from Mount Olympus, Verhoeven doubles down on his heightened approach, slyly depicting Quaid as a kind of four-square Alice in Wonderland, lost in a dream world of strange characters. A TV advert is *Total Recall*'s equivalent of the White Rabbit, leading Quaid on his Martian adventure. There are clues everywhere that what we see is all part of Quaid's fantasy; before he falls asleep in the Rekall dream chair, Quaid sees snapshots of the people and places he'll encounter over the next ninety minutes. At one stage, the guy from the TV advert appears, warning Quaid that he is in the midst of a fantasy; back in the real world, he's still strapped into the chair at Rekall, suffering from some kind of psychotic episode. If Quaid doesn't step out of the delusion, the man says, Quaid will be lobotomised. Look closely at the end of the movie, where Quaid has saved the planet, bested the bad guys and got the girl, and you'll see a blinding white light emanate from the corner of the screen – Verhoeven's subtle clue that the lobotomy is indeed taking place. Quaid chose the seductive fantasy rather than reality; Verhoeven, if you believe this reading of his movie, lobotomised the 1980s biggest action star and got away with it.

Verhoeven continued his subversive style of science fiction with 1997's *Starship Troopers*, which turned the pro-military politics of Robert A. Heinlein's 1959 novel on its head. Heinlein imagined a future where military service is a requirement for citizenship, and where humanity's spread across the galaxy has resulted in all-out war between Earth and giant insects on a distant planet, Klendathu. Verhoeven and screenwriter Edward Neumeier keep that concept, but cast Heinlein's twenty-third-century Federation as blatantly fascist: TV reports resemble Nazi-era propaganda, uniforms resemble those worn by the Third Reich, and Verhoeven consciously borrows shots from Leni Riefenstahl's 1935 film, *Triumph of the Will*.

Taken together, Verhoeven's trilogy of 1980s and 1990s SF films explore how individualism can be threatened by external forces, whether it's corporate greed, technology or, in the case of *Starship Troopers*, fascism and mindless conformity. The thread that runs through all three movies is the role that television media – then still the dominant form of mass communication – plays in allowing those threats on the self to play out, either through pacifying us with false impressions of the real world in the case of news networks or diverting our attention altogether with advertising.

Hilariously, some critics took Verhoeven's depiction of a fascist America at face value when *Starship Troopers* came out in 1997, apparently thinking that the director was asking audiences to side with his airbrushed, daytime soap characters (played by Casper Van Dien and Denise Richards) and their mass slaughter of alien creatures. Unlike *RoboCop* and *Total Recall*, *Starship Troopers* wasn't a huge financial success, perhaps because its distributors simply didn't know how to market it.

With the 1990s over, Verhoeven made one final movie in Hollywood: the sci-fi thriller *Hollow Man*, released in 2000. A sordid updating of H. G. Wells's *The Invisible Man*, the movie was a bigger hit than *Starship Troopers*, but it's a disappointingly conventional, even rote slasher-thriller with little of the verve the director showed in the past; its disquieting central theme of voyeurism is ultimately cast aside for a straightforwardly violent final act. Verhoeven himself admitted that he was dissatisfied with *Hollow Man*, and with studio filmmaking in general; *RoboCop* and *Total Recall* had been made under the aegis of production companies that worked outside the Hollywood machine, meaning Verhoeven was left to his own eccentric devices. By the 1990s, both Orion and Carolco had collapsed, and Verhoeven was left to decide whether he wanted to be a gun for hire working under the watchful eye of increasingly wary studios like Sony, which distributed *Hollow Man* through its Columbia arm. Verhoeven opted to move back to Holland, where he continued making movies at a slower pace: the Second World War drama-thriller *Black Book* (2006) and the 2016 thriller, *Elle*.

The three sci-fi movies Verhoeven made between 1987 and 1997 remain among the best to emerge from American genre cinema. Stylistically they may be products of their time, but the ideas they express remain undimmed; we can still sense Verhoeven, just outside the frame, arms waving, teeth bared, radiating ferocious intelligence.

Selected SF films mentioned in this chapter:

Total Recall (1990)

Starship Troopers (1997)

Hollow Man (2000)

22. Ghost in the cel

AKIRA (1988)

'The future is not a straight line. It is filled with many crossroads.
There must be a future that we can choose for ourselves.'

To the primal clatter of drums, a crimson motorcycle tears through Tokyo streets, its tail-lights leaving neon streaks in their wake. For many in the West, this was their first glimpse of *Akira*, manga artist turned director Katsuhiro Otomo's seminal animated movie. Taking in a slew of influences, from *Metropolis* to *Blade Runner* to the artwork of French comic-book artist Jean 'Moebius' Giraud, *Akira* is a film of extraordinary detail and ambition.

Adapted from Otomo's own manga, first published in *Young Magazine* in 1982 and still ongoing while the movie was being made, *Akira* is a sprawling epic involving government and military conspiracy, teen biker gangs, strange kids with telekinetic powers and apocalyptic destruction.

Akira is a cyberpunk parable about post-war Japan, its rapid progress and those in danger of being left behind along the way. It is deeply cynical about science, politics, religion, military power and the bovine credulity of the masses. If hope can be found anywhere, it's in the next generation of youngsters, and the possibility that they might finally learn from our mistakes.

Japan's artists and writers who grew up during the country's post-war rebirth, understood that while technology had resulted in the bomb that destroyed Hiroshima and Nagasaki, it was by embracing scientific progress – making the transition from an essentially agricultural society to a technological one – that had saved the country from oblivion. *Akira* is perhaps the most famous product of this post-war transition, as British anime expert and *The Anime Movie Guide* author Helen McCarthy points out.

'*Akira* came from that place where technology was both a terrible threat and yet the country's only hope of survival,' McCarthy says. 'The technology that was inflicted on Japan was also the technology that Japan used to claw its way out of the flattened ruins of Tokyo. That was its position when Otomo was writing.'

Just like Tokyo in the 1950s and 1960s, the Neo-Tokyo of *Akira* is rebuilding from a cataclysmic war that left it in ruins. The Olympic Games, due to be held in the city in 2020, are a symbol of Japan's newfound prosperity, just as they were for the country in the 1960s.* But fault lines are shifting beneath the surface of society: there are biker gangs declaring open war on the streets. There are mass demonstrations against an oppressive government regime, while a new religion has built up around a mysterious figure called Akira.

Against this backdrop, a teen motorcycle gang led by the cocksure Shotaro Kaneda comes face to face with a secret government experiment. After a bike accident, Kaneda's childhood friend, Tetsuo, is carried off to a fortified building, where he's subjected to a series of tests that awaken his latent psychic abilities. Gradually, Tetsuo's power grows past the point where he can control it – and, once again, Tokyo teeters on the brink of destruction.

Like Jonathan Swift, Otomo uses his characters to satirise different walks of contemporary life. Nezu is a politician who claims to be on the side of the freedom fighters, but is revealed to be more intent on seizing power and holding onto his money. As if his rodent features weren't telling enough, look at the fate Otomo plans for him: choking to death on an overdose of heart pills – possibly containing Warfarin, the same chemical used in rat poison. Likewise Doctor Onishi, the Einstein-like scientist, who spends the whole movie locked up in his lab, obsessing over computer readouts and paying little heed to the chaos unfolding outside. The great Japanese public are credulous enough to assume that Tetsuo is a returned messiah and follow him blindly to their deaths – as does Lady Miyako, who has little more than a cameo as a shrieking

* See: http://kotaku.com/the-2020-tokyo-olympics-were-predicted-30-years-ago-by-1276381444.

religious leader (in the manga, she's revealed to be one of the government's early test subjects).

Akira, then, is as rich thematically as it is visually. An unprecedented sum of around 1.1 billion yen was spent on drawing and painting its 160,000-plus frames – a budget garnered near the peak of Japan's 1980s prosperity. From 1986 onwards, the country's economy soared, meaning investors suddenly had millions of yen to invest in movies; as a result, Otomo, together with producers Ryohei Suzuki and Shunzo Kato, succeeded in setting up The Akira Committee, a consortium of Japanese companies ranging from Bandai to Kodansha to Toho.

That extraordinarily high budget allowed Otomo and his team of animators to indulge in techniques and ideas that were unprecedented in Japanese animation. Most of the country's animated output, both before and after *Akira*, generally uses twelve images for every second of footage; lower-budget television anime will often use less. *Akira*, meanwhile, uses twenty-four images – or cels – every second, doubling the animators' workload and, by extension, hugely inflating the cost of production. The payoff, however, is one of the most vivid and fluid traditionally animated films ever to emerge from the Far East. In a scene where Tetsuo uses his nascent telekinetic powers to fend off the tear-gas shells fired by a phalanx of soldiers, for example, it's possible to see every lick of smoke and individual particle swirl around the anti-hero's head.

Akira's real genius lies not just in the quality of the animation, however, but its strength as a piece of cinema: *Akira* adheres as much to the conventions of Western live-action filmmaking as it does to anime. There are tracking shots, focus-pulling, canted angles and POV sequences. Otomo draws inspiration from such movies as *The Warriors*, *Blade Runner* and Kubrick's *A Clockwork Orange* and *2001: A Space Odyssey* for his exquisite compositions. He uses that visual language to craft sequences that wouldn't have been possible in the 1980s, and would still be difficult to achieve convincingly with modern CGI: gladiatorial fights between bikers riding at top speed; a child's anguished scream sending the top of a building crashing down on a street heaving with demonstrators; Tetsuo's stricken body bursting out in a fleshy array of bulging limbs.

Indeed, *Akira*'s cinema literacy has had a reciprocal effect on Western film-making; its themes, imagery and style have had an enormous impact on sci-fi and action cinema. The Wachowskis, the filmmaker siblings behind *The Matrix* and its sequels (see Chapter 26); director Josh Trank's teen sci-fi thriller *Chronicle* drew freely on the idea of a Tetsuo-like young man becoming twisted by his supernatural powers. The music video for American rapper Kanye West's song 'Stronger' recreated several scenes from *Akira* almost shot for shot.

Aside from the output of Studio Ghibli and its legendary animator Hayao Miyazaki, few films have done more to establish Japanese anime in Western minds than *Akira*. While such shows as *Battle of the Planets* (known in Japan as *Space Science Team Gatchaman*) aired on American television first, *Akira* was obviously, eye-poppingly different: sophisticated, disturbing and technically dazzling. In the UK and parts of Europe, the success of *Akira* was instrumental in establishing a cult audience for anime, and companies such as Manga Entertainment were founded to cater to that growing market. By the early 1990s, such movies and shows as *Bubblegum Crisis*, *Fist of the North Star* and the controversial *Urotsukidoji* were suddenly available in British stores – and occasionally making headlines for their nudity and graphic violence.

Akira set a new benchmark in animation and, in many respects, it has never been surpassed. In 1991, as the anime scene was getting under way in the UK, Japan's bubble economy suddenly burst. Just as the grotesque swelling of Tetsuo's body preceded a cataclysmic event, so Japan's bursting asset market saw the country fall into an economic abyss from which it would take years to recover. While Japan continued to produce animated movies of all kinds, few directors or studios essayed a film on quite such a scale again.

The film remains a unique artefact from Japan's late twentieth-century history, capturing both its hopes and fears for the future. Its imagery and ideas have remained enduring, to the point where producers in Hollywood have long since taken a keen interest; in 2002, Warner Bros purchased the rights to make a live-action version of Otomo's magnum opus. For years afterwards, the project would linger like a ghost in Hollywood trade papers, occasionally surfacing with a rumour here or news of a personnel change there, but some-how never coalescing into anything remotely concrete. By 2012, a string of directors and writers had been involved in the American *Akira*, while actors as varied as Keanu Reeves, Kristen Stewart and *Tron: Legacy*'s Garrett Hedlund had come and gone. It's as though the producers behind the project recognise *Akira*'s power as a piece of modern pop culture, but can't quite agree on what makes it so unique; is it the vision of a future metropolis beset by protests and gang violence? Perhaps. Is it the city-levelling action, which is now firmly in vogue in mainstream American movies? Possibly. Is it the cool red bike, which appears so prominently on the original film's posters? It certainly doesn't hurt. But *Akira*'s true power emanates from Otomo himself: it's his artwork, his character designs, his extraordinary melange of ideas, that make *Akira* the masterpiece that it is.

As for the film's enduring power, it's Helen McCarthy who puts it best:

'*Akira* has affected the culture in places that never had the nuclear bomb, because Otomo wasn't just talking about the bomb, he was talking about the terror of the moment when you realise, usually in your late teens or your early 20s, that you are never actually going to control anything. Ever, as long as you live. [. . .] That for me was the message of *Akira*: you can't control any of this, but you don't have to let them control it. You can hold onto what you think is important, keep faith with your friends, live your life. You can be your own stability. You can become your own island. That, to me, was the wonderful thing about *Akira*.'

ANIMATED SCI-FI

If Japan has produced more animated sci-fi than any other country on the planet, then that's because its relationship with technology is so completely unique. Whether it's such giant-robot shows as *Tetsujin 28*, *Gundam*, *Macross* or *Evangelion*, we see these themes of threat and salvation played out over and over again in Japanese animated sci-fi. The giant robots (or mecha) designed by such Japanese artists as Go Nagai, Kunio Okawara or Masamune Shirow are majestic and beautiful in ways that Western robots seldom are, yet they are also imbued with devastating power. In Japanese anime, scientific progress can be seen everywhere in their futuristic cities – but those cities are wont to be wiped out in a heartbeat, either by terrifying alien technology or mankind's own hubris.

The past sixty years have proved to be a fruitful breeding ground for great sci-fi ideas in Japanese manga, TV and cinema, and covering it all would require an entire book of its own. Beyond the boisterous and often bloody anime imported to the USA and UK in the 1990s and 2000s, Japanese animators have created all kinds of visually and conceptually imaginative work. The early films of Hayao Miyazaki frequently straddled the boundaries between fantasy and sci-fi to bewitching effect. In *Nausicaä of the Valley of the Wind* (1984), adapted from his own manga, Miyazaki predicts a post-apocalyptic future where huge, mutated creatures roam the plains, and where the remaining pockets of humanity live in medieval-like villages that rely on wind turbines for energy. His next film, *Laputa: Castle in the Sky* (1986), takes the flying island motif from *Gulliver's Travels* to spin another charming eco-fable, this one about an ancient, technologically advanced race capable of building huge weapons of mass destruction. Like so many of Miyazaki's films, *Laputa* is about humanity's tense relationship with the natural world and the reciprocal nature of scientific progress. Its robots and flying islands are organic and beautiful-looking, yet their destructive power is fearsome. In Miyazaki's hands, the flying island becomes a symbol of our collective ingenuity and failings.

The same sense of triumph and despair can be found in *Royal Space Force: The Wings of Honneamise* (1987), directed by Hiroyuki Yamaga and animated by Gainax. Like Philip Kaufman's 1983 film *The Right Stuff*, it's about a nascent space programme, yet *Royal Space Force* is, uniquely, set in a strange parallel world quite unlike our own. As a group of scientists and astronauts attempt to put a man into space, the country around them teeters on the brink of war. Thanks in part to a huge financial investment from Bandai, *Royal Space Force* rivals *Akira* in its exquisite design and animation.

'The details in it are so perfect,' concurs Helen McCarthy. 'Every single thing, from the way cutlery is designed, the way housewares are designed, the way light falls because of the position of the sun and the stars ... . everything in that movie is very, perilously close to perfect. It's just gorgeous, and it's a joy to watch.'

All that detail and ambition didn't, however, translate into box-office success, and neither has *Royal Space Force* succeeded in becoming an *Akira*-level cult phenomenon in the West. Nevertheless, it's a phenomenal work of art and design and, as McCarthy says, it deserves to be regarded as something far more pivotal than a footnote in a studio that would one day make the hit series *Evangelion*; '*Wings of Honneamise* is the first great work by Gainax,' McCarthy says, 'and in many ways, they've been failing to live up to its potential ever since.'

Even in Japan, animated movies made on the scale of *Akira* and *Royal Space Force* are rare, but there are engaging sci-fi ideas to be found at the lower end of the budget spectrum. The Japanese straight-to-video market of the 1980s and 1990s regularly played host to some stunning one-off SF stories; McCarthy cites the gorgeously designed *Dragon's Heaven* (1988), featuring robot designs by Osamu Kobayashi, and *Ai City* (1986) as two less well-known examples. The former is about a sentient robot in a post-apocalyptic landscape; the latter is a Philip K. Dick-esque thriller set in a futuristic city – its twist ending alone makes it one of anime's great hidden gems.

Outside Japan, we have seen animated sci-fi movies emerge from time to time – the classic *Fantastic Planet* (1973), hailing from France, is a key one – but it's only in recent years that they have become more common in the West. Richard Linklater's *Waking Life* (2001) and *A Scanner Darkly* (2006), based on the novel by Philip K. Dick, use rotoscoped animation to blur the lines between delusion, dreams and reality. *The Iron Giant* (1999) takes Ted Hughes's poem and turns it into a Miyazaki-like fable about the duality of scientific achievement: the huge robot of the title is both a terrifying weapon and the loyal friend to its young hero. Overwhelmingly, however, animated sci-fi films made in the United States and Europe have failed to make much traction with their audiences; such films as *Starchaser: The Legend of Orin* (1985) and *Titan A.E.* (2000) have enjoyed cult status rather than outright success. The motion-capture animation *Mars Needs Moms* (2011) was an infamous box-office disaster.

In Japan, meanwhile, anime has continued to thrive, even as it has evolved to take in the latest advances in computer technology. Such directors as

Mamoru Hosoda (*Summer Wars*, *The Girl Who Leapt Through Time*) and Makoto Shinkai (*Your Name*) have told science-fiction stories through anime to hugely popular effect – as of 2017, *Your Name* was the highest-grossing anime feature of all time.

In terms of wider pop-cultural influence, manga and anime have left a profound mark on our consciousness. Directors as varied as James Cameron, Steven Spielberg, Darren Aronofsky, Neill Blomkamp and Christopher Nolan are all either inspired by anime or openly discuss its influence in interviews. And as we'll see in Chapter 26, one Japanese anime in particular – *Ghost in the Shell*, based on Masamune Shirow's manga and directed by Mamoru Oshii – has left an indelible impression on Western cinema.

Selected SF films mentioned in this chapter:

Fantastic Planet (1973)

Nausicaä of the Valley of the Wind (1984)

Starchaser: The Legend of Orin (1985)

Laputa: Castle in the Sky (1986)

Ai City (1986)

Royal Space Force: The Wings of Honneamise (1987)

Dragon's Heaven (1988)

Ghost in the Shell (1995)

The Iron Giant (1999)

Titan A.E. (2000)

Waking Life (2001)

A Scanner Darkly (2006)

The Girl Who Leapt Through Time (2006)

Summer Wars (2009)

Mars Needs Moms (2011)

Your Name (2016)

23. Rise of the machines

TERMINATOR 2: JUDGMENT DAY (1991)

'If a machine can learn the value of human life, maybe we can too.'

Not unlike Fritz Lang decades before him, director James Cameron gradually built a reputation for being a harsh taskmaster. On *Metropolis* (1927), Lang coldly gazed through his monocle as dozens of extras – many of them children – were drenched by the icy jet of a water cannon. For his undersea sci-fi film *The Abyss* (1989), Cameron subjected his actors to a similarly harrowing shoot. Largely filmed in a water tank in South Carolina, the production was both expensive and gruelling, with the cast and crew spending long hours submerged in freezing water. Morale on the set reached a point where crew-members started wearing T-shirts that read, blackly, 'Life's abyss and then you die.'

Although less financially successful than *Aliens*, *The Abyss* was nevertheless another ambitious and often beautiful-looking genre film. While other studios' copycat undersea horror films – *Leviathan*, *Lords of the Deep*, *Deepstar Six*, to name a few – cut corners to create their ocean-bottom sequences, *The Abyss* looked astonishingly real. The cast and crew may have gone through hell to make *The Abyss*, but the results, to use a common Hollywood saying, were all up there on the screen.

The Abyss's centrepiece, in terms of visual effects, lasted little more than a few seconds. It was a sequence in which an alien intelligence, capable of manipulating water, sends a tentacle of liquid wriggling and twisting through an underwater drilling station. When the water tentacle (or pseudopod) encounters a human – Mary Elizabeth Mastrantonio's character, Lindsey

– the tip of it shape-shifts to create a copy of her smiling face. Although brief, the scene was a breakthrough in digital filmmaking, using as it did an early version of a new piece of software called Photoshop.

Photoshop was developed at ILM by John Knoll, a visual effects artist who had previously worked as a motion-control camera operator on such films as *Star Trek IV: The Voyage Home* and Joe Dante's sci-fi comedy, *Innerspace*. *The Abyss* wasn't the first film to feature CGI visual effects – *Tron*, *Star Trek II* and *Young Sherlock Holmes* among others got there much earlier in the 1980s – but its use of CG to create a photorealistic, morphing character was nothing short of groundbreaking.

ILM's work on *The Abyss* earned it an Oscar in 1990, and paved the way for Cameron's next film: a return to the world of killer cyborgs he had first dreamed up at the start of his career. Back when Cameron was writing the original *Terminator*, he'd initially had the idea of a shape-shifting, artificial assassin made from liquid metal, but he quickly realised that it was a concept beyond the reach of traditional movie-making techniques. *The Abyss's* water tentacle proved, however, that such a character could theoretically be created with CGI – even if those scant seventy-five seconds of imagery had proved expensive and time-consuming enough to delay the release of the entire movie.

By the start of the 1990s, the production company behind *The Terminator*, Hemdale, was on the brink of collapse, and at the urging of Arnold Schwarzenegger, independent studio Carolco pushed to acquire the movie rights. Once those rights were purchased in 1990 – for a reported $5 million – production on *Terminator 2: Judgment Day* progressed at an intense pace; the screenplay, co-written by Cameron and his old friend William Wisher, was completed that May. By October, filming was under way, largely in Los Angeles and other locations in California – the aim being to get the movie finished in time for a pre-arranged release date of 4 July 1991.

Time wasn't the only factor bearing down on *Terminator 2*, either. Once its effects, stunts and star salaries were all added up, its budget amounted to slightly more than $100 million – a record-breaking sum for the time. Hollywood trade papers, always on the hunt for a dramatic story, suggested that Carolco could go bust if *Terminator 2* failed. Then there was the matter of the liquid metal Terminator itself, the T-1000. Cameron imagined this new threat, sent back to the year 1995 to kill a ten-year-old John Connor, to be faster, stealthier and more cunning than the first film's T-800. The assassin would also have the ability to assume other identities and completely change its shape, whether that meant transforming its hands into swords or hooks, or sending its body oozing through gaps like a blob of mercury. With *The Abyss*'s digital effects taking six months – and delaying the film's release in the process – the decision was made to get ILM started on *Terminator 2*'s CGI before shooting had even begun. Approximately $5 million was spent on the digital effects sequences in *T2*, which amounted to around five minutes of footage in the finished film. The greater share of *T2*'s effects were practical or photographic, with Stan Winston – who designed the stunning T-800 metal skeleton for the original *Terminator* – returning to help realise Cameron's ideas. Although relatively brief in the context of a 137-minute film, *Terminator 2*'s use of CGI shouldn't be underestimated; as well as those pioneering transformation effects, which saw the T-1000 rise up from a hospital floor and morph seamlessly into actor Robert Patrick, the movie also made extensive use of wire removal and face replacement. Techniques that are commonplace in twenty-first-century movies were still relatively new in 1991, and *Terminator 2* laid the groundwork not just for other effects movies – *Jurassic Park*, *The Phantom Menace*, *The Matrix* – but also an era of filmmaking that was still just over the horizon a quarter of a century ago.

Like *Aliens* five years before it, *Terminator 2* demonstrated Cameron's ability to craft an engaging sequel. Conceptually, *T2* is broadly the same as *The Terminator*: a cyborg assassin is sent back in time to kill a resistance leader before he's reached maturity, while a protector – in this case, Schwarzenegger's reprogrammed T-800, replacing Kyle Reese – is despatched to stop it. But as well as fulfilling the requirements of a Hollywood sequel – bigger explosions, more stunts, glossier special effects – Cameron subtly shifts the story's tone and message. Whereas *The Terminator* was shot through with a broad streak of horror, *T2* is less nightmarish and graphically violent. *The Terminator* was about a doomed love affair and the inevitability of a coming war. *T2* has the

T-800 utter the line, 'It's in your nature to destroy yourselves,' but its overriding message is one of hope. Sarah Connor, John's estranged mother, has become a battle-hardened warrior since the events of the last film, and seems in danger of becoming as harsh and unfeeling as the machines that will one day take over the planet. As *T2*'s story plays out, Sarah reconnects with her son, and ultimately realises the value of empathy and compassion; likewise, the T-800, while protecting John, becomes a surrogate father and begins to display some disarmingly human traits. *The Terminator* concluded with the foreboding clouds of a coming war between humanity and machine; *T2* more comfortingly suggests that nuclear war can be avoided if, to paraphrase Sarah Connor, 'We learn the value of human life.' It's a feel-good message for a bigger, broader summer film, and also one that suited events in the early 1990s; by then, the Cold War was finally over, the Iron Curtain had fallen, and the looming threat of a nuclear calamity was beginning to ebb.

Terminator 2 also marked the beginning of a gradual change in audience tastes. This time around, the visual effects were arguably as big a draw as Schwarzenegger's stardom, even if the Austrian Oak did legendarily get a private jet thrown in as part of his salary. While *The Terminator*'s roots lay in the 1980s era of big guns, muscles and overkill, *T2* also marked the beginning of a new kind of summer film: effects-driven and carried by its globally recognisable branding. *Jurassic Park* and *The Matrix* were just around the corner; the turn of the millennium brought with it the rise of the comic-book movie and the Marvel Cinematic Universe.

The film's unprecedented budget also caused something of a consternation in Hollywood. With a spend of over $100 million including advertising, *T2* had to do huge business in order to make a profit – and, despite forecasts of doom in some quarters, it succeeded. After its release, Cameron showed little interest in continuing the franchise, though he did head up a theme-park attraction with 3D visuals in 1999. After the collapse of Carolco in the mid-1990s, the studio's co-founders Mario Kassar and Andrew Vajna returned with a new company, C2, through which it made 2009's *Terminator 3: Rise of the Machines*. Once again starring Arnold Schwarzenegger, it featured newcomer Kristanna Loken as a female Terminator sent back to kill John Connor (yes, again), now a twenty-something loner played by Nick Stahl. Director Jonathan Mostow attempted to channel the spirit of Cameron's sleek, kinetic film-making in this latest chase saga, but something was missing: perhaps it was the absence of Linda Hamilton (Sarah Connor had died between sequels), or maybe it was the lack of really new ideas – the new Terminator is pretty much the same as Robert Patrick's T-1000, albeit with a skeletal chassis beneath the liquid metal. Whatever it is, a sense of murky inevitability settled over the franchise again from *T3* onwards. In *T2*, Cameron made it clear that there was 'no fate but what we make for ourselves'; in the movies that came after his tenure, Judgment Day is inescapable – it can no longer be stopped, only post-poned. This means that mankind is fated to wrestle with machines for as long as the *Terminator* franchise remains profitable, hence such sequels as 2008's *Terminator Salvation* (released by Sony), a short-lived TV series, *The Sarah Connor Chronicles* and 2015's *Terminator: Genisys*, released by Paramount. The latter once again brought back Schwarzenegger as a T-800 with weathered skin; the cyborg insisted that he was 'old but not obsolete'; audiences, it seemed, were less sure, and the response was tepid to say the least.

In 2019, the rights to the *Terminator* franchise, having been a bargaining chip since the late 1980s, return to James Cameron. Whether he'll have the inspiration to rework the nightmare he created for a new generation remains to be seen. For now, the *Terminator* series is a little like Sarah Connor at the end of the 1984 film: on a dusty road that stretches off to an uncertain future.

THE REAL SKYNET

Don't trust your computer. Keep a beady eye on your smartphone. If you believe some of the more alarmist sci-fi movies made over the past few decades, the machines are biding their time, waiting for just the right moment to turn against their human masters. In *Colossus: The Forbin Project* (1970), a military computer becomes sentient and makes a bid for world domination. Yul Brynner's robot cowboy terrorises a theme park in writer-director Michael Crichton's *Westworld* (1973), anticipating another of Crichton's cautionary fables – *Jurassic Park* (see Chapter 24). In the sordid sci-fi horror *Demon Seed*

(1977), adapted from the novel by Dean Koontz, Julie Christie is menaced by an AI program that takes over all the gadgets in her high-tech house. Christie's character, Mrs Harris, is eventually impregnated by the machine intelligence, named Proteus Four, and gives birth to a bizarre human–machine hybrid. Less physically invasive, but no less terrifying, is the notion that machines might one day trigger a nuclear war, either by accident (as in 1983's *WarGames*) or with the express intention of wiping out humanity (*The Terminator* and its sequels).

None of this is to say that machine takeovers have to be hostile; in his first novel, *Player Piano*, Kurt Vonnegut depicts a post-war future where mechanisation has taken over most of the jobs once carried out by humans. Society is divided between an affluent management class, who oversee the machines that run everything, and the dispossessed former workers, who live a comfortable yet directionless existence. Although published in 1952, *Player Piano's* theme is still pertinent in the twenty-first century. In April 2017, a study emerged that predicted that we're on the cusp of what it called Industry 4.0: an era where human labour will be routinely undercut by machines and computer systems – even in developing countries that currently thrive on the output of cheap workforces.*

Robots in factories, driverless cars and drones are all technologies that could eventually replace human jobs: taxi drivers and couriers, soldiers, labourers or secretaries. We're already seeing how quickly a new technological innovation can change an entire industry – robots have been used in the automotive industry for decades, for example. The smartphone app, Uber, has created an entire network of cheap transport, much to the chagrin of professional taxi drivers the world over. In the military, the last few years have seen the increased use of unmanned aircraft; in 2012, a report revealed that one in three aircraft in the US Air Force was a drone.

Gradually, these advances have filtered into genre cinema and television. The British TV series *Black Mirror*, the brainchild of writer Charlie Brooker,

---

* See: https://www.theguardian.com/technology/2017/apr/04/innovation-in-ai-could-see-governments-introduce-human-quotas-study-says.

casts a satirical and often disturbing eye over the rise of smartphones, digital surveillance and videogames. *Terminator: Genisys* (2015) reworked James Cameron's tech noir for the Web 2.0 era, with the human-hating artificial intelligence Skynet revealed to have its origins in a cross-platform operating system; unwittingly, our species hastens its demise by downloading the latest, must-have piece of software.

The notion that a dangerous new technology might present itself as a protector is a prevalent one in modern sci-fi. In the superhero sequel *Captain America: The Winter Soldier* (2014), an initiative called Project Insight is described as a breakthrough in counter-terrorism by American Secretary of Defence Alexander Pierce (Robert Redford). Connected to the planet's satellite systems, Insight is a hovering weapons system designed to eliminate terrorist threats before they can emerge. It soon becomes clear that Insight is about to be used for a much more fascistic purpose: killing political opponents before they can become a nuisance. Insight is, in short, a military drone on steroids.

'It's a serious issue,' says director José Padilha, whose 2014 *RoboCop* remake dealt with the use of military drones. 'You can think about it like, if America pulled out of Vietnam because soldiers were dying, if robots were there instead, what would have happened? It's true that the automation of violence opens the door to fascism. And it's a real, serious issue. I think in 10, 20 or 30 years, countries are going to start talking about legislation, where they're going to have to decide whether they should allow robots to kill people, or allow law enforcement to become automated.'[*]

Indeed, some academics are already arguing that new laws will need to be brought in to address the rise of automation, both in the military and elsewhere. In 2012, a report called *Losing Humanity: The Cast Against Killer Robots* lobbied for the pre-emptive ban of autonomous weapons – that is, machines that can select and open fire on targets independently from a human

---

[*] See: http://www.denofgeek.com/movies/jose-padilha/29178/jose-padilha-interview-robo-cop-elite-squad-philosophy.

operator.* The April 2017 report mentioned above suggested that governments might soon introduce some form of minimum quota for human workers – a means of ensuring that, say, a factory always has some kind of human presence among all the machines.

In the 1940s, sci-fi author Isaac Asimov came up with the Three Laws of Robotics: a set of rules designed to protect humans from harm by intelligent machines. As a new age of technology changes the way we live, work, communicate and even fight wars, it seems increasingly likely that a similar set of rules will be required in the real world.

Selected SF films mentioned in this chapter:
Colossus: The Forbin Project (1970)
Westworld (1973)
Demon Seed (1977)
WarGames (1983)
Captain America: The Winter Soldier (2014)
Terminator: Genisys (2015)

---

* See: https://www.hrw.org/news/2012/11/19/ban-killer-robots-its-too-late.

24. Bringing back the dinosaurs

JURASSIC PARK (1993)

'We spared no expense . . .'

In the summer of 1993, a Hollywood trade paper ran a photograph of Austrian superstar Arnold Schwarzenegger and a dinosaur. Schwarzenegger points over his shoulder at a huge statue of a Tyrannosaurus rex and laughs derisively, thus providing a perfect illustration of that year's cinematic clash of the titans. In one corner there was *Jurassic Park*, directed by Steven Spielberg and adapted from Michael Crichton's bestselling novel of the same name. Billed as '*Jaws* with claws', it was sold on its special effects and potentially awe-inspiring concept: in a twist on Crichton's earlier movie *Westworld*, it was a cautionary tale about a theme park where breakthroughs in DNA technology bring the dinosaurs back from extinction. And this being a Crichton novel, the dinosaurs refuse to stay cooped up for long.

Running against *Jurassic Park* in the summer of 1993 was Schwarzenegger's latest opus, *Last Action Hero*. Spielberg's movie may have had the high concept, but *Last Action Hero* had the star wattage; directed by John McTiernan – who had scored huge hits with *Predator* and *Die Hard* – it was sold as a comedy adventure that satirised the action genre. From the mid-1980s onwards, Schwarzenegger had starred in hit after hit, with *Conan the Barbarian* and *The Terminator* teeing off a string of action vehicles that included McTiernan's *Predator*, dystopian future sport romp *The Running Man* (based on a novel by Stephen King), Paul Verhoeven's *Total Recall* and James Cameron's *Terminator 2*. At the time, there was little reason to assume that *Last Action Hero* wouldn't be another success for the unstoppable Austrian Oak; that summer, the film's marketing campaign made it just about unavoidable – infamously, *Last Action Hero*'s title was even emblazoned on the side of a NASA rocket. But *Jurassic Park*'s advertising spend was, if anything, even more ferocious, with Universal stumping up an estimated $65 million on marketing. In the end, *Jurassic Park*'s cutting-edge special effects and dinosaurs proved to be the most magnetic draw; as *Last Action Hero* fizzled, *Jurassic Park* soared, besting Spielberg's *E.T. The Extra-Terrestrial* as the highest-grossing movie of all time.

In adapting Crichton's book for the screen, co-writer David Koepp excised some of its gorier and frightening moments – including graphic descriptions of velociraptors disembowelling their victims with razor-sharp claws – and repositioned the movie as an adventure story with a sci-fi horror edge. Richard Attenborough plays billionaire industrialist John Hammond who, with his army of scientists, has managed to create his own Lost World on the remote Isla Nublar somewhere in the Pacific. As a group of visitors – among them investors, scientists and Hammond's grandchildren – arrives to take an early look at Jurassic Park's attractions, an attempt at corporate espionage leaves the island's security fences disabled. Before long, the entire place is overrun by toothsome predators.

Following in the tradition of animators Willis O'Brien and Ray Harryhausen, *Jurassic Park* pushed visual effects into startling new arenas. Initially, stop-motion veteran Phil Tippett intended to bring the film's menagerie of T-rexes, velociraptors and other extinct creatures to life using computer-controlled, animated puppets. Ultimately, however, a new technique was conceived, in which Tippett used something called a 'Dinosaur Input Device' – a puppet that could be physically manipulated by an animator, and its resulting movements mapped onto a digital model of the dinosaur on a computer. Industrial Light & Magic then spent approximately six months developing the film's sixty-three digital effects shots.

Like *Terminator 2* before it, the number of digital effects sequences in *Jurassic Park* was relatively small by twenty-first-century standards, with Stan Winston's full-sized creature effects used in a far greater number of shots; of the fourteen minutes of dinosaur footage in the movie, nine of them were achieved in this manner. The overall result, however, was almost seamless: in those two-or-so hours, it really did look as though dinosaurs had returned from the grave – not through genetic manipulation, but through CGI. *Jurassic Park* marked another step on the technique's evolutionary ladder; where *Terminator 2* used computers to create the illusion of one form morphing to another, *Jurassic Park* proved that a creature made from pixels could look believably realistic, even when placed next to a flesh-and-blood actor.

Jurassic Park therefore heralded not only the birth of a new franchise – one that is still going, with 2015's *Jurassic World* rebooting the series to money-spinning effect – but also sparked a new generation of effects-driven action and adventure movies. Just as breakthroughs in animatronics and makeup effects led to such films as *The Thing* and *An American Werewolf in London* in the 1980s, *Jurassic Park* hastened a revolution that was even more far-reaching: suddenly, it seemed as though just about anything was possible with a little imagination and a lot of processing power.

One filmmaker inspired by *Jurassic Park* was George Lucas, who had founded ILM way back in 1977. He saw those majestic shots of diplodocuses striding across Isla Nublar and began thinking again about his old *Star Wars* franchise; with this new digital technology, he reasoned, he could finally create the fantasy worlds he had struggled to realise through old-fashioned filmmaking. Within two years of *Jurassic Park*'s release, Lucas began work on his first *Star Wars* film in more than a decade: what would eventually become *Star Wars Episode I: The Phantom Menace*.

Between them, *T2*, *Jurassic Park* and 1999's *The Matrix* (see Chapter 26) ushered in a new era of mainstream filmmaking. Techniques such as matte painting, rear projection, miniature effects and prosthetics had evolved, certainly, but the basic technology behind them had remained almost unchanged since the birth of cinema. The digital blockbusters of the 1990s heralded a new kind of movie-making: matte paintings, creature effects, colour grading and even the composition of entire scenes would soon be adjustable on a computer. Phil Tippett, who had worked in visual effects for nearly twenty years by 1993, looked at *Jurassic Park*'s digital dinosaurs and joked that he would soon be out of a job. Today, Tippett's studio has long since branched out to the digital arena.

Jurassic Park also proved that a film could be a major blockbuster without an expensive star attached to it. In *Jurassic Park*, the dinosaurs were the star. The *Jurassic Park* logo became ubiquitous in 1993, appearing on lunch boxes and T-shirts and toys, just like the *Star Wars* emblem over fifteen years earlier. The success of *Jurassic Park*, and the failure of *Last Action Hero*, represented a marked shift in audience appetites; once again, Spielberg had inadvertently fostered a new breed of hit movie – visual, preferably PG-13 rated, and marketable all over the planet.

The shockwaves from *Jurassic Park's* thunderous arrival are still being felt today. Colourful, effects-filled movies, from Marvel to *Star Wars* to Disney's live-action remakes of its old animated classics, are reliably successful at the box office. Hollywood still has its highly paid movie stars, but they frequently struggle to compete with the power of a brand; in the autumn of 2016, the sci-fi romance *Passengers*, starring Jennifer Lawrence and Chris Pratt, failed to make itself heard above the marketing bluster of Disney-Lucasfilm's *Star Wars* spin-off, *Rogue One*.

Digital filmmaking has now matured to the point where young, up-and-coming directors can make their own answer to *Jurassic Park*, even on a tiny budget. Before he emerged in Hollywood as the director of *Godzilla* (2014) and *Star Wars: Rogue One*, Gareth Edwards – a thirty-something filmmaker from Nuneaton – made *Monsters*, a road-trip creature feature set in a Central America overrun by giant beasts from outer space. Edwards shot the film guerrilla-style, with handheld cameras and largely improvised performances from his small cast. When he got back to the UK, Edwards created the visual effects himself for just a few thousand dollars; as he later commented in interviews, anyone with enough money could walk into a shop and buy a laptop with more processing power than the computers used to create the dinosaurs in *Jurassic Park*.

The plummeting price of computers, free editing software and the advent of streaming video sites like YouTube and Vimeo have all contributed to a climate where a young filmmaker can – in theory – create a movie on a tiny budget. Where expensive pieces of equipment like Super-8 cameras were once the preserve of kids from affluent families – Kubrick, Spielberg or J. J. Abrams, say – digital movie-making means that a budding filmmaker from far outside the Hollywood system can put a monster movie on YouTube and wind up with a successful career in the United States. This is exactly what happened to Uruguay's Fede Álvarez, who in 2009 uploaded a sci-fi short called *Ataque de Pánico!* to YouTube. Within weeks, he had been signed up by Sam Raimi's production company Ghost House Pictures, and wound up directing a reboot of *Evil Dead*, released in 2013.

The digital revolution has, therefore, resulted in two very different outcomes. At one end of the movie-making spectrum, the rising number of effects shots in movies means that a summer film can cost hundreds of millions of dollars, with work farmed out to multiple VFX studios to keep up the pace. But at the other end, advances in technology have fostered a climate that would have seemed like science fiction to the filmmakers of the 1970s. The critically acclaimed 2015 drama *Tangerine* was shot entirely on an iPhone. Today, anyone with a smartphone and a story to tell can make their own *Jurassic Park*.

RETURN OF THE MONSTER MOVIE

The popularity of *Jurassic Park* opened the floodgates in Hollywood, and a new wave of monster movies came rolling forth. In the 1998 remake of *Godzilla*, modern masters of disaster Roland Emmerich and Dean Devlin brought the Japanese film company Toho's atomic *kaiju* across the Pacific for a tour of Manhattan. Hollywood producers were trying to gain the rights to *Godzilla* before the release of *Jurassic Park*, yet the resulting film was clearly riding in the slipstream of Spielberg's blockbuster. The rather soulless giant reptile bore more of a resemblance to *Jurassic Park*'s T-rex than the majestic beast in *Godzilla* and, more curiously still, it lay eggs from which snapping, velociraptor-like mini-zillas hatched to terrorise the residents of New York. Worst of all, the film lacked the emotional gravitas of Ishiro Honda's 1954 original or the camp appeal of its sequels.

A much smarter entry in the 1990s monster-movie cycle came from Mexican director Guillermo del Toro, who had come to Hollywood's attention thanks to his ingenious vampire horror, *Cronos* (1993). Del Toro's English-language debut, *Mimic* (1997) was compromised from the start by a meddling studio, yet it's still a satisfying twist on the B-movie staples established by such 1950s films as *Them!* (1954) and *Tarantula* (1955). A deadly epidemic is cured with the help of a new breed of genetically modified cockroaches, but what scientist Susan Tyler (Mira Sorvino) hasn't reckoned on is that these new critters would escape into the sewers of New York and mutate into human-sized, predatory monsters. Del Toro takes this basic idea (adapted from a short story by Donald A. Wollheim) and spins out a sci-fi horror tale full of the rich imagery for which he's now known; the roaches have the ability to pass themselves off as human by wrapping their wings around themselves, thus taking on the silhouette of a tall man in a long coat. A sequence where Tyler encounters one of these figures on an otherwise deserted subway, its 'coat' unfurling into huge, black wings, is a masterful rug-pull moment.

Del Toro also planned for the movie to be more than a straight cautionary horror; the ending he originally devised had the cockroaches survive and vanish among the population of Manhattan – the implication being that they're still out there somewhere, evolving and slowly taking over the Earth. This ending was later dropped in favour of a more straightforwardly happy conclusion; a director's cut of *Mimic*, released in 2010, brought the movie closer to del Toro's original vision, yet the full version of his chilling story is still sadly lost.

Other monster movies of the 1990s revelled in their B-movie status. Director Peter Hyams's *Relic* (1997) pitted Tom Sizemore and Penelope Ann Miller against a Rhino-like monster running around in Chicago's Natural History Museum. Called the Kothoga, the beast is a lizard–insect hybrid from South America, which feasts on the brains of its human victims. The film was a curious departure for Hyams, who had made such smart genre films as *Capricorn One*, *Outland* and *2010*, and it's mostly memorable for Stan Winston's creature design, its eclectic cast and its writing team; husband and wife co-writers Rick Jaffa and Amanda Silver went on to write the new *Planet of the Apes* movies for 20th Century Fox.

One of the smartest monster movies of the new millennium came from South Korea. Directed by Bong Joon-ho, *The Host* (2006), sees a fearsome creature rise from the polluted Han river in Seoul. As the amphibious beast attacks the city's population, the story follows a humble shopkeeper (played by Korean star Song Kang-ho) as he tries to track down his missing daughter, snatched by the creature during one of its rampages. Like *Godzilla* half a century earlier, *The Host* is inspired by a real event in which a surgeon working for the US military released 20 gallons of formaldehyde into the Han river – an incident that prompted minor protests and a swift public apology from an American lieutenant general.* An almost identical spillage creates the toxic monster in *The Host*, leading the American military to use a similarly damaging chemical – a fictionalised version of Agent Orange – in a vain attempt to kill it. Bong's film is, in short, an environmentalist satire where the dumping of toxic waste begets monsters.

The Host is but one example of how the monster movie can be manipulated to explore all kinds of themes; *Cloverfield* (2008), directed by Matt Reeves, taps into post-9/11 traumas. *Monsters* (2010) is about our collective indifference to human suffering; in a strangely prescient image, director Gareth Edwards has the United States build a wall between North and Central America – all the better to keep the *kaiju* at bay. *Colossal* (2017), directed by Nacho Vigalondo and starring Anne Hathaway, is an offbeat tale of alcoholism and disillusionment. Beneath the destruction and chaos, the meanings behind these big-screen monsters are as colourful and varied as the creatures themselves.

Selected SF films mentioned in this chapter:

Mimic (1997)

Relic (1997)

Godzilla (1998)

The Host (2006)

Cloverfield (2008)

Monsters (2010)

Colossal (2017)

---

* See: http://www.waterworld.com/articles/2000/07/us-military-apologizes-for-formalde-hyde-release-in-s-korea.html.

25. Appetite for destruction

INDEPENDENCE DAY (1996)

'Now that's what I call a close encounter.'

On one of his regular strolls through the countryside of Woking, British author H. G. Wells imagined what might happen if an alien armada descended from Mars. That reverie formed the bedrock for *The War of the Worlds*, the defining alien-invasion novel which, in time, would inspire a whole sub-genre of movies about cold-hearted imperialists from outer space.

A century later, German filmmaker Roland Emmerich began thinking about making an invasion movie of his own. Emmerich's writer-producer partner Dean Devlin, with whom he had recently made the sci-fi fantasy romp *Stargate* (1994), was initially unimpressed by the prospect, and argued that the whole invasion genre was thoroughly played out. Like H. G. Wells before him, however, Emmerich had a single, arresting image coalescing in his mind. Emmerich called Devlin over and pointed at the city buildings outside his window; imagine, Emmerich said, a huge alien ship looming up over those skyscrapers, its shadow plunging the city into darkness. Forget the quaint-looking flying saucers of old – these invaders flew around in ships the size of Central Park.

This was the genesis of *Independence Day*, the bombastic summer block-buster that revived not only the invasion sub-genre but also the disaster movie – a genre that had risen in the 1960s and fallen out of fashion again by the early 1980s. Like the films of director and producer Irwin Allen – nicknamed 'the master of disaster' – *Independence Day* introduced an ensemble cast of characters from all walks of life: pilots, scientists, an exotic dancer, even the

President of the United States. As in Allen's disaster movies, trying to figure out who would live and who would die was as much a part of the entertainment as the explosions and special effects.

Those special effects would pose something of a hurdle for Emmerich's idea of a B-movie on an epic scale. Even with a budget of $75 million, the sheer number of effects shots – reckoned to be around 450 – would stretch the studio's coffers to the limit. *Terminator 2* and *Jurassic Park* had hastened a revolution in CGI, yet digital effects were still extraordinarily expensive; one producer put the bill at a horrifying $150,000 per shot. But Emmerich had a secret weapon: back in his native Germany, his teacher at film school had proved to be something of a genius when it came to generating effects on a shoestring budget; Volker Engel had worked with Emmerich on his first feature film, the low-budget sci-fi curio *Moon 44* (1990). To keep costs on *Independence Day* down, Engel pulled together a team of young German film students, and spent several months in a disused aircraft hangar, building scale models of cities, alien ships and their bug-eyed occupants. Ultimately, Engel succeeded in making *Independence Day*'s effects shots for the bargain price of $40,000 each.

There was one special effects shot in particular that had executives at 20th Century Fox rather concerned. In a rough cut of the live-action and effects footage that would eventually be used in the movie's teaser trailer, one sequence showed the White House explode in a blaze of green lasers and crimson fire. It was a disturbing image, the producers thought; perhaps even sacrilegious, like burning the nation's flag.

'It's all great,' Emmerich was told, 'but can you not blow up the White House in the teaser?'

'Well,' Emmerich replied, 'it's in the movie.'

'Yeah, Roland,' Fox executives replied, 'but you're not American. You have to understand this is a very touchy issue.'*

Nevertheless, Emmerich lobbied to keep the shot in the trailer, arguing that it was the disturbing quality that made the scene so effective: it was a

---

* See: http://www.denofgeek.com/uk/movies/roland-emmerich/41605/roland-emmerich-interview-independence-day-resurgence.

simple yet powerful image of the aliens' might. They can hit us where we live.

Independence Day's marketing would prove vital to its success. Aside from Will Smith, who was best known as the star of TV series *The Fresh Prince of Bel-Air*, and character-actor Jeff Goldblum, *Independence Day* didn't have the kind of banner name that could open a picture – like *Jurassic Park* before it, the film relied on the draw of its concept and the quality of its special effects. To this end, Fox spent an unprecedented sum of money on *Independence Day*'s promotion, with $1.3 million spent on airing a single trailer during the 1996 Super Bowl. The exploding White House would prove to be the centrepiece in the film's $24 million marketing drive.

Independence Day was sold as the must-see movie of the summer, and audiences duly flocked to see it. Critics, however, were harder to win over, and widely railed against its stereotypical characters and thuddingly obvious dialogue. An *LA Times* writer dubbed the film 'The Day the Script Stood Still';* another lamented that *Independence Day* was a symbol of everything wrong with the new crop of 1990s blockbusters: glib, devoid of subtext and, perhaps worst of all, cynically aware of its own ephemeral nature.

Where such films as *Raiders of the Lost Ark* and *Star Wars* were praised for bringing old matinee serials into the twentieth century, *Independence Day* was dismissed as a throwback: a pair of genres from the 1950s and 1970s slammed together to make a movie high on sound and fury but low on intelligence. It's certainly a wonder why the invasion movie would make a reappearance at a relatively prosperous time in American history. When flying saucers were last seen buzzing about over US landmarks in the 1950s, they were an emblem of Cold War fears and a reassuring demonstration of American military power; almost without exception, the invaders were repelled in the end. *Independence Day*, on the other hand, plays down the fear factor and dials up the bravery, ingenuity and fortitude of the United States. Emmerich's film may see alien ships hover over the entire planet, yet it's almost exclusively an American movie; the plight of other countries is effectively reduced to a series of

---

* See: http://articles.latimes.com/1996-07-02/entertainment/ca-20348_1_independence-day.

eye-rollingly clichéd cameos. With a charismatic president in the real White House – Bill Clinton – and the economy riding high after a recession in the early 1990s, *Independence Day* served as a monument to the country's prestige and confidence.

There are signs here and there, though, that Emmerich isn't taking the film's jingoism all that seriously; the rousing speech delivered by President Thomas J. Whitmore (Bill Pullman) is served up with a generous side order of ham and cheese. The melodrama, colour and self-aware humour ('Now that's what I call a close encounter,' Will Smith quips after punching an alien) might suggest that Emmerich is attempting to make something approaching big-screen Pop Art. (The unsubtle use of all-American imagery certainly has an air of Andy Warhol about it, and Emmerich himself is an avid collector of icono-clastic artwork.)

Independence Day's conclusion, which is either amusing or cringe-inducing depending on how you look at it, appears to be a playful riff on *The War of the Worlds*. In Wells's story, the aliens are eventually thwarted by their delicate immune systems. In *Independence Day*, they are defeated by a computer virus – a plot development that still leaves computer geeks groaning into their popcorn to this day.

By a strange quirk of Hollywood synchronicity, *Independence Day* wasn't the only alien-invasion movie to hit cinemas in 1996. Directed by Tim Burton, *Mars Attacks!* was an anarchic disaster-comedy inspired by an infamously violent set of trading cards from the 1950s. Featuring a much starrier cast than *Independence Day*, with Jack Nicholson rubbing shoulders with Glenn Close, Pierce Brosnan and even Tom Jones, *Mars Attacks!* offered a more withering view of American might, with its array of military leaders and politicians depicted as a bunch of arrogant neurotics who deserve everything the aliens can throw at them. An affectionate homage to many of the same 1950s movies that *Independence Day* freely referenced, *Mars Attacks!* was an unexpected misfire; audiences, it seemed, couldn't quite get on board with Burton's wilfully gaudy spectacle.

With the benefit of hindsight, *Independence Day* could be seen as a fulcrum in expensive summer movies, both pointing backwards to such movies as

Earth vs the Flying Saucers and *Earthquake*, and ahead to the effects-led, franchise blockbusters of the new millennium. From a technical standpoint, *Independence Day* was one of the last movies to extensively use practical special effects, yet its scenes of city-wide destruction would have a lasting impact on such directors as Michael Bay and Zack Snyder.

Bay's 2007 film *Transformers*, a live-action take on Hasbro's line of toy robots, contains all kinds of ideas from the Emmerich playbook. It's an alien invasion movie and a disaster flick, with giant robots laying waste to entire city blocks. It has an ensemble cast ranging from soldiers to CIA agents to an awkward teenager, played by Shia LaBeouf. As with *Independence Day*, the cocktail of destruction and upbeat, sometimes puerile humour would prove to be intoxicating to audiences – and baffling to film critics. To date, *Transformers* and its numerous sequels have pulled in over $3.7 billion.

The tragic attacks of 11 September 2001 cast *Independence Day*'s events in a new light. For a generation of Americans, the notion that a foreign invader could cause shocking damage and loss of life in its cities was no longer abstract: after the attack on the World Trade Center, it was part of the here and now.

As the George W. Bush administration embarked on its War on Terror, audiences became increasingly attracted to escapism in their movies. In film after film, we've seen America's cities devastated by outside forces but, in every instance, there's a force for good standing between us and the invaders. From 2007's *Iron Man* onwards, Marvel Studios' superhero movies have provided the certainty lacking in the real world. *The Avengers* (2011) sees a team of heroes battling aliens in downtown Manhattan. Huge parts of the city are razed, yet, like *Independence Day*, goodness prevails, and evil is faced down with a smile and a wry quip.

When director Zack Snyder stepped in to bring Superman into the post-9/11 era, he too appeared to draw on *Independence Day*'s template. *Man of Steel* (2013) is another alien-invasion movie, which this time sees Superman (Henry Cavill) fighting the despotic General Zod (Michael Shannon) and his super-powered cohorts from the planet Krypton. Zod plans to use something called a World Engine to turn Earth into a planet habitable by his species, leading to the film's own equivalent of the exploding White House in *Independence Day*.

The World Engine floats astride the city of Metropolis – a fictionalised Manhattan – repeatedly sucking buildings up into the sky and slamming them down again. It's akin to watching the Twin Towers collapse over and over, like a film clip played on repeat.

By 2016, images of splintering buildings threatened to become a cliché of summer movies. Roland Emmerich belatedly returned to the invasion genre with *Independence Day: Resurgence* that year, which saw a new generation of pilots and scientists face an even greater threat from another world. But where *Independence Day* was a novelty twenty years earlier, *Resurgence* was but one genre film in a summer season full of them by 2016. Against the might of such franchise films as *Batman v Superman: Dawn of Justice*, *Suicide Squad* and *Captain America: Civil War*, *Resurgence* struggled to make itself heard above the din. Ironically, Emmerich found his movie upstaged by the brand of larger-than-life spectacle he had helped create.

In the 1990s, the high-concept movie was king; in the 2000s, the franchise had replaced it. The heroes of *Independence Day: Resurgence* managed to repel another invasion, but even their bravery couldn't match the brand recognition of Marvel and DC.

THE SCIENCE OF DISASTER

Stories of disaster are as old as storytelling itself, from the world floods in the Bible and other religious texts to the sinking of Atlantis. We may no longer believe that earthquakes are caused by dragons stirring beneath our feet or that comets are a portent of doom, but our fear and awe of tsunamis, meteor strikes and volcanic eruptions remain undimmed – at least if you believe recent cinema history.

One particular strand of genre cinema deals – either seriously or otherwise – with how science might attempt to save our species from acts of God. *When Worlds Collide* (1951) was a glossy, somewhat thin updating of the Noah and the Ark myth; as a heavenly body from outside our own solar system is discovered to be on a collision course with our planet, scientists construct a rocket designed to carry our best and brightest to the safety of a new world. With seats on the ship limited to say the least, lots are drawn to select the lucky passengers. Needless to say, the outside world doesn't take kindly to this, and mass riots take place around the rocket's launch pad. Slow-moving and stiffly acted, *When Worlds Collide*'s final act brings with it a shot of the assembled survivors on board the ship; all appear to be Caucasian – something a movie would rightly be taken to task for today.

A cheaper but more intelligent film hailed from the UK – a country not commonly associated with the disaster genre. *The Day the Earth Caught Fire* (1961), shot in black-and-white and partly tinted a broiling orange, imagines that repeated nuclear tests have caused our planet's temperature to soar to deadly levels; scientists scramble to reverse the effect, and the world can only look on with baited breath. Unusually, *The Day the Earth Caught Fire* is told not from the perspective of scientists or the military, but hard-drinking, heavy-smoking journalists. It gives the film an unusually grounded, low-key feel, and while it's short on the crashes and bangs of American disaster movies, its dialogue and performances really crackle. The movie also ends on an eerily ambiguous note.

The 1970s cycle of hit disaster movies prompted the making of *Meteor* (1979), a sub-Irwin Allen thriller starring Sean Connery as part of a panic-stricken ensemble awaiting the arrival of a colossal meteorite. An orbiting missile system, the Hercules, is despatched to blast the giant rock into atoms; the complete destruction of Earth is averted, but the slivers of debris left behind spark a string of unconvincing miniature cities to be pounded by fire and waves.

Disaster films were on the wane by the 1980s, but one or two genre pieces kept the flame burning. Perhaps the funniest of the era was *Starflight One* (1983), a TV movie given a theatrical release in the UK. Lee Majors stars as the cool-headed pilot of a new passenger jet capable of flying in Earth's upper atmosphere. Predictably, disaster strikes, and flailing attempts are made to get the cast to safety. The acting is wooden, the effects don't bear up to scrutiny, but *Starflight One* retains a retro, goofy charm. Majors eventually manages to successfully guide his wayward plane safely back to terra firma, which makes a complete mockery of its subtitle: *The Plane that Couldn't Land*.

As digital effects made scenes of city-wide destruction more convincing than ever, the disaster movie made an unexpected return. The late 1990s saw Earth battered by not one but two deadly meteors, as rival Hollywood studios pitted their films against each other. First came director Mimi Leder's *Deep Impact*, which emerged in 1998. The US government tries in vain to hide an impending ELE (Extinction Level Event); when word gets out, the news is greeted with a mixture of terror and philosophising. Michael Bay's *Armageddon* followed that same summer, starring Bruce Willis and Ben Affleck as a pair of drilling experts blasted into space to destroy an asteroid 'the size of Texas'. There are heroics, Russian stereotypes and Aerosmith wailing on the soundtrack.

Movies about disaster from above and below persisted well into the new millennium, as *The Core* (2003) took the *Armageddon* template and combined it with Jules Verne's *Journey to the Centre of the Earth*. Our planet's core has ceased turning, increasing our species' exposure to deadly solar radiation; meanwhile, in a standout scene, a huge flock of confused pigeons causes mass panic in London's Trafalgar Square.

To combat the threat, an affordable ensemble cast – Hilary Swank, Aaron Eckhart, Stanley Tucci – clambers inside a large drilling machine to bore down and get the core going again. If it sounds daft, then wait until you see it; even the effects team couldn't take the story seriously, if one shot's anything to go by – look closely, and you can see a large, raw trout hitting a London café window among all the stuffed pigeons.

Scientific accuracy didn't appear to be top of the agenda in Roland Emmerich's *The Day After Tomorrow* (2004), where Earth is left frozen by a new Ice Age – there's much peril and bravery, but the plot and acting are secondary to the special effects. Five years later, Emmerich returned with what might be his magnum opus of disaster, *2012* (2009). As predicted by the Mayans, that year brings with it an event capable of extinguishing all of humanity: 'The neutrinos,' a scientist explains with a gasp, 'have mutated!'

The cod-scientific jargon is an excuse for a series of earthquakes, volcanic eruptions and tidal waves, making *2012* a bumper compendium of cataclysmic events. This time, John Cusack's the hero charged with keeping his family one step ahead of danger, as a team of scientists launches a flotilla of massive arks out of dry dock.

These are, of course, the very definition of goofy, audience-pleasing multi-plex fodder, but not all disaster films are so purely action-driven. *Children of Men* (2006), directed by Alfonso Cuarón and based on the novel by P. D. James, is a sober and breathtakingly shot thriller that sees humanity threat-ened not by an act of God, but by an infertility epidemic. As our dwindling society shuffles into chaos and despair, the protagonist, Theo (Clive Owen), is charged with protecting a heavily pregnant young woman (Clare-Hope Ashitey) – perhaps humanity's last hope for survival. More than a decade later, *Children of Men*'s depiction of a Britain on the brink of collapse feels chillingly plausible.

Maverick filmmaker Lars von Trier's *Melancholia* (2011), meanwhile, uses a disaster to tell a deeply personal story about depression and inner resolve. It borrows the central concept from *When Worlds Collide*: a planet, Melancholia, is on a collision course with Earth. At an upmarket country retreat, a blackly depressive young woman (Kirsten Dunst) calmly faces the end as her more 'balanced' sibling (Charlotte Gainsbourg) begins to quake with fear. It's an individual, operatic and sometimes darkly funny movie – look out for German character-actor Udo Kier as an incandescent wedding planner. Like *The Day the Earth Caught Fire* before it, *Melancholia* proves that disaster movies can provoke thought as well as thrill the senses.

Selected SF films mentioned in this chapter:
When Worlds Collide (1951)
The Day the Earth Caught Fire (1961)
Meteor (1979)
Starflight One (1983)
Mars Attacks! (1996)
Deep Impact (1998)
Armageddon (1998)
The Core (2003)

The Day After Tomorrow (2004)
Children of Men (2006)
Transformers (2007)
2012 (2009)
Melancholia (2011)
Man of Steel (2013)

26. Through the looking glass

THE MATRIX (1999)

*'You take the red pill, you stay in Wonderland and I
show you how deep the rabbit-hole goes.'*

In the late 1990s, a pair of young filmmakers were pitching Hollywood producer Joel Silver their idea for a highly unusual science-fiction film. It would take in a dystopian future, a simulated version of the present, squid-like sentient robot overlords, kung fu, philosophy and guns – lots and lots of guns. To illustrate what their movie could look like, the filmmakers sat Silver down and showed him the Japanese animated feature, *Ghost in the Shell* (1995).

'They showed me this Japanese cartoon,' Silver recalled in a *Making Of* documentary about the film, 'and they said, "We want to do that for real." '*

And that's exactly what the Wachowskis did.

Born in the 1960s, Andy and Larry Wachowski were steeped in the culture of manga, anime and the fluid fight scenes of Hong Kong cinema. They recognised something unique about comics and animation: their ability to manipulate time and space. In a fight between two characters, a single second could be stretched out over several pages or extended to a minute of slow-motion footage; shorn from the limitations of cumbersome film cameras, which have to be physically handled by an operator, animation can, in the hands of skilled artists, show a continuous stream of movement. Consider the opening motorcycle sequence in *Akira* (see Chapter 22); with animation, director Katsuhiro Otomo pulls off smooth tracking shots that would have

---

* See: *The Making of The Matrix* (1999), https://www.youtube.com/watch?v=8ufqaDx4iuQ.

been unthinkable with the technology available to live-action filmmakers of the 1980s.

The Wachowskis' second feature film, *The Matrix* fuses Western fairy tales, Christian iconography, cyberpunk and myth-making with the visual language of Eastern live-action and animated cinema. It's also a movie for the era of the Sony PlayStation and the growing ubiquity of the internet; it presents a shared, simulated reality that can be hacked and manipulated, just like a video-game. Thanks to movies like *Terminator 2* and *Jurassic Park*, the digital revolution was in full swing by the late 1990s, yet the Wachowskis' use of computer imagery wasn't limited to creating believable creatures or matte backgrounds – rather, they used new innovations in movie-making to make the camera appear to behave like it did in such Japanese animated films as *Akira*, *Ninja Scroll* or director Mamoru Oshii's cyberpunk classic, *Ghost in the Shell*. The Wachowskis' influences, from the writing of Jacques Baudrillard to the heroic bloodshed of John Woo, from anime to *Alice in Wonderland*, all went into a film that would inform the look of American movies for years to come.

Like a Philip K. Dick novel, *The Matrix* is about an everyman who discovers that the world isn't quite as it seems. A programmer and hacking expert, Neo (Keanu Reeves) learns from a mysterious figure, Morpheus (Laurence Fishburne) that what he understands as everyday waking reality is, in fact, a computer simulation. Sentient machines have long since taken over the Earth, enslaved humanity and turned them into a colossal, living battery farm: while the machines suck away our energy, we're kept placated by the Matrix – a shared simulation of the late twentieth century, which leaves us blissfully unaware that we're fleshy batteries trapped in pods. Accepting the call to adventure – illustrated by a Lewis Carroll-like moment involving a choice between a red and a blue pill – Neo escapes the Matrix and awakes to a horrifying reality: a devastated planet patrolled by sentient machines.

The Matrix follows a classic storytelling template that goes right back to ancient myth: a hero journeys into an unknown world and discovers that he's an archetypal Chosen One – a saviour capable of releasing his people from centuries of slavery. Explored at length by such writers as Joseph Campbell and Christopher Vogler, this common narrative – or monomyth, as it's sometimes called – can be seen in everything from Greek myths to *Star Wars* to Harry Potter. *The Matrix* is therefore conventional in terms of story structure; it's in its visual style that it broke new ground. Neo learns how to enter and leave the Matrix at will, and how he can manipulate its physical laws: time can be warped, allowing Neo to dodge bullets in flight or perform gravity-defying kicks and jumps.

To create *The Matrix*'s action scenes, the Wachowskis used an inventive mix of traditional and new filmmaking techniques. The use of cables to allow actors to make superhuman leaps and flying kicks was already a common practice in Hong Kong movies by 1999, but it was relatively unheard of in Western cinema; to choreograph *The Matrix*'s fights, the Wachowskis turned to Yuen Woo-ping, the director and stunt coordinator behind such martial arts classics as *Snake in the Eagle's Shadow* (an early hit for Jackie Chan in 1978), *Magnificent Butcher* (starring Chow Yun-fat) and *Iron Monkey* (starring Donnie Yen). Yuen was initially reluctant to take on the project, and stipulated that he wanted the film's actors to undergo weeks of rigorous fight training before the shoot began; he assumed the Wachowskis would baulk at the thought of this and find another coordinator. To his surprise, they agreed.

Yuen's balletic fight scenes alone set *The Matrix* apart from other American action films of its era; equally revolutionary was its camera work, masterminded by visual effects supervisor John Gaeta – a designer and inventor who had worked with Douglas Trumbull earlier in the 1990s. Like Trumbull, Gaeta had the creative ingenuity to use existing technology in a way that had never been seen before; he devised a rig of still cameras arranged around a subject, each taking a picture in sequence. When put together, these still images created the illusion of a camera moving around a single moment: one of *The Matrix*'s most celebrated – and oft-copied – scenes involves Neo leaning backwards to dodge an evil agent's bullets. For a few seconds, time appears to slow to a crawl as the camera orbits Neo's flailing arms. Although slow-motion sequences weren't without precedent, and other filmmakers had explored similar techniques – including French director Michel Gondry, whose 1996 commercial for Smirnoff predated *The Matrix* by three years – it had never been used so dramatically or effectively in a movie before. (Little wonder, then, that *The Matrix* upstaged *Star Wars Episode I: The Phantom Menace* at the Oscars the following year, with John Gaeta among the team that picked up an award for best visual effects.)

The Matrix may have been but one pre-millennial film that explored the nature of reality (1998's *Dark City*, directed by Alex Proyas, shared many similar themes with *The Matrix*, and the Wachowskis even recycled some of that movie's sets) but it was nevertheless one of the most influential films of its era. A pair of sequels, *The Matrix Reloaded* and *The Matrix Revolutions* (both 2003), failed to make the same impact, but thanks to the Wachowskis, the visual language of anime, manga and American comics took root in American cinema. After *The Matrix*, other Hollywood movies clamoured to create gravity-defying fight sequences of their own; with its comic-book imagery and hyper-stylised action, the film hastened a coming wave of Hollywood superhero movies. Just one year later, 20th Century Fox released its first *X-Men* movie, which, like *The Matrix*, used CGI and wirework to create its larger-than-life action. Sony's adaptation of *Spider-Man* followed, and the stage was set for the Marvel Cinematic Universe, established by the release of *Iron Man* in 2007. Take a look at Marvel's psychedelic superhero movie, *Doctor Strange* (2016), and you'll see distinct traces of *The Matrix*'s reality-warping aesthetic.

The Wachowskis' passion for sci-fi and anime continued long after they had left *The Matrix* behind. In 2008, they made a live-action adaptation of the Japanese animated series *Speed Racer*, starring Emile Hirsch and Christina Ricci; four years later, they made *Cloud Atlas* with German director Tom Tykwer – an ambitious rendering of David Mitchell's epic sci-fi novel of interconnected lives spread across centuries. Neither these nor *Jupiter Ascending* (2015), a marriage of Cinderella fairy tale and bombastic space opera, managed to garner the same critical and financial success as their 1999 blockbuster. But even if the Wachowskis never make another film as popular as *The Matrix* again – Warner Bros is currently planning a continuation of the franchise without their involvement – the filmmakers' contribution to mainstream cinema is plain to see. By looking outwards, to the conventions of Hong Kong martial arts films and the language of Japanese animation, the Wachowskis changed the style and pace of Hollywood movies forever.

Virtual reality

'You can't just plug your brain into this machine and not expect to be affected by it,' went a line in 1999's *The Thirteenth Floor*, a noir-ish sci-fi based on Daniel F. Galouye's 1964 novel, *Simulacron-3*. Sci-fi writers like Philip K. Dick, Frederik Pohl and Galouye had been writing about the possibilities of simulated realities for decades, but by the 1980s and 1990s, advancing technology seemed to imply that such a feat might soon be possible. And if science could create a simulated world as real as our own, what might the implications be?

It's the kind of question that science fiction is uniquely placed to answer, whether it's in literature or cinema. In 1982, Steven Lisberger's *Tron* offered up a kind of *Alice in Wonderland* for the time of *Space Invaders* and *Pac-Man*; a digital fantasy where ordinary mortals can enter cyberspace and become powerful heroes. David Cronenberg's *Videodrome*, released that same year, was in many ways a dark reflection of *Tron*: in it, rival corporations battle for the minds of America with mind-bending television signals that blur hallucination and reality. In one prophetic scene, anti-hero Max Renn (James Woods) puts on a special helmet that turns his hallucinations into a vivid virtual world he can explore and touch. That helmet looks uncannily like the virtual reality devices that caught the media's attention in the early 1990s. VR was a breakthrough that might, news reports excitedly told us, assist surgeons during difficult operations or help therapists cure phobias and post-traumatic stress. As it turned out, the processing power of computers in the early 1990s meant that those predictions were a little wide of the mark; the helmets were big and bulky, the graphics in such games as *Dactyl Nightmare* – which worked on a system called Virtuality – jerky and crude.

Nevertheless, VR fired the imaginations of writers and filmmakers throughout the decade, leading to a wave of techno thrillers, such as *The Lawnmower Man* (1992), in which a childlike gardener is turned into a despotic supergenius through VR conditioning. Directed by Brett Leonard, the movie was noteworthy for its extensive use of CGI – including cinema's first all-digital sex scene – though the story around it is, from beginning to end, pure hokum. Nominally based on a short story by Stephen King, the resemblance was so slim (amounting to little more than a title swipe) that King sued to have his name scratched from the credits.

Such mid-1990s thrillers as *Disclosure*, *The Net*, *Johnny Mnemonic*, *Hackers* and *Virtuosity* all dealt with the dangers of bleeding-edge technology in some way or other, whether it was in relatively believable terms (*The Net* was among the first films to deal with the subject of identity theft) or the far-fetched (*Virtuosity* sees a computer-generated serial killer escape into the real world).

Far more intelligent than any of these was *Strange Days* (1995), written by James Cameron and Jay Cox, and directed by Cameron's then-wife Kathryn Bigelow. It's a thriller exploring the social impact of a device that is capable of recording and playing back other people's memories; these can then be saved to disc to be enjoyed as a first-person experience by other users. Like *Videodrome*, *Strange Days* sees a sleazy anti-hero (Ralph Fiennes's Lenny Nero) drawn into a dark web of murder; the violent death of a prostitute is captured on disc, and Lenny discovers that it's all part of a much larger conspiracy. Thrillingly fast-paced, *Strange Days* explores how technology can be used to satisfy some of our nastier and voyeuristic appetites – and the device at the heart of Bigelow's film is all the more disturbing because it seems so plausible.

Whether it was caused by pre-millennial angst or a mere coincidence, the topic of simulated realities became increasingly insistent as the 1990s drew to a close. Released a year before *The Matrix*, Australian director Alex Proyas's sci-fi thriller *Dark City* saw its protagonist wake up in a benighted metropolis, only to discover that it's not really a city at all. Less action-oriented than the Wachowskis' film, its shadowy images and suspense make for a uniquely disturbing film.

As you would expect from a Cronenberg film, 1999's *eXistenZ* is no less unsettling. Like *Tron* and *Videodrome* before it, *eXistenZ* acts as a kind of distorted negative image of *The Matrix*: more measured, more seductive and deeply thought-provoking. In Cronenberg's near future (or is it an alternative present?), videogame technology has become so powerful that it's created a terrorist opposition group – calling themselves Realists – which aims to stamp it out. When game designer Allegra Geller (Jennifer Jason Leigh) shows up at a town hall to show off her latest virtual reality system, she's narrowly saved from assassination by anxious security guard Ted Pikul (Jude Law). The pair flee into the countryside, Allegra carrying the only copy of the experimental game with her.

Through his fleshy, surreal and often bloody images, Cronenberg wonders aloud just where videogame technology might one day take us. As processing power evolves and graphics become ever more realistic, the possibility that we might one day create a digital world indistinguishable from our own begins to feel less and less like science fiction. Such devices as Oculus Rift and PlayStation VR mark a fresh attempt to introduce virtual reality into our living rooms; one day, maybe we'll see videogames as mind-altering as the ones in Cronenberg's *eXistenZ*: simulated environments that are so seductive that, not only would we want to live in them, we might never want to leave.

Meanwhile, such Silicon Valley billionaires as Elon Musk and Sam Altman are continuing the recurring philosophical suggestion that our own waking reality might be a simulation held inside a *Matrix*-style super computer – and if it's a simulation, they say, then maybe it can be hacked.[*] A coming wave of technology may, therefore, not just change the way we live, but fundamentally alter the way we look at reality itself.

Selected SF films mentioned in this chapter:

Tron (1982)

Videodrome (1982)

The Lawnmower Man (1992)

Disclosure (1994)

The Net (1995)

Johnny Mnemonic (1995)

---

[*] See: http://www.newyorker.com/magazine/2016/10/10/sam-altmans-manifest-destiny; https://motherboard.vice.com/en_us/article/there-is-growing-evidence-that-our-universe-is-a-giant-hologram; http://www.independent.co.uk/life-style/gadgets-and-tech/news/elon-musk-ai-artificial-intelligence-computer-simulation-gaming-virtual-reality-a7060941.html.

Hackers (1995)
Virtuosity (1995)
Strange Days (1995)
Dark City (1998)
eXistenZ (1999)
The Thirteenth Floor (1999)

27. Future shock

MINORITY REPORT (2002)

'Everybody runs, Fletch.'

Richard Dreyfuss's Roy Neary gazing up, awestruck, at a twinkling UFO in *Close Encounters of the Third Kind*. The wide-eyed lost alien in *E.T. The Extra-Terrestrial*. Majestic shots of dinosaurs roaming verdant plains in *Jurassic Park*. Steven Spielberg's early sci-fi films are marked out by an infectious sense of wonder in the face of the unknown. Yet Spielberg's maturation as a filmmaker saw him move away from the warm tone of those movies, with his holocaust drama *Schindler's List* (1993) perhaps providing the turning point in his career. While Spielberg continues to make movies for broad audiences, these are frequently interspersed with movies with much grittier, darker themes: *Amistad, The Terminal, Saving Private Ryan, Munich, Bridge of Spies*.

Meanwhile, Spielberg's genre films also began to take on a darker hue in the new millennium. *A.I.: Artificial Intelligence*, based on a short story by Brian Aldiss and originally developed by Spielberg's late friend Stanley Kubrick, mixes its *Pinocchio*-like tale with moments of jolting violence: sentient machines melted by acid, an android abandoned by its human mother. Critics seemed split over the film's merits on its release in 2001; today, the film appears to be undergoing a much-deserved reassessment.

Spielberg's next film was arguably his heaviest sci-fi movie up to that point. Like Paul Verhoeven's *Total Recall* (1990), *Minority Report* is based on a short story by Philip K. Dick – in fact, it was initially considered as a sequel to that hit, with former cinematographer Jan de Bont once attached as its director. By the late 1990s, however, Spielberg had agreed to make the movie with star

Tom Cruise, resulting in one of the most thought-provoking and satisfying genre films in the director's long career.

Like Dick's original story, *Minority Report* imagines a near-future city – New York in the book, Washington, DC in the movie – where murder has been reduced to zero thanks to a new police division called PreCrime. A battery of Precogs – young psychics capable of seeing the future – are used to prevent crimes before they happen, allowing PreCrime's forces to sweep in and make an arrest before a trigger is pulled or a knife is unsheathed. With the scheme a proven success by the year 2054, the US government is on the cusp of rolling PreCrime out to the rest of the country. A society free from homicide appears to beckon.

PreCrime cop John Anderton (Cruise) has an unshakeable faith in the new system – at least until the Precogs predict that Anderton will murder a man named Jim Crow within the next two days. Baffled and horrified, Anderton avoids capture by his former colleagues and tries to find out who framed him for the crime he hasn't yet committed. Key to the mystery is the Minority Report of the title: a record of the rare occasions where the PreCogs' vision of the future hasn't aligned. Publicly, PreCrime is an infallible system, yet the hushed-up existence of a flaw might prove Anderton's innocence – while at the same time destroying the police unit Anderton has spent years helping to build up.

Like *Total Recall*, *Minority Report* uses Dick's story as a springboard for an exciting action movie with lots of special effects. But once again, the author's philosophical ideas and expert blending of genres – here, sci-fi and detective fiction – shine through, and Spielberg lends the film a starker, more sober view of the future than Verhoeven's outlandish neo-brutalism. Written by Jon Cohen and Scott Frank, *Minority Report*'s adapted screenplay cleverly expands the slight tale on which it's based, providing a more thoroughly fleshed-out impression of a future city, while at the same time creating a more detailed arc for the story's lead character.

In fact, *Minority Report* contains one of the most detailed depictions of a future society ever committed to film; rather than emulate the dark, cluttered future of *Blade Runner*, as so many other filmmakers had since 1982, Spielberg assembled a team of scientists, futurists and designers to make their own attempt at predicting the future.

At a Santa Monica hotel in 1999, these experts spent three days holding round-table discussions about the year 2054 and what technological changes it might bring. In many instances, these advances are extrapolations of things that exist in the present: newspapers connected to the web, magnetic cars, advertising that tailors itself to the viewer. Yet many of the gadgets and ideas depicted in *Minority Report* proved to be surprisingly accurate; the sequences where Cruise operates a computer with hand gestures, for example, predate the kind of touch-screen technology we now take for granted on our tablets and mobile phones.

More importantly, *Minority Report* touches on the implications of those technological advances. PreCrime brings with it a host of moral and philosophical questions: the nature of freewill and the implications of arresting someone before they have committed a crime. The movie also raises an important point about faith in new technology; initially, Anderton's belief that PreCrime is the perfect system appears unshakeable. A government representative sent to investigate PreCrime (played by Colin Farrell) questions the legality of arresting people before the fact, to which Anderton replies that the Precogs' visions are as certain and reliable as the laws of gravity. The rest of the movie tests Anderton's faith in PreCrime past breaking point, as he discovers that the Precogs can be manipulated in ways that he hadn't even considered.

Science may not have granted humans paranormal abilities just yet, but the questions raised by *Minority Report* remain pertinent more than fifteen years later. Spielberg's movie came out long before the dawn of Web 2.0, smartphones and social media – Facebook, for example, didn't launch until 2004 – but the film accurately explores how breakthroughs made with the best intentions can have unforeseeable consequences. When Mark Zuckerberg co-founded Facebook to allow users from all over the planet to share pictures, messages and updates about their everyday life, his aim was to create a friendly global community; what Zuckerberg might not have predicted was how other companies might use the data generated from all that shared information.

Shortly after the inauguration of Donald J. Trump as US President in

January 2017, suggestions began to emerge that a British company may have helped push the billionaire candidate to his unexpected victory by using something called psychometrics. In simple terms, psychometrics is a branch of psychology that analyses massive amounts of data – Google search results, the articles or pictures we 'like' and share on Facebook – and uses it to make deductions about an individual's personality. The kind of music someone likes might provide an insight into whether they're an introvert or an extrovert; the kind of news sites they read provides an indication of their political views and how susceptible an individual might be to new ideas.

The story went that the British company was harvesting data from a variety of sources to build up a psychological model of American citizens and how they might vote.* This model could then be used more accurately to target individuals with political messages based on their hopes and fears. Whether the use of so-called Big Data helped Trump win the election or not, the harvesting of personal information is just one example of how a seemingly benign invention like Facebook can be used in ways its creators hadn't intended.

In 2013, a piece of software called PredPol – short for Predictive Policing – was trialled in the UK.† It uses existing data to provide the police with forecasts of when and where crimes might occur. It's a far cry from the crime prevention depicted in *Minority Report*, but it's another example of how a relatively new technology can affect society in unpredictable ways.

A scene in *Minority Report* shows Anderton walking through a shopping precinct, where moving billboards track and target him with personalised messages: buy this beer, wear that item of clothing. Today, we're used to websites showing us adverts based on our search history; what has only recently become clear is just how valuable – and revealing – the virtual footprints we leave behind actually are.

---

* See: http://motherboard.vice.com/read/big-data-cambridge-analytica-brexit-trump.
† See: http://www.predpol.com/how-predpol-works.

CITIES OF THE FUTURE

Time and again, science fiction has explored how cities might be transformed by technology – and how precipitously things could collapse when that technology fails. The twenty-first-century New York of *Soylent Green* (1973) is a living hell of overcrowding and horrible food; the Los Angeles of *Blade Runner* (1982) is a polluted, fading ghost city where only the eccentric, the vulnerable and the unseemly remain. The London in *Children of Men* (2006) is a grey, depressing police state.

In 1927, *Metropolis* was the first film seriously to depict a futuristic city: in the hands of Fritz Lang's model-makers and artists, the city of *Metropolis* is a giant, multi-layered engine of activity. Vehicles and people scurry to and fro among tall, glittering buildings that eclipse much of the sky; the impression is of a city that is at once beautiful and claustrophobic. Like any real-world sprawl, the city of *Metropolis* looks clean and inviting from a distance, but closer inspection reveals the cracks and divisions; the rich live in airy rooftop dwellings while the poor are packed into slums. The skyscrapers stand as a beacon of progress, yet the workers' revolt and the subsequent meltdown of the city's engine rooms reveal how precarious the whole edifice really is.

In 2007, scientists at North Carolina State University and the University of Georgia concluded that, for the first time in history, more people lived in urban than rural areas.* Since the Industrial Revolution, people have flowed from the countryside to cities in search of education and employment; as in *Metropolis*, cities are engines of productivity and movement. Where the cities of the Victorian era were vulnerable to crime, unemployment and disease, the cities of the twenty-first century are comparatively clean, safe and efficient. But from established economic powerhouses like London and New York to relatively new sprawls like Jing-Jin-Ji in China, cities remain a delicate solution to a modern thirst for expansion and growth. Sanitation and disease may

---

* See: https://web.archive.org/web/20090107023453/http://news.ncsu.edu/releases/2007/may/104.html.

no longer be such present issues, but overcrowding, crime and pollution undoubtedly are.

Even in the most utopian-looking urban spaces, imperfections remain. The twenty-first-century city in *Things to Come* (1936) looks like a shining monument to progress from the outside, but within, pockets of its citizens have begun to tire of the thirst for scientific advancement; 'Is there ever to be any age of happiness?' one character moans. 'Is there never to be any rest?' The film's reply is unequivocal: without progress, there is only stagnation.

Often, however, progress leads to decadence and division. In *Rollerball* (1975), a future of corporate-led super states appears to have created a peaceful equilibrium – our warlike tendencies are played out instead on television and in a deadly gladiatorial sport. Yet the peace has come at a price; the corporations reign absolutely, and in this regimented world, there's little room for an individualist like *Rollerball* star Jonathan E. In *The Hunger Games* (2012), America's elites have created what, for the privileged, is something akin to a utopia. The Capitol is a glistening modern city where the clothes are grand and the food's to die for. The rest of Panem's population, packed into pre-industrial Districts, face the possibility of being wiped out in a heartbeat if they step out of line.

From *Metropolis* to *Children of Men*, sci-fi explores the perils of urban malaise and what happens to those left behind by the march of progress. John Carpenter's *Escape from New York* (1981) imagines a Manhattan so uncontrollably corrupted by crime that the US government has opted to build a wall round the entire island and turn it into a prison. In the early 1980s, the image of a crime-ridden New York wasn't necessarily all that far-fetched; in the place of high crime rates, the gentrification of Manhattan, and the rising cost of housing that goes with it, the city has created a separate issue of its own: social cleansing. From New York to London to Shanghai, areas that were once run-down have been replaced by financial districts or luxury apartments for the wealthy; the results are often clean and beautiful-looking from a distance, but as in *Metropolis*, the poor are pushed to the fringes, and the divisions are plain to see.

In Neill Blomkamp's *Elysium* (2013), this division was taken to a satirical extreme. Earth is a polluted dustbowl, and so the wealthy have migrated to an orbiting space station that looks like Beverly Hills with robot servants.

Strip away the magnetic cars, elevated walkways, moving billboard posters and other futuristic gadgets, and the cities in sci-fi films are much like our own. They are a compromise, a means to an end, and constantly in flux. Architects and city planners may do their best to create urban spaces that balance the old and the new, the rich and the poor, the worker and the boss, but creating and maintaining that equilibrium, even with all the scientific breakthroughs at our disposal, remains elusive. Today, new cities are being planned and built all over Africa; a projection published by CNN in 2013 predicted that the number of people living in urban areas will leap from less than 500 million (as recorded in 2009) to more than 1.2 billion by the year 2050.* As cities continue to provide the thrumming engine of modern society, the questions raised by the smartest sci-fi – pollution, social inequality, crime, a rising global population – remain as pertinent as ever.

Selected SF films mentioned in this chapter:

Things to Come (1936)

Soylent Green (1973)

Rollerball (1975)

Escape from New York (1981)

Children of Men (2006)

The Hunger Games (2012)

Elysium (2013)

---

* See: http://edition.cnn.com/2013/05/30/business/africa-new-cities-konza-eko.

28. Inhuman behaviour

DISTRICT 9 (2009)

'He was an honest man, and he didn't deserve any of what happened to him.'

If science fiction deals with the effects technology can have on society, then it also excels in exploring how basic human instincts remain constant. Even as our computers, phones and cars become more efficient and sophisticated, we still haven't managed to evolve away from some of the darker sides of our being. Like the *Planet of the Apes* franchise, *District 9* provides an unsettling and frank look at humanity's capacity for racism and cruelty – and, once again, the portrait is a less than flattering one.

District 9 is set in an alternate version of the present, twenty-eight years after an alien ship first appeared in the skies over Johannesburg. The occupants of that ship – a spindly, chattering population of insect-like creatures, which humans derisively dub 'Prawns' – now live in District 9, a huge internment camp just outside the city, packed into tiny shacks and shunned by society. By 2010, the camp has become so filthy and overcrowded that the government decides to relocate the aliens to a new area, and the official in charge of the operation is Wikus van der Merwe (Sharlto Copley), who cheerfully leads parties of armed soldiers into District 9 to 'abort' foetuses hidden in the aliens' homes – a brutal means of population control. Petty and spitefully cruel, Wikus is perhaps the vilest lead in a sci-fi film since *A Clockwork Orange*'s Alex DeLarge (1971) – that is, before the story takes a sudden and ingenious turn. During his tour of the township, Wikus comes into contact with an alien liquid, which gradually mutates him into the very thing he loathes: a creature shunned by his colleagues and subjected to cruel experiments by scientists.

Fate therefore drags Wikus, kicking and screaming, to something that at least vaguely approaches redemption; turning against his former employers, Wikus helps an alien, Christopher (a motion-captured Jason Cope) and his young son find a means of leaving Earth.

Like Ridley Scott before him, South African director Neill Blomkamp got his start in advertising, where he specialised in making slick promos that fused live-action footage almost seamlessly with digital effects. One of his most widely noted commercials was for Citroën, which showed one of the manufacturer's cars transform into a dancing robot. Evidently a fan of anime, manga and the movies of Paul Verhoeven, Blomkamp's short films garnered plenty of attention online; like his commercials, they showed extraordinary ingenuity on a tight budget, whether a film depicting rabbit-eared robots patrolling the streets of Johannesburg (a nod to the manga *Appleseed*, by Japanese artist Masamune Shirow) or *Yellow*, an intense little film about rogue droids. Along with Gareth Edwards, Blomkamp is one of a new generation of filmmakers that instinctively weave CGI into the very fabric of their work.

It was Blomkamp's short films that caught the attention of Peter Jackson, the New Zealand director who had just come off the *Lord of the Rings* trilogy and his sprawling 2005 remake of *King Kong*, and had recently struck a deal with Microsoft to produce a movie based on the hit videogame, *Halo: Combat Evolved*. Initially offered to director Guillermo del Toro, *Halo* instead went to Blomkamp, who began working up his own version of the first-person shooter's sci-fi universe.

During pre-production, however, funding for *Halo* fell apart. The uneasy three-way alliance between Microsoft, 20th Century Fox and Universal, who had agreed to share the cost of making the movie, turned sour and, by 2007, Blomkamp was left with a stack of production designs for guns and sets but no movie. Like Wikus van der Merwe, however, the *Halo* project gradually mutated into something new. Casting around for story ideas, Blomkamp turned to one of his earlier short films, *Alive in Joburg*, a faux documentary in which interviewees describe the grim fate of alien visitors, who have been thrust into internment camps, brutally mistreated or pressed into service as slave workers. How Blomkamp acquired these interviews was chillingly effective: the interviewees weren't actors, but ordinary people, and the victims they talked about were real Zimbabwean refugees who fled to Johannesburg in the late 1980s and early 1990s.

What began as the $125 million *Halo* adaptation at Fox therefore became the much leaner, $30 million *District 9*, co-written by Blomkamp's wife Terri Tatchell and produced by Peter Jackson's Wingnut Films. Shot with the same handheld, documentary style as *Alive in Joburg*, *District 9*'s sense of realism – at least in the movie's first half – is a world away from the formal polish of, say, J. J. Abrams's *Star Trek* reboot or James Cameron's *Avatar*, also released in 2009. Filmed in and around a real Soweto township, *District 9* has an almost tangible sense of grittiness. The immediacy of Blomkamp's filmmaking is in the vein established by found-footage horror phenomenon *The Blair Witch Project* (1999), but it also keys into the post-YouTube era of ubiquitous recording devices and citizen journalism.

With the film beginning as a documentary, of sorts, following Wikus around on what should for him be a regular day's work, *District 9* echoes the everyday realism of H. G. Wells's *The War of the Worlds* – a first-person account of alien invasion – and also, glancingly, British TV comedy phenomenon *The Office*. Wikus is the equivalent of David Brent, the vain and oddly childlike middle manager played by actor and writer Ricky Gervais; like Brent, Wikus evidently loves the attention lavished on him by the camera and, initially, it's satisfying to see such an unpleasant character dealt a sharp karmic blow. There's certainly a hint of comedy in Sharlto Copley's superb performance, which phases from smarm and maliciousness to fear and regret. That Copley improvised much of his dialogue also adds to the movie's sense of off-the-cuff authenticity. Remarkably, *District 9* represented Copley's first role in a feature film; while he had always harboured a love of acting, he had instead moved into the VFX business. In his early twenties, Copley founded a television production company, and often let Blomkamp, then still a teenager, use his firm's computers and help out with advertising projects.

Blomkamp had only just turned thirty when he made *District 9*, and there's an unmistakable youthful energy in the film's grotesquery and violence. Wikus's transformation is pure Cronenbergian body horror, while the heavy artillery, exploding bodies and moments of black comedy are straight out of Paul Verhoeven's school of filmmaking. And like *RoboCop* and *Starship Troopers*, the social commentary beneath the comic-book violence is hard to miss: *District 9* deals quite explicitly with the kind of segregation and racial cruelty that left a blight on South Africa's history – and placing them in the context of a sci-fi action film brought those topics to a young audience who probably wouldn't queue to see a movie about apartheid in their local multiplex. *District 9* was far from the first movie to deal with these themes – *Alien Nation* (1988) was also about racial tensions between humans and extraterrestrial visitors – yet its unflinching honesty and technical ingenuity certainly set it apart.

Regrettably, *District 9* isn't entirely enlightened in its outlook; after its release, the movie was criticised for its portrayal of a group of Nigerians, who are roundly depicted as violent and superstitious.[*] Flawed though it is, the movie nevertheless strikes at the core of a human failing that refuses to go away: our innate xenophobia. It's no coincidence that the aliens in *District 9* are imagined as insect-like and loathsome, since history is filled with periods where people of other races were treated or described as less than human. Jews were subjected to dehumanising propaganda by the Nazis in the 1930s – an act which prepared the ground for even more horrifying atrocities later in the Second World War. As the number of Middle Eastern migrants trying to cross into Europe threatened to grow into a humanitarian crisis in 2015, several British newspapers described those people – many of them parents with small children – as a 'swarm': a word more commonly associated with locusts.

Given that *District 9* was an original concept with an unknown cast, its financial success was all the more surprising. The movie also struck a chord with voters at the Academy Awards, since it went on to become one of the rare genre films to receive Oscar recognition, including a nomination for Best Picture.

To date, Neill Blomkamp has continued to make sci-fi films with political themes, all starring his collaborator Sharlto Copley in some capacity. *Elysium* (2013) was an action fable in which our planet's wealthiest 1 per cent have

---

[*] See: http://africasacountry.com/comment-district-9-and-the-nigerians.

decamped to an orbiting space station (the titular *Elysium*, based on an iconic, torus-shaped design by Syd Mead), leaving the rest of us to scrabble around in the dust and decay. A lowly factory worker named Max, played by a shaven-headed Matt Damon, takes up arms against the wealthy after an industrial accident leaves him deathly ill. Like Wikus, he's initially motivated by self-preservation: Max wants to get to Elysium, where potentially life-saving technology awaits. In the end, Max winds up fighting for a greater cause, which brings him face-to-face with the cold-hearted bureaucrat Delacourt (Jodie Foster) and her psychotic foot soldier, Kruger (Sharlto Copley).

Visually, *Elysium* matched *District 9* in terms of its detail and technical surety. Yet Blomkamp himself later admitted that *Elysium*'s plot was a little undernourished; the concept of Elysium, a Beverly Hills gated community in space, is a fascinating one, but largely relegated to a background detail as the gun-heavy action takes centre stage. The film is, nevertheless, packed with some ripe moments of satire: a tech CEO (William Fichtner) so obsessed with the bottom line that he won't let a sick employee lie on a sickbay couch for fear of sullying the sheets.

Blomkamp's brand of violent social commentary continued in *Chappie* (2015), about an artificially intelligent robot and his growth from childlike innocent to violent gangster. The bones of the plot are straight out of the 1980s family film *Short Circuit*, yet Blomkamp and his writer partner Terri Tatchell bend the formula to comment on the way human growth is affected by its environment. Kidnapped and trained by a pair of Johannesburg criminals (Ninja and Yolandi Visser of South African rap group, Die Antwoord), police robot Chappie (a motion-captured Sharlto Copley) gradually takes on the slang and violent tendencies of his adoptive parents. The film's rather cluttered mix of action and eccentric ideas – including Hugh Jackman as a devoutly religious ex-soldier and engineer who thinks artificial intelligence is an abomination – didn't exactly endear critics to its cause, and neither did *Chappie* capture the public's imagination like *District 9*. All the same, Blomkamp's ability to get original, quite personal sci-fi films made in an increasingly cautious movie business shouldn't be overlooked; nor should the individual use of CGI in his movies. James Cameron's motion-captured *Avatar* (see Chapter 29) may have pushed boundaries with its photorealism, yet *District 9* did something equally important: it took computer-generated characters out of the clean environs of a sound stage and into the real world. The integration of *District 9*'s aliens into the shacks and garbage of a South African township was key to the film's realism; the idea was pushed even further in *Dawn of the Planet of the Apes* (2014), where digital apes blended seamlessly with the mud and bracken of a North American forest. Technically dazzling, gleefully violent, yet also satisfyingly intelligent, *District 9* remains one of the most distinctive sci-fi films of the new millennium.

Sci-fi at the Oscars

At the 44th Academy Awards in 1972, *A Clockwork Orange* received a nomination for Best Picture – a recognition seldom bestowed on a science-fiction genre film, even from a director as celebrated as Stanley Kubrick. Both before and after *A Clockwork Orange*, awards bodies such as the American Academy of Arts and Sciences in the USA and BAFTA in the UK tended to restrict their admiration for sci-fi to technical awards: *Forbidden Planet* was nominated for Best Visual Effects at the 1957 Oscars, for example, but lost to Cecil B. DeMille's *The Ten Commandments* and its parting of the Red Sea sequence. *Planet of the Apes* was recognised for John Chambers's makeup effects (he received an honorary Oscar) and received nominations for Best Costume and Best Original Score; similarly, *Star Wars* received accolades for its editing, sound design, visual effects and art direction – but no nod for director George Lucas. (*Star Wars* was, however, lavished with praise at the Golden Globes and BAFTAs, with nominations for Best Film from both bodies.)

Science fiction isn't the only genre that tends to be overlooked by the Academy – comedy and horror arguably have it worse – but it remains the case that some of the most dazzling SF films have lost out in favour of more grounded dramas; perhaps the most famous example was *E.T. The Extra-Terrestrial*, another rare genre film to be nominated in the Best Picture category. Ultimately, Richard Attenborough's three-hour biopic *Gandhi* took away the Oscar; Attenborough later opined that *E.T.* deserved the win.

Thanks in no small part to the work of directors like Kubrick and Spielberg, sci-fi has approached something close to mainstream respectability over the past twenty years, which is reflected in the kinds of awards the Academy sends in the genre's direction. The tide began to turn in 2009, when both *District 9* and *Avatar* were nominated for, among other categories, Best Picture. That the Academy had increased the number of possible nominations in the Best Picture category, precisely to heighten the chances of more leftfield choices appearing on the list, certainly helped. Yet the presence of *Avatar* and *District 9*, placed alongside Pixar's animated fantasy *Up* and Quentin Tarantino's war film *Inglourious Basterds*, suggested that Academy voters were more willing to engage with movies outside their regular purview – such uplifting or powerful human dramas as *The Blind Side*, *An Education* or *Precious*.

Ultimately, neither *Avatar* nor *District 9* won Best Picture; Cameron lost out to his ex-wife Kathryn Bigelow and her Iraq War thriller, *The Hurt Locker*. Eight years later, Cameron might have had *Avatar* in mind when he grumpily argued, in an interview with the *Daily Beast*, that the Academy 'doesn't regard the films that people really want to see'.* That Cameron's 1997 period romance *Titanic* won Best Picture might fly in the face of that theory, however, as might the nominations that came along after *Avatar*'s nod for Best Picture. Since 2009, such SF films as *Inception*, *Gravity*, *Mad Max: Fury Road* and *The Martian* have all received nominations in the Best Picture category; in 2017, director Denis Villeneuve's profoundly moving drama *Arrival* received no fewer than eight nominations, including Best Picture and Best Director.

Cameron may have a point, however, about the kinds of movies that tend to take home the Best Picture award at the end of the night. He points out that the majority of the Academy's members are actors, and have a tendency to back films that celebrate their craft; with films that are more technical, or rely more heavily on special effects, Cameron says, 'they say, oh, that's not an acting movie'.

Yet even this attitude may change in time. To see how the film industry's thinking can shift to embrace developments in filmmaking, take a look back

---

* See: http://www.thedailybeast.com/articles/2017/01/29/james-cameron-on-the-trump-administration-these-people-are-insane.html.

to 1982 and Disney's sci-fi fantasy, *Tron*. It made pioneering use of CGI – as well as a liberal use of cleverly integrated photographic and animation techniques – to bring its artificial world to the screen. The extensive use of CGI in *Tron*'s effects was so new, in fact, that the Academy didn't consider the film eligible for a nomination in the Best Visual Effects category – because, as director Steven Lisberger later put it, using computer graphics was considered 'cheating'. While this may not have been the Academy's official stance, there was a certain distrust of computer-driven effects in Hollywood at the time; within Disney, the use of computers in traditional 2D animation was met with some resistance, since it was feared that it might put traditional artists out of a job. In any event, *Tron* had to make do with nominations for Best Costume Design and Best Sound in 1982; it was only in 1996, when the film's pioneering status was more widely respected, that the Academy gave the film a belated award for technical achievement.

Today, both audiences and the film industry at large are well used to the presence of CGI in movies. Such directors as David Fincher and Denis Villeneuve regularly use computer graphics for background details that are all but invisible to the untrained eye: set extensions, digital matte paintings or, in *Arrival*'s case, the addition of expensive military hardware like tanks and helicopters. With a growing acceptance of digital filmmaking, maybe one day we'll see a sci-fi film finally win Best Picture.

Selected SF films mentioned in this chapter:

E.T. The Extra-Terrestrial (1982)

Tron (1982)

Short Circuit (1985)

Alien Nation (1988)

Elysium (2013)

Gravity (2014)

Chappie (2015)

The Martian (2015)

Arrival (2016)

29. Digital domains

AVATAR (2009)

'Sometimes your whole life boils down to one insane move.'

Having spent months submerged in freezing cold water for his 1989 sci-fi opus *The Abyss*, Cameron pretty much did the same thing again on the set of his 1997 period romance, *Titanic*. As Cameron put together his tale of the doomed ocean liner, grim news stories began to emerge of unhappy actors, cost overruns, a tyrannical director and a bizarre poisoning incident involving lobster chowder and the drug phencyclidine – or PCP. Hollywood trade papers, predicting that *Titanic* would be a colossal failure, began to salivate. In the face of these gloomy predictions, Cameron managed to steer his ship to success, and *Titanic* went on to become the late twentieth century's *Gone with the Wind*: both hugely profitable and popular at awards ceremonies. In an industry where reputations hinge on success, Cameron found himself at the top of the Hollywood power list; in 1998, when the director pronounced himself 'King of the world' at that year's Oscars, he had reached a position that most filmmakers can only dream of: like Kubrick, he had the clout to make just about any movie he felt like.

Cameron therefore returned to a story idea he had outlined before he had embarked on *Titanic*: a sci-fi action adventure called *Avatar*. Originally planned to begin shooting in 1997, after *Titanic* was finished, *Avatar* instead remained in stasis for almost a decade; Cameron's ambitious plan to make a movie with digital characters simply couldn't be done, he said, with the technology available at the time. For the next few years, Cameron busied himself with making documentaries, including *Aliens of the Deep* (2005), which showcased his newfound love of deep-sea diving.

Convincing 20th Century Fox to bankroll a movie with a potentially huge budget – research and development for the *Avatar*'s 3D camera systems would run into the millions, some of it paid for by Cameron himself – was also a tricky proposition, even with Cameron's post-*Titanic* clout. It wasn't until the spring of 2007 – a decade after the release of his period disaster epic – that filming finally began; with a reported budget of $237 million, Cameron was banking his career on his sci-fi fantasy becoming a success.* In an interview with the *Independent*, Cameron later admitted, 'We were three years and $150m in before I saw the first shot that convinced me that we actually had a movie.'†

This might explain why, as work on *Avatar* got under way in a huge Californian aircraft hangar, Cameron's no-nonsense approach to movie-making resurfaced with a vengeance. A leading *Avatar* actor once claimed that Cameron took a ringing mobile phone off someone on the set and affixed it to a wall with a nail gun (the director later denied the story).‡ Gradually, however, it became clear that the years of research and development were beginning to pay off; the virtual camera system created for the production allowed for a new kind of digital filmmaking, where Cameron and his team could film a virtual landscape as though it were a real location. In practice, this meant that actors in motion-capture suits could be filmed fighting with sticks in a cold hangar, while through his monitor, Cameron could see in real time what the digital characters looked like against a lush alien landscape.

Cutting-edge cameras notwithstanding, *Avatar*'s story is an old-fashioned one. Heavily inspired by Edgar Rice Burroughs's Barsoom series of books, which began with *A Princess of Mars* in 1912, *Avatar* is about a former soldier who meets and falls in love with a noblewoman on an exotic planet. There are strange creatures, despicable villains and plenty of bracing action sequences.

---

* See: http://www.businessinsider.com/james-camerons-avatar-not-as-expensive-as-originally-stated-2009-3?IR=T.

† See: http://www.independent.co.uk/news/people/profiles/james-cameron-dont-get-high-on-your-own-supply-8650777.html.

‡ See: http://www.independent.co.uk/news/people/profiles/james-cameron-dont-get-high-on-your-own-supply-8650777.html.

What Cameron brings to this pulpy adventure are his own concerns about the environment and American foreign policy, as well as a sci-fi conceit that could have come from an online videogame.

Avatar is set on the distant planet Pandora, a world prized by Earth's government for its rich supply of a material called Unobtanium (curiously, there was a substance with the same name in 2003's quirky disaster flick, *The Core*). As the planet's mined under the watchful eye of the military, represented by the cold-hearted Colonel Quaritch (a beefed-up Stephen Lang), a separate initiative takes place to win the 'hearts and minds' of the planet's alien race, the Na'vi – a tall, blue-skinned race with feline eyes and tails, who live peacefully among the trees. In order to mingle among the locals, scientists and soldiers are mentally twinned with artificially grown bodies identical to the Na'vi. Strip away the sci-fi, and you have the story of a disabled human soldier, Jake Sully (Sam Worthington), who's reincarnated as a ten-foot-tall alien; mentally, he's still an earthling, but now he can, as it were, walk a mile in a Na'vi's shoes.

Living among the Na'vi, Jake begins to see their plight first-hand, as their land is gradually taken and torn apart by Earth's mining activities. As Jake falls for Neytiri (Zoe Saldana), the chief's daughter, he becomes a member of the tribe, and winds up in a pitched battle against Earth's mechanised forces.

If anything, the pre-release anticipation surrounding *Avatar* was even greater than the curiosity that built up around *Titanic*. For Hollywood's press, there was its colossal budget and renewed suggestions that Cameron might have finally overreached himself this time; word was that *Avatar* would have to make $500 million just to break even. For devotees of Cameron's earlier genre movies – *The Terminator*, *Aliens*, *T2*, *The Abyss* – *Avatar* had its own magnetic allure. As we've already seen, those films were not only wildly popular but, in their own way, defined the look and feel of movies and videogames for years afterwards. The question was, could *Avatar* do the same thing again?

Like the earthly forces in the movie itself, Fox were determined to win hearts and minds with their multimillion-dollar fantasia. And so it was that, in August 2009, months before *Avatar*'s scheduled release, the studio launched the first trailer to a clamour of online interest: the promo was downloaded an estimated 4 million times on its first day of launch, and almost broke Apple's servers in the process. For most, this was their first glimpse of Cameron's new opus, and the director's affection for military hardware and gun-blazing action seemed present and correct – but what to make of all the tall blue aliens and gaudy fauna, like something from a 1970s prog-rock band's album cover? By the time Fox had presented fifteen minutes of footage to journalists and bloggers at IMAX cinemas the following day, uncomplimentary comparisons were already being drawn to such movies as *Dances with Wolves*, *The Last of the Mohicans*, *Pocahontas* and *FernGully*. Indeed, charges of derivative storytelling and, worse, its place in a long line of 'white saviour' narratives clung to the movie after its release in December 2009. Cameron may have been well-meaning in his story about earthly corporations destroying environments and displacing communities in search of profits, yet its central thread of a Caucasian male 'going native' struck several film critics as a rather uncomfortable racial fantasy. ('It rests on the assumption that non-whites need the White Messiah to lead their crusades,' was how the *New York Times*'s David Brooks put it in 2010.*)

Avatar, was, however, as much a showcase for Cameron's new technology as his storytelling prowess. Filmmakers had toyed with 3D since the dawn of cinema. In the 1950s, 3D was one of several answers to the growing threat of television; in 2009, would-be cinemagoers had more reasons than ever to stay at home rather than take a trip to see a movie. *Avatar*'s eye-popping stereoscopic imagery gave consumers a new reason to leave their homes and visit their local multiplex; televisions may have been getting bigger, videogames may have been getting more realistic, yet *Avatar* provided an experience that could only be found in a cinema. This selling point, far beyond the film's casting, its storytelling or even the reputation of its director, was what made *Avatar* a box-office phenomenon in late 2009. By the time *Avatar* got a second release in 2010, with its extra footage pushing its duration to an indulgent 171 minutes, the movie had long since crossed the $2 billion mark.

Avatar led to a brief yet intense rekindling of industry fascination with 3D, as other studios clamoured to add an extra dimension to their movies and

---

* See: http://www.nytimes.com/2010/01/08/opinion/08brooks.html.

manufacturers rushed to get 3D working on their televisions. Cinema owners certainly loved the 3D revolution, since they could add a surcharge for the stereoscopic experience. Producer and DreamWorks co-founder Jeffrey Katzenberg even proclaimed that *Avatar* was 3D's *Citizen Kane*.

Avatar's more profound and lasting contribution to cinema was arguably its breakthroughs in motion capture. Although the movie was far from the first to use the process, the advent of virtual cameras and photoreal digital characters was unprecedented, and paved the way for equally ambitious films still to come – not least the rebooted *Planet of the Apes* franchise.

As for James Cameron, he's taken a path not unlike the one taken by his hero, Jake Sully. Bewitched by Pandora, he's since immersed himself in it: in 2010, the director announced his decision to turn *Avatar* into a trilogy, with *Avatar 2* said to be scheduled for 2014. When that year finally arrived, Cameron announced that the sequel was being pushed back, and that the franchise was instead set to grow, with *Avatar 2* pencilled in for 2016 and two further movies released each year thereafter. Two years later, he announced a further delay, and revealed that he was no longer making four sequels, but five. The first of these is now scheduled for Christmas 2020.

Assuming Cameron sticks to his most recent plan, he will have spent more than twenty years on making *Avatar* movies. Like George Lucas, Cameron seems lost in a world of his own making; Francis Ford Coppola once commented that when Lucas made *Star Wars*, we lost a great filmmaker. By a similar token, we can only wonder what other movies Cameron might have made had *Avatar* been only a moderate hit.

The question is, do audiences have the same appetite for more movies in the *Avatar* universe as Cameron does? Certainly, *Avatar*'s annexing of our popular consciousness has fallen far short of *Star Wars*. A few years after its release, the stream of merchandise, books and spin-offs petered out; tellingly, there is no annual *Avatar* equivalent of *Star Wars* Day. *Avatar* showed up at a unique moment in history; shortly after a disastrous stock-market crash, when audiences were in the mood for something colourful and escapist. In the intervening years, we've seen the rise and rise of Marvel's superhero movies; Disney-Lucasfilm's rebooted *Star Wars* franchise means that space opera is again breaking box-office records – and, thanks in no small part to *Avatar*, now available to view in 3D. *Avatar* may have been a game-changer in 2009, but the success of the sequels will almost certainly hinge on whether moviegoers are interested in a second, third, fourth or even fifth visit to Pandora.

However the sequels turn out, Cameron still seems intent on pushing the technical envelope: his *Avatar* sequels will, he says, create a 3D world without the need to wear special glasses.

THE RISE OF MO-CAP

Since the dawn of cinema, filmmakers have sought to find ways of bringing the creatures in their imaginations to life. Winsor McCay's 1914 film *Gertie the Dinosaur* was a groundbreaking mix of animation and live performance, in which McCay appeared to interact with a friendly animated diplodocus. Stop-motion pioneers Willis O'Brien, Ray Harryhausen and Phil Tippett evolved the process of putting hand-animated models in the same frame as real actors. These techniques, constantly refined though they were by generations of artists, remained broadly unchanged for almost a century, until the advent of computer-generated imagery began to offer filmmakers a whole new toolset from which they could draw.

Expensive and time-consuming to generate, CGI was initially restricted to brief sequences in movies of the 1970s and early 1980s, such as the computer displays in the *Westworld* sequel, *Futureworld* (1976), and the celebrated Genesis sequence in *Star Trek II: The Wrath of Khan* (1982). Such pioneering movies as *Tron* (1982) and *The Last Starfighter* (1984) made far more bold, extensive use of CGI, however, with *Tron*, in particular, pushing the boundaries of what was possible with contemporary technology: although simple, Bit, a kind of talking sidekick to hero Flynn (Jeff Bridges), was the first CGI character of its kind in a full-length feature film. Look at *Young Sherlock Holmes*, released just three years later in 1985, and it's clear just how quickly these techniques were progressing; in one imaginative sequence, a stained-glass window depicting a knight in armour comes to life and menaces a vicar.

Although lasting mere seconds, the sequence took months for Industrial Light & Magic's digital arm to design and animate – at the scene's helm was John Lasseter, who would later go on to direct the pivotal CG animated films *Toy Story* (1995) and *A Bug's Life* (1998).

Digital characters increased in their complexity and photorealism through the 1990s, taking in the landmark *Jurassic Park* (1993), *Casper* (1995), featuring a talking, CGI lead character for the first time in cinema history), and *Jumanji* (1995), with its computer-generated animal stampede. The use of motion capture (mo-cap) to record an actor's movements and transfer them to a CG character also began in the 1990s, with sci-fi horror *The Lawnmower Man* (1994) using an early form of the technique. The decade's highest-profile use of CGI, however, was arguably in George Lucas's *Star Wars* prequel, *The Phantom Menace* (1999); in the run-up to the movie's release, much was made of Jar Jar Binks, an all-digital character based on the voice and movements of actor Ahmed Best. Like Yoda a generation earlier, Jar Jar was something of a creative risk: the character would have to walk and talk alongside actors Ewan McGregor and Liam Neeson; if Jar Jar didn't look entirely photorealistic, the results could be disastrous. Briefly, Jar Jar was the poster boy for *The Phantom Menace*'s marketing drive; his smiling, duck-like face even appeared on the cover of *Rolling Stone* shortly before the movie came out.

As it turned out, photorealism was the least of George Lucas's problems. Jar Jar looked convincing enough, but the reception to the squeaky-voiced, clumsy sidekick drew responses that ranged from the irked to the positively outraged – some critics condemned Jar Jar as a racist caricature, which Lucas strenuously denied. Characterisation aside, Jar Jar Binks was nevertheless a considerable achievement in technical terms; had he been more warmly received, it's even possible that Binks's contribution to cinema would be as widely recognised as Gollum, the CGI character brought to life by mo-cap actor Andy Serkis for director Peter Jackson's *The Lord of the Rings* trilogy. Instead, it was Serkis who became known as the ambassador for mo-cap as a new and vital frontier in acting; in the wake of the first *Lord of the Rings* movie's release, *The Fellowship of the Ring* (2001), there was even talk of Serkis receiving a Best Supporting Actor nomination for his performance. (*The Fellowship of the Ring* was nominated for thirteen Oscars and won four, including Best Visual Effects.)

Together with New Zealand-based effects studio Weta Digital, Serkis has helped bring more digital characters to the screen ever since. He reunited with director Peter Jackson for the remake of *King Kong* in 2005, in which Serkis played the giant ape from Skull Island, and reprised his role as Gollum in the *Hobbit* trilogy, which ran from 2012 to 2014. Serkis's finest work to date can be found in the *Planet of the Apes* movies, starting with *Rise of the Planet of the Apes* in 2011. Weta's use of CGI to create Caesar, a photorealistic digital chimpanzee, is stunning – but it's Serkis's humane, subtle performance beneath the effects that creates such an unforgettable character.

Today, motion capture is such a common technique in movies that it's barely commented on by critics. In 2016's *Star Wars* spin-off, *Rogue One*, for example, Alan Tudyk plays an all-digital droid named K-2SO. Blending seamlessly with the actors around him, K-2SO's digital origins are so subtle that they almost pass by unnoticed. At the same time, the performance beneath the effects shines through: as a surly machine with a disquietingly frank manner of speaking, he's one of the movie's highlights. Motion capture has ceased to be an eye-catching novelty, or a hook on which to hang a film's marketing; it's now an accepted part of movie-making.

Rogue One also – somewhat controversially – used CGI to bring the late actor Peter Cushing back to life. Using motion capture and digital manipulation, actor Guy Henry's performance was recorded and overlaid with Cushing's computer-generated likeness – thus bringing the villainous Grand Moff Tarkin back to the screen for his first speaking role since 1977. Although approved by Cushing's estate, the use of his image sparked some debate over the ethics of using a deceased actor's likeness. While CGI hasn't yet reached the point where a digital human actor looks indistinguishable from a real one – *Rogue One*'s Tarkin has a certain glassiness around the eyes and a stiffness in the jaw – the future depicted in director Ari Folman's 2013 sci-fi film *The Congress* seems to be drawing ever closer. Based on a story by *Solaris* writer Stanisław Lem, it concerns a middle-aged actress (played by Robin Wright) who agrees to have her likeness scanned into a computer for use in the movies. The upside is that she'll be paid handsomely; the downside is that she can never physically appear in a film again.

Only time will tell where motion capture will take cinema in the future. For now, mo-cap actors and effects studios are simply doing what Winsor McCay, Willis O'Brien and Ray Harryhausen were doing all those decades ago: using technology to bring imaginary characters vividly to life.

Selected SF films mentioned in this chapter:

Gertie the Dinosaur (1914)

Futureworld (1976)

Star Trek II: The Wrath of Khan (1982)

The Lawnmower Man (1994)

Toy Story (1995)

A Bug's Life (1998)

Star Wars: The Phantom Menace (1999)

King Kong (2005)

The Congress (2013)

Star Wars: Rogue One (2016)

30. Dream logic

INCEPTION (2010)

'What is the most resilient parasite? Bacteria? A virus? An intestinal worm? An idea . . . Once an idea has taken hold of the brain it's almost impossible to eradicate.'

Storytelling ideas bounce back and forth down the ages, leading to places that even the most prescient sci-fi writer couldn't predict. *Flash Gordon* begat *Star Wars*; *Star Wars* begat *The Matrix*; and *The Matrix* led indirectly to *Iron Man*, *The Avengers*, *Guardians of the Galaxy* and the Marvel Cinematic Universe. Yet as movie-making budgets have soared and profit margins have narrowed in the twenty-first century, a falling number of directors working in the American mainstream have acquired much in the way of creative freedom; such writer-directors as Shane Carruth, Jeff Nichols and Alex Garland have made original, challenging films at an independent level, yet Hollywood studios are often loath to risk putting millions of dollars into a genre film that isn't based on an existing novel or comic book.

British writer-director Christopher Nolan is one of a handful of directors who can command the kind of creative control that Spielberg and Kubrick enjoyed a generation earlier. From his beginnings as the maker of low-budget thrillers like *Following* (1998) and *Memento* (2000), Nolan successfully navigated Hollywood's trap-laden corridors of power. A gun-for-hire studio thriller – a remake of the Danish film *Insomnia* (2002) – led to his first big-budget film, the superhero reboot *Batman Begins*, in 2005. Since then, Nolan has deftly interspersed popular franchise material (itself peppered with sci-fi ideas) with more personal but similarly broad filmmaking. Period thriller *The*

Prestige (based on a novel by Christopher Priest) followed *Batman Begins* in 2006; *The Dark Knight*, which broke attendance records in 2008, was followed by the complex genre piece, *Inception*, in 2010.

With his precisely combed hair and smart suits, Nolan has cultivated the image of a mainstream filmmaker with the coolly intellectual air of a university professor. Nolan's movies, which he makes with his producer wife Emma Thomas, reliably share common themes: most prominently, that of a deeply flawed protagonist who retreats from reality, whether it's through the persona of a costumed vigilante or via a cutting-edge dream machine.

Like *Dr Strangelove* before it, *Inception* wears its sci-fi cloak so lightly that a casual glance might leave you asking whether it belongs in the genre at all. Yet while the film is undoubtedly a thriller – a high-concept heist movie, specifically – its ideas pivot on a futuristic piece of technology that could easily have emerged from a novel by Philip K. Dick or William Gibson. Indeed, Nolan's 'Pasiv' device, which allows its users to enter, explore and even distort a collective dream space, is so redolent of the ideas in Philip K. Dick's novels *Ubik* and *The Three Stigmata of Palmer Eldritch*, David Cronenberg's *eXistenZ* (1999) and Japanese director Satoshi Kon's animated feature, *Paprika* (2006), that some critics have speculated over the creative debt *Inception* might owe to those earlier works. Whether Nolan – who wrote as well as directed – was aware of them or not, it's perhaps fairest to say that he's swimming in the same creative ocean that storytellers and philosophers have splashed about in since the beginning of civilisation; thinkers as diverse as Plato and René Descartes often wrote about the porous nature of reality. Macabre writer Edgar Allan Poe famously wrote, 'All that we see or seem / Is but a dream within a dream' a full 150 years before Nolan sent Leonardo DiCaprio tumbling into a Matryoshka doll of imaginary spaces.

DiCaprio plays Cobb, a dapper criminal who owes his career to the existence of a new piece of ex-military technology: using the Pasiv device, he specialises in entering the subconscious minds of his targets and stealing the information they have stored away. Cobb is therefore a valued freelancer for, say, global energy corporations, who are willing to use his unique form of espionage to stay ahead of their rivals. It's exactly this kind of corporate intrigue that drives the thriller element of *Inception's* plot. Japanese billionaire Mr Saito (Ken Watanabe) wants to prevent a rival energy company from gaining a damaging monopoly, so he employs Cobb to target his rival's young boss, Fischer (Cillian Murphy) and plant in his mind the idea of splitting up his company. This planting of an idea, a process called inception, is considered so difficult that most believe it to be impossible; Cobb, expert dream manipulator that he is, thinks he knows how to pull off the perfect mind crime.

What follows is a kind of sci-fi take on *Oceans 11*, in which Cobb assembles a team of specialists to help catch Fischer unawares, put him to sleep, enter his dreams and plant the seed for his company's break-up deep in his subconscious. Unlike the surrealist landscapes of Hitchcock's *Spellbound* or Satoshi Kon's *Paprika*, Nolan's dreams are presented as concrete and almost mundane; the idea being that Cobb's targets don't even realise they are dreaming. Instead, the dreams in *Inception* have to be constructed by the intruder, like mazes or the paradoxical artwork of M. C. Escher; Nolan illustrates this with some quite breathtaking effects sequences, the most celebrated – and, more recently, oft-copied – being a scene in which the Paris skyline is folded over onto itself. *Inception's* dream spaces look concrete, but they can also be bent and distorted, not unlike Neo's manipulation of the simulated world in *The Matrix*. Another key sequence sees actor Joseph Gordon-Levitt fighting a group of villains in a hotel corridor, their bodies appearing to defy gravity as they jump from wall to ceiling, trading punches and kicks. Taking inspiration from Stanley Kubrick's *2001: A Space Odyssey*, Nolan and his team – including special effects designer Chris Corbould – built a 100-foot-long corridor set on a huge rotating platform.

In some respects, however, the action-thriller elements of *Inception* are its least interesting attributes. There may be shootouts, car chases and an endlessly long snow sequence that pays homage to the James Bond film *On Her Majesty's Secret Service*, but Nolan seems more smitten by the human aspect of his story – certainly, it's *Inception's* more intimate moments that stick in the mind long after all those chases have finished.

The complication for Cobb is his long history with the dream technology at *Inception's* centre. Years earlier, Cobb's wife Mal (Marion Cotillard) committed suicide – specifically, we later learn, because of the years they spent together in the dream realm. In short, Mal spent so long in an unreal sphere that she began to reject reality itself; most tragically of all, she believed that her own children were artificial constructs. Years after her death, Mal still appears in Cobb's dreams – often fulfilling the role of a disruptive femme fatale in the midst of his mind heists. Like Hari in Stanisław Lem's novel, *Solaris*, Mal is a projection of Cobb's memories, yet appears to exist as a living entity with her own (highly unpredictable) freewill. Cobb's motivation may be to pull off his act of inception, but his true goal is self-forgiveness; only by confronting his guilt, and moving on from it, can he lay Mal to rest and get on with his life.

The film's final image is that of the spinning top – a totem once used by Mal (and later, Cobb) to determine whether they were dreaming. If the spinning top falls, the reasoning goes, then they must be awake. Like the origami unicorn at the end of *Blade Runner*, *Inception*'s closing shot therefore leaves us with a nagging question: Nolan doesn't show the top falling over, so does that mean the happy ending, in which Cobb is reunited with his children, is merely another dream? Certainly, the film as a whole contains a fair bit of dream logic – we might ask, for example, how Mr Saito can magically clear Cobb's criminal record with a single phone call – and it's certainly possible to read *Inception* as an account of a grieving widower working through a traumatic experience via his dreams.

Yet *Inception* can also be interpreted as a postmodern comment on the process of filmmaking itself; if sitting in a cinema is akin to dreaming, then Cobb's the equivalent of a director, manipulating and planting ideas from behind the scenes. The concrete nature of Cobb's dream spaces is akin to the suspension of disbelief we experience while watching a movie; we may know that vast spaceships and four-legged tanks in a *Star Wars* movie can't exist, but while the lights are down, we choose to accept the version of reality presented to us. As Cobb tells Ariadne in one key line, 'It's only when we wake up that we notice anything strange.'

Inception therefore taps into the distinctly human need to make and share stories – to create imaginary spaces where we can explore our hopes and anxieties. Long before humanity put an astronaut on the Moon, we first dreamed of space travel in books and movies. More than a century before genetic engineering or robotics, Mary Shelley wrote about the creation of artificial life. Even in the twenty-first century, with release schedules commonly filled with sequels and remakes, intelligent, thought-provoking sci-fi movies still break through. As well as *District 9*, *Avatar* and *Inception*, we have seen the likes of *Moon*, *Elysium*, *Ex Machina* and Christopher Nolan's space odyssey, *Interstellar*. *Gravity*, a sci-fi disaster thriller directed by Alfonso Cuarón, broke new ground in its use of digital filmmaking, with CGI used to create the illusion of a movie shot with a single, floating camera in one take. *Arrival* (2016), directed by Denis Villeneuve and adapted from 'Story of Your Life' by Ted Chiang, is a tense thriller about alien visitation, but it's also a deeply moving portrait of grief. Ridley Scott's *The Martian* (2015), adapted from Andy Weir's novel, is about human ingenuity in the face of almost certain death.

As this book has shown, making original sci-fi films carries a certain amount of risk for the people who invest in them. *Metropolis*, *Blade Runner* and *The Thing* are highly regarded today, yet they were hardly financial successes at the time of their release. In the present, we've seen such high-concept movies as *Jupiter Ascending* (2015), a sci-fi take on Cinderella by the Wachowskis, struggle to make back its gargantuan budget. Likewise *Tomorrowland* (also 2015), Disney's family adventure about a futuristic utopia. Every so often, however, a sci-fi film comes along and captures the cinema-going public's imagination, and *Inception* is one genre film that garnered both critical acclaim and huge success at the box office. Perhaps it's because it satisfied an ever-present need for spectacle and escapism, while at the same time exploring themes that are rare in a typical big-budget action thriller: bereavement and guilt, certainly, but also the indelible power of dreams, imagination and storytelling.

Now wait for last year

In the early part of the twentieth century, cinema was the new medium; a form of both entertainment and communication that quickly built up its own language to tell stories and impart ideas – cutting, composition, close-ups, music, colour and sound. Filmmaking takes in an array of disciplines, from art to design to writing to science and, as we've seen, looking at a century of sci-fi movies provides a useful lens through which we can see the development of cinema as a whole.

Beyond the techniques of filmmaking, sci-fi movies also reflect more than a century of social and cultural change. Through the genre's prism, we've seen space travel, the advent of the atom bomb and the dawn of the computer age. We've seen how technology can bring about wonderful new possibilities and horrifying destruction.

As cinema has matured, however, it's also had to adapt to changing audience tastes and rival forms of entertainment. Just as the cinema eclipsed the theatre as populist entertainment, so television began to compete with movies for the public's attention in the 1950s, 1960s and 1970s – hastening the introduction of colour, surround sound, widescreen and 3D. Next came videogames, first in amusement arcades and then on home computers and consoles; today, cinema must compete with the ubiquity of smartphones, YouTube, Netflix and social media. Only time will tell how the medium will mould and change to absorb these and other future developments.

It's a common complaint that the more clichéd scientific breakthroughs predicted by the genre – jetpacks, flying cars, food in pill form, colonies on other planets – haven't come to pass. But what's worth noting is that the concerns so commonly explored in sci-fi are still as urgent as ever. The grim visions of a nuclear apocalypse conjured up in *Dr Strangelove* and *The Terminator* haven't happened but, conversely, the missiles that could end our civilisation still rest in their silos. For all our scientific progress, the divide between rich and poor touched on in Fritz Lang's *Metropolis* still hasn't been solved almost a century later; as a film like Neill Blomkamp's *Elysium* suggests, progress has a tendency to enrich one end of society while leaving the other more impoverished than ever. To these concerns we could add global terrorism and global warming; the rise of digital surveillance, where everything from our interests to our physical movements can be tracked through our phone signals and our internet histories; the militarised use of unmanned vehicles; the loss of jobs as more vocations are taken up by machines and software. Science fiction is uniquely positioned to explore these fears, whether it's in literature, as in Dave Eggers's disturbing Silicon Valley dystopia, *The Circle*, or in videogames, television and movies.

More than this, sci-fi can also show humanity at its most intelligent, progressive and compassionate. Amid their scenes of tension and disaster, such films as *Arrival*, *Interstellar*, *Life* and *Gravity* show people of different genders, races and backgrounds uniting for a common cause. As actress Rebecca Ferguson points out, science fiction – whether it's *Star Trek* or a sci-fi thriller like 2017's *Life*, in which Ferguson plays a quarantine officer – is capable of looking at our species with a utopian sense of hope. Through space exploration, adversity on other planets or the study of an alien specimen on the International Space Station, as in *Life*, we catch a glimpse of what a humanity without prejudice, 'without borders' might look like.

'On the ISS, there is no hierarchy,' Ferguson said. 'Gender equality is basically there – it doesn't matter if you're a man or a woman. You're there because you're the best person for that job. Without one of them, the mission can't work [. . .] It has to be all of us together. Then there's the cultural mix. The ISS represents what I wish the world was today: without borders, without limits, with curiosity and welcoming of everyone's thoughts and ideas."*

The *Star Wars* franchise, once populated overwhelmingly by white male actors, has evolved to reflect the diversity of its audience; 2015's *The Force Awakens* features a British female lead (Daisy Ridley), a black co-star (John Boyega) and scene-stealing support from Guatemalan actor Oscar Isaac as an effortlessly cool X-Wing pilot. Movies such as these – and many others like them – suggest that at least some progress is being made in a largely male-dominated industry.

More than a century ago, a French entertainer fused conjuring tricks with cutting-edge technology to create a new form of magic. Georges Méliès was among the first to recognise that a film camera could do much more than

---

* See: http://www.denofgeek.com/uk/movies/rebecca-ferguson/48137/rebecca-ferguson-interview-life-acting-in-zero-g-sci-fi.

capture everyday reality – it could also be used to transport us to another realm where anything is possible. From Fritz Lang and Thea von Harbou in Germany to Andrei Tarkovsky in Russia to Neill Blomkamp and Terri Tatchell in South Africa, filmmakers have used science-fiction cinema to give us new ways of viewing both ourselves and the world around us. Where the next hundred years will take our planet is impossible to predict; whatever happens, we'll always have science fiction to light the way ahead.

Selected SF films mentioned in this chapter:

Gravity (2013)

Interstellar (2014)

The Martian (2015)

Arrival (2016)

Life (2017)

Bibliography

Big Screen Scene Showguide (April 1968).

Bogdanovich, Peter, *Who the Devil Made It?: Conversations with Legendary Film Directors* (London: Arrow, 1998).

Buhle, Paul and Dave Wagner, *Hide in Plain Sight: The Hollywood Blacklistees in Film and Television, 1950–2002* (New York: Palgrave Macmillan, 2005).

Clute, John, *Science Fiction: The Illustrated Encyclopaedia* (London: Dorling Kindersley, 1995).

Dowd, Vincent, 'Kubrick Recalled by Influential Set Designer Sir Ken Adam', *BBC World Service* (16 August 2013), http://www.bbc.co.uk/news/entertainment-arts-23698181.

Fordham, Joe and Jeff Bond, *Planet of the Apes: The Evolution of a Legend* (London: Titan, 2014).

Goldman, Harry, *Dr Frankenstein's Electrician* (Jefferson, CA: McFarland, 2005).

Hoberman, J., 'The Cold War Sci-Fi Parable that Fell to Earth', *New York Times* (31 October 2008), http://www.nytimes.com/2008/11/02/movies/movies-special/02hobe.html?_r=0.

Hochscherf, Tobias and James Leggott, *British Science Fiction Film and Television: Critical Essays* (Jefferson, CA: McFarland, 2005).

Kaplan, Mike, 'Kubrick: A Marketing Odyssey', *Guardian* (2 November 2007), https://www.theguardian.com/film/2007/nov/02/marketingandpr.

Keegan, Rebecca, *The Futurist: The Life and Films of James Cameron* (New York: Three Rivers Press, 2010).

Lyons, Barry, 'Fritz Lang and the Film Noir', *Mise-en-Scène* (1979), https://cinephiliabeyond.org/mise-en-scene-fritz-lang-invaluable-short-lived-magazines-article-master-darkness.

Miller, Frank, 'Metropolis', *TCM* (30 May 2014), https://web.archive.org/web/20140316012144/http://www.tcm.com/this-month/article/25817%7C0/Metropolis.html.

Murray, Scott and Peter Beilby, '*Mad Max* Production Report', *Cinema Papers*, no. 21 (May–June 1979).

Nathan, Ian, *Alien Vault: The Definitive Story Behind the Film* (London: Aurum Press, 2011).

——, *Terminator Vault: The Complete Story Behind the Making of The Terminator and Terminator 2: Judgment Day* (London: Aurum Press, 2013).

Owen, Jonathan, 'James Cameron: "Don't get high on your own supply"', *Independent* (8 June 2013), http://www.independent.co.uk/news/people/profiles/james-cameron-dont-get-high-on-your-own-supply-8650777.html.

Powell, Helen, *Stop the Clocks! Time and Narrative in Cinema* (London: I. B. Tauris, 2012).

Rushdie, Salman, 'Talks with Terry Gilliam', *Believer* (March 2003), http://www.believermag.com/issues/200303/?read=interview_gilliam.

Schlosser, Eric, 'Almost Everything in "Dr. Strangelove" Was True', *New Yorker* (17 January 2014), http://www.newyorker.com/news/news-desk/almost-everything-in-dr-strangelove-was-true.

Stern, Marlow, ' "Mad Max: Fury Road": How 9/11, Mel Gibson, and Heath Ledger's Death Couldn't Derail a Classic', *Daily Beast* (16 May 2015), http://www.thedailybeast.com/mad-max-fury-road-how-911-mel-gibson-and-heath-ledgers-death-couldnt-derail-a-classic.

Stern, Marlow, 'James Cameron on the Trump Administration: "These people are insane"', *Daily Beast* (29 January 2017), http://www.thedailybeast.com/james-cameron-on-the-trump-administration-these-people-are-insane.

Taylor, Chris, *How Star Wars Conquered the Universe: The Past, Present and Future of a Multi-Billion Dollar Franchise* (London: Head of Zeus, 2015).

Wells, H. G., 'Metropolis Review', *New York Times* (17 April 1927), http://www.laphamsquarterly.org/roundtable/mr-wells-reviews-current-film.

Wise, Damon, 'Metropolis: No 2 Best Science Fiction and Fantasy Film of All Time', *Guardian* (21 October 2010), https://www.theguardian.com/film/2010/oct/21/metropolis-lang-science-fiction.

Acknowledgements

This book wouldn't exist without the help, support and generosity of a great number of people – too many to list fully here, in fact. But briefly, I'd like to offer my sincere thanks to Duncan Proudfoot, Amanda Keats and Emily Byron at Little, Brown, both for commissioning this book and for their time and effort during its writing, to Nazia Khatun, for publicity expertise, and to Howard Watson, for his invaluable advice and the laser precision of his copy editing. Warm thanks to Helen McCarthy and Professor Will Brooker, whose knowledge and passion for anime and science fiction proved so vital to my research.

Then there are my family and friends: my longsuffering partner Sarah Carrea, who has provided so much patience and kindness, before, during and after the writing of this book. My mum and dad, Kathy and David, for their love and encouragement. Nathan Gibson, Marc Bazeley, Geoff and Sue Carverhill, John Cox and James Peaty, whose friendship has kept me going from the first chapter to the last. The late Peter Naylor, whose intelligence and mentorship guided me for so many years.

Finally, I must thank *Den of Geek* editor Simon Brew, who gave me my first writing job and has championed my work for more than a decade.

Writing may be a solitary pursuit, but I'm forever indebted to the people who have helped me on this strange and fantastic voyage. May the Force be with you – always.

Index